Corpse Fauna

OTHER TITLES BY JAMES CHAMBERS
The Engines of Sacrifice
Resurrection House
On the Night Border
On the Hierophant Road

KOLCHAK THE NIGHT STALKER
The Forgotten Lore of Edgar Allen Poe
The Faceless God

OTHER ESPEC BOOKS TITLES BY JAMES CHAMBERS
THE CORPSE FAUNA SERIES
The Dead Bear Witness
Tears of Blood
The Dead in Their Masses
The Eyes of the Dead

SYSTEMA PARADOXA SERIES
Devil in the Green (Volume 6)

VOX ASTRA
The Black Box
When Clouds Die

OTHER ESPEC BOOKS INCLUDING JAMES CHAMBERS
After Punk
The Side of Good/The Side of Evil
Gaslight & Grimm
Best of Bad-Ass Faeries
Awakened Modern
Society for the Preservation
of CJ Henderson

DEFENDING THE FUTURE SERIES
Dogs of War
Man and Machine
In Harm's Way
Best of Defending the Future

BEYOND THE CRADLE SERIES
If We Had Known
Footprints in the Stars

JAMES CHAMBERS

BRAM STOKER AWARD-WINNING AUTHOR

THE CORPSE FAUNA CHRONICLES

NEoPARADOXA

PENNSVILLE, NJ

PUBLISHED BY
NeoParadoxa
a division of eSpec Books LLC
Danielle McPhail,
Publisher
PO Box 242,
Pennsville, New Jersey 08070
www.especbooks.com

ISBN: 978-1-956463-13-2
ISBN (eBook): 978-1-956463-12-5

All persons, places, and events in this book are fictitious and any resemblance to actual persons, places, or events is purely coincidental.

Copy Editor: Greg Schauer, John L. French
Interior Design: Danielle McPhail

Cover Art: Glen Ostrander
Interior Art: Jason Whitley
Cover Design: Mike McPhail, McP Digital Graphics

For Cedrick, CJ, and Rob, who were here for so much of this; I wish you were here for the finale.

Contents

The Dead Bear Witness / 1

Birch's Refugees / 67

Section Afterword:
Escape from the Prison of the Blind Dead / 103

Tears of Blood / 115

Dead-End Street / 207

Section Afterword:
A Zombie Ate My Boarding Pass / 223

The Dead In Their Masses / 233

Passengers / 323

Section Afterword:
The Distance to Lohatchie / 345

The Eyes of the Dead / 353

Lohatchie Coda / 463

Section Afterword:
The Dead Won't Die / 483

Bonus Story: Body / 489

About the Author / 505

About the Artists / 507

Our Legion of the Undead / 508

THE DEAD BEAR WITNESS

For Chris and Vince,
walking dead men
'til the end

THE DEAD BEAR WITNESS

CORNELL:
ONE

Four guys committed suicide today. One managed to do the job right.

A wiry kid in for possession doused his clothes in turpentine from the shop, then set a match to his shirt. The screws displayed uncharacteristically good sense letting him burn a while so he wouldn't rise up again after they hit him with fire extinguishers.

Another made a grab for a guard's gun, forcing a shootout. The hacks fought his corpse into submission long enough to set fire to it.

Number three swallowed most of a box of rat poison, told no one, and died on his feet washing breakfast dishes in the kitchen. He bit through the throat of the inmate next to him before the other cons cleared out, and two guards returned with scatterguns to rip the dead bastards to pieces.

The fourth grabbed a knife during lunch and cut his own throat. Panicked inmates stumbled over each other trying to get away, blocking the screws from reaching the body before it switched on again. He killed two more inmates and wounded a guard before they pinned down all four of them and dragged them to the infirmary for chopping up.

Nightmare fuel that made me homesick for solitary.

I'd spent a month there only to emerge into the devil's definition of a life-and-death struggle, and I honestly could not say which side I preferred.

My stint in the hole came by way of punishment for breaking the collarbone of some Aryan Brotherhood asshole who wanted to "protect" me. Show no weakness to those white supremacist fucks—they *will* make you their dog or kill you trying. Warden Lane Grove knew it as well as I did, but I was fresh blood and a media darling, and he wanted to teach me a lesson about getting cocky.

Last thing the warden told me before he slammed shut the cell door was, "You think you're someone special, son? Someone different and unique? You're nobody special. You're only clay like all the rest of us. Sooner you accept that, better off you'll be, because if you think my punishment is harsh, you'll find an even ruder surprise waiting for you in the next world if you don't change your ways."

Worst thing for me about solitary was that there was nothing to occupy my mind but thinking about how horribly I had screwed up when I was on top of the world. They wouldn't allow me my books or even a Walkman—nothing but the searing brightness of the cell's single bare bulb lit twenty-four, seven. That and all the time I needed to pick over the carcass of my memories, like the last time I saw Evelyn or the look on the bank manager's face when three slugs from my Beretta M9 bored through his gut. Sometimes I got to wondering how it might have gone if I'd been just a few seconds faster.

That's when I came to understand what Evelyn meant when she used to say the world is a smiling jackal eager for its chance to tear out your throat and lap up your blood. Most people don't see it coming for the clutter in their lives, like politics or religion or trying to make a decent living with the deck stacked against them. Evelyn fand I never had much use for all those things telling people the "right" way to live. Better to take what we needed and be long gone when the man came around to collect his due.

I believe Evelyn held to that right up to the moment I dropped my guard and got her and our baby growing inside her killed.

TWO

When my four weeks in isolation ended, Officer Paulson and Officer Gamewood yanked me out of the hole and dragged me down the hall to the infirmary, while I chased dime-sized ghost glares burned onto my retinas by the bulb in my cell. Wasted from hunger and not having slept more than an hour at a time since they tossed me down there, I wasn't so far gone I didn't notice Paulson's sickly tremors or the glistening film of sweat coating his pale face, or how he mumbled into the empty air, not talking to me or anyone else really.

"Whole world's over. End of everything," he said.

I figured the whole thing was a sick joke, a head game, more of my continuing education according to Lane Grove. Or maybe Paulson liked to get a little high on the job. Had second thoughts about all that after the horror show at the infirmary.

While I lay on a gurney with an IV of saline solution plugged into my arm to treat me for dehydration, a couple of hacks brought in Sammy Costa, ashen-faced and bleeding like a New York City fire hydrant in July. He was a snub-nosed car-thief on a ten-year chip for his third strike. He was a stupid man with a smart mouth. So, it was no surprise someone had decided to slice him open and make good work of it. The guards hefted him onto the gurney beside mine, but the two-foot wide puddle of blood that Sammy's wounds spilled onto the floor made it obvious there was no saving him. Doctor Foley took one look, shook his head, and called the time of death. Then he set to work with the nurse and guards ripping Sammy apart like the devil's pit crew.

They used bright scalpels and whirring bone saws. Blood spattered and flesh tore. Muscle snapped like strands of aged chewing gum. Translucent flaps of skin peeled back from bone and sinew. Joints cracked, and foul patches of gas belched from the recesses of Costa's body. His left arm came loose and a guard dropped it into a thick vinyl bag, sealed the bag shut, and tossed it into a waiting laundry cart. Next went Sammy's legs, each one amputated below the knee, wrapped in separate containers then tossed on the pile. Every few seconds the nurse called out the time, counting it down. Sweat dripped from Doctor Foley's face.

It mixed with Costa's blood and ran in milky rivulets along the doctor's silver tools.

Costa's right arm vanished into a plastic sack.

Guards yanked on his thighs and spread them until his hip joints surrendered with a loud snap.

"One minute," the nurse said.

Thirty seconds later they finished. Foley hunched over Costa's face, sliced a scalpel through what was left of his neck, and then wrenched the car thief's head free from his body. Two guards slipped a body bag over his torso; another held one open for the head. All that was enough to make me think I'd died in the hole and woken up in some insane hellish version of reality, but then as Sammy's lifeless, gray face vanished into black plastic, his smartass eyes flicked open and stared right at me. They gleamed like polished ivory in the last beam of light that touched them. They were cool as December, like all was right in Sammy's world. Soon as that bagged head crowned the pile of body parts, the aluminum cart shimmied and rattled. Slow at first, like when a truck rolls by a house and shakes the pictures on the walls, but then each black bundle wriggled, shifted around, twisted and turned like a caged rat. The canvas liner bulged as the severed limbs squirmed around each other.

The nurse screamed "Incinerator, now!" and sent the guards rushing the cart from the room.

The infirmary air swelled with the foul odor of raw flesh and the pungent stink of sleepless terror. I'm well acquainted with the scent of fear. It's a mixture of clean, dried sweat and the kind of body odor that comes from an adrenaline rush. Except for being so depleted by my hitch in solitary, I would've caught it wafting off my escort. I would've gagged on it rising from the medical staff when I entered the room. But it took the icy dread of seeing Sammy Costa ripped apart to make me realize fear's choking perfume tainted the entire prison. Now that I'd scented it, I couldn't ditch it.

I grabbed the nurse by the arm. Her nametag read Oberon. My voice came out like a rasp scratching across oak. "What in holy hell was that all about?"

"Shit," the nurse said. "You been living in a cave for the last month?"

THREE

Later, with a clean bill of health—aside from dehydration, sleep deprivation, malnourishment, and the general stress that comes from existing in a windowless three-by-five cell for a month—they sent me back into general population.

It was afternoon recreation period, so I went to the television room. It was empty. That time of day, the place should have been full of soap opera fans, but there was nothing but snow on every channel. I stretched out on the couch and relished its coarse comfort. I rested my eyes in the cool stillness of the room. Visions of Sammy Costa flashed through my mind, mixed with Nurse Oberon's weary eyes, and the sickly look on Paulson's face. I tried to pinpoint the exact moment when sanity had deserted the world. I couldn't do it.

Footsteps scuffed the tile floor. I shot upright and opened my eyes. A long-timer called Old Corntooth waved me back down and then shuffled to the table by the sofa. He sat on its corner and gave me the once over. I'd seen him around a few times, one of those guys who's been inside so long, he's like a ghost. He smiled, showing me how he'd earned his name.

"Been in solitary, ain't you?" he said. "You're out of touch, I suppose. Don't know the score anymore. Bad way to be in here. Uninformed, I mean. Lot's changed in a little time. You ought to watch this."

He handed me an unlabeled DVD in a clear plastic case.

"Television signals died two weeks back. All we's got left is a DVD-DVR machine in here. Got a couple of old football games up on the shelf, a couple of musicals, one of them Adam Sandler movies, but this here's the only one you need. It's the only one that means much. When you're done, stick it in the crack between the wall and the cabinet. I'll fetch it later. We ain't supposed to have it, y'know? Warden don't like this to circulate."

Old Corntooth left the room without looking back. I stared at the square of shining plastic in my hand, the silver circle inside it. Wasn't unusual for contraband skin flicks or movies the warden deemed objectionable to circulate in secret, but no one was likely to waste their time singling me out for something like that. Couldn't think of a good reason anyone might single me out at all. It's best in prison when no one pays any attention to you whatsoever. I wondered who'd sent it, knowing by the broken-down look in Old Corntooth's eyes that he'd never have bothered with me on his own.

I slid the disc into the player and sat back.

What followed: Two hours of raw, fucking chaos.

One-hundred and twenty minutes of madness.

Seventy-two-hundred seconds of death, blood, and blind panic.

That's what this movie was about.

The plot was shit, but the rest of it was convincing as all get-out. Someone had recorded it all while channel surfing and news channel or not, every damn broadcast was the same: the corpses of the dead now rose within four to ten minutes of death and hunted the living with a savageness of insane dimension. It was worst in the cities where mobs of the dead swarmed the streets, but inside a few of days it had spread everywhere. The corpses moved with desperate purpose, heedless of their own safety, ignorant of any injury, and their growing numbers replaced the lost two to one. Nothing stopped them but fire or cutting them to pieces. The hunger so clear in their blank eyes drove them to consume the thing they'd once been: the living.

The reporters all asked the same question, "Why?"

Sure enough there were theories: radiation, disease, voodoo, parasites, the Apocalypse, Wi-Fi, genetically modified tomatoes, RFID chips, iPad mind control apps, and on, and on. No one had figured it out by whatever day the broadcasts had been recorded. Not that it mattered. The people on television worried about stopping it before it was too late, but it seemed like that point had come and gone and caught everyone with their pants down.

Except for me.

I got to watch the whole thing as if it was taking place right then. I pictured people outside fighting for survival against the mobs of walking dead. I thought of cities packed with panicked crowds, hospitals overrun with corpses that wouldn't stay down, and roads choked by cars, trucks, and useless ambulances. My imagination ran away a touch, I admit, but I've always been that way. Thing was, what all the other men had experienced over the past weeks, locked up helpless inside while the rest of the world died, I put myself through in two hours, catching up fast. And I understood that all that was in the past, that with the dead spreading as fast the reporters said, any frantic battles for life were all over and decided by now. What had been a month in the hole for me must have seemed like years to the people outside. And that bastard Grove had let me stay there to rot as if the end of it all was no concern of mine, as if I were the ultimate outsider, living in my own world. Maybe he was right.

The DVD ended with a blank blue screen that matched the empty patch in my memory from my time in the hole. Damn video did wonders for my doubts about my sanity.

We'd been safely locked up, a thing for which not a man among us would have been grateful five weeks ago. And I wondered how many felt differently now. What was there to look forward to after we did our time: families, homes, girlfriends, money? Shit, some of us had lost all of that long before resurrection fever began firing up the dead. They say there's nothing more dangerous than a man with nothing left to lose, and here I was penned up with a prison full of men, nothing in any of our futures but rot and darkness. I almost wished I'd never been dragged out of my rational, little cube in solitary.

FOUR

Hit the exercise yard to shock my muscles out of the atrophy of confinement. Physical exertion clears my head. I had a hunch I was going to need my wits as much as my strength soon.

Outside was cool and dry, the kind of spring weather that makes you want to drive a hundred miles an hour with the top down. For half a heartbeat I wondered if the world had really changed. Here it was: alive and untouched for all I could see, free of nightmares other than the ones we bring to life ourselves. Then I smelled the lingering odor of decay in the air and heard the low undercurrent of voices echoing in the yard, coming not from the prisoners but from outside the prison walls. Rifle reports snapped from the perimeter stations at irregular intervals. The gunshots mingled with the crash of hammers. At one end of the yard, workers were erecting a structure with lumber that had been meant for the new storage shed. A hill of old junk and debris was piled up beside it.

I settled onto the bench and began pumping through my first set. The heft of the barbell laced strands of pain through my chest, but the grimy iron felt good in my hands. A con came over to spot me, looking grateful for the break in his boredom. He smoked a cigarette while I went through two more sets. My muscles warmed to the exertion with the last one, so I switched to smaller weights and kept at it, boiling off the cold dread gathered at the base of my spine. I worked my body until the knots in my gut melted to nothing, and then I sat there panting while the breeze licked the sweat from my back.

That's when Klug approached me, stopping here and there along the way to bum a drag off someone's smoke, gab with other cons, or tie his shoe, the whole time keeping his eyes on me with a gaze like a stream of ice water. Coming slow so as not to scare me but letting me know I'd better sit tight and wait for him.

Klug was near seven-feet tall and built like a linebacker, big with much more muscle than fat. His clean-shaven head glistened in the sunlight. A bright cobra hood tattoo adorned the back of his neck and skull. Nobody fucked with the King Snake. There was no point. Not a man in the yard could take him one-on-one, and Klug, for his part, liked his privacy. A genuine live-and-let-live arrangement, which from what I could see, worked fine. Klug had been high up on the food chain before the cops brought him low on a bogus firearms charge, and he went inside with solid connections. Even the supercops kissed his ass. Klug returned the favor by using his influence to help maintain order when it suited him. That kind of shit made for easy time, I suppose, but shots like Klug do you a favor just to obligate you. My first day in I'd elected to do everything possible to stay off his radar.

Guess I screwed the pooch on that plan. Klug stepped up beside me, and the temperature dropped three degrees in his shadow.

"Hear you're a Lohatchie boy," he said.

"Yeah?" I asked. "Where'd you hear that?"

"Don't much matter. I grew up in Lohatchie, too. Spent my summers playing around the 'Glades, running airboats for Gator Joe's. Lived down on Kettrick by the rail yard till I left when I was sixteen. You look about the right age. Imagine we might have passed each other on the street more than once."

"Probably did. Gator Joe's went out of business long time ago, you know."

"I heard. Too bad about that. Joe deserved better than the shit he wound up eating."

A flurry of gunshots crackled on the wind. Klug craned his neck, intent on the vibrant sky like he was waiting for the answer to some unspoken question. Behind his careful expression his eyes hinted at the rapid-fire thoughts gamboling through his mind. Whether or not the answer ever came to him, I don't know, but he met my gaze again and put a hand on my arm, squeezing the muscle tight.

"Waste of good ammo," he said. "Nothing stops them short of incineration or blowing them into very small, very immobile bits. Slice them apart, their arms and legs will come after you as best they can. We're lucky the fuckers are so slow and stupid."

I thought of Sammy, a man in pieces, still kicking.

"Old Corntooth told me he showed you the news, so you know what's what now," Klug said. "Could be we're the only ones left, I suppose. Likely there are others out there in situations like ours, but there's no way to know. Ain't no real communications left working. Warden Grove carried things on like normal for a few days, but when it was clear this thing wasn't going to turn around, he locked us down drum tight. No one in, no one out, no exceptions. Not even the guards' families. The screws looked ready to mutiny at one point, but Grove kept enough of them loyal to hold the lid on. Pretty soon they all realized that whatever family they'd left behind would probably best be forgotten. So, now, except that they got all the guns, they're prisoners here, too, like us."

"I'm tickled by the irony."

Klug cracked what might have been a smile, but I wouldn't swear to it.

"You ever eat down at Mona and Joan's on Banyan?"

"More than a few times," I said. "Damn good fries."

"Yeah. And milkshakes. Nothing beat their chocolate shakes."

"Screw chocolate. Strawberry-banana. Joan's specialty. The ultimate shake."

"Shit, I'd fight my way through a dozen men for one of those right now." Klug smiled for sure this time, parting his lips and licking his broad white teeth like he could taste the food right then—golden crisp and steeped in oil and salt, sugar sweet and creamy cold. "Yeah, it's good to be talking to a Lohatchie boy. Man, I bet we're the last two left. Funny us both winding up here. Especially since word is you got a place in the wilderness down there, where if you'd have made it before the Feds caught up with you, they might not have caught you at all."

That knocked the wind out of me. I couldn't imagine how Klug or anyone else here knew about that.

Klug read my expression.

"I been in here long enough, I can tell you not to expend a lot of energy keeping secrets. It ain't possible, least not from me."

"Suppose it's true. So what? It'd have to be hundreds of miles away from this shithole, from anywhere, in fact, wouldn't it?"

"Most of this sorry lot in here haven't caught on yet to the warden's grand plan." Klug paused to light a clove cigarette and exhaled a sweetly acrid cloud over my head. "Understand this: That man will see to it none of us ever leaves this prison alive. We have provisions stockpiled for another week, maybe two if they get stingy, and we got generators for power, but fuel is running low. He can't keep us here long without thinning the population or recruiting men to forage for supplies. He doesn't have enough guards to send any away scavenging, and he sure as hell won't trust any of the cons to do it. He knows—walking dead or not—they'd never come back once he let them outside the walls.

"Even if he could make a go of it, he wouldn't bother. When the dead began to walk Grove declared it the End of Days. He curled up squarely in the pages of his Bible and he hasn't come out since. We all had to find some way to cope. The ones that didn't aren't around anymore. For a man like Grove, with that big a hard-on for God to begin with, this has got to seem like some seriously momentous shit. Protecting us is keeping us from God's righteous judgment. Sealing us up in here to ride out the storm would be holding us back from the world as the Lord hath remade it. So, he won't let anyone out to hunt or try to find out what's happening. We could be living like princes here, but he lets the wormfeeders collect up around the walls because he believes most of us are meant to die at their hands. It's just a matter of time before he decides to throw open the doors and let us all get cozy with God's latest plague upon humanity."

"Why hasn't he done it already?"

"Wants to prepare us before we go, make sure we repent our sins and all that happy horseshit. A few of us have decided to be elsewhere when this particular shit hits the fan. The wormfeeders go where the food is, meaning where we are. There must be six, seven hundred outside, scattered around the countryside, pressing at the gates, homing in on us. Ten, fifteen, twenty more show up every day. From where I don't know because the nearest town is thirty miles away. They're damn tough to kill, and they make more of themselves fast. Couple weeks back a busload of people came banging at the door. Grove refused them entrance then ordered the guards to open fire. The ones killed by bullets got up and started eating the live ones. Fifteen minutes later, the whole lot of them had joined the big dead party."

"Break out and where do you run?" I said. "You figure if you can get far enough away, maybe someplace like my alleged hideaway, they won't pick up the scent."

"Scent, noise, psychic vibration, whatever the fuck they get off on. Got to be a limit to their range. That's my theory, anyway. Figure I'm better off out there testing it than rotting in here waiting to die."

"What if I'm not interested?"

Mild surprise ran through Klug's face. "I hadn't considered that. I will if you really need an answer."

I shook my head. "Leaving here sounds fine. How many?"

"Nine, including you and me."

"Too many. Needs to be less when we get where we're going. It ain't exactly a mansion."

"Well, such things have a way of working themselves out." Klug took a last drag on his cigarette, dropped it to the ground, and stamped it out. "I know I can trust you to keep this quiet, Lohatchie boy. Tonight, after Grove's dog-and-pony show, go back to your cell, wait one hour, then meet me in the cafeteria. It's been arranged."

Klug blended into the crowd. Another burst of faraway gunshots ripped through the afternoon.

Feeling exposed and weak in the hot sun, I watched the men work away building the structure. Feverish chills ran through my body. I feared I was coming down sick, but then I realized I was shivering because I'd recognized what Warden Grove was constructing down the yard.

He was having a gallows built.

FIVE

I sat alone at supper.

It was a pleasant change.

My first day in, everyone had wanted a piece of me. They had seen me on the news for weeks: "the modern-day John Dillinger," the bank-robbing folk hero who relied more on his wits than his gun and made monkeys out of the cops. Yeah, it was a healthy dose of exaggeration, but there was some truth in it, too. I robbed more than a dozen banks over two years and came away clean with more cash than Joe Six-pack could make in a decade worth of overtime. Still got a fair amount of cash safely stashed, all of it about as valuable as dirt in the current state of the world. When I did a bank I did it in style, and I did it smart. Jumped from state to state, kept a low profile, used a different crew each time, different methods, wore disguises, did everything I could to erase my signature. I enjoyed a fair amount of luck, too; whenever I was on the job things seemed to break my way more often than not. Simple things, like a guard taking an unscheduled bathroom break, or the bank not being full of customers, or hitting all green lights on the way out of town. Little things made a difference when it came to a clean getaway.

I hit nine banks before anyone connected the first four. Most of them had been fast, in and out, grabs off the tellers, but the time could be stretched, maybe take some of the vault, and I did that a few times for the big hauls. It wasn't hard with Evelyn on my side. Girl like her made information easy to come by, so we could go in on the guard's coffee break or avoid banks that rigged cash with GPS chips and dye bombs and marked bills.

The best part—at least until my last job—was no one ever got hurt. That lone fact had a good portion of the public on my side by the day the news broke that the Feds had connected all my robberies, admitting in the process that they'd been outsmarted for a solid eighteen months. I won over even more people by the time they caught me, having accomplished some conspicuous good deeds with portions of the take. Call it buying good publicity, because that's what it was. Mug for the camera, flash a nice smile, let them see you're just an average guy, and it reminds them all how much they'd like to buck the system the same way you did if they only had the balls and the smarts. That's the beauty of mass communication. Blur the lines enough then real life vanishes and people think they're watching a movie. Bank robber? No, sir, not me! I'm the next great, misunderstood, anti-hero "victim of a heartless society driven to a life of desperate crime." I was a modern-day Robin Hood driving a late model Lexus SUV, proving anyone can have anything they want if they only have the stones to take it. Even the most law-abiding drones respond to that with hope and envy, if only on a subconscious level. When the Feds caught me, though, I was still reeling from losing Evelyn. Hell, I got more than a thousand consolation cards while I was on ice waiting for my trial, plus half a dozen offers to go on talk shows and tell my side of events so "the people could understand." All they really wanted was to pick me apart like a new toy that fascinated them as much as it disgusted them.

None of that crap interested me.

I missed Evelyn too much. I thought I deserved to suffer for letting her down so I pled guilty.

The court handed me a life sentence for killing the bank manager and two security guards. My public defender threw his arms up in frustration at me copping to a rap he thought we could beat down to manslaughter. Only thing that kept the needle out of my arm was a spark of mercy fanned by the fact that one of the men I killed had just shot my pregnant wife to death. The model definition of a "fucked-up chain of events," I suppose.

And consider this: if I'd walked, or kept myself tied up in court on appeal, I'd probably be dead now, tromping around rotting in the sun.

Tempts me to start believing in fate.

Let me assure you, though, that it's a bad thing to come into stir with a reputation of any kind. Others feel duty-bound to take you down a peg or two, see if you got any real juice. That made my life difficult at best until I lost my cool with that skinhead punk. While I was in the hole, word had traveled about what I had done to get there. That told everyone else—except people like Klug—to keep their distance. My first night back no one seemed itchy for a scrap. The whole cafeteria was so damn subdued it made my skin crawl, and I knew it was those wooden beams raised above the prison courtyard that dominated the thoughts every of man around me. We were to assemble in the yard for a special service following dinner. Warden Grove's orders. They hadn't strung the ropes before mealtime, but we all knew they'd be hung in time for the night's activities.

Old Corntooth parked himself beside me as I sucked down a forkful of red Jell-O.

"Klug got you, huh? Shots like him usually get what they want," he said.

"Don't know what you're talking about, old timer."

"Uh-huh." His railroad track smile faded. "I'll tell you the same thing I told Klug. Skip it. It ain't gonna happen. You're better off here, cause no matter what they throw at you, you can always find a way to keep your head down and tough it out. You try and force 'em to play by your rules, they just going to smash you down. I been in near thirty years, and I know what I'm talking about."

"You don't even know what time it is. This play is for everything. Keeping a low profile ain't going to save your skinny ass this time. But maybe an old fart like you ain't too concerned about that."

I dropped my spoon and broke Old Corntooth's grip where he'd clutched my wrist. He poked a finger against my chest.

"I'm supposed to be out in six months. You hear me? Then I go free, I get my life back, and this shit has to go down, now." He coughed. Tears welled in his drooping eyes. "You and Klug and them, you all carrying on like it ain't nothing. It ain't fair."

I felt the supercops' eyes checking up on us, so I stood up to leave, lingering long enough to whisper, "What's changed, old man? The world is full of empty-headed bodies colliding off each other the way it always was. Gotta find an angle and make it work for you. Give up fighting and you're like those bastards outside: dead. Most of the ones out there—hell, most *in* here— were dead a long time ago. Only they were too fucking stupid to lie down and stop breathing."

Corntooth shook his head. "No, no, it ain't like that."

I pushed past the old man as gentle as I could and left him with his shoulders sagging like a week-old balloon. A crowd began filtering out to the yard, and I had gotten my fill of the somber efficiency of the cafeteria. I wanted to raise my eyes and see stars instead of a greasy stone ceiling for a change. I followed the others into the rose-amber glow of the raging bonfire that now consumed the junk pile beside the gallows. I stood in the shadow of a watchtower manned, as they all were, by men with automatic rifles. The firelight made the sky hazy, but I picked out enough stars to satisfy me. Fifteen, twenty minutes ticked off before everyone was gathered there, grim-faced, determined not to betray the slightest bit of fear but failing. A crowd that big keeping that quiet unnerved me. I scanned around for Klug but caught no sign of him.

Thundering music exploded from the loudspeakers, slow and funereal, some God-awful classical shit that filled us with a sense of powerlessness. Warden Grove possessed quite a touch of showmanship, having once been a revivalist preacher, and he played the part well. Ten figures marched onto the platform: three inmates bound in shackles, escorted by two shotgun-toting hacks apiece. A stocky, dark-suited man with his mouth hidden behind a blue surgeon's mask followed them; no question, he was an executioner. One-by-one the cons took their places below the gallows poles, all three of which now hung with coarse ropes tied in nooses that swayed a little in the breeze.

Warden Grove entered like a prince deigning to address his frightened subjects. The bastard telegraphed everything there was I hated about people like him.

"I will waste no time, men." He spoke into his microphone, and his voice boomed from the public address system. "Time is now more truly of the essence than ever before in life. Now it is the hour and the day of the master's return, and if you have not kept your house in order, then let this be your last chance to put your soul right. Tonight, three sinners stand beside me, gazed upon by a host of sinners. We all are sinners in the eyes of God. All of you, to the last man, bend beneath the weight of your guilt. I see it, men. I do. It burdens you like foul mud staining the fabric of your spirit. The Good Book promises that on judgment day there will be a reckoning, and on that day the dead shall rise from their graves. That day is at hand. No longer can you afford the luxury of your craven ways. It's time to repent as these three brave souls behind me have done."

Grove poked the microphone toward the first inmate's face. "Your name, son?" he said.

The man was so beaten and bruised he could only stand propped up by his escort. Grove shoved the microphone closer.

"Again, son. Your name?"

"Donnie...uh, Don Cooper," he said.

"What path have you chosen, Mr. Cooper?"

"God's path. I've chosen to...repent my sins. To go to the Lord...with a clear conscience."

"The Lord has forgiven you, Mr. Cooper, as he is willing to forgive all sinners. Now that you've taken God into your heart, it's left to you to see that your soul remains in its current state of grace, that you don't backslide and once again become one of the fallen. Would you do me the humble honor of accepting my assistance in assuring this?"

"Yeah...uh, yes, please," said Cooper, struggling as if to remember lines.

Grove asked the same questions of the other two men and got the same canned answers, though none of them looked like they understood what was happening. They'd all been pounded hard, broken down, and driven to submission. They would have agreed to almost anything only to put an end to whatever Grove had been doing to them.

"God so loved Mankind, he gave unto us his only Son, and sacrificed him for our sins," Grove said. "It is our duty to follow his example, by sacrificing ourselves to redeem our tainted spirits. These men are here tonight as examples for you all, guides to show you the way to light, truth, and salvation."

The executioner draped velvet hoods over the head of each supplicant and fitted nooses around their necks.

"Donny?" one of the men called. "Donny, I can't see you. What's happening?"

"It's okay, Arthur. I'm still here, and this shit...this shit is almost over. You just...keep your head together," said Cooper, his voice muffled by his hood.

"Men, pray now for your fellows that their souls might find peace," said Grove.

"Donny!" the con screamed.

The executioner sprang the trap doors. The three convicts dropped into air. The sound of their necks snapping seemed small and insufficient for such a terrible thing. Their bodies dangled, bobbing and swaying like mute wind chimes. I'd never seen a man hang before, and I'll tell you it's not quick and clean like they show it in the movies. Matter of fact, it's a damn messy, nasty way to die, unless it's done to perfection. And how often does perfection happen in this world?

Quiet reigned a long time over the crowd. The crackling of the fire was the only sound to be heard aside from the moans of the restless dead traveling on the wind. A number of men looked at their watches, some stared at their shoes. Everyone knew what was coming. No one stirred. A few minutes passed, and then the corpses jerked to life with clumsy, sweeping kicks. They wind-milled their arms like marionettes, and in the firelight, it looked like they were dancing in air to some slow music only they could hear. Grove let the show go on awhile. Later a bunch of hacks came and took position above each hanging body, three to a man.

"The unrepentant man is doomed to eternal flesh and carnal punishment," said Warden Grove. "Such is the fate of the worldly. Only those who choose forgiveness may transcend to a higher existence."

The screws hauled the flailing bodies up, each grabbing a limb or two, while another yanked the noose free. I was grateful for not having to see the dead men's blank eyes beneath their hoods, for knowing they couldn't see the rage and horror in our faces if they could see such things at all anymore.

"Free these men of their flesh!" Grove shouted.

The guards heaved the first of the struggling bodies onto the bonfire. It burned slow like green wood and wet leather, as it kicked and burrowed deeper into the trash heap. The others followed. All three tunneled their way toward the heart of the conflagration like they were drawn to the heat at its center. Disgusted cries and impotent curses rose from the crowd.

"These men have been saved and their souls are set free." Warden Grove swelled with pride. "Who would like to be next?"

I never before heard a silence like the one that answered him; it was heavy and hard and full of hot shock and burning hatred like a firestorm waiting to gush down and incinerate everything it touched.

"Men, I anticipated your reluctance to join the ranks of the saved tonight. To resolve spiritual matters often requires preparation and deep contemplation. I understand. So this will now be part of our daily routine, until each man among you worthy of saving has made his peace with the Lord and been safely sent to his eternal reward. Remain here for one hour. Reflect upon what you have seen. Then you are to return to your cells. Those of you who choose salvation may tell any prison official at any time in order for the appropriate arrangements to be made."

Grove descended the platform and disappeared inside, leaving us to perspire for sixty minutes in the warm night and the heat of the bonfire. Within the flames, the three corpses grew thin and black until not a scrap of flesh remained on their charred bones.

Then, finally, they ceased to move.

SIX

Later I lay in my cell, thinking how smart my pedophile cellmate, Baldwin, was to leave me undisturbed. On my third day inside, after catching him using my comb, I'd promised to make sure he didn't live to see the end of summer. Can't say I really meant it, as repugnant as he was, but the threat stopped him from interfering with me or my things.

I worked at reading the tattered copy of *The Subterraneans* I'd gotten from the prison library before being dumped in solitary, but mostly I stared at the ceiling or glanced at my watch, waiting for the hour to pass. When it was almost time, I dropped to the floor, snaked my hand into the narrow space between the metal leg of the bunk and the wall, and tapped until a loose chunk of masonry slipped free. A beat-up paperback of Faulkner's Light in August waited wedged inside. Hidden within it, where I had hollowed out some pages, was the jagged half of a snapped penknife blade, bound with duct tape to part of a wooden spoon handle. It wasn't much, but it was all I'd had time to acquire before my stint downstairs. I slipped it into the waistband of my shorts, enjoying the nervous glance Baldwin flashed at the sight of me with a shiv in my hand.

Sickly-looking Paulson came by on his rounds, pausing at my cell to unlock the door. He tipped me a nod then went on his way. I waited a minute before I crept out. I ignored the hatred and envy that poured from of the eyes of the insomniac men in the other cells. Any one of them would've been glad to trade places with me as the King Snake's new favorite. I reached the end of the cellblock and walked deeper into the prison. Along the way, I passed three guard stations, each one deserted. I encountered no one in the halls. The Cobra lived up to his reputation. In the darkened cafeteria, the scent of his clove cigarette filled the air.

His voice poured from the shadows. "That display tonight changes things. We can't wait till next week. We got to move right away."

"Move where?" I said.

"You'll find out soon enough."

Klug stepped into the faint glow from the corridor lights and gestured for me to follow him. He led me through the kitchen to a passage that connected with a hallway to the administrative wing. There I hesitated.

"No one will see us," Klug said. "It's taken care of for an hour at least. No worries. Come on."

We crept across the linoleum floor and ducked inside a stairwell that led up to another level. From there we mounted two more flights of steps and then emerged outdoors atop the wall below one of the guard towers. Two people waited there. One was a guard whose badge read Combest; the other was a nurse from the infirmary, Townsend. I had seen her before but never so close. When the breeze tossed her dark hair, I found myself staring at the curve of her jaw where it sloped down from her ear. In that shadowy light, she looked a lot like Evelyn.

"You're late," said Combest.

"No, we're not," Klug said. "Where are the others?"

Combest indicated the tower and a metal ladder up to the observation deck. We climbed single file. Inside the glass walls of the watch room waited another guard, Mason, and two cons hunkered down out of sight on the floor.

"This him?" said Mason.

"That's him, Mason."

"I read your file, college boy," Mason said. "That pretty face of yours may play with dumb-ass TV reporters and overfed sheeple, but it means nothing in here. If you go grandstanding on us I'll have no hesitation putting a bullet in your head. Understand me?"

"Well," I said, "you can try."

Mason withdrew a step. A flicker of uncertainty lit his eyes.

"No time for this crap, Mason," said Klug. "Cornell's with me. He's one of us. And right now we have business to discuss."

I recognized the two on the floor, Jaime and Scopes, enforcers for Klug. They pulled me down beside them.

"Keep out of sight, asshole," Jaime said.

Klug squatted, too, unfolding a piece of paper from his shirt pocket. He flattened it out on the floor, providing us with a rough map of the prison. He took us step-by-step through the plan. We would leave by the west loading docks, which Grove had sealed up when deliveries stopped arriving. The whole area was shut down, lightly guarded at best, and that would give us a fair chance of slipping away unnoticed. There were three trucks there. Tomorrow night, Combest and a guard named Georges would sneak in, siphon the gas from two of the trucks, and store it all in the third. Meanwhile Townsend would pack medical supplies boosted from the infirmary. Later Combest would meet with Paulson and gather provisions from the kitchen, where Paulson supervised the afternoon work crew. Mason would see to weapons.

We would leave between eleven and midnight, with Klug making arrangements for clear passage from our cells to the loading dock. Money was worthless, but there were other forms of bribery and coercion, and I had no doubt Klug was expert at them all. The last piece fell on Paulson, who sometime in the evening would secure the keys and punch codes for the garage doors and perimeter exits. After that all we had to do was ride, and I got to play navigator.

"We go in two days," said Klug. "Before *Preacher* Grove gets a chance to save our souls for us."

Mason waved me over to the window. "Come here."

I looked out over the north field. Mason switched on a spotlight. The beam slashed the night and illuminated the aimless wormfeeders shuffling along the fence, circling what must have seemed to them a butcher shop late to open for business.

"I know you've been in the hole, so I want to make sure you see what we're up against," Mason said.

"Shut that fucking light off," said Klug. "You'll get us noticed."

"Nobody's gonna notice. Nobody's gonna care. Get bored up here, and it's time for a little target practice. We all do it. Happens every night," Mason said. "Here, look."

He handed me a pair of binoculars.

Except for their decay, the dead things resembled drugged mental patients, empty and tuned into a frequency the living could not hear. Mason hefted his rifle and sighted through the scope. The slug caught one of the corpses in the eye and exploded out the back of its head. The body fell over and rolled around in the dirt, its stained necktie flapping like a tongue.

Mason squeezed off another round, but aimed wide and split the calf of a dead woman passing behind his target, knocking her over. He fired again, taking out necktie's other eye, flattening him to the ground, where he flopped around and tried to get up.

"Doesn't stop them," Mason told me. "They still smell us fine, or sense us, or whatever, but it evens the odds a bit if they can't see to chase us."

I scanned the herd of wormfeeders, seeing many empty eye sockets that had been blown out by rifle fire.

"I wanted you to know I'm a damn good shot," said Mason.

"You missed that second one," I said.

"Think you can do better?"

"Hand me the gun."

"Fuck, no."

"Gonna have to trust me sooner or later."

"Enough," Klug said. "We need to get back now."

I shrugged. What the hell? I'd have my contest with Mason another time. I was sure if we spent any amount of time together—sooner or later—it would come.

Klug and I clambered down the ladder with Jaime and Scopes, quiet as we could. The administration wing stood as empty and still as we'd left it. At the cafeteria, the four of us split to return to our cells. Klug and Scopes headed off into the darkness; Jaime and I moved together toward our cellblock. We didn't speak, but Jaime helped me find my way back along a path different than the one I'd taken to meet Klug. It led to a hallway that connected to the cellblock on the other side of my cell, and that's where they jumped us: two Aryan Brotherhood shitheads, looking for me for payback.

One of them took Jaime off his feet with a pipe to the back of his legs, and the other threw his weight at me, trying to connect with a makeshift sap of rocks stuffed into a rag. He was fat and slow and I dodged every shot, sliding along the floor until his mass shifted enough that I could free my shiv. The fat man dripped sweat and squawked about what he was going to do to me once he made me his punk, how my ass would be his to peddle to all his friends, and his first customer would be Baldwin. Turns out scaredy-cat Baldwin had slipped them as many cigarettes as he could scrounge together to take me out before I killed him. Fat man gave me more than an earful before I thrust the broken penknife blade into his neck and forced it until the tip broke out the back. He cried out and then dropped his dead weight on me like a falling cow.

I fought my way loose from his bulk, figuring his partner would be done with Jaime soon and coming for me. What I found when I crawled out from under, though, was Jaime propped up against the wall, both knees shattered, but the bloodied pipe gripped tight in his hands. Beside him, laid out with a shattered skull, stretched the second skinhead.

"Shit, brother," I said. "Your legs are all fucked up."

"Get out of here," Jaime said, wheezing from pain. "The King Snake's gonna need you. You got maybe four minutes before these fucks get up again. I ain't going anywhere with broken knees, so fucking leave me like you never met me. Go! Now!"

I've never been one to argue with good sense. Jaime was a lost cause as far as escaping and that meant he was as good as dead. It wouldn't do anyone a damn bit of good for me to be found covered in blood and out of my cell after lights out. I wrenched my shiv free from fat man's throat and threw it to Jaime.

"You might need this," I said.

"For them?" Jamie said. "Or for me?"

"Your choice."

I jumped shadows back to my cell. When I got there I pressed a pillow over Baldwin's face without even slowing down and beat him until my knuckles got raw. I made sure he knew how the dogs he'd sicced on me had died and how I held him responsible for losing Jaime. Only thing that kept me from killing him then and there was knowing the son of a bitch wouldn't stay dead.

SEVEN

That night I dreamt of Evelyn rising from her grave, pleading with me to find her, and I tried to, I really did, but the harder I looked, the more she faded away until she vanished altogether. After that I wandered through a field of mist, where foggy gray eddies hid something right beyond my sight. Giant fleeting shapes moved by me and strange masses passed overhead.

Voices called out, speaking names I didn't know. I walked for what felt like hours, lost, aimless, until I tripped over something hard and fell to the ground.

Lying on my back, I looked up and watched the mists peel away. Hundreds of pairs of eyes stared at me through the gray haze. They floated in the gloom, dim constellations of observance, of judgment, all of them focused on me. I covered my face with my hands to blot them out and scrambled to my feet. When I dared to look again, the mist and the eyes were gone. The world revealed was like it always had been, except that everyone was dead and decomposing: grinning corpses drove cars, worked in stores, walked in and out of office buildings. A baby rolled by in a stroller with a bottle of blood clutched in its pudgy gray hands. Its mother smiled as she pushed the stroller around a corner. By the time I realized who they were, they were already gone. I searched for them, but the streets of the city went on forever like a wild maze of hot concrete and shining steel radiating out from me. Alleys became dead ends. Bars appeared in windows. Sidewalks circled back on themselves. The air grew wet and suffocating. I found a deep, empty doorway and sunk into it, pulling out from the flow of dead life that coursed through the streets.

I snapped awake with Evelyn's laughter echoing in my head. Lying in the dark, listening to my memories, thinking of Evelyn and all I'd put behind me and all that lay ahead—that was the first time in my life the notion of suicide ever sprang to mind.

Well, I thought, *fuck that.*

DELLA:
EIGHT

Della Townsend only ever trusted two men in her life and both had died long before the dead plague began. No matter how much she missed them, she was grateful her brother and her father had not lived to see what became of the world. Six months back Della had lost her mother, too, and she had thought she could not get any more alone than that. Life had proven her wrong when it stranded her, one of three women trapped in a prison full of violent men under siege by the walking dead. It did not matter that Warden Grove gave the women secure, private quarters and declared them off limits to protect their so-called virtue. His word was insufficient to stop the propositions and insinuations, the leers, and crude gestures, and the surreptitious gropes whenever an opportunity presented itself. That Della did not get along with the other nurses—Lucinda Tancredo and Sue Oberon—was no help to her situation either. Lucinda and Sue were young and naive enough to believe the dead plague would blow over and pretty soon life would go back to normal.

They flirted with the guards. To get things they wanted and make sure they had protectors, they even fucked some of them, taking care to keep it secret from the warden. Della did not do such things. She worked in the infirmary, sometimes sixteen hours a day, and when she was not working, she kept herself closed off in the cell she had been given as living quarters. Not a man inside failed to remind her in some way of her two ex-husbands, and those men had taught her more than a few hard lessons. She knew it was inevitable, though, that men would come for her, probably two or three at once to make sure she could not resist. She had already broken the nose of one guard who had grabbed her ass and smacked another who had propositioned her, and she had even seen a strange light in Warden Grove's eyes when he looked at her the last time he visited the infirmary. She knew men like this resented her for holding back. Sooner or later, they would want to put her in her place. She hoped she would be long gone before that happened.

If she really needed help, there was Combest. He liked to come by her cell, tapping his club against the bars, smiling while he waited for her to invite him in, like he was doing now. She nodded for him to enter because it was easier than running him off. She thought she knew what Combest wanted, but he was too soft to take it from her. Still, she sat up straight and smoothed her skirt down to cover her thighs. No reason to encourage him.

"What do you want, Randy?" she said.

"Came to see how you're doing with everything we got going on. Things got a little tense in the tower last night. Thought you might be nervous. Thought we could talk some."

"All right, have a seat."

Della kept a folding chair in her cell, and Combest liked to settle into it like it was made of glass. He set his hands on his knees. They were trembling.

"Think we can do this?" he said.

"We have to, unless you prefer hanging."

"Maybe there's another way. Behind closed doors, Grove's talking like there's going to be something after all this. He's asking some of the guards to delay their salvation so they can help him do God's work later on."

"He ask you?"

"Not yet."

"Not ever. You're not the missionary kind."

Combest tilted his chair back on two legs and balanced there with his head touching the cement wall behind him. He always sat like that, like a submissive dog on its back.

"Bet he asks you."

Della scowled. "I'm not the missionary kind, either."

"Tell you what, though, to his eyes, you're more pure than Lucy and Sue. He knows they're catting around. Doesn't like it, but he figures it cuts the tension among the guards if some of them get a little release now and then. Makes those gals tainted, though. You, on the other hand, he considers a real woman, mature. He has moments when he stares out his office window, pining over his lost Missus, and I swear he's got you on his mind too. Wants you to be the good woman behind the great man."

"I'd just wind up stabbing him in the back. He's cracked. I don't want any part of his work." Della glanced at her watch. Almost 8 a.m. She was due at the infirmary soon.

"You might change your mind if he asks you."

"Not likely. What do you care anyway?"

Combest shrugged. "Figured if you had his ear, you might put in a good word for me."

"You backing out of Klug's plan?"

"No. But I wonder if it's smart. I really want to know: Do you think we can do this thing?"

Della nodded.

"Not sure I trust the King Snake," said Combest.

"Don't. Not even a little. But if anyone can get us out of here, he can. Once we're out, though, watch your back, and be ready for a double-cross."

"I don't like working with cons, especially Klug's thugs, and this new guy, Cornell. Some of the guards aren't much better."

"Mason's solid," Della said. "I knew him a little back in high school. He played football. He was a family man."

"Not anymore."

"No."

"Sad thing, that."

"We're living in sad times."

Combest stood and folded the chair. "I'd feel a lot better if I could get a beer. Used to head home from here at the end of the day, fire up the charcoal grill in the yard, and sit out there with a cold one until sunset. Maybe listen to a little music, or maybe only to the breeze rustling the trees. On Fridays, I'd have a couple of the neighbors over. Sure took the edge off things."

That day, watching Combest fold the chair and lean it against the wall, Della saw him in a different light. He always left her cell with a longing look in his eyes, and she often pitied him for it, thinking it spoke of a base desire, but today it made her wonder what kind of man he had been in the old world. Maybe she had read him wrong. Maybe he was not after her, but only looking for a neighbor to talk to and a normal conversation to make life seem a little less insane.

"What kind of music?" she asked.

"Blues." Combest laughed. "Cause, you know, I thought life was hard back then."

"Randy, did you have family out there?"

Combest straightened, keeping his back to Della. He did not answer her right away. He seemed so still that she felt a twinge of guilt over maybe touching a raw nerve.

"Everybody had family out there," he said. "Everybody has someone."

He moved toward the door, keeping his face turned away, and left. As Combest's footsteps diminished along the corridor, Della thought, *everybody but me.* Then she stood and readied herself for work.

NINE

The dead and dying came in all day that day. A nasty flu had been going around, and there was no medicine to fight it. Most with the virus recovered after a few days; some did not. People whose bodies had not yet picked a side filled the beds. Doctor Foley hardly had any regular patients to treat anymore. He bitched about his infirmary having been turned into a disassembly line, his examination tables into chopping blocks. He could take apart a body in under two minutes if he wanted to, but when the fourth corpse rolled in before noon that day, he started playing a game, using every last second, timing his final snip of the spinal cord with the moment when the dead man's eyes flashed open and his jaw began to click. Foley's game spooked the guards on duty, Calderon and Hammond, as well as Sue Oberon, and it frightened Della. It was not the risk that bothered her so much as it was the change in Foley's demeanor. He declined her offer to take over for a while so Della let it go and kept working until her white dress was stained almost solid red.

Every chance she got, she slipped a few more items out of the medicine cabinet and hid them in her clothes. The cabinet should have been locked, but Foley was too distracted or too tired to care about such details. She had already collected antibiotics, sterile gauze and bandages, analgesics, surgical thread and needles, and a thermometer, and she planned to lift more things later. She wanted to take some morphine and Valium, but those supplies were running low, so she would have to wait until the last opportunity or their absence would be noticed. Mason, the third guard working chop duty that day, ran interference, distracting the others and blocking Della from sight whenever he could. Of all the men trapped in the prison, Mason was the only one Della liked, but he was so immersed in anger and grief, she thought it might end him.

Mason went off duty at 4 p.m., and by then, Della had doubled the supplies she had already lifted. The stream of incoming dead dried up, although more would no doubt come later. Tancredo and Oberon left for the cafeteria, and Foley went into his office to nap and closed the door, leaving Della and

Mason alone in the gore-stained room. Della took cleaning supplies out of a closet, set them on a countertop, and prepared to scrub. She saw Mason heading for the door and caught him by the arm on his way out.

"Hey," she whispered. "Thanks. Got us a good stash going."

"We'll need it," Mason said.

"I want to ask you something," she said. "Why don't you ever talk about it?"

"About what?"

"The day the bus came. If I were you I'd have died that day."

"Dying doesn't mean what it used to."

"You know what I mean." Della let go of Mason's arm and then lifted two bottles of ammonia from the mop bucket. "You ever want to talk it out, I'm here. Okay?"

"Tell me something. You hear a lot of guards talking about who they lost? About their families, wives, girlfriends?"

"Not too many."

"Because they don't know what happened to them, and long as it stays that way, maybe what's keeping them going is hoping that *their* family, *their* wife, *their* girlfriend got lucky, that someone who loves them is hiding someplace safe, waiting for them to come home. Me, *I know.* I saw them at the end, standing proud and beautiful while that insane, self-righteous shitsmear had them murdered in front of me."

Della felt foolish and clumsy. She did not comprehend the depth of bitterness and grief in Mason's voice. It was like a deep vein of toxic metal running through the earth.

"You remember what Grove said when it happened?" Mason asked.

Della had rushed up to the tower with Doctor Foley that day to argue that if Grove would not let the people on the bus into the prison then he should at least allow Foley out to treat their injured. Grove hadn't even let Foley speak. He had been preoccupied with Mason, who had gotten there first to plead for the lives of his family. The warden ranted like a true fire-and-brimstone preacher, but she could not recall what he had said. Too many people had been shouting. She shook her head.

"I remember. He said, 'There's the world out there, and it has its sinners, and here inside these walls, we have ours. For now the world out there is dead to us. That's God's plan. You and I aren't to question it,'" Mason said. "Then he gave the order to open fire."

Della remembered Mason screaming after that, almost as loud as the gunfire, his voice echoing in the watchtower.

"Don't know how much you saw then or if you knew who was who. My boys survived the gunfire. My wife didn't. The dead got up and finished off the wounded."

"I'm sorry," Della said. "I...I shouldn't have asked."

"S'all right. I know you meant well," Mason said. "I'm coping as well as any man could. Okay? So don't fret about me cracking when we bust out of here."

"I won't. I wasn't."

"The thing I can't stop thinking about is how Melissa and the boys must have felt so relieved when they reached the prison, thinking they'd found sanctuary, only to have it yanked away from them. Every time I close my eyes, I see her, how she stood with my sons, while all the people from the bus pounded on the gates. She knew I was watching, and she wouldn't cry or show fear. Maybe she believed I'd find a way to come through and get them inside. Whatever they'd done to make it this far, whatever they'd suffered, they'd only fought for a chance that never existed. I won't be surprised once we leave this place, if we find ourselves in the same position."

"Mason." Della placed her hand on his arm.

"You know when it was all over that bastard Grove had the nerve to say a prayer for them?"

Della remembered that part. It had sent Mason into such a violent rage that the other guards had cuffed him and dragged him into a cell to cool down.

"I keep my mouth shut," Mason said, "Because I don't want to take anyone else's hope away. In a perverse way, I'm one of the lucky ones. The wondering is over for me. I know. *I. Know.* I owe that to Warden Grove. So, if you think you're going to cozy up and comfort me, and we're going to bust out of this place running together for some happy ending, you'll be a lot better off sticking to your bandages and your medicine."

Mason shook free of Della's hand and left.

Della sank to a chair and cried.

When she looked up again, Foley stood in the open door of his office, staring at her with wet, bloodshot eyes. He was looking at her hip. Della glanced at what had caught his eye. One of her lab coat pockets had split, and a wad of antibiotics packets was poking out.

"Shit," she said.

TEN

"Don't think I don't know what you're planning." Foley closed his office door behind him and Della. "I don't know the details, but a breakout is a breakout, and I understand now more than ever why people want out of here. Hell, a few weeks ago, I might've asked to come with you. So keep taking what you need on the sly, and I'll keep pretending I don't notice the missing inventory and how things have been rearranged on the shelf to make it look like there's more than there is. That isn't why I wanted to talk to you."

"No?" Della said.

Foley opened a drawer in his desk, removed a bottle of scotch, and set it on the blotter in front of him. It looked like smoky gold. He placed a paper cup beside it then filled the cup and offered it to Della. It surprised him when she accepted it. He produced another paper cup and poured a drink for himself.

"Bottoms up," he said.

Foley and Della drank. The doctor refilled their cups then put the bottle away.

"Sip this one," he said. "Don't know where or when I'll ever find more."

Della studied Foley's tired eyes. She knew he had become jaded—that had been inevitable—but she still saw a spark there of the compassionate, intelligent man she had met when she first started working with him. She had recommended to Klug that they include Foley in the breakout, but Klug had rejected him. Too independent, too high minded, too likely to be a problem, he had said, and she could not persuade him.

"If you're lighting out for the territories," Foley said, "there's some information you really ought to have."

"Like what?"

Foley hesitated. He looked Della up and down, and for half a moment, she feared he was going to proposition her or try to blackmail her for sex. Instead, he only nodded to himself as if he had answered an unspoken question. Then he reached under his desk and produced a black briefcase. He opened it and removed a case-hardened laptop. Della felt a gasp of air pass between her lips.

"You know you can't tell anyone I have this, right?" Foley said.

"I know," Della said. "Grove would punish you. Not that it's worth a damn since the 'Net went down."

"This one happens to be worth far more than a damn," Foley said. "The truth is, the 'Net may be down, but it isn't dead and buried yet."

He typed on the laptop keyboard then swiveled it around to show Della the screen. A Web browser displayed a grid of thumbnail images, links to videos, photo galleries, and documents.

"What the hell?" Della said.

"Don't get too excited. The public 'Net is gone. This one will be too soon. But for now it's still cooking, although there's nobody minding the shop. Doesn't matter. Very few people can access it. You need government or military clearance, an encrypted satellite connection, and last but not least, one of these spiffy combat-grade laptops."

"Why do you have that?"

"Got it from the CDC," Foley said. "I never meant to make a career out of being a prison doctor. I was on track for a research post in Atlanta, as of eight months ago. The Army drafted me for a little advance field work. Hooked me up with this. Had me filing data based on my observations here. They were interested in everything from basic vitals to illness trends to psychological conditions. Never told me why. I didn't ask. That comes with the job I'd applied for, so I think this was something of a trial run. But none of that's important. Look here."

Foley moved the cursor over a grainy thumbnail and clicked the link. A video player replaced the grid. A fuzzy image filled its screen. Beneath the image were the words "Posted by Birch," followed by a date from last week. Foley clicked play. The image sprang to jerking motion. A pair of eyes peered out from rotted flesh. The focus was poor, but the eyes swiveling in their sockets were vibrant and white. They glistened. Della did not understand. She glanced at Foley, who directed her back to the screen. The movie focus blurred then sharpened and the view inched back. The eyes diminished in the frame. The skin around them shifted and wrinkled. Movement came into the top of the frame. It took Della several seconds to realize what she was looking at. It was a dead man restrained in chains, facing away from the camera, and snarling as he tried to look over his shoulder. The eyes at the center of the image were embedded in his back, below the base of his neck. The video ended and froze on the same image with which it had started.

"What...?" Della said. "What is that?"

"Damned if I know," said Foley. "But it's something real. I know Birch. He's a doctor and a military officer. I've traded a few e-mails with him, but he's finicky about keeping in touch. Remember when this all started and we figured somewhere someone was holed up working out a solution? That's Birch. The punch-line is he's stumped. But he's gone further than anyone else trying to decipher this nightmare. So when he posted this, I...well, I didn't know what to think. I've seen this twice in the last few days. An eyeball where it shouldn't be. In someone's foot the first time. In a kidney the second. I figured it was some anomaly, tissue growing where it shouldn't, like cancer, but tissue shouldn't be growing at all in the dead. I don't want people asking me any more questions I can't hope to answer so I kept it quiet."

"Why are you telling me?"

Foley closed the laptop, slipped it back into its case, and stuck it under his desk. "You're going out there. You need to be prepared. You need to know."

"That the dead have eyeballs in strange places?"

Foley shook his head. "That the dead are changing."

CORNELL:
ELEVEN

Figured I was done for the next morning when the screws caught sight of beaten and bruised Baldwin, but he covered up best he could, hid the limp I'd given him, and said nothing. He'd had one shot in him and it had failed. That sad son of a bitch would've eaten glass and stuck his hand in a blender if I told him to after that.

Gave me a scare, though, when the screws fetched me away from breakfast for an audience with Warden Grove. Two of them brought me to the administration wing and planted me on a bench outside the warden's office. After awhile another con came out, blubbering like a baby, eyes swollen, face red and purple. He clutched his left arm against his chest as he stumbled off in the direction of the infirmary.

My turn next.

Standard procedure for an audience with Grove meant standing stiff-backed and motionless in the warden's office while he reclined in a leather chair, puffing on a cigar, and two guards stood watch. Today it was Gamewood and Hammond. They ushered me in and Grove made me wait a little longer while he stared me down. Behind him a window looked out over the south lawn, where the road to town cut a dusty scar through the fields. Wormfeeders dotted the grass like a herd of strange livestock.

"Good morning, Mr. Cornell," Grove said. "Good of you to take the time to see me."

"Yes, sir."

Grove blew a cloud of smoke toward me. It drifted up and across the room's sparse decoration—a wall of framed photographs of the warden from his days as a preacher, stumping at the pulpit, shaking hands with local bigwigs and state politicians. He had a few diplomas mixed in, and here and there pictures of his family. I wondered how he felt about losing them. Probably pleased as fucking punch that they were united with God and looking forward to joining them.

"After a good many years preaching, I felt the need for a new challenge," he told me, noticing my interest. "Ten years ago I came here to shine the light of truth on the wicked. It has been most rewarding. Now, you may be wondering what this has to do with you. Well, given recent events, it seemed appropriate you should have the same chance for salvation as any other man in my keep. I let you witness my good works in the yard, and I hoped you would be swayed by them."

Grove took a thick file from his drawer and dropped it on his desk blotter. He opened it and leafed through a stack of clippings and photocopies covering my story.

"Then I realized that I was mistaken. You're a different kind of man than most incarcerated here. Your road to redemption cannot be as simple as theirs. You're an intelligent, capable fellow, Mr. Cornell. But I believe you're crippled by a towering sadness."

He lifted a scrap of newspaper with a photo of Evelyn. The picture had been in a camera I had when the police arrested me, but Evelyn had been dead by the time it was published.

"Could I be correct?" Grove said.

The warden was good, I'll grant him. He sniffed out my weak spot like a crow digging for grubs. I didn't answer.

"Tell me about her," he said.

"Nothing to tell anymore."

"Did you love her? She was with child when she died, wasn't she? Was it yours? A new life. Were you happy about that or did it terrify you? Maybe both?"

"I don't want to talk about it."

Grove snapped his fingers. Gamewood slammed his club into my kidney. The pain buckled me to my knees. I clenched my teeth against a scream.

"I'm a patient, understanding man," said Grove. "Share your grief with me. Share it with the Lord. Let go your burden and cleanse yourself."

Gamewood struck again, glancing his wood off my shoulder blade. Fresh hurt blasted through me like slivers of hot glass.

"The way to redemption begins with the admission of sin," Grove said. "Do you hate yourself for leading your woman to a wretched life that got her killed?"

Despite my throbbing aches, I laughed. No one had ever led Evelyn to do anything.

"No? The child, then? Help me out here, Mr. Cornell. We both know you don't lose any sleep over the money you stole. That was only ever a means for you, not an end. Such pedestrian transgressions are of little interest to either one of us, I think."

Hammond's boot slammed my stomach, lifted me onto my side, and left me gasping for air.

"Whether you know it or not, choose to accept it or deny it, you've arrived at a crossroads. Your body will die and rot, as all men's bodies do. The question is whether your soul will remain trapped within it after your death or be freed to obtain its heavenly reward. I offer you salvation, Mr. Cornell. You suffer no easy pain, but time heals all wounds. I can give you the opportunity to lick yours and knit your soul back together."

A fist crushed the back of my neck and drove me to the floor. I smacked my forehead, bit my tongue, and saw stars.

"You're a charming, gifted young man with the ability to secure people's loyalty and capture their imagination as well as demand their attention and obedience. These are skills I'd find most useful in my upcoming mission. My work here will end soon. Last night commenced the final stage. Those who can be saved here will be, and those who cannot be saved will be sent to their eternal damnation. When that is done, I'll lead a group of men into the world to free those worthy of redemption and guide any we might find still living toward their everlasting rewards. There are many, many good souls trapped in foul decaying flesh. God has charged me with their rescue."

I clawed onto all fours, only to feel Gamewood's baton lash into my thigh. It knocked me sideways, and I gasped.

"You possess the elements of a leader. With your charisma you could have been a businessman, an entertainer, even a politician. But life dealt you a bad hand, didn't it?" Grove skimmed pages in his file and pulled out a copy of an old police report. "A good student with and aptitude for language and science, until at age 17, you were arrested for armed robbery, carrying a busted gun that couldn't even be fired. Bet you got a story to tell about that. Your two friends took pleas, fingered you as the ringleader, and did eighteen months in juvenile detention. You took your chances with a jury and wound up sentenced as an adult. Served nine years. I imagine you learned an awful lot about robbing banks in that time, and maybe made a few useful connections."

Grove stacked the papers and closed the folder.

"There's something better than that inside you. You need some time to find it and let it out. Why not do some good while you get your soul right? A man like you could help sustain my men's commitment and help me win the trust of the wanting multitudes."

My thoughts whirled like mud in a rain-swept river. Pain rose in me like floodwaters. I clung to a flotsam desire to lighten the burden I'd borne since the day Evelyn died and part of me began to buy into Grove's insanity. He was right about one thing: I needed to face my guilt for letting down Evelyn, for betraying us both through my failure. I'd fooled myself long enough about that. I could never straighten myself out in prison, cowering and scraping to survive when I should be running circles around these madmen and losers. "Play by your own rules," Evelyn had always said, but I'd given up. I'd forgotten and hobbled myself, thereby making my debt to her a thousand times worse.

Grove offered a way out—except I already had that, I reminded myself, unless I get beaten so badly I can't walk. Like Jaime. Then that door shuts forever.

"Evelyn…" I said, gasping for air. "I promised Evelyn…two things. Protect her always…and never…kill a man…in cold blood. Broke both…the day she died."

It was the truth. Grove would've known if it wasn't. But speaking those few words hurt more than any beating ever could. I had fired on the bank manager in a blistering rage after he shot Evelyn, but those two rent-a-cops had been as shocked as I was when their boss drew his weapon. They would've backed down. I didn't need to kill them. I wanted to do it because all the light had left my world and cast me in such despair that killing seemed like no big thing when in fact it was of such a magnitude that it threatened to overwhelm and obliterate me even now. That's how the jackal snares its prey; it waits for that solitary error, that wrong turn from which there's no recovering.

"Thank you." Grove waved off the guards. "I appreciate your honesty."

He circled his desk, lifted me under the arms, and helped me to a chair. He took a handkerchief from his pocket, wiped the blood from my face, and left the cloth in my hand. He poured a glass of water and held it to my lips so I could sip from it. Every inch the Good Samaritan.

"Who decides?" Needles of pain flared behind my eyes. Blood oozed down the back of my throat. "Who says...who's worth saving...and who gets damned?"

"God has appointed that burden to me." Grove's quiet, unbreakable voice made me feel like worms were eating their way out of my stomach. "I'm here to do His work, and I shall not flinch from my duties."

"When you're done?"

"We all go to our reward someday."

It's only another way out, I told myself. That's all. A back-up plan. Make no more of it. Break out with Klug or throw in with this lunatic, once I'm on the other side of the walls, I can get away clean, no problem. Sometimes it's okay to play by the crazy man's rules, long as you don't forget your own.

"You'll begin your mission tonight. You'll assist me at the gallows. The men have heard the Word from me too often. They resent it. A new voice must deliver them the message of salvation. It has to come from one of their own, now," Grove said.

I hadn't anticipated that.

Damn jackal had pounced when I was down, and his hot breath was steaming at the back of my neck.

TWELVE

Things didn't go well for Jaime.

The guards found him fighting off the resurrected skinheads with my shiv in time to keep him alive, but his blood drove one of the bastards to gnaw clean through his leg above the knee. Damn shame a right guy who could fight like that losing a leg. Least he didn't have to live with it long.

That night he came propped up on crutches with the first group of penitent convicts Warden Gove paraded onto the gallows. Jaime played along with Grove's theatrics. When the executioner fitted his hood, he welcomed it with an oddly gratified expression, like he'd finally gotten the answer to some question that had been itching away under his skin for a long time. I saw it because I was standing three feet to his right. Then the traps opened, and Jaime and his two companions dropped into oblivion. Grove let them hang a while, before the hacks untied them and threw their quaking bodies on the bonfire.

Better than spending your last days a cripple lying around waiting for the end, I suppose.

Others had the same idea. The beaten man who'd passed me outside the warden's office that morning was in the next trio, with his busted arm in a sling. Some of the cons had bought into Grove's proposition, and the warden couldn't have looked more pleased with how it was going. But every time he flashed his swinish grin, I thought of Combest and Georges, who were right at that moment siphoning gas in the loading dock. By the end of the day tomorrow, Warden Grove would be another bad memory in the back of my mind.

Midway through the service Grove had the guards usher me to center stage, where I spouted the words Grove had scripted, mixing them up like he'd asked to make them sound like my own. When you rob banks for a living, you become attuned to the sensation of having people's attention, and I had plenty of it that night in the form of seething hatred and unfettered disgust from the convicts who thought I'd flipped to save my own skin. Guess they were right, even if the words meant nothing to me. But I didn't care what they thought. There was no reason for me to play it their way and wind up dead. Them judging me made them no different than all the other people I'd known wanting to tell me how I ought to live and resenting me for not buying their bullshit code. That night I saw no difference between my fellow inmates and the men who'd locked us all away, or even the hungry, mindless dead. Shit, at least the goddamned wormfeeders didn't lie about wanting to eat you.

After my speech, three cons took the platform. They were different than the others. They'd been beaten and crushed, all right, but anger still smoldered in their expressions. If they could've gotten loose, they'd have torn me and Grove and everyone else on the platform limb from limb. The supercops had to drag them out in cuffs and hold them tight while they roped them up. Grove kept right on preaching.

"Words do not allow me to adequately express how pleased I am that some of you have chosen to accept my aid in securing eternal salvation. I have faith that more will make the same decision. But I understand that some among you are incorrigible and incapable of repenting your ways, and I have elected to waste no time with men of such disposition, men like this trio of unrepentant sinners behind me. Witness their fate. It is the end of all those who choose the path of sin over forgiveness. May they do some good by their example."

The hatches popped open and the men dropped through. I felt a genuine pang of loss watching those unbroken spirits die. Felt a little sick when their corpses began to twitch around at the end of their ropes. Grove left them there for a time, making us all watch, and then the screws came, hauled them up, and dragged them away. It was not to the bonfire they took them but to a steel pen erected beside the gallows to Grove's left-hand side. In they went, tumbling over each other as they clambered onto their feet. They reached through the bars, straining toward the crowd, their heads tilted at strange angles on noose-snapped necks. They couldn't see through their hoods, but there's no doubt they still knew we were there. No doubt at all about their hunger.

THIRTEEN

Next day came the day of the four suicides, and my sudden yearning to return to solitary. Watching that wiry kid burn I suffered my first real pangs of doubt about our chances. I shrugged them off, though, and took heart in how all that hubbub made a fine distraction for Paulson and Combest sneaking provisions from the kitchen and Della slipping medical supplies out of the infirmary. That afternoon I crossed paths with the King Snake in the yard.

"Don't cross me, Cornell," he said. "Your song and dance for Grove better be nothing more than an act."

"Do I strike you as the preaching type?"

"Heh. No," Klug said.

"Grove dragged me into his office and gave me an ultimatum. Had a couple of hacks sweet talk me with batons, too, as you might have noticed," I said. "This shit is only me going along to buy time."

"I know all about it. You did what you had to. Kept your mouth shut, too. Okay. Right now I still trust you. So you keep doing what you have to. Word is out you're still under my protection no matter what your fellow inmates would like to do to you for turning Judas on them. So, stay tight with Grove for now. Just makes it all the sweeter when we pull this off right under his nose. But if you try to fuck with me, I will turn your skull into my personal piss pot."

Klug moved on before I could answer, not wanting to be seen talking to me too long. He never mentioned Jaime.

DELLA:
FOURTEEN

The afternoon before the breakout, blood coated almost every surface in the infirmary. No one bothered cleaning up right away, especially after the run of corpses that had come in that morning and afternoon. Fights were breaking out every few hours, now, and more than a few of them resulted in at least one fatality. Everyone knew there would simply be more dead later or tomorrow or the next day, until Warden Grove finished his work or the last shred of order broke down inside the prison and the bodies lay where they fell until they got up again. Rumors were some of the gangs were planning mass killings of rivals to throw the prison into chaos so they could seize control. Grove had clamped down so tight, though, that no more than fifty inmates were out of their cells at any one time during the day. As Della watched Calderon and Gamewood cart away the latest pile of bagged, twitching body parts, she hoped everything would hold together for one more night. She did not know how many more bodies she could stand to cut apart. She was almost as fast as Foley, now, but she lacked his detachment. It still hit her hard doing it every day. Foley moved like a machine and between corpses he shut himself off in his office, leaving Della and the other nurses to treat the few cons and guards who came in with everyday ailments.

Late that afternoon the hacks brought in three inmates and a guard, all dead in the wake of a spontaneous suicide in the cafeteria. At the sound of the commotion, Foley shuffled out of his office.

"Only four?" he said. "Piece of cake. Everyone take a body and start carving."

Della, Tancredo, and Foley grabbed tools and moved to work on the dead cons. All of them stopped short when Sue Oberon screamed. She had gone to work on the guard, Phil Hammond. Her knees bent, and she fell against the stainless steel table that held Hammond's corpse. She buried her face against his chest and screamed into it. Clothing and dead flesh muffled her voice.

"We don't have time for this," said Foley. He glanced at the clock as he took Oberon by the shoulders and drew her away from the dead body. "There's nothing you can do now, Sue. Sit this one out, okay? Give me a few minutes, and then I'll get you something to take the edge off."

Oberon erupted with a shout and twisted away, shoving Foley aside. She grabbed a scalpel from a tray of surgical tools and waved it in front of her. "Don't you fucking touch me! Don't anybody touch me. And nobody touches Phil."

"Sue, please," Della said. "He's gone, honey. I know how you felt about him, but the man you knew is dead. And you know what he's going to be when he comes back."

"I don't care." Oberon backed up against Hammond's table and grabbed his pale hand. "It's not right. It shouldn't be him, not Phil. We were going to stay together when all this bullshit blew over. We were going to be together outside."

"That was never going to happen, Sue," Foley said. "This won't ever blow over. The dead plague isn't going away, but if you don't put down the scalpel and let us do our jobs, you, me, and everyone in this room stands a good chance of winding up like Phil right now, today."

"Go ahead. Do what you want to the others. No one touches Phil," Oberon said.

Foley sighed. "All right people, watch the clock. Della, Lucinda, start on the others. Gamewood and Calderon, grab blades and start cutting."

"Fuck that, I don't know what to do," said Calderon.

"It's not surgery, Raul. Just slice them apart," Foley said. "Work fast. Immobilize them. Sever the joints."

The clock over the door loomed like the noonday sun. Beneath its steady ticking, the nurses and guards became blurs of motion, blood-smeared uniforms tipped with surgical steel edges that bit into cooling flesh.

Foley approached Oberon. "Sue, drop the blade now. You're a good nurse. I can't afford to lose you."

"Fuck you. Stay away."

"Please, Sue."

"No," she said. Her voice lowered to almost a whimper. "Maybe...maybe Phil will be different when he rises."

"He won't be," Foley said.

"You don't know for sure. You can't know."

"Don't be childish. It's not like Hammond was your only boyfriend. Everyone knows how you are. Someone else will take his place inside of a week, and you'll forget all about Hammond. You're in shock now. Put it in perspective. He didn't really matter to you that much, did he? He gave you nothing you won't be able to get from the next man in line you let into your bed."

Oberon gaped as if she had been slapped.

Della cringed at the cruelty of Foley's words, but sometimes that was what it took to reach people who were not thinking straight. Oberon wavered. Her hand holding the scalpel dipped. Tears streamed from her eyes. Foley edged closer. Della released the deep breath she had been holding, but then the hand she was cutting away from its wrist jerked to life and its clumsy fingers grabbed at her. Too much time had passed.

A moment later, Hammond's corpse jerked sideways, dropped halfway off the table, and grabbed onto Oberon as it slid the rest of the way over the edge. The dead thing pulled the nurse to the floor with it. Oberon screamed, the sadness in her voice replaced with terror. Foley rushed forward, grabbed Oberon's arms, braced his foot against Hammond's dripping torso, and tried to pull them apart. The dead man sank his teeth into the nurse's back and clamped down. Oberon flailed as Hammond's mouth ground down to her bone. She panicked and slashed the scalpel, slicing Foley's arm. The doctor swore and jumped away. Blood welled up along a six-inch gash down his sleeve.

"A little help?" Foley said.

Calderon and Gamewood had cut every joint on one dead con and were helping Tancredo finish off another. Della worked on the third with a cut through the neck and spine. All three dead men bucked on their tables, broken bodies drawn toward the living flesh beyond their reach. Della darted across the room and grabbed Foley, shoving his sleeve up to examine his cut. It was clean and shallow but bleeding fast. She pulled adhesive pressure bandages from the cabinet and began slapping them on in a row up Foley's arm like giant stitches.

Calderon shouted and swung a motorized surgical saw, aiming for Hammond's neck. Gamewood came from the other side with an electric bone saw and pressed the whirling blade into the dead guard's shoulder. The saws cut flesh and sent blood spurting onto Oberon, starting her screaming again.

"Somebody get her clear," Gamewood said.

Tancredo grabbed her friend's arm and tried to pull her loose, but Oberon sagged, dead weight. Her eyes blanked out. Calderon wrenched his saw free and swung again, trying to sever Hammond's neck, but the dead man lurched sideways and the saw blade punched against Oberon's skull, biting through bone and deep into her head. Tancredo screamed and scrambled away.

"Oh, shit," said Calderon.

Foley pushed past Della and shoved the stunned Calderon aside. He pulled the saw out of Oberon's skull, drawing soft flecks of brain and blood-matted hair with it. Grabbing Hammond's head with one hand, he sawed at the neck with the other.

"It's a saw you fucking imbecile. Not a machete," Foley told Calderon. "What are you so afraid of? How's he going to bite you with his teeth buried in Sue's back? It's a wonder someone as stupid as you remembers to breathe."

Foley drew the saw back and forth twice more; Hammond's head popped loose from its body. Foley yanked it free from Oberon's back, tearing out a chunk of flesh with it. He hurled the head into a corner. Gamewood had severed one of Hammond's arms and now he started on the other. Foley turned to the legs. A minute later, Hammond's corpse lay in pieces on the blood-slicked floor. The room quieted, and the only sounds came from the corpses rattling the tables and Oberon's shallow gasping. She was deep in shock, and she had lost a lot of blood. Tancredo knelt and cradled Oberon's head in her lap.

"Let's finish up here, folks," said Foley. "Clear out the dead. We've got more work ahead of us. Sue's not going to pull through, in case any of you were wondering." Foley was right. Oberon lingered for fifteen minutes, during which time Della and Foley worked with Calderon and Gamewood to bag and dump the four corpses they had cut to pieces. Tancredo stayed with Oberon, waiting until she breathed her last, and then she called Foley. The doctor declared her time of death, and with help from Gamewood, lifted her body onto a table. He took Oberon apart with unexpected gentleness. No one spoke. Everyone wanted her bagged and dumped before she started twitching. No one wanted to watch her resurrection. They almost made it.

Afterward Foley looked at Della with a wild gaze. "Getting out of here is a damn fine idea," he whispered to her. Then he went in his office and shut the door.

FIFTEEN

Having lost a guard and a nurse from his staff, Warden Grove came to visit the infirmary. He surveyed the gore and bits of dead flesh everywhere, looked at the damage done to the cabinets and tables, and shuddered at the sight of Gamewood and Della, both painted nearly black with drying streaks of blood. He bowed his head and prayed. His lips moved soundlessly for several minutes. He looked humbled. Della stopped mopping and waited in silence until he finished his prayer.

Grove lifted his head. "Where are the others?"

"Calderon went to change his uniform. Tancredo walked out. Don't know where to," said Gamewood.

"She and Sue were close," Della said. "Sue died in her arms."

"Doctor Foley?"

"Resting in his office." Gamewood gestured at the door.

"I'll get to him in a minute, then. Tell me how it happened," Grove said.

"Yeah, the kitchen crew brought in four bodies," said Gamewood, but he stopped when the warden waved him silent.

"Your story I'll read in your report, Mr. Gamewood." Grove took the mop from Della's hands and placed it in the bucket. "Are you injured?"

"No," Della said.

"That's good. Would you tell me what happened? Are you all right to talk about it?"

"It's like he said, they brought in four dead," said Della. She leaned back against the countertop and explained to Grove how Sue's reaction had endangered them all and led to her death.

"The wages of sin," Grove said when Della finished. "And incompetence, from the sound of it. Consider Calderon permanently off chop duty. I'll find him something equally unpleasant but better suited to his poor skills. Thank the Lord no one else was hurt."

Grove's gaze made a circuit of the room as if he were searching for something or cataloging the ruin. The rotten aroma of dead flesh and eviscerated bodies filled the air. It was like the constant taint of decay that hung in the atmosphere but a thousand times more potent.

"This is no place for a woman," Grove said. "Bless you for the good work you do, Ms. Townsend."

Della stiffened. "Thank you."

"God willing, you won't have to do it much longer. I'm confident the Lord above has other plans for someone as strong as you."

"I wouldn't pretend to know what the Lord has planned."

"It's true, his ways are hard to know, but the death and suffering that fills our days has sharpened my senses. I feel closer to God now than I have in years. He's shown me that I have a road to follow beyond these stone walls and iron bars. There's work for me in the outside world. God has entrusted me with a sacred duty. Thankfully, it isn't one I must undertake alone. I'll have a chosen group to share my burden. I want you to be a part of it. My work here will be finished soon. Then it'll be time for me and a few others to leave. I'd like you to be at my side, not just as a nurse, but as a friend, a colleague, and maybe, given time, something more."

Della slid along the counter away from the warden. She bumped the mop handle and spilled the bucket in which the mop stood. Bloody cleaning fluid gushed onto the tile. Della snatched up the mop and used it to keep the water and detergent from spreading too thin. The soap and bleach cut streaks of clean floor through the blood. Della pushed the mop around, concentrating on the floor to avoid the warden's stare.

"Give it some thought," Grove said. "I'm not asking a small favor. It's a true commitment to me, to the Lord, and to His work. But make sure you consider your options before you answer. You might find them less appealing than a life of righteous service."

Grove crossed the room and knocked on Doctor Foley's door. "Doctor Foley, open up," he said. "It's Warden Grove. Let's talk, son." Foley didn't answer. Grove turned the knob, and shouted, "Wake up, Doctor."

The door cracked open. Grove pushed it inward and leaned into the opening. A hand jutted out and seized him by the hair, tugging hard enough to pull him off balance and send him tumbling to the floor. Foley lurched into view, stumbling over Grove. The doctor's face looked ashen and flaccid, his eyes glassy. He moaned. In one hand he clutched the bottle of scotch he had shared with Della, empty now. His foot caught on Grove's elbow, and he tripped and landed on his knees. He dropped the bottle then and wrapped his hands around one of Grove's legs. His mouth stretched open to bite into it.

Grove shouted. He forced himself onto his back, breaking Foley's grip.

"Lord, help me!" the warden cried.

Gamewood rushed across the room and kicked Foley in the chest, tumbling him backward into the office. Grove scrambled away on all fours, slipping on the wet floor, dropping back onto his hands and knees each time he tried to stand. Gamewood grabbed him under the arms, helped him up. Foley's moaning, hissing corpse filled the doorway then staggered toward Gamewood. The guard stood with his back to it, off-balance while he stretched to support Grove. Della swung the mop around, planted the head against Foley's abdomen, and shoved with her full weight. The doctor jolted into his office again, tripped over a chair, and landed on his back on the floor.

"Stop him," Grove screamed.

Della withdrew the mop. The sight of Foley dead crushed her. On his desk a bottle of pills lay turned over, its contents scattered. Beside it was a hypodermic needle, a bubble of fluid still in the syringe. *Bastard*, Della thought, and then she slammed the door closed.

Seconds later, the dead doctor banged against the other side.

"What happened?" said Grove.

"He died in there," Gamewood said.

"Obviously, you idiot. But how? Heart attack?"

"The dead nurse cut him," Gamewood said. "Did he bleed to death?"

"The wound wasn't that bad," Della said.

"Did one of those things bite him?"

Della did not want to tell them what she had seen or what Foley said to her before he closed his office door for the last time. The urge to sob, to break down crying almost overwhelmed her, but she held it in check through her anger. Although a small part of her understood it, Foley's cowardice infuriated her. She had believed he was a better man, a stronger one, but he was like almost every other man she had ever known and dared to admire: weak and selfish. Della checked the clock. In a few more hours it would be time to meet the others at the loading dock.

"Did one of those things bite him?" Grove asked again, but no one answered. "I suppose it doesn't matter. Dead is dead. What do we do with him?"

Della said, "Unless you plan to grab a knife and start cutting, *we* do nothing. Gamewood and I, however, will dispose of Doctor Foley's corpse properly."

Grove scowled at Della. He noticed his suit was streaked with blood from his scramble across the floor. He swept a red clump from his sleeve.

"As you wish, Ms. Townsend. The infirmary is now yours to run. Let's you and I talk again soon, in my office, where we won't be interrupted."

Grove walked out. Della stared at Foley's door.

The thing on the other side pounded against it with a rhythm like a slow, steady heartbeat, and Della almost laughed at the irony.

CORNELL:
SIXTEEN

One of the first supplicants at that night's service was a low-level drug trafficker I'd met a few times many years ago and hadn't seen or heard of since. He winked at me and said how it was good to go out with a familiar face nearby. He was small and he burned fast in the bonfire. I hoped they'd all go quick and easy like that so I could be done, keep my rendezvous with Klug and the others, and get gone for good from living in the shadow of Warden Lane Grove.

The second wave included Baldwin, crossing the platform as straight and tall as he could, looking like one of the few who hadn't needed the warden's gentle coercion. I suppose I'd helped out somewhat in that department. He stared me down the whole time, and when the executioner fitted his hood, he flashed me a final smile that said he'd found a way to cheat me out of killing him. Guess it meant something to him, then, how he died. I wasn't sorry to see him go. He deserved to die uglier than he did.

Eighteen more cons took the long dive that night.

One prayed up until the moment the noose choked his throat closed.

Another pranced around and flipped us the bird while he shouted about how he'd see us all in Hell. That one landed in the pen.

There were nine wormfeeders crowded in there, bouncing off each other like catalyzed molecules, but the cage was too strong for them break free. Most of them had worked their hoods loose by now, and they never took their eyes off the crowd, never stopped staring at the living with that stark need that somehow crept up from their empty guts to shape their contorted expressions. I knew, then, the real reason for Mason's brand of target practice. We watched the dead die. They watched us live. A man could only be looked at that way for so long before he needed to react. I was glad I'd be leaving soon.

My first chance to slip away came when the service ended and Grove left the platform. Before I made it, one of the guards caught me dead on, and said, "Warden wants to see you."

Walking through the quiet corridors, I wondered what new torture Grove had devised for me, and I swear I heard the sniff and sensed the heat of the jackal's breath at the side of my face. I felt him nearby almost every hour of the day now, a dark, patient presence waiting for the weight of the mistakes I'd made to finally trap me for him. I promised myself—whatever came, whatever Grove threw at me—I wouldn't go down without a fight. One way or another, I would put my days of self-despair and licking my wounds behind me. Guess I should've known better than to go making promises to myself where the Warden Grove was involved. Down in his office he waited for me with half a dozen hacks, and I knew it had all gone to shit when I saw Old Corntooth cowering in a corner with a bitter, self-satisfied gleam in his wrinkled, dewy eyes.

"Think they're worried about you yet?" he asked. "Mr. Klug and the others don't like to be kept waiting, I'd imagine."

"Don't know what you mean," I said.

"Don't lie to me, Mr. Cornell. You can't protect them. Your old acquaintance already told us about the breakout, but he doesn't know the specifics. Now, I've seen a side of you that others have not, and so I'm willing to give you the benefit of the doubt and believe you were with left no choice but to go along with Mr. Klug's desperate scheme. Now, please, justify my faith in you, and tell me where to find these unrepentant sinners?"

Smart thing to do would have been to give them up to work myself in tight with Grove and bide my time till we left on his mission. I owed Klug nothing. He had only drafted me for his plan and would never have bothered with me if I didn't have something he wanted. It wasn't misguided loyalty that led me the other way. I'd simply had my fill of letting other people call the shots for me. Even if I went down right then, Klug's group would still have a chance to escape without me, and there had to be places other than Lohatchie that might be safe. Mostly, though, I hated to see some tired, broken-down pussy like Old Corntooth get a leg up on the few people I knew who weren't afraid to keep pushing for something other than the shit deal life handed them. And, of course, I had a singular dislike of the warden.

"Nobody's breaking out," I said. "What's the point? Where would they run?"

"Once down this road should've been enough for you, but I see we haven't made the progress I'd hoped." Grove waved on the guards. "I've never been one to shy away from a difficult case, though. All dogs can be trained."

No way was I going to let them kick the shit out of me again. I kissed a little farewell off to Evelyn, an apology for letting it end like this, so pitiful and mundane. I wondered if she might be waiting for me on the other side, not that I believed in all the God and afterlife hoodoo that Grove liked to shill—but damned if that wouldn't make everything all right and send all the pain away if I got to see her again.

Three of the hacks slid batons from their belts.

One tried to draw me out with a loose snap on his holster, an exposed gun inviting me to grab it and give them a reason to start pounding me. Then I wondered why they needed a pretense when the only law left was Grove's and he had brought them all here to beat on me. I glanced at the hack's badge: Georges. The only guard in on the breakout I hadn't yet met. The King Snake's specialty was making things happen; he was as much a clockmaker as a killer. There was no signal in Georges's steady gray eyes, but there couldn't be. He needed me to make the first move. Wouldn't pay for him to blow his cover if I wasn't smart enough to follow his lead and ballsy enough to risk the only option left for me.

Either way the gun offered me a way out.

I prayed it was the one I wanted.

When Georges raised his stick, I seized his automatic, dropped to the floor, rolled, and fired four shots. Three hit home and three guards went down. Before I had time to finish wondering if I'd made the right choice, Georges clubbed the fourth guard to his knees. The fifth froze in his tracks, confronted by the barrel of the gun in my hand. Georges produced a pistol from his back-up holster and aimed it at the warden. The amount of blood staining Grove's carpet told us at least two of the men I'd shot were dead. We all realized it together. Every man in the room glanced at the clock above the door. The countdown began.

Grove stood solid and stone-faced behind his desk. "What exactly do you think you're doing, men?"

"Fuck you, preacher," Georges said. "Consider this a changing of the guard."

"You won't accomplish anything this way except a lot of bloodshed," said Grove. "I'm not afraid to die. How about you? Or you, Mr. Cornell? You going along with this nonsense? Hell, boy, you're one of the few in this place who's actually got a future ahead of him."

I squinted, amazed. "What future? Prancing around like your trained dog?"

"Doing the Lord's work in these trying times. Working toward your redemption."

"Shit!" Georges shouted. "We don't have time for this! And I got no patience for snitches."

He whirled and fired a round into Old Corntooth's head. The impact from the slug knocked him hard against the wall. He slid to the floor, smearing a track of blood behind him. His eyes and his gap-toothed mouth hung wide open.

"I'm sorry, Fredericks. You threw in with the wrong side," Georges said to the last guard. Then he shot him in the chest.

"Cool it, man," I said. "Don't screw things up now."

"You don't tell me what to do," Georges said.

He lunged across Grove's desk and whacked the warden behind the ear with the grip of his pistol. The blow staggered Grove. Georges grabbed him and dragged him out of the office. I followed, slamming the door behind us.

"Leave Grove," I said. "He'll slow us down."

Georges' eyes narrowed, and he glared at me. "Who the fuck asked you, pretty boy? You do what I say."

I was grateful to be out, but Georges was feeling the strain, and I had no idea how high his breaking point was. So I shut up and let him take the lead. We followed the safest route from Grove's office off the administration wing, keeping out of sight along shortcuts and back corridors that Georges knew. Closer we got to the delivery docks the more deserted the way became. The entrance was right where Klug had showed us on his map and the whole area seemed utterly abandoned. In the garage and loading area were only Mason and Combest, piling packages of food onto the back of the truck.

When Mason saw Grove, he dropped the box in his hands. It split open against the floor. A can of peaches rolled out.

"What the fuck is he doing here?" Mason said.

"Klug here, yet?" said Georges.

"No," Mason told him. "Now, tell me why Grove is."

Georges kicked Grove down the stairs. The warden stumbled then fell to the concrete floor where he lay on his back, groaning.

"Get me some rope, Combest," Georges said.

Combest dug a line out of the supplies in the truck and handed it over. Georges tied Grove's hands behind his back, knotted his feet together, and dumped him in a corner.

"Dammit," Mason said. "I'm not playing with you. Why is Grove here?"

"I don't answer to you," Georges said. "Wait for Klug. Let him do the explaining."

Mason didn't like it, but he didn't press things with Georges. I figured he knew the man well enough to know how close he might be to snapping. The way he paced the room while I helped Combest and Mason pack the truck, I figured it couldn't take much more to push him over the edge.

Mason had come through with a stash of rifles, shotguns, and pistols. I tossed Georges empty weapon on the pile. With visible reluctance, Mason handed me a fresh automatic, and—damn the irony—it was a Beretta M9.

"Like you said, gonna have to trust you sometime," Mason told me, flashing a weather eye on Georges.

Fuck, I thought, *how long can these shitkickers keep it together?*

I made sure the Beretta was loaded, thumbed off the safety, and tucked it into my waistband.

Scopes and Della arrived next with two satchels of medical supplies, which Della locked in a chest built into the back of the van. She also brought a black briefcase, which she stowed in the truck. That made all of us, except for Klug and Paulson, and so we sat in the dimly lit garage and waited, most of us maybe wondering what kind of world we'd find outside the walls.

Not me, though.

I knew better.

The world I knew had been stillborn, except for the few shining lights I'd found in it, and I'd allowed the brightest of those to be snuffed out. I didn't expect to find much different out there from when I'd first left it other than a harder road to survival. I didn't care. All I wanted was my freedom. I'd come to prison wanting punishment for letting Evelyn down. Instead I got the same bullshit that kept me from living my life in the first place. Debasing my spirit was never going to help me reconcile my broken promises. Evelyn would've wanted me to live the best life I could on my terms, and that was exactly what I planned to do, what we all planned to do, for as long as we could among the dead. Too bad that jackal sniffing his hot nose through my hair didn't give a puddle of piss about our plans.

SEVENTEEN

We knew right away something was wrong when Paulson shuffled onto the loading platform stiff-legged and gray.

"Shit, he's dead," Mason said. He braced a rifle against his shoulder and squinted into the sight. "No one will hear if I fire. No one's even in this end of the building."

No one objected. Bullets gouged through Paulson's eyes and ripped open most of his skull. He crumpled then rolled over and dragged himself forward, falling from the loading platform to the floor with a wet splat.

"How do we get out of here? Paulson was supposed to have the keys," Combest said.

"Doesn't matter. Wait for Klug," Georges said.

"Maybe Paulson got the stuff before he croaked," Mason said. "Son of a bitch looks like he died on his feet. Must have been sick or something."

"Yeah, he was," I said, remembering how he'd been sweaty and trembling the day he brought me out of solitary.

Mason got a shotgun from the truck and edged toward Paulson. He pressed the barrel against the dead man's left hip and fired, nearly severing the joint. The shot knocked Paulson flat, and Mason shifted the gun over the dead guard's right shoulder and took off an arm. He reloaded and blasted the other, then sighted on Paulson's neck, and ripped the corpse's head most of the way loose. It didn't stop Paulson but he couldn't move very well after that, and Mason found little trouble beating off the advances of the dead man's wiggling limbs while he searched his uniform.

"Got it," he said.

An overloaded key ring dangled from his fingers. In the same hand, he clutched a blood-spattered notebook. He wiped it clean on his pants and opened it. The punch codes were written inside.

"We got everything we need," said Della. "Let's go."

"No!" Georges said. "We do nothing without Klug."

"Klug could be dead or worse," said Della. "The longer we wait—"

Georges slapped her. The smack resounded through the garage. Della staggered.

Mason and I moved at the same time, but I was closer and that's why Georges wound up on the floor with my foot on his throat rather than with a bullet in his head. Mason sure as hell meant to kill him. Someone needed to take control of this free-for-all before things got out of hand.

"Mason," I said, "point your gun somewhere else, give Combest the keys then get the truck ready."

"Fuck you, con. Step aside," said Mason.

Falling back on the tone of voice I'd used to corral terrified bank customers, I looked Mason in the eye, and said, "Mason, you dumb, ugly motherfucker, this is where things either break our way and we make a daring escape into the night or they go to shit and we all die really fucking painful deaths. Give Combest the keys and get the goddamn truck ready. Now!"

He hated me and he didn't want to do it. The give and take passed through his eyes while he weighed his response. I could almost read his thoughts in his face. He was thinking he could kill me and Georges easy with two or three quick shots, but then he'd have to answer to Klug and maybe the others. He lowered his weapon and did what I'd told him. For a moment, I felt like maybe we had a chance of getting out of there.

Combest took five tries to find the right key and open the lock on the loading dock. The electric doors crawled upward. Night poured in, and a narrow driveway stretched out toward it, turning into the darkness in the direction of the prison gate. I expected that fresh air to smell like freedom. Instead I choked on its stench. We couldn't see the wormfeeders, but we could smell them.

"What the hell?" Scopes said.

Three figures drifted toward the open doors. Four more followed. Scopes grabbed a flashlight and caught one full on in the beam—the fat Aryan punk whose neck I'd gouged. His partner trailed behind him. More figures staggered into the faint light. Among them were the victims of some of the cons who'd committed suicide, inmates who'd died less publicly than those in Grove's showcase sacrifices, and some guards who'd maybe refused to go along with the warden's plan. Guess he'd dumped them all here for cheap security in case anyone tried to do what we had in mind. About fifty of them blocked our path. Grove must have started stockpiling them early.

"What do we do, now?" Combest said.

"First of all, close that goddamn door." Klug's voice boomed down from the loading platform. "And Cornell, get your foot off of Georges."

The King Snake approached like his namesake: sly, easy, and lethal. He crouched over Warden Grove and lifted his face from the ground.

"Gotcha, motherfucker. *I win*," he said. Then he punched Grove in the nose and bounced his head off the floor.

Georges got back on his feet. "Son of a bitch, it worked."

"Damn right," the King Snake said. "Now get those guns off the truck and get ready. Y'all ain't going anywhere."

"What the fuck are you talking about?" Mason said.

"We have Grove. That means this whole fucking pit is ours," Klug said. "We put the warden out for show on his own damn gallows, hang his ass out where anyone who wants to can beat his twitching carcass with a stick day and night until it rots away to scraps, and every man in this place will be in our pocket. I have men waiting for my signal. Now I have guns to give them. We're going to turn this place into a fortress."

"And the King Snake will take his throne," I said.

Klug smiled, missing my sarcasm or ignoring it.

"What about escaping?" Della asked.

"To some cabin in the woods? When we can stay here, forage in town, and build an empire? I never wanted to leave, sweetcheeks. Just wanted Grove looking the other way long enough for us to get close to him. Knew he was interested in Cornell so I played that card for what it was worth, and it paid off better than I expected. Escaping was a last ditch backup plan. If shit went south, we could always run." Klug glanced at me and winked. "Sorry I couldn't let you in on it, brother, but I needed you believing we were leaving for real when Grove moved on you. Now, you all can do what I say and come along for the ride or you can die right here and go sit outside with the rotbags."

"This is bullshit," Mason said.

"Think so?" Klug asked.

He took Georges's gun and fired before anyone could stop him. Combest screamed once then fell, clutching at his chest. Klug moved across the room, kicked Combest's body outside then hit the door switch. The panels crawled downward. Combest was still alive, moaning, too shocked to move, as the door shut him out of sight.

"I said close the fucking door," Klug said. He removed the keys from the control box and put them in his pocket.

It wouldn't have hurt the King Snake to let us go, but he wasn't one to give anything away for free. Maybe if he'd known that Mason's family had been among the bus refugees turned out by Grove at the prison gates, he'd have tapped someone else to secure his arsenal, but even I didn't know that then. If Klug had he might've understood Mason felt the same way I did: he only wanted his freedom and he didn't care what anyone else thought he ought to be doing or what anyone else wanted. Damn hard to bully someone who's got nothing to lose and nothing really to gain. No past, no future. A man in that position tends to hit back where it hurts most.

"Well fuck you, too!" Mason yelled.

He raised his shotgun and blew away most of Lane Grove's face in spray of shot and red gore that drenched the concrete.

Klug gaped. "Motherfucker!"

Not even the King Snake could think of everything.

Scopes charged toward the stash of weapons on the truck, but Mason opened up the other barrel and blasted his legs, crippling him.

Georges pulled a snub-nose from his ankle and fired wild, shattering one of the truck windshields. Shots ricocheted off the masonry and everyone ducked. I grabbed Della's arm and pulled her around the far side of the truck we'd loaded. Mason vanished behind one of the other vehicles, firing fast to force Klug and Georges behind a stack of crates in the opposite corner. They left Scopes writhing in pain on the floor. When the echoes of gunfire ceased I heard two things: the lazy thumps of wormfeeders beating against the garage door and the angry voices of living men coming from the inside corridor.

Up to then that jackal breathing down my neck had only been playing with his food. Now his hunger had finally outweighed his boredom, and his jaws were closing.

The inside doors of the loading area exploded with a crash and a whoosh of hot smoke. Six guards burst through in a gray haze. Klug and Georges opened fire before the hacks got their bearings, forcing them back. Two of them dropped on the platform. Georges spread some cover fire while Klug wriggled out and grabbed an automatic rifle off one of the dead, and then the King Snake unleashed his fury. The guards fired back. Bullets whined through the air. Sparks flew as lead pocked the metal doorframe. Bits of concrete spun loose from the walls. Klug's mouth hung wide in a silent scream. He paid no attention to a shot that grazed his shoulder and left a trail of blood soaked into his singed shirtsleeve. Below the crossfire Paulson's head wobbled like a rolling bird's egg. His eyes strained for sight of food. His limbs flopped and squirmed around him like suffocating fish.

Klug and Georges would run out of ammo soon at the rate they were firing, and when their guns died, the guards would advance. Seemed wasteful and stupid until I understood they were watching the clock, holding off the hacks till the dead men on the platform got up and started running interference. Might have done the same myself. That thought got me moving, because I knew the next step would be to get to the weapons, and unless Klug's disposition had gotten a whole lot cheerier as a result of being shot and losing his sacrificial prize pig, that meant going through us. Mason and I made eye contact, drawing the same conclusion: our only way out was the yard.

We had the truck. Klug had the keys to the door.

"Can you shoot?" I asked Della.

She nodded. I shoved my gun into her hands and told her to cover me.

"Okay," she said.

She handled the gun with confidence, getting a shot off every few seconds to keep Georges from turning his attention our way. I slipped into the exposed opening at the back of the truck and found the three spare fuel cans that had been stocked up. I lined them up within reach of the door, grabbed one, dropped to the floor, ducked, and crab-walked toward the yard exit. The pungent fumes burned my nose when I opened the cap. I tried not to splash fuel on myself as I emptied the can to make a puddle halfway along the length of the door. The wormfeeders stood just inches away on the far side. Their sad moans drifted through, and the metal rattled under their fists.

Running back to Della, I saw Warden Grove's corpse stand up. The remains of his head poked upward like a broken flower-pot, and he shuffled his way toward the nearest food source: Scopes. Grove pounced on the wounded con like a rat, ripping his flesh with his splintered teeth. Scopes fought but he had lost a lot of blood and was weak. Probably slipping into shock, too, and likely run through with horror at watching himself being eaten. He only stopped screaming when Grove chewed his throat open and champed down on his larynx.

The gunshots died down. Georges had emptied his snub-nose and produced yet another weapon, and I wondered where the hell he hid them all. A truck engine rumbled to life. Mason sat behind the wheel of the vehicle he'd been using for cover. I had time to wave to him once for luck before he revved the motor, popped the clutch, and blasted in reverse across the loading area. The truck body smashed through the crates that had shielded Klug and Georges. Chunks of wood whirled in every direction. Klug twisted around, his face a contorted mask of surprise as the back bumper caught him below the waist, lifted him and pinned him to the cinder-block wall. His rifle sailed loose and disappeared below the wheels. I thought the impact might cut him in half, but then the truck came to an abrupt halt.

The crash left Georges sprawled sideways in a mess of broken crates. He tried to aim his gun when Mason climbed out of the cab, but his hand drooped from his broken wrist like a useless toy. Mason shot him, hitting him in the neck. Georges pressed his shattered hand against the wound and tried to hold back the gout of blood streaming out.

I grabbed a shotgun from the stash and trailed Della to the corner. We got there in time to watch the King Snake realize that he was trapped unarmed with a corpse that would soon be hungry for his flesh and that we were going to leave without him. He didn't like either circumstance.

Mason shoved his hand into Klug's sweat-dampened shirt pocket, fishing for the keys. When he found them, he took them straight to the control box. We needed to run. Soon it would dawn on the supercops in the corridor that they weren't being shot at anymore, and then they'd recover their bravery.

"You can't leave me here, Cornell," said Klug. "I know this shit wasn't supposed to go down this way, but we've got to put that behind us. C'mon, man. I never did you no wrong. Used you a little, yeah, but you were going to be there with me at the top. Ain't no part of Lohatchie left but you and me. We got to stick together. How else we gonna survive this crazy shit? Just fucking help me, man, all right?"

Felt like I should've had something smart to say then, but nothing came to mind. I stared at Klug like he was a bug pinned to piece of corkboard. His face screwed into a twisted wreck of anger and pain, and then all at once let it go as he started laughing. Only took me a moment to catch onto the joke.

I ducked sideways with maybe a half second left to avoid the gore-drenched hug of Warden Grove approaching me from behind. Klug stopped laughing when Grove's momentum carried him into the wreckage. The dead preacher tripped, plunged forward, and started scrabbling his way toward the King Snake. After all, what's the difference between Klug and me to a wormfeeder? Fresh meat is fresh meat.

With the corner of my eye I spotted the two dead hacks dragging their pale bodies upright on the platform.

Scopes would be next.

Time to move.

Della sent a couple of potshots at the guards to keep them hiding then ran to the truck. Mason was ready at the control box.

My first two matches extinguished in the gas puddle, but the third ignited a low wall of blinding hot flame that licked at the door. Mason hit the switch and we hauled back to the getaway truck as the door inched up. The fire spread down a ten-foot length between us and the yard, and as the opening widened, the first wormfeeders pushed inside. They burned like jack o' lanterns, and the aroma of cooking flesh polluted the air. Others fell into the conflagration and drove the flames higher. The smart ones trailed around to the clear end. Soon nearly all the corpses had shambled to one side and the yard emptied out in front of us.

The first wormfeeder to reach the truck knocked on the passenger side window and Mason gave him the finger. Della hunkered down behind the seat and I sat behind the wheel with the engine running. Only three wormfeeders stood in our way when I gunned the motor. Heat rippled through the truck as we breached the waist-high fire. The dead things crunched under the tires, bouncing us like speed bumps, as we emerged into the yard. Then Mason was pulling my arm and screaming, tugging on the wheel so we swerved right and smacked more wormfeeders off our fenders.

Combest's body appeared in the glow of the headlights.

The punch codes.

I slammed the brakes hard and brought the passenger side as close to Combest as I could. The truck skidded. For a fleeting second two right tires left the ground, and I felt certain we'd tip and crash, but then gravity sucked the vehicle back down and it jolted to a shuddering stop. Mason popped the door and dropped to the ground. He fired on the closest wormfeeders, launching chunks of flesh into the darkness, then rifled Combest's shirt. The notebook was gone. He heaved the body over and patted the dark grass, feeling for the paper and cardboard. The wormfeeders closed in. I slid into the passenger seat and blasted them with the scattergun. Stale blood spit from their wounds, but they kept coming. In moments they'd overrun us.

"Forget it," I shouted. "We'll crash the gate."

"No!" Mason called back. "Got it!"

Combest grabbed him before he could stand. His body shivered as movement returned to it, and he came at Mason with his mouth open, teeth bared. Mason tripped trying to scramble away. He strained to aim his gun at Combest, but they were pressed too close together. The other wormfeeders closed on them. In the half second I took to think of leaping out of the truck and helping Mason instead of hitting the gas and running, Della raised her gun and fired into Combest, forcing him away from Mason.

The next moment, Mason was back in the cab, shoving me toward the driver's seat and tugging the door closed behind him. I punched the gas and we rocketed into the yard, plowing through wormfeeders. The truck jounced and skidded. Twice, bodies caught up on the wheels almost sent us out of control, but after that the ride smoothed out as we raced down the hard pavement of the driveway. The first fence loomed ahead, a darkened guard post beyond it, and I skidded us to a halt two inches from the heavy chain link.

Mason leapt out, clutching the wet notebook and punched in the codes. The wormfeeders came faster than I thought they could. A dozen wobbled toward us.

"Shit, there are more of them?" said Della.

Mason sidestepped the rolling gate to enter the pen, and I edged the truck in after him. I jumped out with a rifle once we were in the tight space of the checkpoint. The fence slid closed after us. We sat sandwiched between the yard and the outside world. We looked at our exit, sealed by a single chain-link gate topped with razor wire, the only thing between us and the whole goddamn, dead-infested world. There, beyond the gate, seventy, eighty, a hundred wormfeeders glommed against the aluminum mesh like they'd been expecting us all along.

Mason roared and fired round after round into them till he emptied his magazine. I thought he might reload and keep firing, but instead he slung the rifle over his shoulder and rubbed his eyes.

"Fuck. How the hell do we get past them?"

Della climbed out of the cab. "What now?"

"Now," I said. "We blow up the truck."

I don't know why I said it. It was the first thing I thought of and it struck me as the kind of rare inspiration that should be trusted even if you can't quite picture how it's all going to work out. I didn't know what chance we'd have on foot outside the prison walls, but I heard Evelyn's voice in my mind telling me not to give up, happy again because I'd stopped lying down to take whatever came my way. Or as Lane Grove might have put it, the Lord helps those who help themselves.

"That's the best you can come up with?" Della said.

"Yeah," I told her. "Go back, we die. Stay here, we die. Only choice we've got is keep going forward. We've come too far to do anything else. Unless we take out a whole bunch of the dead in our path all at once, going forward is going to be a tad difficult."

She turned to Mason, who shrugged.

"I got nothing better to suggest," he said.

"Sonofabitch," she said. "Couple of geniuses I wound up with. Let's make it work."

"We take what we can carry," I said. "Then light the gas tank, open the gate, and hide in the station booth. Let in as many wormfeeders as will fit and wait for the fuel to blow them to cinders. Then we run out through the visitor's door and haul ass across the meadow behind them. They've been gathering around the prison for so long, maybe they won't be so dense once we get some distance."

The guard station included a small airlock type of arrangement that protruded beyond the gate. It was used to admit people on foot without passing them through the pen. It wouldn't protect us for long, but I hoped it wouldn't have to. The chain link on either side of us buckled under the weight of the dead. They saw us. They wanted us. On the yard side, I saw Scopes and Grove in with the crowd, and I saw Klug in the distance limping along with half his torso shorn open. Seeing Grove's ruined body lurch against the fence, I wondered if the warden had met his god now, even though there was no bonfire for him, only the pen.

"Town's thirty miles north of here," said Mason. "Gonna be a hard run across countryside crawling with wormfeeders. My house is less than half that distance east. We make it there, we can get a car."

"All right," I said. "Mason's serving breakfast. Let's start packing."

We took guns and extra ammo from the truck. Della insisted on bringing the medical supplies. I figured any wound you couldn't walk off was as good as being dead, but I didn't argue. We stowed enough food to hold us for at least three days, and Della retrieved the black briefcase she'd brought.

"What's in there?" I asked.

"Information," she said. "Doctor Foley's laptop. It's a piece of military equipment with a link to a satellite network."

"How the hell did Foley come by that?"

"Worked for the CDC," she said.

"Hunh. Maybe it'll be useful," I said. "Hope you remembered to grab the charger."

Della's face blanked for a moment before it twisted with anger. "Dammit," she said. "Sonofabitch."

"Don't sweat it. We'll figure something out. If not, it looks heavy—you can use it as a club."

Fuming, Della put the briefcase with the rest of our things in the airlock, and then we prepared the truck.

Fetid hands clawed the chain link on both sides of us. The cries and groans of the dead filled the air. Mason and Della put our gear in the guardhouse while I tied together strips of padding from the truck and soaked them in gas to make a fuse. I threaded it into the truck's gas nozzle and shoved it down as deep as I could with my rifle barrel. Della took the third can of gas, jumped up on the hood of the truck, and splashed fuel over the mob of wormfeeders until they were soaked and dripping, shining in the moonlight. Mason entered the code for the gate and punched the button. It creaked sideways, squealing under the weight of the dead.

I lit the fuse. We ran into the booth.

Wormfeeders stumbled in, pushing and shoving, tripping over one another in the confined space. The gates spread and more followed, clotting against the front of the truck and blotting out the headlights. The pen became a writhing tangle of shadows creeping toward the guard booth, where we crouched below the window level. I crossed my fingers hoping the wire-reinforced glass would hold up to the explosion.

Damn good thing it at least proved bullet resistant.

Three shots must have struck it before we realized we were under fire.

The spotlight in the nearby guard tower flickered to life and we saw hacks up there pointing down at us.

The light drew the attention of the wormfeeders away from the booth, but there were so many of them, there was no way to return fire without exposing ourselves. We were stuck waiting, and it was taking a hell of lot longer than I had expected for the gas tank to blow. We heard the dead right on top of us, lowing like sick cows and batting weak fists against the windows. They knew we were there and it was stoking their hunger. Every few seconds another shot from the guard tower ripped through one of the dead and sprayed blood onto the window glass, turning the glow from the spotlight beam ruby-red in our dark hiding space. The gunshots came faster. The windows couldn't hold much longer. Splinters of glass cracked loose and sprayed around us. We grabbed our weapons and prepared to fight the living and the dead.

Night erupted into blinding day.

A wave of heat cascaded over us.

The weakened glass shattered, and heavy, webbed chunks rained down. Burning metal and flesh flew into the room and crashed against the far wall.

The explosion had been less powerful than I expected. The truck went up like a charcoal barbecue doused with too much lighter fluid rather than a bomb, but it achieved the desired effect. All the wormfeeders in the pen lit up from head to toe, packed so close together that the flames danced among them, reaching out to those still beyond the gate, racing through the dark to turn the mass of them into horrible scarecrow torches. The confines of the pen had driven much of the explosive force upward where it hit the guard tower. The spotlight went dark when a piece of debris shattered it. Patches of flame burned in the darkness above us.

We ran.

Four wormfeeders lingered outside the visitor's door. Mason shoved his shotgun into one's mouth and fired. The corpse's decomposed skull muffled the blast as it burst. Della shot another one in the leg and toppled it. I pounded at the other two with the stock of my rifle, beating them aside and forcing them to the ground. More wormfeeders came toward us, but we batted them away or shot their feet out from under them. The farther we moved from the prison, the fewer we met. Most of them had their attention elsewhere. Trundling toward the gate were two ragged lines of walking dead coming around the prison walls, drawn by the light and noise or beckoned by those who'd been there first. Their horrible voices filled the night.

We followed a path through the woods, one Mason knew well enough to navigate in the dark, and came out on the road two miles away from the prison. It was deserted. At a steady pace, we'd reach Mason's house by morning. There we could figure out what came next. One thing Klug got right was my hideaway deep in the Everglades north of Lohatchie. If all the world proved a cesspool of decaying flesh and cannibal corpses, then we could head there, leave it all behind us, and maybe make a new life. Maybe not. I wasn't one to count on a happy ending, no matter how simple it sounded.

Walking along in the moonlit stillness, I tasted air free of rot and fear for the first time in weeks. I knew again how it felt to be my own man. Somewhere that smiling jackal laughed over the good scare he gave me, knowing all along it was only a matter of time before he decided to deliver what he'd promised. For now, though, it was enough that I could no longer hear Evelyn's voice in the back of my mind. That's how I knew she was pleased.

BIRCH'S REFUGEES

DAY 16, 6:03 P.M.

A man in ragged, red clothes walked among the dead.

No, *not* a man. A corpse.

That James Birch thought of him as a man at first glance made him extraordinary. He didn't move like the other walking corpses, who wandered the field below the hospital like shell-shocked survivors, tripping over scattered piles of fallen bodies. Rather, the man in red moved with a purpose and an alertness alien among the living dead. But Birch had no doubt he *was* dead; the signs of decay on his face and arms were modest but unmistakable. And any living man who walked that field would've been quartered and devoured by the dead in minutes—yet they paid no attention to the man in red. To them he was only another rotting body among the dead masses.

His actions astonished Birch more than his appearance. As he worked his way across the field, he knelt beside one damaged corpse after another, lingering long enough only to press his fingers against each one's eyes, like a priest delivering a final blessing. Hundreds of bodies littered that field, decay hardened, capable only of twisting and wriggling in the mud because their legs and arms had been shattered or severed in a battle Birch hadn't witnessed; from the hospital roof, they looked like frantic, broken ants. But once the dead man knelt by them—once he touched them—they turned stone still and didn't rise.

Truly dead.

Birch would've killed or died to know how to do what the man in red did. Almost any living man would've.

The cloudless afternoon darkened for a breath, and Birch shivered. A kind of energy radiated from the strange dead man, rising in ripples of palpable cold that sought something, sought...*life*. It connected with Birch in a jolt at the base of his neck, the touch of a desolate consciousness swollen with hatred and insatiable hunger.

The man in red looked up and met Birch's stare across the haze.

Birch froze.

Behind him, a motor started. Propellers whined as the pilot prepped the helicopter for take-off. The soldiers were loading the cargo space with boxes of supplies foraged from the hospital laboratories. Birch held a box of unused Petri dishes filled with agar jelly. He should've been helping to load the huey but he couldn't move. The strange dead man's intense gaze pinned him in place. Worse, it felt familiar.

While his lifeless eyes remained on Birch, the man in red reached for the next corpse: a woman in a torn workout suit, so mottled with stains it resembled a lizard's skin, bisected at the waist. Yet drawn by the helicopter noise and the activity on the roof, her two halves tried to claw and squirm their way toward the hospital and the sounds of life. Then the man in red touched her eyes, and the woman flopped to the ground, both parts of her dead for good. Her savior awaited Birch's reaction, but Birch only gaped, too stunned to express anything. He doubted his own senses. No one else seemed to notice the man in red, not the soldiers hurrying around the rooftop, not the two snipers posted to watch the hospital grounds. Maybe after weeks of haunting his sleep, Birch's dreams of the dead now leaked into his waking life. Or maybe this was another vision, another glimpse between the cracks of reality that only Birch saw.

A cluster of walking corpses mobbed the hospital entrance now. They beat themselves against the doors, pounded them with weak fists, and even the dead who couldn't move yearned to join them. They hungered for flesh, thirsted for blood. Birch wondered if the dead felt pain when they starved. Even severed arms, legs, and heads still shifted around on the ground, worms in the mud, hands dragging themselves forward on rotting fingers, driven by an incomprehensible need to find life and consume it. And at the center of the field, the man in red put down another shattered corpse. Then another. And another after that. Miraculous. Birch wanted to know what the dead felt in the last seconds before their wasting bodies stopped moving, if they felt anything at all.

The man in red held nothing in his hands. He did no more than brush his gray fingertips across the eyes of those he released. Birch wished that power flowed through him.

Certain he had seen the man's face before, he dredged his memory but couldn't recall from where he knew him. Rot obscured his features, and no one ever looked quite the same in living death as they had in life. The cold energy flowing between them surged, driving a frigid spike through Birch's head. He winced as silent words sprang into his thoughts: *You* will *remember me. You killed me. You wouldn't let me serve the living, so now I bring mercy to the dead. Soon you and everyone else will be part of my ministry.*

The voice echoed in Birch's mind, shallow, distorted yet almost recognizable. Another blast of pain expanded in his head. He flinched and dropped the case in his hands. Plastic and glass cracked when it smacked the ground, and the lid snapped open. Birch glanced down at the box then back to the field.

The man in red was gone.

The cold energy dissipated.

"Sir?" Private Lou Nelson stood at Birch's side, eyeing Birch's shaking hands. "You all right, sir?"

Birch hesitated then shook his head. "Fine. Just... tired. I was up all night." He folded the box shut and lifted it.

"See something down there?" Nelson asked.

"Thought I saw a living man walking around."

"Living? No way, not down there," Nelson said. "Some of the rotters still look pretty good, I guess. Probably that's all you saw."

"Maybe."

Birch wanted to find the man in red and make him tell how he killed the dead. If he insisted on what he'd seen, he knew the men would believe him—that they'd hunt for the strange dead man, fight through throngs of the walking dead, even die if he only told them that's what it would take to end the dead plague. Even as Birch thought that, a shred of hope glimmered in Nelson's eyes, so faint the private probably didn't realize it'd crept into his expression. Birch took it for hope that maybe he really had seen something that could help them down amidst the horror.

Maybe I have and maybe I haven't. I don't know what's real anymore.

"A good-looking rotter," he said. "That had to be it."

He stared across the field, the wind of the chopper blades beating at his back. Layered strands of gold and orange clouds stacked on the horizon.

"Sir, just so you know the chopper's loaded, and we'll go whenever you're ready. But, sir, if you don't mind me saying, we'd all like to make it back to Vanguard before sunset."

"Right, me too," Birch said. "Let's split."

He followed Nelson to the helicopter, crouching low as he boarded and shoved the box into a space in the cabin. As the whirlybird rose, Birch studied the field. He'd seen it from the air several times on runs to scavenge supplies, but it had never seemed so placid. Despite the dead clamoring at the hospital doors and the wrecked bodies twitching in the mud, the wide swath of corpses stilled by the man in red made the field look like an overturned graveyard.

If the strange dead man were someone Birch had killed that hardly narrowed the field. He had done a lot of dirty work in his day. He couldn't remember everyone who'd died because of him, and, if he was being honest, he didn't even know who they all were.

He nudged Nelson, sitting beside him, and pointed out the band of unmoving dead bodies. "What do you make of that?"

Nelson shrugged. "Guess they rotted out."

The chopper angled away, and the field dropped from sight. Birch closed his eyes.

The memory of the strange corpse's words stoked his anger. Hard enough these days to sustain belief in life as something worth preserving at any cost, he didn't need the dead invading his mind. He didn't want the dreams and visions of them that came almost every night, didn't want to be the only man with answers for the living. He no longer held any certainty that the answer to the dead plague could ever be known—until today, when he saw what the man in red could do. If all that proved only a waking dream, he feared it might crush his faltering hope for good. The dead had risen and taken over the world, the living were in decline, lights out, curtains closed.

Maybe that was all there was to it.

DAY 17, 1:15 P.M.

The soldiers flattened the dead with tanks; the treads crushed them to dust and jelly, leaving only a scattering of fingers and toes twitching in the mashed earth. Weeks ago, Birch had suggested using lengths of cable to corral the walking corpses and then crushing them with the four M2A3 Bradley's Major Alan Novak commanded. Now the procedure anchored the daily routine at Vanguard labs, and the men cleaned away the remains with flamethrowers. Although not enclosed, the biolab facility stood far enough from the nearest town that not too many corpses found their way there. The "wrap and smash," as the men had named it, had won Birch the Major's confidence. Now he sat in Novak's commandeered office, watching the operation through a window. He admired its simplicity. A direct solution for a clear-cut problem, the absolute opposite of the dilemma he faced in the lab and the favor he hoped Novak would grant him.

"The *Clostridium tetani* produces a neurotoxin, called tetanospasmin," Birch told Novak. "It ravages living muscle and skeletal fibers, causing the muscular contractions and lockjaw of tetanus. Theoretically, a modified form of the bacteria could produce an attenuated toxin that might explain the controlled movements of the walking dead. They could mimic life through bacteria-driven muscular contractions."

"It's mutant tetanus? That's the cause?" Novak jotted notes on a pad at the center of his well-ordered desk. "Can I report that to General Collier?"

"No. Nothing's certain. The bacteria and toxin are present in the tissue samples I've studied, but the rest is only a hypothesis," Birch said. "Part of one, at least. It doesn't explain why they attack and eat the living, why they move around like they do, why they migrate, and why they're not rotting on their bones. If reanimation was due to bacteria alone, their movements would be random, and they'd be decomposing at a normal rate. This might be *how* the dead are walking, but it isn't the only factor. It isn't *why* they're walking."

"What's the difference?"

"You drop a bomb on a target, that's *how* you destroy it, right?" Birch said. "The reason you drop that bomb, the reason it exists in the first place, those are separate things. The bomber might not even know why he's using it. To him, the bomb is only a tool."

"Are you telling me this is an attack, the bacterium is a bioweapon?"

"No. This wasn't created in a lab."

"Fuck's sake, Birch. Make yourself clear. I've been cutting you serious slack since I got here, because you were Special Forces back in the day and you seem like the only one with his head screwed on right about this clustershtup. But I need results. The brass are getting nervous, and when the brass get nervous, I get nervous, and that upsets my stomach, which means I can't enjoy that oh-so-important, first cup of coffee in the morning, and that puts me in a rotten damn mood all day, every day. That's no good for anyone. So, fix this shit already, you fucking mad scientist egghead, because I want to know that all is right in the world again so I can enjoy my morning coffee."

Birch waited for the major to smile or laugh; he didn't.

An improbable burst of admiration for the man filled Birch. Confronted by a set of insane circumstances, Novak boiled things down to a simple benchmark for success. That kind of thinking made him an effective soldier, but it would only work for so long. Birch had known other soldiers like Novak, and he knew what might happen when they exhausted their coping mechanism.

"Doing my best, sir." Birch considered telling Novak about his visions, the things he saw in his dreams, even about the dead man in red, but Novak wouldn't believe him. It would only give him cause to doubt Birch's sanity and that would complicate everything. "This thing isn't exactly in the textbooks."

"Did it evolve?" Novak said.

"Everything evolves. But, no, not how you mean, centuries of genetic processes happening in days like in some mindless, Hollywood blockbuster, and not because it had a will to evolve or some other nonsense. If it really is the *Clostridium tetani*, it evolved because something in its nature gives this strain an edge in reproducing. If that's where it came from we've been living with it for a long, long time. It's possible. There could have been an animal reservoir before it made the jump to humans, but we'd have seen isolated cases before the dead plague, maybe going back decades, maybe without knowing what they were. It's possible we did and they were misidentified, but I find that unlikely. The symptoms of reanimation are… acute. Anyway, the dead plague wouldn't have come on all at once, spreading in days like it did. It would've taken months, maybe years. Tetanus doesn't spread like the measles."

"Listen, I need something to report," Novak said.

"I know. Thing is, the toxin should be impotent in dead flesh. *Clostridium tetani* is anaerobic. Its spores can survive in dead tissue if it isn't exposed to oxygen. Spores are a far cry from the dynamic bacteria we've found under the microscope, though. You get tetanus when you step on, say, a rusty nail, because it punctures your flesh, delivering the bacteria from within the rust inside your body to an environment that allows it to grow. Something has to be putting this modified bacterium into dead bodies at almost the exact moment of death. Then it replicates and spreads in minutes through the dead tissue in sufficient volume to reanimate the corpse. In my clinical opinion, that's fucking nuts."

"Maybe it's already there when people die. Someone aerosolized it, dispersed it, and people inhaled it."

"No. The fundamental nature of the C. tetani hasn't changed. It's still anaerobic. Prolonged exposure to air would destroy it. I've been taking blood tests from everyone who'll let me, and I haven't found a single living person with it in their system."

"What about your control?"

"Decomposing nicely, no bacteria present, but he hasn't provided any real clues."

"So, what, you hit a dead end already?"

"I've only been at it for two weeks."

"Time is not on our side."

"Talk to Gochek. Talk to Friedman. See what they've learned."

Novak dropped his pen on the desk and leaned back in his chair. " Friedman's got nothing and admits it. Gocheck says it's space dust we picked up from a passing comet."

"He's making that up because you scare him."

"Yes, I do, and that he is. He's an engineer not a biologist, so what can I expect? I have to make due with the available resources. Everything crashed so fast, there was no time to prepare. You're the only one bringing in anything I can wrap my mind around. And here's a sobering thought: you may be the only one in the country with a grasp on this thing. You're the hot ticket. I report to my boss, he reports to his, and he calls the President. You make sense of this thing."

Birch shuddered. "Do I?"

"A mutant bacterium? Yes, I understand that."

"That's not what I said."

"That's what it sounded like. At least, it's a start."

Novak stared Birch down, and the scientist checked himself from disillusioning him. Novak trusted him, and Birch could not say he was wrong. Maybe what he'd learned so far would lead to answers or even a cure.

In the meadow outside, soldiers scrambled near the complex's main entrance. One group provided cover fire for another uncoiling cable between two Jeeps. The shooters destroyed legs and joints with controlled bursts of gunfire, immobilizing the dead, easy prey for the tanks. The line of bodies in the scorched grass reminded Birch of the field outside the hospital, and he thought of the dead man in red, walking from one twitching corpse to another, stilling each one he touched. The key to the dead plague hid in that touch.

"We may have to move soon," Novak said. "The dead are starting to turn up here in bigger groups."

"Let's hold out as long as we can. There's no other lab in this state—hell on this coast—with the equipment we have here. Very little of it is mobile."

"My men are doing their best."

"They're doing incredible. They've kept us safe."

"Another week, though, who knows?" Novak said.

Birch cleared his throat. "One other thing. O'Neal's doing well. She'd like to go back to her room now. That okay with you?"

Novak's expression hardened. "She all healed up?"

"Getting there. She's fine. Really, she is."

Novak shook his head. "Talk to me when her scabs are peeling."

DAY 17, 2:30 P.M.

Birch stood in the parking lot and watched soldiers tighten a cable around thirty or so dead. The corpses moaned and swiped at the living with stiff hands. Then the cable dropped and the group began to push apart, but the tanks rolled in too fast and pressed them to the ground. The Bradleys grumbled with solid, mechanical certainty, leaving behind a slick of decomposed muck and splintered bones. Afterward the soldiers hosed down the tank treads to clean away bits of bodies and clothing. Then they torched the remains left in the grass.

Birch knew Novak's commanders had only sent the tank unit to Vanguard in the first days of the dead plague because they expected equally definitive results on a grand scale. Vanguard specialized in bioscience with military applications, everything from better anthrax vaccines and organic sutures to weaponized allergens and untraceable, fast-degrading bioweapons. Over a decade, the Army had sunk a fortune into the company. As its vice president of research, Birch knew well the give and take of dealing with the military. Their protection would last only as long as he could produce. Until yesterday, he'd feared he'd reached a dead end.

He returned to the main building, to the sub-level where he kept his specimens, carded into the secure corridor, and then waded into a gut-churning stench. The first door on his right led to O'Neal's room, a storage area converted into makeshift quarters. Birch knocked then entered, pushing the door open against towels jammed at its base to block out the smell. O'Neal sat on her bed reading a Douglas Adams paperback. She lowered a cloth soaked with water and perfume from her mouth. Birch sniffed its faint sweetness.

"Please say you've come to bring me upstairs," O'Neal said.

"Novak won't budge until your scabs are peeling."

Birch examined O'Neal's bandages, lifted some to check her wounds.

Wormfeeders had bitten her thirteen times in a dead attack the day Novak's unit arrived. At one point her wounds turned black with infection and O'Neal had languished, feverish, for days, dozens of tooth marks oozing pus and blood, but she'd recovered.

"You're still a little on the wet side, so no go for now. Sorry. How you feeling?"

"Bored out of my skull. At least I barely notice the stink anymore."

"Any cravings for the flesh of the living?"

"I might bite Major Novak's ass if he doesn't let me out of here soon."

"He's playing it safe. Look on the bright side: You've proven the bites themselves aren't fatal or contagious. The risk if you're bitten is dying of blood loss or infection."

O'Neal dog-eared the page she was reading and dropped the book on her bed. Birch picked it up.

"*Life, the Universe, and Everything*? Self-help?"

O'Neal laughed. "I wish. Robbins loaned it to me, but he doesn't have the first two in the series. I read them in high school. Funny stuff. Thought it might cheer me up."

"Don't panic," Birch said.

"Words to live by," O'Neal said. "You need a hand wrangling your specimens?"

Birch shook his head. "No. I only came down for some samples from Dickie, and he's still a well-behaved corpse."

Birch and O'Neal walked to the next storeroom, where Dickie Stein's body was stored. There were five storage rooms in a row along the hall, and the other three held Birch's specimens of the reanimated dead. Sometimes they moaned and banged listlessly on the doors, but now they were silent. Birch looked in on Stein's body. A foul blast of air crept from the room. Birch coughed.

"Still dead," O'Neal said. "Here, use this."

She handed Birch her washcloth. He held it loosely over his mouth and nose, and it filled his nostrils with the sugary aroma of cheap perfume. It cut down the rotten stink, allowing Birch to collect hair and tissue samples from Stein's corpse. Stein, a Vanguard janitor, had dropped dead from a heart attack six days ago while mopping up the labs—but he never got up again. So far Birch had found very little active *Clostridium tetani* in his body. When he had what he needed, Birch slammed the door and returned the cloth to O'Neal.

"I'm so sorry you have to sleep next door to that."

O'Neal shrugged. "Duty calls. Sometimes duty stinks. Besides, it's not a whole lot worse than a boot camp locker room in August. Just has a different *tang* to it."

Birch and O'Neal laughed as they returned to her room. O'Neal flopped onto her bed and whistled. Birch noticed a clean uniform hanging from a hook in the corner, and under it, propped against the wall, stood O'Neal's rifle. One of her fellow soldiers had brought them, a sign they hadn't given up on her. Birch envied her the camaraderie.

"How's life topside?"

"Fine. Except for all the walking dead."

"Worse than mosquitoes."

"We're attracting attention. Fifteen miles from the nearest anything, but we've got more showing up every day. As much as they can know anything, they know we're out here."

"How long can we hold out?"

"Another week, maybe."

O'Neal sat up. "What happens to me if we need to leave in a hurry?"

"You'll be clear in a couple days. If we need to leave before then, I'll come get you myself."

"Thanks. A girl can stand just about anything but to be forgotten."

"No one gets left behind," Birch said. "God only knows where we'll go, though. Hey, you know, I don't even know where you from."

"Virginia."

"Been there a few times."

"You?"

"Long Island."

"We're both pretty far from home."

"You itching to get back there?"

"Yes and no. I've got a big family. I try not to think about what happened to them. Maybe it's better if I never go back. I'm not sure home exists anymore."

"Sorry. Stupid question."

"Forget it. I'm sure you've got the same worries."

"Not really. I haven't had a family for a long time." Birch gathered his samples from where he had set them on the floor and backed out into the corridor. "Rest up. I'll see you later."

Ignoring the awkward sympathy in O'Neal's expression, Birch closed the door behind him.

DAY 25, 9:32 A.M.

Wrapped inside a heavy-duty trash bag, the thing on the worktable thrashed sideways and fell to the floor. The four soldiers who'd set it there seconds ago rushed to retrieve it and replaced it where it belonged. The thing inside twisted and fought, but they held it down tight on the steel table. One of its hands ripped through the bag and clawed at a soldier's wrist with cracked fingernails too weak to penetrate the man's thick work gloves. All of the soldiers wore them, as they wore bandanas across their faces to dampen the stench.

"Hold it in place," Birch said. "I've got to strap it down."

He wore the same type of heavy gloves as the soldiers, the material so thick that his scalpel looked like a toy between his bulky fingers. He sliced away part of the plastic bag, exposing the thing's head and neck. The dead man stared at him with sunken eyes and ground its yellowed teeth. Birch ignored him.

He grabbed one of the nylon straps he'd rigged to the table, pulled it snug across the thing's forehead, and tightened it in place. He drew a second strap across its jaw. Then he cut away more of the plastic bag and strapped the dead thing's shoulders down. With the soldiers' help, he worked his way along the rest of the writhing corpse, pinning it to the worktable, using cuffs for the thing's hands. He stopped at the waist, but only because nothing remained below that. The dead man's legs had been crushed to pulp and amputated during the morning wrap and smash, his upper body preserved from destruction only because Birch had requisitioned a fresh work sample, as he'd done every day for the past five days, since he discovered the first anomaly.

"All right, he's secure," Birch said.

The soldiers backed away to the room's four corners, following Major Novak's orders never to leave Birch unguarded with an active specimen. Lang and McCormick, Birch's assistants, prepared the body for dissection. Lang scissored away the remnants of its clothing and cleaned it of sticks, dirt, and other debris. McCormick set up a video camera on a tripod by the worktable. The dead man's sallow eyes tracked everyone who passed it. Behind its crooked teeth and disintegrating lips, its black tongue rustled and squirmed. The thing moaned, a low, gravelly noise, unbroken even to take a breath, carrying on, rising, falling, producing garbled sounds that sometimes mimicked speech. Birch wadded up a rag and shoved it into the thing's mouth, muting it. He traded his thick work gloves for sterile latex and then approached the specimen.

Birch glanced at the camera. "Tissue samples and general observation of one of the reanimated dead, day 25 of the dead plague. Specimen is male, adult, age...," Birch eyed the corpse for a clue, but found nothing, "...indeterminate. Specimen gathered at Vanguard location during routine security procedure. Time of death and duration of reanimation unknown."

The dead thing showed no reaction when Birch pushed the scalpel into its flesh and cut downward along its chest all the way to its waist. The partly-decomposed skin split like leather. Birch kept up a steady verbal description of his work, recording it for future reference, as he'd recorded dozens of similar dissections. The familiar red light of the camera blinked at him like a metronome. *As if anyone will ever want to watch this.* Still, if he missed an answer right under his nose, he wanted to make sure he had a second chance to find it.

He cracked the body open and began to remove its organs, placing each gray, shriveled piece in containers that Lang readied and then removed. He stacked them on the counter for study later. The heart, lungs, and most of the intestines were gone when Birch noticed the pronounced bulge, like a massive cyst, in the thing's liver. It rotated beneath the surface. Birch set down his scalpel, wiped his face with a paper towel, then rubbed his eyes. He hoped that when he looked again, the thing would be gone.

It wasn't.

About the size of a golf ball, the bulge shifted, rippling the dead flesh that encased it. Birch gestured for McCormick to focus the camera's lens on the liver then he retrieved his scalpel and sliced open the bump. The blade nicked dead meat, and the thing's motion ceased. Birch hesitated. He dreaded what was coming next. The liver parted along the circumference of the cyst; it opened like an eyelid and revealed a dead, white, eye peering straight at Birch. Under the brightness of the laboratory lights, its pupil dilated to a pinpoint. It counted as the seventh out-of-place eye Birch had found since the first one appeared.

"How in holy hell do these things get in there?" McCormick said.

He stepped around the camera for a closer look. Lang leaned in from the other side. The soldiers inched in from the corners. Birch waved them back.

"Stay in position," Birch told them, and then to Lang, he said, "Bring a container."

Birch worked with the scalpel to remove the liver. The eye tracked the motions of his hand and the shining movements of the blade until the liver sliced free from the body. Then the eye blinked shut. Birch placed the dead organ in the container, set the specimen under a lamp on the counter, and studied it. Except for decay and the out-of-place eye, the liver appeared normal. He prodded it with the tip of a pen. The eye flinched but didn't open. Birch pressed the flesh around the eye; it gave like dried-up jelly in a balloon. The eye opened again, stark and expressionless. Birch made sure McCormick got a clear shot of it while he flashed a penlight into it and watched it follow the beam. Then he cut into the dead liver, excavating a space around the eye. The flesh came away in soft clumps. Birch exposed the entire eye, including a rudimentary optical nerve trailing from its anterior, buried in the meat, connected to nothing. After wiping off clinging bits of dead flesh, Birch placed the eye in a specimen jar and sealed it.

"How do you think they get there?" McCormick said.

"Indigestion," Lang said. "He ate someone who disagreed with him."

"You're joking, but you could be right," Birch said. "Dead limbs stay reanimated when they're separated from their body. Why not a dead eye after it's been devoured? Except look closely. It shows no signs of damage or decay. It wasn't chewed. And encysted in the liver like that? It's like it grew there."

"That couldn't happen, it growing there. That's not possible, right?" McCormick said. "Could that happen?"

"You still hung up on what's possible?" Birch said. "Thought we'd all gotten past wasting time on whether or not weird shit's possible. How is an eye growing inside a dead man's liver any harder to accept than the fact that the dead man in question is still moving and would take a bite out of any one of us if he could?"

Birch resumed dissecting the body. He removed half a dozen more organs before he found a second eye, this time embedded in a kidney. He, McCormick, and Lang repeated what they'd done with the liver and set the new eye beside the first one.

McCormick and Lang worked in silence after that. Birch sensed tension and fear in the soldiers. They'd crossed an unexpected threshold, stumbled upon something that made their nightmare a thousand times stranger and more frightening than only a few days ago, and Birch, in whom they'd entrusted all their hopes for an answer, couldn't yet explain it. Maybe he never would. Instead he kept dissecting the specimen, afraid that if he stopped, all of them in the room would crack up trying to make sense of something impossible to understand.

He found two more eyes before he finished.

After he cataloged and stored all the specimens, scrubbed the lab clean, and sent his assistants away, Birch uploaded a video clip of one of the eyes to the remnants of the Internet the government had protected. He posted it without comment as he had clips of the other anomalies he'd found in the last few days. He felt like a savage falling back on faith, casting a prayer into the ether, wishing for someone or something greater and wiser than himself to whisper back the truth in his ear.

DAY 27, 10:53 P.M.

Miniature stars of blood flickered in the air. Streaks of it whirled around Birch in the pattern of distant galaxies he had seen in pictures taken through powerful telescopes. He stood at the center of the swirling storm, desperate to keep clean and dry but failing as the blood spattered against him, a sideways rain, slicking him red. Wherever he moved, the vortex moved with him, its center locked on him, and both him and the storm trapped in a white, unfurnished room, a space lit by a gelid glow that emanated from its pristine walls.

Outside the room, people screamed.

Guns fired. A muted explosion erupted. Ground quaked.

Sticky fingers clutched at Birch's hand. Friedman had dragged himself across the floor, trailing broken legs and a double stripe of blood behind him. Strips of shredded, bloody cloth dangled where the dead had ripped through his clothes and gouged into his flesh. He was straining to reach Birch. Crimson bubbles danced on his lips as he tried to speak. Then his face twisted into a wretched expression, and he dropped and lay still.

The roar of the spinning blood rose until it drowned out the sounds of combat. Disoriented, Birch staggered around Friedman's corpse. An exit awaited on the far side of the room, a black rectangle cut into the shining, white wall. Fiery lightning-flashes lit it. Shapes moved through the darkness on the other side. Birch called out to them, but no one answered, or if someone did, the hissing storm of blood drowned it out.

Birch reached for the gun at his waist, but he wasn't wearing it. Almost too late, he remembered Friedman and turned back. The dead man was pulling himself along the floor toward him, moving faster than Birch would've expected. A kick to the head jolted Friedman onto his back, and then Birch bolted for the door. Crouching low, he fled the white room. As he entered the gloom outside, the spinning blood stilled, and the roar of the vortex died. All the blood dropped to the floor in a barrage of splashes.

Silence, now.

No gunshots or screams.

No muzzle flashes or explosions of light.

Gun smoke mixed with the stink of fresh blood, and the scorched scent of burning metal lingered in the air.

Behind Birch, the door to the white room blinked shut. Darkness crept in around him, leaving only a faint glow bobbing somewhere up ahead. Birch approached it, finding an electric lantern rolling like an egg on the floor. He didn't have to look far to see who'd dropped it. A soldier lay motionless up ahead, his hand reaching for the lantern handle. Lifting the light, Birch examined the dead man. His throat was torn out. Something blunt had been pounded into his chest, cracking his sternum, dragging bone and muscle with it when it was removed, leaving a gaping black cavity emptied of its heart. He read the name "Alvarez" stitched on the dead man's uniform but didn't know him.

He wandered, using the lantern to find his way. Its light drained into the shadows. Birch walked toward a steady plinking sound, tracking the noise down the rough, sloped floor of an earthen tunnel. The air swirled with a weak breeze rich with the scent of damp soil. Insects and vermin, invisible in the blackness, scuttled underfoot.

At the end of the tunnel, the lantern light touched a pair of booted feet swaying in the air. Birch inched forward, bearing the lantern like a shield. The light revealed another uniformed body, a familiar name stitched over the breast pocket. Birch hesitated. Sadness welled up in him, but he needed to know what held her up, why she danced and jerked in mid air. He lifted the lantern a few inches more. Two of the walking dead hung down like rats through the dirt ceiling of the tunnel roof, their gray, rotting hands buried deep in Private O'Neal's flesh, holding her close to their mouths so they could bite into her face and skull, into her neck and shoulders. They snarled at Birch, their rotting faces ripe with hunger. Their hair fell out in muddy clumps; maggots nested in what remained. The dead hissed at the light then continued feeding. Birch turned and ran, only to stumble hard and crash to the ground, smashing the lantern.

The dark came alive around him. He knew without seeing them that a ring of the dead tightened around him like the cables the soldiers used to herd the walking corpses. He wished for a weapon. He would've run back to O'Neal's body and taken her pistol, but he'd lost his sense of direction and had no idea where to go.

Then the darkness lifted. Everywhere Birch saw points of dull, white light like the afterimages of fireworks burned into his retinas. More blinked on each second. In the vast darkness Birch felt tiny and cold like a man adrift in space, surrounded by distant stars he could never reach, each one a sun that lit him with hatred as his life bled into the frigid vacuum. A faraway voice rumbled, deep and slow—calling to him.

He recognized it: the voice of the man in red.

Though distance muffled his words, his hatred and fury struck Birch like freezing water. Icy winds blew across his neck and face. He trembled from the cold.

The lights neared him, and he saw they weren't stars but eyes, thousands of pairs, peering out from the mist of a black corruption, their stares burning through him, making him feel like a ghost. Maybe that's all he was now, what all the living were in this world of the dead—remnants haunting a place to which they no longer belonged, a place that rejected them. The faraway voice came clearer: *You owe the dead everything. And they will take what is theirs.*

A door slammed shut with a sharp crash.

Real light returned.

Birch snapped upright and nearly toppled backward in his desk chair. He blinked against the harsh glow of the overhead fluorescents. He was in his lab. His back and neck ached with stiffness. McCormick and Lang, his assistants, busy at one of the tables, stopped work to stare at him.

"You okay?" Lang asked.

"What happened?" Birch said.

"You nodded off. We let you sleep. Figured you needed the rest."

Birch checked his watch. He had slept for twenty minutes.

"You're pale, man." McCormick held half a sandwich, munching on it while he worked. "Do you get any real sleep at all? I mean, fuck's sake, you need to take care of yourself. What if you'd nodded off like that while you were driving?"

"You idiot," Lang said. "Who drives anymore?"

Birch moved to the door. "I need some air. I'll be back."

Birch walked outside and tried not to think about what the dream meant, if it meant anything at all, if it wasn't only a nightmare born of stress and fear, if the man in red wasn't only a creation of his subconscious terror. Birch found the pressure harder to bear every day. The shit rolled downhill harder from Novak, who was being pressed for results by General Collier, who in turn was sweating it with his boss and the president, but Birch had little more to offer them. Everything he learned about the strange bacterium was measured and analyzed, and still all Birch's data divulged no secret. Standard tetanus treatments didn't affect the bacteria strain, and every new approach he conceived proved useless. He had been unable to come up with any explanation for eyes found inside the corpses, and that seemed to bother Novak more than anything else. They'd already stayed at Vanguard a week longer than they should've. Their isolation no longer protected them as much as it had. The dead were getting harder to manage and more numerous. Soldiers ran "wrap and smash" ops four or five times a day. They put their lives at risk so Birch could keep working in the best facility possible.

They held out so he could stop the dead from walking.

Except he no longer believed he could, at least not by any means discoverable in a laboratory. He could devise no scientific explanation for why the dead returned to activity nor any meaning for the eyes embedded in their corrupt flesh. The face and voice of the man in red haunted him, inescapable, inevitable, a glaring reminder of his failure, a sign of what Birch suspected was the immutable truth—that the dead couldn't be stopped by the living.

The tide of nature had turned to favor them, forcing the living to run and hide, but for those at Vanguard, it was too late even for that. Leaving for a more secure location now would be a bitter pill, not only for Birch's failure, but because Birch knew people would die on the way, lives sacrificed to buy him extra time that had led nowhere.

He crossed the big lawn toward the main entrance, aiming for the bright dots of a night patrol's flashlights. Too much light attracted the dead, so they kept the parking lot street lamps dark and avoided using spotlights. Ahead of him, Birch saw a cluster of little lights indicating soldiers gathered near the dense hedge that edged the parking lot.

He veered for it then halted when a feathered slash of fire streaked the night, igniting a body Birch hadn't seen in the dark. The burning corpse shuffled in circles for several seconds before it collapsed. A second blast of flame touched it. Birch waited for others to show. Remembering his latest dream, he touched the gun at his hip and found its cold presence reassuring. Only the crackle of flames disturbed the night quiet, not moans from any other nearby dead. When the corpse burned long enough, the soldiers hosed it down, spewing up a cloud of gray smoke. Birch approached as they began to beat the charred remains with axes and iron pipes, breaking it to pieces.

One of the soldiers, with a pair of night vision lenses hanging from his neck, met Birch and waved him back. "Sir, you shouldn't be out here."

"Yeah, tell me about it, but I had to get out of that lab and get some air before I snapped," Birch said.

The soldier lifted his flashlight, briefly blinding Birch, then lowered it to paint Birch's ID badge hanging from a lanyard. "Sorry, Dr. Birch. Didn't realize it was you."

"No problem. Lot of them coming in?"

"Thirteenth one tonight. It's more than last week, sir, and a hell of a lot more than the week before. We get a lot more coming in groups now, too. Hard to spot them at night, they're so damn quiet sometimes. Infrared is useless, but we can see them with our night eyes. I don't know if they can talk to each other, but if they can I'd say word's out that we're the graveyard hotspot. Anyone who's anyone who's dead wants in here."

Birch nodded. "Or it could be there's so many dead now, they're spreading everywhere in larger numbers."

"Thanks for that depressing alternative, sir."

"Sorry," Birch said. "Private O'Neal on duty tonight?"

"Checkpoint Echo, sir. You heading over there?"

"Yeah. Echo's the west gate?"

"Yes, sir. I'll radio over, let them know you're coming," The soldier handed Birch a flashlight from his belt. "Take my backup. You'll need it."

"Thanks." Birch clicked on the light. The beam lit up the name stitched across the soldier's shirt: Alvarez.

Birch spoke the name without thinking.

"Yes, sir?" Alvarez said.

Birch couldn't reply. Bloody, dream images of Alvarez flashed back to him, transposed over the man standing before him. Birch couldn't remember ever meeting Alvarez before tonight, yet in his dream he'd known exactly what he looked like, even down to the way the man wore his uniform.

"Sir?" Alvarez asked.

"You're Sergeant Alvarez. We haven't met before."

"No, sir," Alvarez said. "Is something wrong?"

"No. Major Novak speaks highly of you. That's all. It's good to meet you."

"Good to meet you, too. I'll radio Echo, now."

Birch crossed the open lawn toward the west gate. Halfway there, he realized that with so little light from the normally bright complex, hundreds, if not thousands, more stars occupied the night sky. Their light fell on his face. He felt naked and exposed. Vulnerable. Thoughts of swirling blood and constellations of eyes and a voice that spoke to him from the void came to mind. He kept his fingers crossed that O'Neal would have a little time to talk. She was a good listener. He hoped he'd be able to put the dream image of her dead out of his mind while he was with her.

He knew he wouldn't.

DAY 35, 11:37 A.M.

Birch embraced O'Neal then kissed her, but she pushed him away and backed against the wall. Puzzled, Birch sat down on the bed. O'Neal held a manila envelope in her right hand. She and Birch hid out in the storeroom where she'd convalesced; they'd been using it to slip away together. The stench that had clung to the room weeks ago lingered no more. Dickie Stein's corpse next door had decomposed past the point of stinking, and Birch's living dead specimens down the hall had hardened into a state of arrested decay. No one upstairs remembered they'd put a bed down here. O'Neal usually showed up for their rendezvous smiling and bright, happy to lock the door behind them and shut out the awful world for awhile. In only the past few days, though, the number of dead wandering into the Vanguard complex had doubled, putting everyone on edge. Still, O'Neal seemed more shaken now than Birch had seen her since she'd been wounded by the dead.

"What's in the envelope?" he asked.

"Photos."

Birch held out his hand. "Let me see."

O'Neal held them back. "You don't have clearance—but I think I'm supposed to give them to you anyway."

"What do you mean?"

O'Neal frowned. She crossed the room, sat beside Birch on the bed, and leaned her head on his shoulder. "We knew it wouldn't last. You knew that, right? This thing we have, our escape? It's been fantastic. You've been fantastic. With everything falling apart and dying, I never thought there could be anything like what we have. But it couldn't last, could it?"

"What, are you dumping me?" Birch said, and then he laughed. "Or are you pulling out? Did Collier change your orders?"

"No. Orders are to stay put, hold the complex, keep you online working. They're desperate, and they won't let go. They figure you have the best chance of success here with your equipment."

"Then, what is it?"

The way O'Neal shuddered against him made the room feel cold like a cell, and for a moment, Birch thought of himself as trapped, a prisoner. Then he took the envelope from O'Neal's hand. She let him.

"Major Novak called me into his office this morning to review patrol schedules. That was bullshit. All he talked about was you. He knows about our affair, but he doesn't care. He thinks you're our best hope of ending the dead plague, so whatever it takes to keep you happy, keep you functioning is worthwhile, including me. I was insulted at first, but then I realized he meant we have to protect you. We have to keep you going until you find the answer."

"I'm not sure it's there to be found," Birch said.

"Novak got up and went to get coffee. Took almost ten minutes to do it, and he left what's in that envelope out on his desk in the open, where he knew I'd see them. He *wanted* me to see them. I *think* he wanted me to take them. After I saw them I couldn't do anything else. When Novak came back, he acted like he didn't even notice they were gone. I'm supposed to warn you. Look."

Birch slid out a handful of 8 ½ x 11 pictures printed on glossy photo paper and spread them out on his lap. Dated between 12 and 14 hours ago, satellite images of the Vanguard complex and its vicinity showed crowds of walking dead flooding the land like an invading army fifteen to twenty miles northeast of the complex. The sequence of images illustrated them moving closer. Birch examined the pictures twice. In eighteen to twenty hours the dead would overrun the Vanguard complex. Birch's fingers brushed a slip of paper taped to the back of the most recent image, a note scrawled in Novak's handwriting: "Take your equipment and whomever you need. I'll leave you a van and weapons by the south exit. Head out before dawn."

"I didn't see that before." O'Neal read the note and let out a long breath. "I was afraid I'd screwed up."

"Collier and the others know we can't survive this." Birch stood and paced the room. "They have to know. But they're keeping us here anyway."

"Maybe they don't know what else to do."

"We leave. Hide somewhere else."

"You told them there's no place with equipment as good as what you have here."

"It's worthless. I won't find the answers in my lab. It's something beyond that."

"Maybe they think Novak's men can protect us."

"Are you kidding?"

"These guys are sitting it out in a bunker somewhere. You think General Collier's ever worked 'wrap and smash' duty? Bastard probably hasn't ever come within three feet of one of the rotters, probably hasn't ever even smelled one."

"We should warn everyone. Get them all out of here."

"No. You'll force Novak to stop us. He won't disobey orders. He won't run from a fight, even if he can't win."

Birch wanted to argue that reason and common sense would prevail, but then he remembered Novak's rant about his first cup of coffee in the morning. Some boundaries the major wouldn't break. He would follow orders to his last breath.

"Why is he giving me an out?" Birch said.

"He believes you can end the dead plague," O'Neal said. "And he knows losing you will cost us our best chance. Maybe, he doesn't want to risk that. If I were a betting woman, I'd wager Collier ordered him to protect you to the best of his ability, not keep you prisoner. There's enough wiggle room there even for Novak to rationalize warning you."

"I guess. But, Joan, if there's a solution, it's outside my capabilities to discover it." Birch wished he felt the clarity of purpose he saw in O'Neal's eyes. " I don't mean it's too advanced. I mean it's unscientific. They don't need a biologist to figure this out, they need a, a...fucking magician, or a theologian."

O'Neal's expression soured. "Don't give me that cop-out bullshit. You got further than anyone else. There were others working on this. No one got into it as deeply as you did." O'Neal held Birch's hand. "It's only a matter of time. Something hasn't occurred to you yet, you haven't found all the information you need. Even if you're right, so what? You want to die here and become one of those things? Novak's giving you an escape. Don't squander it."

"Everyone left behind will die."

"Maybe not. They're good fighters."

Birch pushed the photos into O'Neal's hands.

"They are. They're the best. But there aren't enough of them for *this*. Not by a fucking long shot. Ammo is low. They won't last a day."

O'Neal scowled and tossed the pictures to the floor. "Figure out what you need and who should go."

"You. I need you," Birch said. "Come with me."

"Are you sure?"

"I won't leave you behind. I won't forget you."

"Okay," O'Neal said. She drew Birch down onto the bed beside her. "But first, because who knows when we'll have another chance to be alone like this...."

Birch slipped his arms around O'Neal and held her. He tried to mask his anxiety, but he knew she could feel it, even as he felt how badly she wanted to ease it, to make him see things in the same clear-cut way she did. Her touch drove some of the tension from his body. She gave him the last light in a dying world. He wouldn't let go of her; if he had to flee the dead and abandon the living to stay with her then he would.

DAY 36, 1:07, A.M.

Every night between 12 a.m. and 5 a.m., the labs closed and all nonessential equipment powered down to conserve generator fuel. The research crews bunked in an ancillary building and half a dozen field tents that Novak's men had pitched on the back lawn, leaving the main facility empty. The corridors of the lab center stretched into a fragile stillness. Birch and Sergeant Alvarez found their way through it by flashlight, Birch still using the one Alvarez had given him the night he'd first dreamt of the soldier's death—and O'Neal's.

Similar dreams had come to Birch many times in the past weeks, all of them brutal and disturbing. Alvarez, Friedman, and O'Neal appeared in some of them, dead or dying, or even as one of the walking dead, mindless and ugly. So Birch had decided to take them all with him when he left, hoping to spare them from the dead horde, and maybe save their lives. Others had appeared in his dreams too. Lang and McCormick, Private Nelson and Private Robbins who'd made chopper runs to the hospital with him, all of them doomed in his visions. He wanted to take them all. Assuming his dreams were premonitions, perhaps he could save their lives. If he kept them nearby, maybe he could protect them. Maybe not. But anyone who stayed behind would certainly die. Sometimes, the dreams were only jumbles of faces and bodies, men and women with guns, children, soldiers, moving through a landscape jammed with rippling, infinite crowds of the living and the dead. Always, Birch heard the voice of the man in red, low, deep, and muffled, like the hum of a distant machine. But it was growing louder. Coming nearer as if the dead pressed harder against Birch's consciousness the closer they came to the Vanguard complex.

Alvarez stopped at the door to Birch's lab. Birch tried not to look at his face. When he did, he only saw his dream vision of it, broken and bloodied, haunted by the frozen stare of its dead eyes. Birch unlocked the door. Alvarez pushed it open and washed the room with light.

"Clear, sir," he said.

Birch entered and walked to his desk. He unplugged his laptop, coiled up the charger, slid it into a case, and placed it on a table by the door. He took two empty boxes from the closet and set them beside it, then he gathered items from the lab and packed them. He took four more laptops, along with a stack of notebooks, and a thick, fanfold spreadsheet printout. He gathered up test tubes, microscope slides, and ampoules, then packed them in and padded them with scrap paper pulled from the trash bin. Alvarez monitored the corridor, but no one came. They heard only the faint voices of the night patrol calling as they lit up the latest dead arrival at the perimeter. Birch slung three of the laptops from his shoulders and picked up one of the boxes. Alvarez took the other box and the remaining two computers.

"I want some things from Friedman's lab," Birch said.

They walked to a lab at the far end of the corridor. Friedman's space stank of formaldehyde. A chemist, he worked on ways to accelerate physical decomposition, trying to create a powder or spray to turn the walking dead into instant rot. Birch found another box and placed two microscopes into it then took Friedman's laptop and another one, splitting them up between him and Alvarez. He stacked the new box on top of the first one and let Alvarez lead the way. The men strained from the load they carried.

"Can I ask you a question, sir?" Alvarez said.

"Shoot."

"Why me? Private O'Neal told me how Novak warned you and all, but I don't see why you picked me. You could've taken anyone. You hardly know me."

"I trust you," Birch said, afraid to admit the real reason. "You gave me your flashlight."

"That's it?"

"Isn't that enough? I had to pick someone."

"If you say so, sir."

They turned down another long hallway and followed it to a side exit that came out away from the front parking lot and the tents at the rear. The van stood fifty yards away across the grass, parked at the end of an access road that led to a small equipment shed and vehicle area used by Vanguard's maintenance crew. A dirt trail beyond the shed led to a back road that connected with the highway five miles south. Birch had sometimes used the route as a shortcut home. He and Alvarez loaded the boxes and computers into the truck.

"Seems like not much to take, sir," said Alvarez.

"It'll do. The really powerful stuff is too big or too sensitive to move. Let's go round up O'Neal and the others."

Birch and Alvarez headed for the tents, careful to stay quiet. O'Neal had already gone to rouse Friedman and enlist his help in gathering the rest of the group. She was to make everything sound like an order from Major Novak so no one would argue much about being woken in the middle of the night. Three figures emerged from one of the tents. Birch whistled. The trio stopped and waited for Birch and Alvarez to catch up to them—O'Neal, Friedman, and Lang, the latter two clutching backpacks and briefcases.

"Birch!" Friedman looked disheveled and worried. "What the hell's happening?"

"No time to explain, Carl," Birch said. "We need Robbins, McCormick, and Nelson, fast as we can find them."

"Is the perimeter breached?"

Birch said, "Not yet."

The group crept past the darkened tents, stopping at two more, while Private O'Neal went in to wake the last three people. Packed with equipment and baggage, the small van could hold eight. Birch had chosen his list from his best researchers and those he'd seen most often in his dreams. He wanted to take so many others, people he'd worked with every day for years, people he trusted, people who deserved better than the fate he was leaving them to. But really everyone deserved better than that, and for those left behind, their end would be no different than that of almost everyone else in the world. On the road, his band of refugees could wind up dead before they reached the highway for all he knew.

At the van, Private O'Neal opened the doors. Friedman spotted his computer and lab samples.

"You raided my lab?" he said. "This has gone too far! No doubt I speak for all here when I say there's no way in hell I'm getting in this van until you explain what the fuck is going on."

"We're relocating," Birch said. "Novak's orders."

"Stealing away in the middle of the night? With research and equipment that legally belongs either to the Vanguard Corporation or the U.S. Army? You'll have to lie better than that."

Most of the group stood around Friedman, their curious expressions angled at Birch, all of them weary and sallow in the van's weak light. Only O'Neal and Alvarez stood with Birch. They were armed, and Birch knew they'd comply if he asked them to force the others into the vehicle. Instead he reached into the van and pulled the envelope of satellite photos from one of the boxes. He passed around the pictures, told how O'Neal had gotten them, embellishing as if Novak was as eager to save Friedman as he was Birch. If Birch could win Friedman's support, he'd help him convince the others.

Birch waited while it sank in. He watched the black horizon, the shadowed squares of the Vanguard building, the faint lights of the night patrols. He smelled burning flesh and hair and knew another dead invader had been eliminated. An aroma of decay came on the breeze. It hadn't been there yesterday, and Birch thought how close the huge march of the dead must be by now. His hand shook. He willed it steady, but it didn't work.

Friedman touched his shoulder. Birch saw a fresh, wet redness in the man's eyes.

"God damn it," Friedman said. "God damn the dead."

The others were already boarding the van.

Alvarez, behind the wheel, started up the engine. Birch nodded at Friedman, took the photos, and the two men got in the van. Friedman squeezed into the back. Birch took the passenger seat beside O'Neal, who sat in the middle. The last door shut. Alvarez pulled out, waiting until they'd rounded a bend in the road before he switched on the headlights. In the woods, the light did little to cut the dark. A minute later they passed the shed. The smooth road ended, and the van jolted over rough dirt. Birch watched clear sky dappled with stars roll past above jagged tree shadows. O'Neal held his hand. The van jolted, slamming its passengers together. Something glass shattered in one of the boxes.

"Shit," McCormick said. "I hope that wasn't anything contagious."

"You idiot," Lang said.

The ride smoothed out. A black road stretched into the darkness. Birch focused on the broken white line down its middle and watched the van devour it.

DAY 36, 1:12 P.M.

Birch snapped awake with sun in his eyes. He had fallen asleep around dawn, while Alvarez picked a slow route along a highway littered with abandoned vehicles. The motion had settled Birch, allowing exhaustion to overtake him. He didn't feel rested for having slept, though, only achy and dried out. His head throbbed.

"Why did we stop?" he said.

He reached for O'Neal, but she wasn't there.

"Bathroom break." Alvarez reclined in the driver's seat, hands behind his head. "We didn't want to wake you."

Birch straightened himself. The others were standing in front of the van, talking and stretching. O'Neal appeared from the thick brush at the side of the road, buckling her belt as she emerged. The van sat parked on the shoulder above a pit dotted with mounds of dirt, sand, and lime, and gouged with shallow trenches. There were no cars around. A bulldozer and a digger occupied the pit's far side along with a steamroller. Construction equipment lay scattered around them. Stuck to the ground at the center of the pit, a scrap of white cloth fluttered in the breeze. The edge of a golf course was visible through the trees. Farther up the shoulder sat a trailer, its windows smashed, its door hanging from one hinge. A lopsided sign beside it announced a building project, but only the words "Coming Soon" and the torn, faded picture of a clubhouse remained visible. The grass and weeds around the trailer lay trampled flat, a web of tire tracks sculpted in the dried mud. Beyond it, the road—a two-lane strip of cracked pavement— curved around a bend and vanished into dense woods.

"Why are we off the highway?" Birch said. He reached into the back of the van, took a bottle of water, and drank most of it.

"About an hour after you crashed, it got impassable," Alvarez told him. "Cars and trucks jammed up everywhere. Clusters of the dead got thicker. Some were hiding in the cars. We couldn't go any farther. Had to find another way. We're kind of making it up as we go along now, but the driving's been smooth. We've been traveling south. Put about 300 miles between us and Vanguard. We'll need gas soon. I've already used one of our spare cans."

"Okay," Birch said. "We'll take care of it."

"The map shows a town a few miles down the road. Chances are we can fuel up there."

"Good."

"Sooner or later," Alvarez said, "we have to decide where we're going."

"We will," Birch said. "One thing at a time."

He stepped out of the van and blinked at the daylight. O'Neal came and hugged him, and Birch kissed her. It felt good to hold her in the open air and the warmth of the sun.

"We made it," she said.

Birch took a head count. No one missing.

"So far, so good," he said.

Birch walked to the bushes to relieve himself. When he finished and turned back toward the van, the sun caught his eyes and filled his sight with a hazy whiteness. The light flared magnesium bright and stabbed through his skull. Sharp pain blossomed in his head and throbbed with a frantic beat. An unwelcome murmur filled his thoughts: the voice of the man in red. Birch didn't understand the words, but the voice called to him. He felt made of paper and air, like he might float away on the breeze or catch fire and burn in an instant. The world spun. He dropped to his knees, tilted sideways to the ground, which seemed ephemeral, as if he would pass right through it, and fell. O'Neal shouted, her voice dim, faraway. Birch glimpsed the others rushing toward him, shimmering like mirages in a burning whiteness that saturated the world.

Then they were gone.

A whooshing roar rose in Birch's head, blood pulsing through his arteries like a rushing river.

Whiteness surrounded him.

Nothing beneath his body.

He floated.

Black specks broke the whiteness.

The specks blinked.

Eyes.

They stared at Birch, a negative of his dream of drifting in space surrounded by constellations of eyes. Birch tried to touch them, but they blinked away. The man in red's voice grew louder, clearer, as if it came from everywhere.

Don't fear this new world. I'll protect you. In the end, you'll be at my side. I'll make sure of it. You are my witness, but only you, and you alone.

The pain in Birch's head spiked.

He moaned and rolled over, sensing the ground beneath him again; grass folded under his hands and rocks bit into his back. Blue sky and swaying green leaves replaced the white light. Birch glimpsed flashes of motion. He heard gunfire and shouting. O'Neal screamed. Someone was crying. Birch dragged himself onto his knees. The man in red stood over him, staring into Birch's face with a pallid expression that mingled hatred, anger, and sorrow. Birch stared into the dead man's face, his mind aching to recall it but producing only the vague resonance of a memory. Red rags fluttered on the dead man's body. Fresh blood ran down his hands. He touched Birch's forehead with one finger and smeared blood there.

"No!" O'Neal shouted. "Get away from him!"

O'Neal fired her gun. Bullets slashed the air, but the dead man in red disappeared.

O'Neal saw him touching me. O'Neal saw *him. He was really* here, *and he touched me.*

O'Neal hefted Birch onto his feet and pulled him toward the van. The dead were everywhere, and the rest of Birch's crew was already dead or fighting for their lives.

Birch struggled to clear his head. He leaned against the van and pulled his gun.

The dead poured out of the nearby woods. They rose from shallow trenches in the pit, where they'd been buried under layers of lime and sand. It dawned on Birch that what had been a construction site had been converted to a burial ground, probably in the early days of the dead plague before anyone realized how useless it was to bury the walking dead. With no living people to draw them out, the dead had simply waited beneath the sand and soil. And Birch's refugees had roused them. Corpses surrounded the van and drew the circle tighter around them. *Wrap and smash.* Robbins and Nelson lay facedown in the road. The dead dragged them over the pavement, pulling them apart piece by piece and eating them. Lang ran across the pit, dodging walking corpses, nowhere for him to go. More of the things spilled out of the woods and clambered up from the shallow mass graves. Birch heard McCormick, who'd climbed up a tree to escape, crying. Part of his intestines hung down from a bloody wound in his stomach. The dead tugged on it even as McCormick tried to gather it up and shove it back inside his abdomen. Only Alvarez and Friedman remained in the clear, hunkered along the front of the van, firing round after round into the approaching wall of corpses.

"Get in the van!" O'Neal shouted.

She shoved Birch through the open side door then climbed in after him and yanked it closed. Alvarez and Friedman worked their way along opposite sides of the van; Alvarez scrambled into the driver's seat and Friedman the passenger's. The motor revved. The van jolted as Alvarez floored the gas and drove into the line of the dead. The van thumped into body after body, knocking them aside, grinding them under its wheels, but there were too many. The dead piled up, and their bodies jammed the tires and stuck to the chassis. The van shuddered then skidded sideways before it stopped.

Alvarez pumped the gas, but the vehicle's wheels only spun in dead flesh like soft mud. Dead fists pounded on the doors, on the windows.

The passenger side window shattered, spraying cubes of glass onto Friedman. Half a dozen hands thrust through the opening and grabbed his head. On the driver's side, the door cracked ajar. Alvarez fought to close it, but the weight of the dead over-powered him. Gray, rotting hands reached through the cracks and pried the door open wider. Birch and O'Neal crab-walked to the back of the van. O'Neal reloaded her gun.

Alvarez's grip on the door slid loose, and it sprang back, exposing him. A mob of writhing, grabbing dead bodies with black mouths stretched wide swallowed him up.

Friedman screamed as the dead ripped away his hair and part of his scalp. He shoved his gun through the window and fired until it was empty. Five shots. The reports exploded inside the van, almost deafening Birch. He barely heard Friedman's shrieks when the dead forced the passenger side door open and dragged him away.

He looked at O'Neal. She clutched her gun and stared at the rotten, gray faces pressed against the windshield. She was braced to fight, her face slick with sweat, her chest heaving as she breathed. The dead climbed in through the front doors.

"Come on," Birch said.

He grabbed O'Neal's arm and pulled her to the side door, threw it open, and leapt to the ground. The dead were thin there, most of them drawn to the fresh bodies on the ground by the front of the van. Birch didn't think he and O'Neal could escape, but he preferred to go down running and fighting rather than trapped in the back of the van. He wanted to see blue sky and sun and green leaves dancing in the wind as he died. With O'Neal close behind him, he picked a path through the gray crowd. The only way led down to the pit, where more of the dead waited. Birch spied the empty golf course beyond and thought if they made it there, they might have a chance.

In the pit, the sand slowed them down. Birch twisted and weaved to avoid dead hands that grabbed for them. The dead seemed lethargic even for corpses. Some of them even staggered away from Birch as he neared—as if avoiding him. Birch wondered why, but he didn't care if it meant he and O'Neal would reach the far side of the pit.

Then O'Neal screamed.

Her hand jerked free from Birch's.

Birch slid to a stop and turned back, only to face a wall of the dead gathered behind him; they swarmed over O'Neal, taking her away.

Birch threw himself into the dead, pushing, fighting, digging his way past them, but there were too many. He couldn't shove through them. They no longer moved out of his way. O'Neal screamed. Her voice cut Birch to his soul. He glimpsed her face, saw her fists flying, feet kicking, but dozens of the dead fell onto her, scrabbling for a piece of her. Through a gap in the crowd, Birch glimpsed a flash of red, and then the hole closed.

A dead hand waved past his face; an eye stared out from its palm.

From the back of one of the dead, three eyes blinked open and looked at Birch.

Eyes appeared on the legs of one corpse, in the cheeks and forehead of another, on the chest of a third.

Wherever the dead eyes blinked open, they turned toward Birch and burned him with their stare. Even as the dead wandered the pit or fought over the scraps of Alvarez, Friedman, and the others, the harsh, angry eyes that popped open on their rotting bodies locked on Birch. It was horrible to be seen by them. Birch tried again to reach O'Neal. He couldn't get past the dead. Then O'Neal's screams stopped. Birch dropped to his knees in the sand and waited for the dead to take him.

They didn't.

They moved around him like he wasn't there.

Like he was one of them.

Birch rejected that. He was alive.

He was still alive.

He stood and walked into the densest throngs of the dead. They stepped aside; they ignored him when he hit them. When he grabbed one, shoved him to the ground, and kicked him, the dead thing only rolled over and worked to get back on his feet.

"You've killed everyone else," Birch screamed. "Why won't you kill me?"

The dead didn't answer.

A hand fell on Birch's shoulder.

He whirled around.

O'Neal.

Her face was ashen and blank, a ravenous slate. Blood smeared her torn uniform. Her throat had been ripped out, and all over her body were fresh cuts and gouges, where the dead had eaten bits of her. Her hair was matted with sand and gore. Her lips moved but no words came. Birch reached to touch her then snatched his hand back. He didn't want to feel her cold, dead skin. This wasn't O'Neal any more, wasn't anything he'd ever loved or cared about; it wasn't anything human.

O'Neal shuffled closer.

She opened her mouth. Hunger filled her eyes. Her gaze seemed to cast out past Birch, who was invisible to her now, her dead stare seeking some unattainable, faraway thing beyond the horizon, beyond the world.

Then O'Neal's eyes rolled back in their sockets. Her body collapsed, and she dropped to the sand, where she lay dead still.

The man in red stood behind her, his hand lingering where he'd touched O'Neal.

Birch flinched at the sight of him.

I give her the gift you cannot. In the end it will be only you and you alone.

The man in red vanished.

Birch knelt beside O'Neal's body and stared at the sky. It was the same as it ever was, and that seemed utterly wrong. Three sparrows glided by, circled, and then flew into the shadows of the trees.

Birch wept.

DAY 36, 3:27 P.M.

Only you.
And you alone.
Birch wiped his face and stood. The dead thinned out and scattered into the woods or along the road. Clusters of them lingered over the bodies of Birch's fallen friends. All of them but O'Neal had reanimated, their bodies so damaged they would never get up and walk.

Birch returned to the van, and as he cleared the stuck bodies from the wheels and the bumpers, not one of them tried to bite or grab him. When he finished freeing the van, Birch got in and started the engine. A second later he shut it off. He left the van, walked across the pit, and took a shovel from the equipment near the construction machines. He chose a place on the edge of the woods, a patch of ground beneath three tall oaks, and he dug. His body protested the effort with aches and pains, but Birch ignored them. When he was done, he took O'Neal's body in his arms, carried her to the grave, and buried her. It was twilight when he emptied the last shovelful of dirt onto her.

He thought he should say something, but he could barely think or feel anymore and only "Don't Panic" came to mind so he left her in silence.

Back in the van, he glimpsed himself in the rearview mirror and saw a man crusted with sand and dirt and gore and drying sweat. Deep red, almost black on his forehead glistened the smear of blood the dead man in red had put there.

That was why the dead wouldn't touch me. I've been marked, claimed, and god help me whatever that means.

Birch glanced at the fuel gauge and remembered Alvarez's warning about filling up with gas in the next town. Then he drove down the road, hoping to escape something he could never outrun.

ESCAPE FROM THE PRISON OF THE BLIND DEAD 21ST-CENTURY REDUX

THE ORIGINS OF CORPSE FAUNA

The Corpse Fauna story cycle was born in 1997, but it's taken more than a few years (a couple of decades now as of this edition) for it to grow up and come into its own. That year was a big, chaotic year for me. I quit a job editing comic books in Florida, moved home to New York, found a new job, got married, moved again, launched an independent comic book series, *Shadow House*, with writer Christopher Mills, and settled in to get serious about writing prose fiction. Looking back, it's a miracle I survived. It's only the resilience of youth that allowed me to take on all the stress, sleep deprivation, and surprises that year brought me; it's only the ignorance of youth that made me confident enough to take all the *risks* involved with doing those things. Which isn't to say I wouldn't do it all over again because I certainly would. Yet even with all that going on, I had other ambitions in the works.

One of those was a comic book project to follow up *Shadow House*.

A one-shot titled, *Zombie Hell*.

The idea was Chris's, but it was born at least in part from the many conversations we'd had about our love for zombie* fiction in all its forms. At that time, that meant primarily George Romero's classic dead movies, Skipp and Spector's *Book of the Dead* anthologies, and the comic book series, *Deadworld*. This was before Zak Snyder remade *Dawn of the Dead*, before Romero returned to the *Land of the Dead*, before *The Walking Dead* became a hit comic and television show, before even the influence of Brian Keene's landmark novel, The Rising, was fully known. Today, even the Centers for Disease Control are in on the action, using the zombie apocalypse in public service announcements about disaster preparedness.

Chris and I had no idea in 1997 how timely the idea for *Zombie Hell* was.

Who can say what might have been if we'd followed through and published it?

Possibly, there would be no Corpse Fauna series today. That's because the germ of what has become Corpse Fauna was in one of the stories I would've written for *Zombie Hell*. It would've been an eight- or ten-page story about an old-timer in prison when the zombie apocalypse occurs, an old-timer due to get out of prison in only a few weeks, but who sees his last chance for freedom vanish into the mouths of the hungry hordes of the living dead.

Sadly, it was not to be.

Shadow House proved to be a critical success but not a commercial one. The artwork was stellar, created by Dan Brereton, Pat Broderick, John Estes, Fred Harper, Art Nichols, and Kirk Van Wormer, all of whom graced the book with their spectacular talents. The book received good reviews and great comments from people like Brian Michael Bendis, Barry Lyga, and William F. Nolan. But even with those things in our corner and strong support from Diamond Distribution, *Shadow House* never quite broke the sales threshold necessary to keep it alive.

---

* I recognize the distinction between a true, traditional zombie and the walking dead, a line that has become thoroughly blurred in popular culture. For convenience's sake, I refer to the walking dead as zombies in this afterword, but they are not called zombies in the *Corpse Fauna* stories, and I don't consider them true zombies. In my mind, they are, simply, the dead, and they owe much more to George Romero and Dan O'Bannon than to Papa Legba and Baron Cemeterie.

In other words, Chris and I were going deeper into debt with each issue, and orders—though rising—weren't rising fast enough. Then logistical and personal issues weighed in and made it more and more difficult to produce each issue.

Shadow House ended with issue five, one issue shy of completing our first story lines, two issues shy of the single-issue epic crossover Chris and I had planned for issue seven.

With the demise of *Shadow House*, the idea for *Zombie Hell*—and a few other projects Chris and I were planning—were consigned the morgue of dead concepts.

THE DEAD RESURRECTED

The morgue is where my "old-timer in prison" zombie story might have stayed if not for Vince Sneed. Vince and I had met through comics. Vince liked *Shadow House*. I liked Vince's comic *Forty Winks*, drawn by John Peters. It didn't take long for me and Vince to figure out we had a lot of common interests in comics, literature, and movies—including zombies. We got to talking, and sometime in 2001 (I don't recall the exact date), Vince asked me a fateful question. He'd gotten a hankering to do some publishing and was looking for some fun material for his first chapbook. He asked me, "You got any ideas for a zombie story?"

"Actually, yes," I said. "I've got this idea for a thing with zombies in prison."

By the end of the conversation, the chapbook was planned. Vince was calling it "Prison of the Blind Dead" (mostly, I think because the infamous Blind Dead movies had recently been released on DVD and Vince had blind zombies on the brain). He even sent me a logo design for the title only a few days later. As I commenced writing, my comic book short story evolved into a much longer prose piece, and the old-timer faded into the background in favor of a new character, Cornell. The old-timer, Old Corntooth, is still there, still largely the way I originally envisioned him, and unless you're reading this Afterword before you read the novella, you've already met him—and you know the story simply outgrew him.

I sent Vince the manuscript with a new title, "The Dead Bear Witness."

Vince (begrudgingly) agreed to the title change and in 2002, the story was published by Die, Monster, Die Books, the inaugural publication of Vince's new publishing venture. It featured a wonderfully lurid cover illustration by Kirk Van Wormer and an interior illustration by Carla Speed McNeil. "The Dead Bear Witness" helped pave the way for Vince's first book project, *The Dead Walk!* (2004), an anthology of zombie stories. That book reprinted "The Dead Bear Witness" and included another of my zombie stories, "Resurrection House." By small press standards, it was a hit, and if you were at the Horrorfind Weekend in 2004, chances are you remember the surfing zombie T-shirt that promoted the book with the caption: "Zombie summer would never end."

Die, Monster, Die went on to publish several more anthologies, novellas, and novels. Vince edited a follow-up anthology, *The Dead Walk Again!* (2007), published by Padwolf Publishing, which included the next major Corpse Fauna story, "The Dead in their Masses." An early version of a third Corpse Fauna story, "Crying Tears of Blood, Sweet like Honey," appeared in *Bare Bone*, issue nine, in 2006, edited by Kevin L. Donihe and published by Raw Dog Screaming Press.

Not bad for a story idea that once seemed doomed to the dustbin of creative dreams.

The long con for all this was a meaty collection of all the Corpse Fauna stories in definitive, expanded versions, with new material in a single volume that would complete the Corpse Fauna story cycle. It was to be published by Die, Monster, Die Books.

As with *Shadow House*, though, an array of intruding realities led to the end of DMD before that book was realized. Corpse Fauna once again found itself on the slab.

THE DEAD WON'T DIE

Enter Dark Quest Books.

Many Balticons ago, publisher Neal Levin and I were talking about how e-books were changing the nature of publishing, opening new opportunities, keeping authors and publishers on their toes, and generally shaking things up. Neal mentioned he liked publishing novellas, and in short order I proposed publishing the complete Corpse Fauna stories as a series of expanded novellas with additional short stories. Discussion ensued, a formal proposal was presented, Neal agreed, and Corpse Fauna returned to stalk the living.

That incarnation of the series included some previously published material, all of which was revised, refined, and greatly expanded. The version of "The Dead Bear Witness" published in the first Dark Quest volume, for example, was more than double the length of the original story, fleshed out with greater characterization, a deeper look into the Corpse Fauna world, and a little added weirdness. "Birch's Refugees" was published there for the first time.

I realized working on Corpse Fauna again that the world had changed since "The Dead Bear Witness" was first published. That posed one of the biggest challenges in preparing these stories for fresh publication. Given how much zombie fiction has been published and how many zombie movies were released in the past decade was Corpse Fauna still relevant?

Corpse Fauna has its roots firmly planted in the territory blazed by George Romero, Lucio Fulci, Skipp and Spector, Stuart Kerr and Vince Locke, but in many ways the state of zombie fiction has moved beyond that. The basic survival story that shaped many a classic tale of the zombie apocalypse has been retold to near exhaustion, and the race has long been on to redefine zombies and find new ways to make them interesting, frightening, or even lovable. Dan Waters' *Generation Dead* is a great example of taking the idea of the living dead into fresh, uncharted territory, and Corpse Fauna is nothing like it.

I asked myself if Corpse Fauna was still relevant.

The answer came in how easily I slipped back into writing the characters that inhabit these stories, how quickly my concern for them sprang back to life, and also in the fact that while there are some classic genre conventions at play in these stories, no one yet has told a zombie story quite like this one or taken the living dead to the places Corpse Fauna goes. The point of any story isn't necessarily how new or innovative it gets with its genre elements, but what it uses those genre elements to say about the world, about humanity. It matters how much the author and reader care about its characters more than how far the rug can be pulled out from under people's expectations. Although the latter is a good thing to do, and I think Corpse Fauna does it well.

At least I hope so on all those counts.

Fair warning, for twists and surprises, here there be tigers. When I first started writing Corpse Fauna, I set some basic ground rules intended to push these stories in a new direction. For example, the walking dead in Corpse Fauna cannot be killed by a shot to the head, infection is not transferred by a bite, and, as is revealed in this volume, the Corpse Fauna walking dead possess a weird and inexplicable (for now) trait unique in zombie lore.

To me, Corpse Fauna feels as fresh now as it did when I first started it.

ANOTHER CHANCE FOR THE UNDEAD

Zombies truly are hard to kill.

Corpse Fauna returned in two volumes published by Dark Quest Books, *The Dead Bear Witness* and *Tears of Blood*, each with a striking cover by the supremely talented Glen Ostrander. They received a positive reception and shambled along through the genre world for a time. The third volume, *The Dead in Their Masses*, was written and planned for publication, and Glen painted yet another horrifying masterpiece for the cover.

Then the world turned yet again.

For reasons upon which I won't speculate, the publisher of those editions ceased almost all communication, stopped paying royalties, and went underground. I stopped publication of the third book (and remain unsure to this day if it would ever have seen print anyway) and reclaimed my rights to books one and two.

Corpse Fauna was once again consigned to the morgue of dead projects.

Afterward, I moved on to new stories.

With two failed attempts to bring Corpse Fauna to realization under my belt, I decided to let the dead lie. There were enough zombie books in the world for those readers hungering for more tales of the walking dead, and maybe Corpse Fauna's time had passed. I wanted to tell other stories, try my hand at new genres and characters, and so I did. I left a door open in the back of my mind for the possibility of completing the series one day in the future and publishing the whole thing, maybe through Amazon for the sake of finality, to get to the end of the story. But I didn't. For a variety of reasons, I probably never would have. Corpse Fauna for the most part looked really dead this time.

Until, that is, Greg Schauer and Danielle Ackley-McPhail approached me about bringing the books back into print with eSpec Books.

Before I answered, I experienced all the same questions and doubts yet again.

I've moved on in my writing in many ways. Zombies no longer hold the same appeal for me they once did. They no longer hold the same appeal for many readers. And with the world yet even more changed since the last revival, did Corpse Fauna still hold any relevance? Thankfully, once again, I realized the stories are as much fun as they once were, and that what I loved best about these stories are the characters. I spent a lot of time with Cornell, Della, Birch, and a bunch of others readers will meet in the forthcoming volumes—and I missed them to some extent. Even more I felt I owed it to *them* to finish their story. I had always had a grand plan for how the varied Corpse Fauna characters would come together and reach their fates, and I could almost feel them asking me to bring them all the rest of the way home.

Thus, grateful for the opportunity to do so, here I am bringing the dead back to life once again with the expert help of eSpec Books.

I believe these characters still speak to the contemporary world, and in some ways, more now than they did in the past. The world has changed much and not all for the better. The push and pull to preserve individual freedom in a world ruled by vicious mob mentalities in particular seems more poignant now than in the past and sharp parallel to hordes of invading corpses. And there's more to come in the other stories.

So my heartfelt thanks to you, readers, who have picked up this book.

I hope you'll stay with us for the rest of the story and help me see it through to the end this time.

As for zombie lore at large, it's up to you to decide where Corpse Fauna falls in the grand chronicle of the living dead, but regardless, I hope you enjoy the journey.

—James Chambers,
June, 2011
Risen from the Grave / February 2019

TEARS OF
BLOOD

This book is respectfully dedicated to those
who fed my appetite for zombie fiction in the days
before zombies were the new vampires:

John Skipp and Craig Spector;
Stuart Kerr and Vince Locke;
Dan O'Bannon; and of course, George A. Romero.

Whitley 2019

TEARS OF BLOOD

IN THE SHADOW OF THE STRANGER
ONE

Vale spotted the stranger cutting the blazing horizon like a black blade, a tall man striding unaccosted through an amber-tinted orchard of restless corpses. Sunset made a mad jumble of the shadows, but where the stranger walked there emerged a sort of order. The dead made way for him. They fell into ranks like rough soldiers at attention, framing serrations against the fiery sky before drifting back to a lethargic chaos after he passed. A hundred yards out from the barbed-wire perimeter, the stranger shifted toward the airport and crossed through the overgrown grass. Gazing down from the air traffic control tower, Vale watched him through binoculars.

The stranger looked like a weary traveler coming to the end of a long, grimy trail; a wanderer in black, mud-spattered slacks and a threadbare white shirt. His torn leather jacket flapped from his narrow shoulders like a battlefield standard. Vale thought he must be dead to walk through a field infested with wormfeeders without igniting a feeding frenzy, but he didn't look dead. He didn't move like the dead—stiff and aimless—nor did he resemble them—gray and blemished with rot. His bright eyes were focused on the path before him, and his cheeks burned red in the dry, gritty wind.

He stopped at the barbed-wire coils staked to the ground. The low sun cast his silhouette through the loops of razor-edged steel, through the chain-link fence behind them, and onto the high, dusty grass between the runways. When the stranger raised a hand to push the hair from his eyes, the shadow of his fingers reached for the terminal like a crow's beak. Then, with a shrug, he resumed walking along the perimeter toward the makeshift guardhouse, where Duncan and Tomaselli were on duty.

Vale snatched up her walkie-talkie to warn them but hesitated. She didn't know what to make of the stranger. Tourists simply didn't exist these days. The last had come more than nine weeks ago, driving a beat-up U.S. Postal Service delivery truck; sick, starved, and dehydrated, he'd died the same day, and they'd burned his corpse so he wouldn't become a wormfeeder. Since then, only the dead came. They looked through the fence with inexplicable eyes that stared from their arms and legs, from their torsos, necks, and hands. Their idiot moans chased the quiet from the night, and their stench poisoned the air. Most of the people sheltering in the airport believed they were the last of the living in the area, and Vale couldn't imagine where the stranger had hidden or how he'd survived on his own. *Maybe he really is dead,* she thought. Maybe her eyes were tricking her in the twilight. But, no, the way he'd stopped and pushed the hair from his face was a gesture only a living man would make.

She raised Tomaselli on the walkie-talkie. Standing orders required them to burn any of the dead who strayed too near the gate, and with the setting sun at his back, the stranger would be easily mistaken for a wormfeeder.

Tomaselli's voice came back: "We see him, Vale. We're not blind."

"Don't cook him," she said. "He's a tourist."

After a pause, Tomaselli said, "You positive?"

"I didn't take his pulse," Vale said, "but he sure as hell looks alive."

"Why aren't the dead tearing him to pieces?"

"I don't know."

"Doesn't matter," Tomsaelli said. "Alive or not, no one's coming through that gate except Campbell and his team. If they ever make it back."

"*When* they make it back," Vale said.

"They should've been here already. Dark soon." Tomaselli gave a humorless chuckle. "Only people outside after dark are fools and the dead, and all the fools died a long time ago."

"Anything on the radio?"

"Dead air and static."

Vale grimaced. The prospect of losing Campbell, of him becoming one of the walking dead, disgusted her. He had pulled the surviving airport people back together after Morgan almost destroyed them, and they were counting on him to lead them through the worst of what was to come. If Campbell didn't return, the little hope left among them would falter and die. Vale didn't want to even contemplate who would fill the vacuum Campbell's absence would leave. She whispered a wish for his safety, but the stranger's arrival was a bad omen.

"Vale? You got us covered?" Tomaselli said. "He's almost here."

"I'm on him," Vale said. "You'll get a closer look than me. Do what you have to do, but keep in mind if you torch him, you're probably burning him alive."

"Don't get your panties in a wad. We won't be inviting him in for dinner, but that doesn't mean we're going to roast his ass."

Vale signed off, set down her walkie-talkie, and then swapped her binoculars for the scope on the .50 caliber rifle mounted in the tower. Wind whistled across the open window in front of the gun. Vale placed the stranger in her crosshairs and rested her finger on the trigger. The rifle felt like an extension of her hands and eyes, like she could reach down through it across any distance and touch the stranger or anything else she saw. At her best, she could take the man out with a single shot to his spine, immobilizing him, her aim so accurate and sure she sometimes spooked the others, which was why no one minded how much time she spent in the tower. She settled into the shooting nest and tracked her target as he moved into the glare of the guardhouse floodlights.

The stranger cupped a hand over his eyes and stopped outside the gate. The chain-link barrier was mounted on wheels and reinforced with sheet metal and fuselage scraps torn from the dead, metal birds that littered the airport. The ground before it was a black wash of charred earth. The stranger stood at the center of the dead zone. Wind snapped the ragged hem of his coat. He glanced over his shoulder at the charnel mob then heeled around and peered through the chinks in the barrier. Nothing else stirred but the biting wind and the restless dead spread across the darkening meadow.

When Duncan emerged from the guard shack with a shotgun braced against his hip, Vale exhaled and caressed the trigger, ready to fire. His cap pulled low over mirrored sunglasses, Duncan approached the gate. Vale knew he would turn the man away. Everyone at the airport had agreed they would take in no more tourists, not after what had happened back before the perimeter was erected—back when there were more than a hundred of them instead of only eighteen. That was Morgan's fault, and now Morgan and so many of the others walked with the dead. Some days, Vale saw Morgan in her sights and thought about putting him down, but she preferred not to waste the ammunition. She wouldn't hesitate, though, to spend a round on the stranger if he became a threat.

Vale read Duncan's body language: *Go away. You're not welcome here.*

The stranger stayed.

He looked at the fading sky then turned back to the gate, waiting. A ghost noise hummed in Vale's ears, a phantom vibration that ran through the tower and into her body. She risked a glance east toward Actsburg.

Beyond the runways and the meadow, on the far side of the concrete loops of the highway, lay the dim and lifeless city, sprawling like a spent lover between the airport and the wild, gray ocean. Vale saw nothing there. The hum became a buzz, then a faint rumble. Vale snatched up her walkie-talkie to check in with Tomaselli, but the crack of gunshots snapped her attention back to the meadow. The rumble became the growl of a motor, and Vale sighted on the airport access road. Cresting a hill, an armored pick-up truck sped into view, jolting over cracked pavement as it slalomed through rows of shambling corpses.

Campbell was back.

Vale watched him through her scope. Hunched in the truck bed amidst crammed-in boxes and packages, he clutched a rifle and fired at the dead swarming toward him.

TWO

Putrefying wormfeeders ruptured when the truck smashed into them with the metal T-bar affixed to its front bumper. The ram bristled with jagged bits of scrap metal welded onto it. Blood and entrails painted it black and purple. Torn-flesh streamers flapped from the fenders and a scalp, dangling by a thread of knotted hair and leathery skin, bobbed in front of the license plate. The body of the truck, armored with pieces from a 747's skin, was mottled with smears of blood and clumps of gore. *Dawson's going to be pissed when Campbell returns it to the garage,* Vale thought. It would take days to clean. But that didn't matter. *Campbell was back.*

His rifle popped with a sound like hail pattering on a car roof. Vale felt the urge to open fire on the dead in the truck's path, but her duty was to cover the gate. She couldn't risk taking her eyes off the stranger for more than a few seconds. He was inching closer to the entrance despite Duncan poking his shotgun through a slit in the armor and yelling at him to go away. Tomaselli came from the guardhouse with a flamethrower strapped on his back and climbed to the top of the ten-foot-high scaffolding that served as the fire post. He crouched there, behind a sheet metal barrier topped with barbed wire and lit the flamethrower's nozzle. Its fiery tongue lashed the dusk.

The truck jounced off the road into the well-worn ruts of a shortcut across the meadow. Excited by the activity, the wormfeeders were converging fast on the pick-up. It wouldn't be long before enough of them gathered to stop it. The truck surged past them, ran over them, and Campbell shot. Here and there, the dead fell. A single bullet couldn't destroy them, but Campbell tried to hobble their feet and legs. "Kneecapping the dead," they called it. Firing from a moving vehicle, he was lucky to hit the very few he did, but how the dead mobbed together made it hard to miss completely as long as he aimed low and fired often. Vale wondered why only Campbell was shooting. Burnett was probably driving, so Reading should've been riding shotgun.

The dusk flared as Tomaselli triggered the flamethrower and burned the first of the wormfeeders to approach the gate. They always came in close when they sensed it was about to be opened. The flame ignited them and drove them back. Vale thought, if it came to it she might shoot the stranger to spare him being eaten alive, but the dead passed him by as if he wasn't there. Even as smoke spiraled around him, rising from the dead zone, where the cinders wouldn't ignite, the stranger stood his ground, serene, unshaken. As if he were somehow immune to the chaos all around him. A chill ran through Vale, and she wondered if this was how she looked to the others when they saw her shooting the dead with cold, mechanical accuracy.

The truck zigzagged around the thickest groups of wormfeeders, bounced hard over a low hill, and Campbell tumbled out of sight in the cargo bed. Moments later, he was up again, hanging onto the side, struggling to get back into shooting position. The truck swerved toward the gate, sending him off balance again. Smoke from the burning wormfeeders corkscrewed in its wind as it crashed through the last line of the dead and broke clear for the entrance.

Vale refreshed her aim on the stranger.

In a flurry of motion, Duncan raised the bracing bar, withdrew his gun, and rolled the creaking gate wide. The truck sped through. Rubber bit pavement. Brakes screeched as the vehicle skidded to a stop. Duncan slammed the gate shut behind it and clasped the lock. The routine was well-practiced and there hadn't been any wasted motion—but still Duncan had proven too slow.

The stranger stood inside the barrier.

Vale blinked.

She had seen the man in her scope one moment, gone the next, but she hadn't seen him move. She put him back in her sight, and she ought to have fired then, but an overwhelming feeling that it would be a mistake stayed her trigger finger. The stranger didn't present an immediate threat. He only stood still and watched the other men with calm, fearless eyes until Tomaselli aimed the torch at him, and then he simply sat cross-legged on the concrete, placed his hands palms-up on his knees, and bowed his head. Vale thought she understood, given his options of crossing back through the crowds of the dead or taking his chances with living people. Yet, as unthreatening as he seemed, there was something to his posture, to how he moved that set Vale's hairs on end.

Without noticing the stranger, Campbell clambered down from the pick-up bed then reached back and dragged a bundle onto the tailgate, knocking a box to the road, where it broke and spilled out cans of food. The cans rolled and scattered, forcing Burnett to step around them as he rushed from the driver's seat to help Campbell ease Reading to the ground. His clothes were soaked with blood. Campbell began CPR, while Burnett tried to use Reading's blood-sopped shirt to pack a wet gash in his midriff where loops of pale, gray intestine peeked out. Putting the stranger back in her sight, Vale radioed the terminal to send Farley, the paramedic who'd become their doctor. It would take him minutes to reach the gate. Vale didn't think that would be soon enough. Campbell's upper body fell and rose with each compression, but Reading looked so pale, Vale couldn't imagine there was barely more than a drop of blood left in him.

A distant car motor coughed to life then rumbled as Farley's compact started on the far side of the terminal.

He was already too late.

Burnett dropped the bloodstained shirt and gripped Campbell's arm. Campbell stopped the chest compressions. Reading's blood pooled around him in a growing sheet as it hemorrhaged from a wound that had been much too big, much too deep. Burnett checked his watch then signaled the start of the countdown. Campbell unholstered his pistol, and Tomaselli stood ready with the torch. Duncan and Burnett drew their guns. And while they were distracted by the shock of Reading's death, the stranger leapt up and rushed past them to the body.

He knelt by Reading's shoulders. Campbell, Tomaselli, Vale— any one of them should've blown him away then and there, but they were too stunned to react and the stranger moved so fast it was hard to follow him. The gaunt man set one hand on

Reading's forehead and caressed his empty eyes shut. He lowered his head, shoulders swaying while he blessed Reading with the sign of the cross. After that, he stepped away and raised his hands in surrender.

Duncan dragged him off the tarmac and shoved him to the dirt. The stranger tried to get up, but Duncan prodded the back of his neck with his shotgun to keep him down. Unsure of what she'd witnessed, Vale kept the stranger in her scope, telling herself he was trouble, that she should take the shot, take him out—and yet she couldn't make herself fire. From the back of her mind, the voice that had helped her stay alive since the day she left her apartment told her the stranger was somehow important, that he was necessary, although for what, she had no idea. Burnett waved for Tomaselli to torch Reading's body. The stranger pleaded with them to wait. He tried to shove himself in front of the flamethrower, but Duncan kicked him back. From the tower, it was like watching a silent movie with everyone waving their hands, and their faces drawn in exaggerated expressions, their shouts silent across the distance. Tomaselli pointed the barrel of the torch at Reading, but then, like Vale, he faltered. Vale wondered if he sensed, as she did, that there was something extraordinary about the stranger.

Two minutes passed.

Seconds ticked by.

Another minute, then two. Reading should have risen.

The threshold for reanimation passed, and the world seemed to sputter except for the keening winds and the drone of Farley's approaching car.

Reading didn't rise.

His eyes didn't flutter open, nor did his body spasm and snap upright; his black, blood-caked mouth didn't grind to life with a hunger for hot blood and human flesh. His lips stayed shut tight. All the men at the checkpoint—except Duncan—lowered their weapons and stared at Reading's corpse.

Campbell's voice crackled over Vale's walkie-talkie. "Vale, you got this tourist in your sights?"

"Tight on him," she said.

"Figured you would've capped him by now."

"So did I," she said. "But it didn't seem like the right move. There's something about this guy, Campbell."

"What is it?"

"I don't know. A feeling."

"Good or bad, darling?"

Vale considered the question then said, "Neither. Only that...he matters. You should've seen him cross the meadow. He was like a ghost. The wormfeeders cleared a path for him. And what he did to Reading... If he can stop the dead from rising then I'm not sure we should hurt him or turn him away until we understand how he's doing these things."

Vale watched Campbell, his long shadow stretching into the gloom while he thought. She admired how he weighed what he knew, considered all the angles, and yet could still make snap decisions when needed. It was a quality that had saved lives and earned him Vale's trust.

"Goddamn funny thing is," he came back, "I got the same feeling. Except maybe for Duncan, so do the others. Everyone's hair's on end."

"Where's this guy from?" Vale asked. "Has he said anything?"

"Only that he's here to help us, that all he wants is shelter. Says we're in danger."

"I could've told you that," Vale said.

"Listen, I want to take this guy in and talk to him but on my terms. We don't need another riot and public display of stupidity. He goes to the pen in Hangar Four, not to the terminal. We'll hear what he has to say then decide what to do with him."

"The others won't like it," Vale said.

"Let them bitch," Campbell said. "Turns out this guy has nothing to offer, I'll cast him out myself, and they'll never even meet him. But I need your help. Anything goes the slightest bit wonky, if he lays a hand on any one of us down here, tries to make a signal, or moves for a weapon, for anything, you shoot this bastard to pieces. I'm not fucking kidding. Got it?"

"Not a problem," Vale said. "Be careful."

Campbell approached the stranger, who stood under guard between Duncan and Tomaselli, and then without warning punched him square in the face. The stranger's head snapped back, and he crumpled to the ground. Campbell struck him twice more on the back of the head and then kicked the man until he lay face down on the concrete and stopped trying to get up. Campbell jabbed a knee against the stranger's back, pinning him while he went through his pockets and clothing. He found nothing. Burnett and Duncan tied the stranger's hands, and then they loaded him into the truck and climbed on after him, squeezing in with the goods packed there. The stranger sat in the truck bed, head tilted upward as if he was admiring the beauty of the blazing sunset, and Vale wondered how he could be so peaceful and brave after being beaten and bound. Campbell slid into the driver's seat, and then the vehicle rolled away. Vale watched it pass Farley's car as the medic parked along the edge of the road. Then she relaxed and lifted her eye from her gun's scope.

Farley got out of the battered compact. He nudged Reading's body with his foot then gave it a cursory check. Afterward, he collected the fallen cans and wiped them off on the grass before he stacked them back into their broken box. He carried the box to his car and, once he was clear, Tomaselli showered Reading with flame. The corpse ignited in a shimmering wave of heat and a cloud of smoke that added to the haze from the burning wormfeeders. The tower stood downwind. Vale tugged the bandanna around her neck up over her mouth and nose and looked away. The flesh of someone really dead, someone who hadn't been resurrected, smelled very different when it burned. It was an odor she'd never get used to. She watched the pick-up truck cut left across a runway toward Hangar Four then checked the clock she kept propped up on the blank radar display.

One hour left in her shift.

One hour left to watch the dead.

THREE

In darkness, Vale crossed the derelict tarmac riddled with weeds; the chill wind ferreted out the gaps and bare spots in her clothing, but the cold and solitude suited her. She felt weary enough to go crash at her sleeping place in the international departures lounge, but at the same time, she was too curious and wired to sleep. She hiked toward Hangar Four with her Ruger Mini-14 in her hands. At least there she could avoid another night of sitting around the terminal, listening to everyone pining for the world to go back to how it had been before the dead walked.

Vale's fingers and toes were numb when she reached the hangar. She slung her Ruger across her back and pushed through the door. The pen stood under rows of lights at the opposite end of the otherwise empty space. A breeze whistled across the building's upper reaches. Armed with shotguns, Burnett and Duncan lingered on the fringes of the lighted circle around the pen. They nodded as Vale passed them. A generator hummed outside, and when the wind slacked, the moans of the dead reached even here.

The pen was an ugly but sturdy cage cobbled together from fence scraps, reinforced with strips of metal from the scavenged jets and laced with lengths of razor wire dangerous to anyone inside it that didn't keep toward its center. The stranger sat there on a desk chair with one broken arm. On the other side of the wall, Campbell sat across from him, looking worn out yet unflinching as he returned the prisoner's stare. Vale guessed the interrogation had gone sour.

Bad shit to deal with after losing Reading.

"So?" Vale said. "What's his story?"

"Not much of a conversationalist, this one," Campbell said. "Tells me we've lost our way, and he wants to set us back upon a righteous path. Apparently our souls are in as much danger as our bodies. Fucking head case."

"He have a name?"

"Everyone has a name," Campbell said. "He's keeping his to himself."

Something about the stranger nagged at Vale. His eyes were deep and tranquil, and when she looked into his face, a warm, friendly feeling came over her. It made her uncomfortable. The stranger smiled. She turned away.

She said, "What happened to Reading?"

Campbell sighed. "We were overrun. The dead were in the storeroom at Food Wizard. We tried to go out the back, but they were in the alley, too, so we cut through the pharmacy next door.

We stood in the front window and let them see us, trying to draw them to that spot so we could make a run for it out the side door. One of the plate glass windows gave out under about fifty or so wormfeeders. A big shard of it tore through Reading. He was standing between it and me. Probably saved my life. I got him to the truck while the dead were still picking themselves up, but we barely made it out of town. They were everywhere, more than I've ever seen at one time before."

"Reading was a good man."

"Yes, he was."

"How'd this guy stop him from rising?" Vale asked.

Campbell shrugged. "He won't say."

He stood up, gestured for Vale to follow him, and then they left Burnett and Duncan to watch the prisoner. Vale trailed Campbell through the dark expanse to an office used as guards' quarters when the pen was occupied. Campbell lit an electric lantern and hung it from a coat rack. In the shaky light he took Vale in his arms and kissed her. He smelled of sweat and dust and blood. Driven by relief that he was still alive, Vale responded, her fingertips dallying at the back of his skull. Then she broke away. She knew where this would lead, and she didn't want to go there. Not again. Not now, anyway, and certainly not in this place.

Vale glimpsed the hurt in Campbell's eyes as he turned away and flopped onto a chair behind the desk, but when he spun around to face her, his expression was as strong and focused as she'd ever seen it. She had told him she wanted time, but she hadn't told him that she regretted what they'd done, that she saw no point in relationships. They'd only ever held her back in the past, and she didn't see how they could last in the present or the future. Her perspective set her apart from the other airport people, who believed that all they really had left was each other. She wondered if Campbell understood. She wondered how long he might wait for her to come around or if she ever would.

"Food Wizard is pretty much picked clean," Campbell said. "We got the last of the canned stuff out of the warehouse today. We'll get the rest of the bottled water next time. Then Corrigan's going to hit the medical supply store across town. After that all we need is more camping equipment, batteries, clothing, and we're ready to move."

"Another week or two, then," Vale said.

"Give or take," Campbell said. "I miss Marcus. We'd be done by now if we still had a pilot."

Marcus had taken people on forays into town in the helicopter parked on the other side of the airport, but he'd died in Morgan's disaster and left them earthbound. Later they found him wandering along the fence and because everyone had liked Marcus, they burned his corpse to bone and ash.

"You still sure this is the right time to go?" Vale asked.

"What do you mean?"

"We've got a good thing here at least as far as shelter and security. It isn't perfect, but we can sleep safe and sound most nights. Why not ride out the cold weather here and head out come spring?"

"We won't last the winter here," Campbell said. "Food will be scarce by New Year's. Making it into Actsburg and back won't be possible on icy, snow-packed roads that no one will ever plow. The generators will die before February unless we turn up another tanker of gas, and good luck with that. You've seen how everyone is. They're past being on their last nerve. And, damn me for admitting it, but so am I. If you're sleeping soundly at night, you're the only one. You think being cooped up here three, four more months, while we run out of everything, and the days get short and dark that one or more of us isn't going to snap? Then what? We start attacking each other? Or someone opens a gate in the middle of the night and lets the wormfeeders in?"

Vale flopped onto a creaky office chair and checked the magazine in her Ruger. Campbell was right. Waiting would gain them nothing but misery. It didn't matter where they went; they couldn't stay here.

"Last I knew you were itching to be out of here more than any of us. Onward, upward, and don't look back. That's your philosophy, right? Now you're sounding like Morgan's right-hand asshole," Campbell said.

"Don't even mention that moron in the same breath as me," Vale said. "I'm nothing like him."

"No. You're not. He was in a category of one. I'm sorry," Campbell said. "But that doesn't change anything. We won't last the winter here."

"It was a passing thought, is all," Vale said. "I'm not thinking straight. That tourist out there screws with my head."

"It's how he stares you down," Campbell said. "Makes you want to trust him. Makes you doubt yourself. You're right, there's something to him. He matters in a weird way. But I can't figure out how, and he's not offering much insight."

"Maybe he's mad you punched him the face," Vale said.

"And also the back of the head before I kicked him. Yeah, guess I'd be pissed off too if I were him." Campbell rubbed his eyes then slouched in his chair. "I don't like it. You know that, right? I don't like being hard like this, using violence as my default position. It's not who I am or who I want to be. I wish things could be different. All the bad things I do are only because I don't see that I have a choice."

"I know that," Vale said. "It's us or them, life or death, and we do what we have to do. We all wish things could be different. But you know what? I bet we all wished that even before the dead started walking."

"True," Campbell said. "But as much as I complained about how shitty I had it back then, I'd trade the dead plague for my bitchy ex-wife and too much overtime in a heartbeat. I guess we all would."

"Maybe." Vale shrugged. "Sometimes people get what they wish for."

Campbell pushed his hair back and yawned. "I should let this guy rest tonight," Campbell said. "Try him again tomorrow with a clearer head."

"Get some sleep," Vale said. "You need it."

"Vale, listen, don't lose hope. Even with the roads as bad as they are, we can make it down the coast in two or three weeks once we leave here. Another few days to make our way inland and we're home and warm. My uncle's farm was still running when I was there last year. Even if he and his family are all gone, there'll be food from last season's harvest, maybe livestock and supplies. All we have to do is raise some barriers, ride out a soft winter, and then come spring we'll make ourselves self-sustaining. It'll be better there. Everyone will be so busy working to survive they won't have time to crack up. As long as we start out in another month, we'll beat the really cold weather. So hang in there."

Before Vale could respond, a hollow, rasping voice interjected from the darkness outside the office: "Anyone who's still here tomorrow night will die and become one of the walking dead."

Campbell and Vale erupted from their seats, grabbing their guns as they rose, and faced the stranger standing framed in the black rectangle of the doorway. His cracked lips curled in a ghost grin; his hands hung at his sides, palms out, facing Vale and Campbell. A deep, black spot, like an ancient scab, marred the center of each one. With the shadows falling across his face, the stranger's eyes looked like steel pellets. Vale lowered her weapon. She couldn't help it. She already knew she wasn't going to shoot him.

"How the fuck did you get loose?" Campbell rushed across the office, waving his gun in the stranger's face. "On your knees! Now!"

The stranger complied. Campbell slipped behind him and pushed the mouth of his gun against the back of the man's skull. Then he leaned out into the void of the hangar and called for Burnett and Duncan. When the echo of his voice died, the darkness returned only whispers—and the faint sound of... crying?

"Hold him here," Campbell said. Vale hesitated, and Campbell's face reddened. "Vale, put your fucking gun against his head and make sure he goes nowhere."

Campbell's tone jarred Vale. She took up her position. The stranger seemed unconcerned by the touch of her gun at his back. Campbell walked into the gloom of the hangar. His voice reverberated as he called to the others. Vale watched his shadow cut the glow from the lights around the pen, and then he fell out of sight when he rounded the cage. Faint voices came through the darkness: Campbell, Burnett, Duncan. More whispers, too soft to reach Vale.

A shotgun blast rocked the hangar.

Vale jolted and squeezed her gun.

"No! What the hell?" Campbell shouted. "Duncan! Drop it!"

"Campbell!" Vale called.

No answer.

A lamp clanked, flashed as it teetered, then fell and cast a whirl of shadows before it smashed on the ground. Duncan howled. Campbell shouted something raw. Vale heard a scuffle. She seized the stranger by his jacket and tugged him onto his feet. With her gun jabbed against the base of his neck, she marched him toward the pen.

"Campbell?" she called. "You all right?"

The sound of flesh smacking flesh came in three short bursts. Duncan cried out. Vale's pulse raced. She stroked the trigger of her Ruger as she steered the stranger into the illuminated zone. Duncan was on his knees, clutching his head, tears streaming down his cheeks. Blood ran from a gash beneath his right eye. Burnett lay behind him, most of his skull and brain splattered across the floor. His shotgun lay next to him. The door to the pen hung open. Campbell stood over Duncan, holding the sobbing man's shotgun in one hand, his other bloodied from punching Duncan's face. Duncan's sunglasses lay in pieces on the ground.

"Oh, god," Vale said. "What happened?"

"They were standing here, crying, and then...he shot him! Duncan shot Burnett," Campbell told her. "Then... he tried to kill himself."

The stranger rushed away from Vale and crouched next to Burnett's body, where he said a prayer and made the same gestures that had spared Reading existence as a wormfeeder. Campbell proved less forgiving this time. He stormed forward and raked the stranger's head with the butt of Duncan's shotgun, knocking him down.

"What did you say to them?" Campbell kicked the stranger in the stomach, and then furious, he turned to Vale, and said, "They released him. They opened the fucking lock and let him go. He talked them into it, convinced them there was no point in holding him, no point in going on living, or some kind of bullshit. Burnett said he wanted to die, and then Duncan just turned and...he just...fired. There was nothing I could do. Burnett didn't even try to move. He let it happen, like he really did want it."

Campbell whirled and dragged Duncan to his feet.

"Why'd you do it?" he said. "What's wrong with you?"

Duncan trembled. His breaths came fast and shallow, and when he tried to speak his lips quivered, and he said only, "I...I...I...I...." Vale thought he might be going into shock. Campbell repeated his question, shouting, but Duncan couldn't answer. Campbell shoved him into the pen and then locked the door. He stepped back to the stranger and kicked him in the ribs. The stranger jerked sideways, tumbled away from Campbell, and then pushed himself off the floor and sat up, indifferent to the beating.

"What did you say to them?" Campbell shouted.

"I told them what I was about to tell you." The stranger's voice resonated, like a cello string holding a long, deep note. It penetrated Vale, impossible to deny; its power made her shiver. "I didn't mean for this man to kill his friend, but death comes to us all, and there's no predicting when or where, even as there's no predicting how anyone will react to the truth. Sometimes the truth has unintended consequences. Both hope and despair can rob a man of his soul. We make our choices alone. These two men were not prepared to hear the truth. Maybe you aren't either."

"What the hell does that mean?" Campbell said. He grabbed the stranger by the shoulders and thrashed him. "Who are you? Why'd you come here? Tell me!"

Campbell shoved the stranger across the floor. The man rolled into a bank of lights that clattered to the ground and shattered. A narrow arc of illumination came from the one remaining lamp. Campbell raised the shotgun over his head like a club and surged after the stranger. Vale bolted between them and forced Campbell back. He tried to yank free of her, but she refused to let him go. Knowing he'd never hit her, she coaxed him away from the stranger, step by step, and then she slid her arm around his back and held him, stroking his head, until the razor edge of his anger dulled.

She understood his rage. Burnett and Campbell were friends from the old world, and losing him and Reading in a matter of hours had dropped their number to sixteen—thirteen men, three women. And the stranger—but Vale didn't see much chance of him filling anyone's spot. They needed three trucks to carry all the food and supplies bound for the farm, twelve people to man the trucks and guns in shifts, and then there would be casualties after they left the airport perimeter. The fewer people there were, the less their chances of survival. The cold calculus of the situation flashed through Vale's mind, even as she saw Campbell reaching the same conclusion. The plan he believed in, the plan he wanted Vale and everyone else to believe in, was in danger of falling victim to a crazy man spreading madness among Campbell's people. He couldn't allow it. He pumped the gun to clear the shell Duncan had fired and reload the chamber. Then he circled around the stranger and prepared to execute him.

FOUR

The stranger said, "If you destroy me, all your people will be lost."

He didn't even flinch when Campbell touched the back of his head with the barrel of Duncan's shotgun.

"Shut up," Campbell said.

"Bad hours are coming your way. Shooting me won't help you weather them," the stranger said.

"I said, *shut up*, tourist."

Campbell snapped the gun against the stranger's head, but he didn't fire, and Vale realized he felt the same thing she did. An aura of power that emanated from the stranger. The gravity of his presence. The sense that the secrets revealed by shooting him might be worse than those discovered if he lived. Executing him was a rational choice. He wasn't one of the airport people. They owed him nothing, and his presence threatened them all; it had already led to Burnett's death. Yet something beyond reason had stopped Vale, and probably Tomaselli too—and now it seemed even Campbell—from pulling the trigger. The stranger stirred fears of the unknown consequences of killing him, of never learning who he was or why he'd come to them, or how he stopped the dead from rising.

"The dead are on a pilgrimage," the stranger said. "You're in their path. When they get here, they'll do to you and everyone else hiding here what they do to all of the living. They'll make you like them."

"No more talking," Campbell said.

He shut his eyes and averted his face, as if he could break the stranger's power over him if only he didn't look at him. His hands shook the gun, the barrel tapped the stranger's head, and Vale sensed the effort Campbell was exerting trying to squeeze the trigger. He wasn't grappling only with the stranger's power but with himself and his uncertainty about how best to protect the people he led. Vale went to him. She placed her hand on the shotgun and helped him lower it.

She spied a flicker of fear in Campbell's eyes when he opened them. His inability to follow through with his decision to shoot the stranger frightened him as much as what that revealed about the stranger's influence. Vale knew the touch of that fear and turmoil, but such inner conflict was a rare experience for Campbell.

"You wanted him to talk, so, okay, he's talking now. Hear him out," Vale said. Then for the stranger's benefit, she added, "If he jerks us around anymore or we don't like what he has to say, I'll shoot him myself."

Campbell nodded. Then with his foot, he shoved the stranger in the shoulder. "Say your piece."

"A hundred thousand or more of the damned are on the march," the stranger said. "And they'll cross this ground. I've witnessed them. They're north of here, maybe a day, a day-and-a-half's walk. It won't be long before they overrun you. There are already more and more of them in this place every day, and when the full host arrives, it will take them days to pass over this land. No fence you build will keep them out. No gate will hold them back. No weapon will stop them. There is no shelter from the dead."

"Why are they coming here?" said Campbell.

"The red man is calling them south," the stranger said.

"Who's that? What are you talking about?"

"Do you think the dead have no purpose? No fate to which they aspire? Do you think they rose from eternal rest without an objective? Have you never wondered what they see with the eyes that stare out from their withered flesh? So few living remain to sustain them, now, to satisfy their greed, their hunger. All that's left is for them to carry out the destiny they've chosen."

"Like I told you, a fucking head case," Campbell said. "Tell me your name. Tell me something that makes sense. Tell me how you came across so many wormfeeders in one place and escaped. Or better yet, tell me how you walked in here without the dead ripping you apart."

"The dead are more than their appetites. They aren't so different from the living in some ways. There is power in understanding what they see when they look at living people with their multitudes of eyes. There is peace in knowing the depths of their corruption and the shallows of their souls," the stranger said. "Their souls aren't like the souls of the living. They aren't the souls of the people they were before they died. But they're souls nonetheless. The power of the lost, scrabbling for new flesh to call its own. The dead who've risen are those who found no God awaiting them in death, no salvation, no respite, no Heaven, no Hell, not even oblivion. They've come back to claim their afterlife from the living."

"Bullshit," Campbell said. "Enough nonsense. Time to put you down before you spook anyone else."

"What if he's telling the truth?" Vale said.

"About the souls of the dead and Heaven and Hell? Give me a break. They're fairy tales," Campbell said.

"You don't know that."

"Yes, I do," Campbell said. "Because I've never seen or heard or felt anything to prove otherwise, and if those things exist, then where the hell is God and all his angels or even the Devil himself while the entire human race is being wiped out by living corpses? You going to tell me that it's all part of some divine plan? I can't believe you of all people would buy into this garbage."

"How do you explain why the dead can walk? Or why they have eyes in places they shouldn't?"

"I don't need to. That's not my job," Campbell said. "My job is to keep us alive and safe. And this tourist is making that difficult. He's playing us. He's a sick fuck who thinks he can work an angle."

"He might be telling the truth about the dead heading this way. How many wormfeeders have turned up out there in the last couple weeks? More show up every night. You said you saw more than ever before in Actsburg," Vale said. "What if he does know why the dead are walking? Your job is to protect people. Do you want to kill this guy or toss him out on his ass before learning a couple of really fucking useful tricks like he knows?"

"No, I don't." Campbell rubbed his forehead. "But what makes you think he'll share what he knows with us?"

"He said he came to help us." Vale faced the stranger. "Isn't that right?"

"Yes," the stranger said.

"So help. Tell us how to be invisible to the dead, how to keep people from rising after they die."

The stranger didn't answer.

"See?" Campbell said.

"Please." Vale approached the man. "Help us, help yourself. Tell us how to survive. If everything else you said is true, we're going to need to know."

"The knowledge alone can't save you," the stranger said. "The ability isn't something that can be taught; it must be earned. Or given as a blessing. You have no time for the first and little hope for the latter."

"Total bullshit," Campbell said. "There's nothing but trouble and riddles with this guy. If you don't want to kill him, we can take him back to the gate and toss him out on his ass. Let him sleep with the wormfeeders."

"We should take him to the terminal," Vale said. "Let him speak to the others. Hear what they think."

"Since when do you give a shit what the others think?"

"I don't, all right? But I don't know what to make of *him*," Vale said. "He hasn't attacked us. He didn't kill anyone. Until Duncan calms down, we won't really know why he did what he did. Maybe he snapped. You said yourself it could happen. This tourist could really be here to help us, and we could be digging our own graves if we ignore him. Maybe someone else will have some insight or think of something we're missing. Maybe he'll open up to one of the others. It can't hurt to find out."

"No," Campbell said. "Cast him out. Be done with him."

"Campbell."

"It's a bad idea. No."

"What if it turns out he's right?" Vale said. "We'll be throwing away a chance to save lives."

Campbell shook his head. "I don't believe him."

"I'm not sure I do, either," Vale said. "But I'm afraid of what'll happen if we do nothing. We can dig in and hide. We can prepare for the dead, and if he's wrong, if an army of the dead doesn't turn up in the next day or two, then we'll all be tired and pissed off and laugh about it in a week, and who cares? But we should act while there's still time."

"There's time for only some to be saved," the stranger said. "Some here may yet live. Some are meant to die; some are always meant to die. And although not all who die must rise again in death, some can never be saved."

Campbell glared at the stranger. "Enough from you. Close your mouth."

"What are you going to do?" Vale asked.

"What he says makes no sense. Ignore it. We're so close to being ready to leave here, to finding a safe place and making a better home," Campbell said.

"God, Campbell, that's so far away," Vale said. "Why do you put all your hopes into that?"

Campbell frowned. "We've got nothing else to hope for *but* that. Why risk it all for some crackpot with crazy stories?"

"All right, fine," Vale said. "We'll know one way or another in a day or two."

"Vale."

Campbell reached for her. She twisted away.

"Shit," Campbell said. "You win. I don't know, okay? I don't have the answers at my fingertips. None of this adds up. Maybe you're right. He could be giving us a real shot to save ourselves. Cuff the stranger, cuff Duncan. We'll drag them in and talk to the others. We can lock up the hangar and send a fire crew back to burn Burnett."

It dawned on Vale then that if not for the stranger's intervention, Burnett would already have risen in death. "Burnett won't rise," she said. "We should bury him."

"No," Campbell said. "Burning's better. Safer."

"We should at least wait to see if any eyes appear on him," Vale said.

"I'll ask the fire crew to check before they torch him," Campbell said.

He snatched Burnett's shotgun from the floor, then stepped over the dead man's body, and set the weapon beside Duncan's on an empty chair. The stranger, kneeling where Campbell had left him, watched Vale with placid eyes. Vale tried to read the soft expression on his face, but she didn't recognize the emotion she saw there.

FIVE

The walk to the main terminal took almost twenty minutes in the dark and moving with two prisoners chained together, but Campbell and Vale knew the path well enough to navigate by flashlight. Duncan whimpered the whole way. Vale wished he would shut up. He sounded like a wormfeeder with half its throat torn out. The stranger, on the other hand, said nothing. He had bounced back from Campbell's beating and appeared as spry and as strong as he had when he arrived except for his arm, which had proven only strained not broken and nested in a makeshift sling. In the distance, the wind howled, and the barbed wire and the chain-link fence clanked. The dead moaned and grunted. The noise would go on all night.

Halfway to the terminal, Vale said, "Campbell, I'm sorry."

"For what?"

"I guess for arguing with you, for forcing you into this," she said, but that wasn't it. There was another thing, prodding from the shadows of her mind, an instinct not yet realized that made her regret how she'd handled the situation. She felt that an unseen balance between her and Campbell had shifted.

"You didn't force me into anything. You persuaded me. There's a difference," Campbell said. "Anyway, you got what you wanted didn't you? Don't go asking for forgiveness on top of it."

Vale said nothing. Campbell didn't know the first thing about what she wanted. Despite his effectiveness as a leader, Campbell still thought in terms of the old world. His escape plan, with its caravan and the farm, represented nothing but a route into the unrecoverable past. He and the others hadn't yet come around to accepting that the world now belonged to the dead. But Vale had. *The stranger has, as well,* she thought. She sensed he saw the world much like she did. Maybe that was the thing about him that got under her skin. She had considered him a bad omen when she first saw him, and it had proven true, but at the same time, he was the first man she'd met who seemed to be living in the world as it was, not as he wished it to be.

"You know what, though?" Campbell spoke into the darkness. "I need you with me when we get in there. I have to keep everyone together and focused on what's best for us all. We can't be choosing sides and having shouting matches and bullshit drama. The others may not like you much, but they respect you. If you stand with me, Malloy won't get a foothold trying to turn this to his advantage. If you really want to save lives, you'll follow my lead. Can you at least do that?"

"Sure," Vale said. "I can do that."

"Well, thank God for small favors," Campbell said.

"Grow up, Campbell," Vale said. "If you don't want to do this, don't. I won't fight you over it. Take him to the gate right now and throw him out of here. Or shoot him. Is that what you want?"

Campbell stopped walking, forcing the prisoners and Vale to stop with him. He turned to face Vale, letting his flashlight point at the ground. He looked like a shadow rising from a puddle of light.

"No," Campbell said, his tone calm and certain. "It's not. I happen to think you're right that we shouldn't take a chance ignoring him, crackpot or not. When I think about walking into the terminal with him, letting him meet the others, all I can picture is the last day Morgan was in charge, the assembly on the tarmac, and how people looked when they realized what was happening. We can't afford to lose control like that again, or we're finished. Something like this could spark a fire we can't extinguish."

"I know," Vale said. "It's a risk."

Campbell raised his light and resumed walking.

They moved in silence for a while, and then Vale said, "I've got your back. Whatever happens in there, I won't let you face it alone."

As they approached the entrance, Vale used her walkie-talkie to call Gordon and Schutt, who were guarding the door. Then they stopped twenty feet out and waited for the floodlights to paint them. Vale and Campbell looked down and shielded their eyes. When the lights flared to life, Duncan screamed and jumped, then tried to break away, but the chains around his wrists and waist jerked tight and held him. Campbell yanked on them, pulling Duncan to his knees. Duncan's sobbing verged on hysterical. He was mumbling over and over that he didn't want to go inside, didn't want to face the others, that he wanted to die before the dead came. Campbell pulled him back to his feet. The stranger remained impassive.

The door's triple locks click-clacked from inside, and then it swung open. Gordon and Schutt appeared, armed with rifles. The shadows of others moved in the passageway behind them. Inside the entrance was a small landing at the base of two flights of stairs that led to the main floor and an access point protected by another heavy security door. The passageway was one of only four of the main terminal entrances left open. The others were welded tight or blockaded. At the sight of Gordon and Schutt, Duncan's sobbing faded to a whimper. He wiped his mouth and nose with the back of his hand and straightened his shoulders.

"I thought we all agreed no more fucking tourists," Schutt said. "Who the hell is that guy?"

"He's a gold club frequent flyer," Campbell said. "Beyond that, we're still working on the details."

"Where's Burnett?" Gordon asked.

"Dead." Campbell nodded back the way the group had come. "In Hangar Four. In the pen. He didn't rise. Need to send a fire crew out there for him to be sure, though."

"He didn't rise?"

"That's what I said."

"Dammit," Schutt said. "I'm sorry, man. We heard about Reading too. Tragic. They were good men."

"It's been a rough day," Campbell said.

"Did the tourist kill him?" Schutt asked.

"No. Duncan did."

"What? Why? I don't get it," Schutt said.

"Hey, Danny," Campbell said. "As much as I'd love to stand out here giving you my personal testimony for the record and all, maybe you could let us in and then come hear the news with everyone else? That way I can get warm and I only have to go through it once."

"Sorry."

Schutt cleared the doorway to let them pass. Gordon stood opposite him. The prisoners walked between them. Gordon paled when she glimpsed the stranger's face. At first Vale thought she was upset over Burnett or Duncan, but the stranger's affect on her was clear. Gordon tracked him with her eyes.

"Gordon?" Vale said. "Everything all right?"

"Yeah, fine," she said.

"You know him?"

"No. He... looks like someone I knew once," she said. "It caught me off guard."

"You sure?"

"Yeah, totally." Gordon ducked Vale's gaze and scanned the darkness around the terminal. "Better go on in. You got an escort waiting."

Vale entered the terminal. Carlson and Domenico had joined Campbell and were ushering the prisoners upstairs. Thurston stood by the upper door. All of them carried a rifle or a shotgun and wore a handgun and knives on their belt. They brought the prisoners into the corridor and waited for Vale to catch up.

"Put Duncan in the cell. We'll work out what to do with him later." Campbell unlocked the chain from Duncan's cuffs and waited for Carlson to take his arm. The chain remained attached to the stranger like a leash. "We'll wait here."

Carlson led Duncan a short way down the corridor then turned out of sight into a connecting passage. The cell—a private bathroom with no windows—was in a back office, with no way in or out except one door, reinforced and rigged to lock from the outside. Two minutes later, Carlson returned, and then the group marched the stranger to the main pavilion, a sprawling concourse lined with shops and restaurants.

This time of night, everyone who wasn't on guard duty would already be there. Windows on both sides of the concourse looked out over the tarmac with a clear view of the land surrounding the airport. It served well as an observation platform. During the day people kept watch here to make sure the dead stayed on the far side of the fence; at night, they studied the dark city and the black horizon, hoping to see lights that never came. It was pushing midnight, but everyone was still awake. They all had private space in other sections of the airport, but they spent most of their time together in the pavilion. Even when it was safe to be alone, it never felt like it, and nobody slept like they used to. A table of spare weapons, some gathered from a souvenir sword display in the duty-free shop, provided an extra touch of security.

When Campbell and Vale walked the stranger into the pavilion, the entire group was gathered at Gate 13. Their expressions were angry and curious. Frightened. Stoic. Guarded. Vale thought she knew what was going through their minds. *Tourists are bad. Awful things happen when we take in strangers. Only the group who survived together can be trusted. Everyone else is an outsider. Everyone else brings death.* They had all said things like that in the days after Morgan's disaster. They had said them standing over the charred bodies of lost friends, said them standing by the fence watching dead people walk by who had once lived alongside them. They had said them while they pieced their lives back together and figured out how to go on. They spoke the words so often that in time they took on the force of law. Now Campbell was breaking that law, and they wanted an explanation.

Campbell gave it to them. He cuffed the stranger to a chair then told everyone what had happened since the man's arrival. They had already heard from Farley and Tomaselli about how the stranger had stopped Reading from rising, but Campbell told them anyway; he told them all the things the stranger had said and all the things he'd done to the man to make him talk. No one interrupted. Vale stood at Campbell's side and studied the faces in the crowd. She found Malloy and glimpsed the greed and violence in his eyes. Beside him stood Estevez, his face a predatory mask, waiting for Malloy to tell him what to think and do. Behind the group, someone moved: Gordon drifted along the back of the crowd, studying the stranger through the spaces between the others, her eyes glued to his face.

Drawn by more than a mere resemblance, Vale thought.

When Campbell finished, the group broke into half a dozen conversations all at once; people called out questions and demanded answers. Campbell gestured for them to wait. When they kept talking, he shouted them down.

"The point of this," he said when he regained their attention, "is to give this man's warning a fair hearing. I've told you what he said, but I wanted you to hear it from him for yourselves. There's no harm in being prepared for the worst. Listen to what he has to say. I want to know what all of you think before I make a decision about what to do with this man and how to protect us."

The crowd quieted. Malloy whispered to Estevez, and then Estevez glanced at Campbell and laughed. Campbell ignored them. Gordon threaded her way through the crowd to the front of the group.

"Talk," Campbell told the stranger.

The stranger faced the people and said, "An army of the dead is coming here. A hundred thousand, maybe more. They will be here in hours, and you—"

"Don't listen to him," Gordon said.

"...you must prepare to leave here," the stranger said. "All of you may not survive if you flee, but if you stay..."

"Don't listen to him!" Gordon shouted.

"What the hell is the problem?" Campbell said.

"I know him. I thought I was wrong. I hoped I was. But I'm not. It's him. I don't know how it's possible, but it is," Gordon said. "Don't listen to him. He's lying. He wants to trick us."

"Why do you say that?" Campbell asked.

Gordon answered. Chaos erupted in the room.

Vale perceived much of what happened next only in flashes of sound, impressions of faces, and blurs of motion. She saw weapons drawn, and then people slammed into her, knocking her sideways as the waiting area surged with activity. Vale couldn't tell who was trying to escape and who wanted to reach the stranger. Some of the men grabbed her, and she fought them off. She tried to focus on Campbell's voice, but there was too much shouting, and she lost track of him. Then a streak of silver cut the air.

The blade of a replica katana from the duty-free shop, grabbed from the table.

It was in Campbell's hands, and he was swinging it toward the stranger's neck, poised to slice his head from his body.

To Vale, the rest of the world seemed to freeze and fade away then and everything slowed until the spaces between heartbeats seemed like minutes. Her eyes tracked the blade as easily as if Campbell was using it to cut paper. Vale's eyes flashed to the stranger's, and his power touched her. She didn't understand why, but she felt desperate to protect him. She drew her gun, took aim, and shot Campbell in the thigh to stop him from striking the stranger. Screams followed the gunshot. People piled onto Vale and dragged her to the floor. She struggled and fought back, but there were too many to fight. They wrestled her guns from her hands, and then they beat her into a black nothingness, while Gordon's screams echoed through her mind: "I know him! I know who he is! I saw his body! He's one of them. He's one of the dead!"

VALE'S DARK DAYS
DAY 1

Vale snickers along with everyone else at the first videos of reanimated corpses that run again and again on television and online. Dead bodies, dressed in open-backed hospital gowns rise in morgues. The dearly departed clamber from coffins in funeral homes. Their figures wasted, their flesh sallow, the dead move like their skin is made of old leather ready to crack and break, but it doesn't stop them from attacking people. Their teeth and jaws and fingers are strong.

Vale watches the first dozen videos then gives up before the steady stream of camera-phone images and shaky digital movies becomes a flood of meaningless horror. It must be a hoax or a stunt. An Internet meme taken to extremes. Someone's sick idea of a joke or an early Halloween prank. It can't be real. Dead is dead. Vale learned that lesson when she was a child and spent two hours trying to resuscitate her dead cat only for her mother to yank it away as soon as she walked in the door from work. Dead is final. Dead gets burned or buried. Dead rots. There's no coming back from dead.

Yet that's what everyone says is happening.

It's seems like such a serious thing, yet no one takes it seriously. Newscasters make only half-hearted efforts to hide their smirks when the first reports of the walking dead scroll across their teleprompters, and the videos provide rich fodder for late-night TV comedians. Vale watches them all because she can't sleep, but their top ten lists and cracks about the dead squatting Wi-Fi at Starbuck's don't make her laugh. Instead she feels numb and frightened, how she feels when a harsh storm comes and the power goes out, only this time she's sad, too, and she wishes she could sleep through it.

Vale switches to a cable news channel after the late-night talk shows end. Around 2 a.m., while a woman from the Centers for Disease Control and Prevention drones on about target cells and airborne vectors and risks of contagion, Vale nods off, hoping this thing with the dead will be like the bird flu and swine flu scares that terrorized so many but in the end amounted to so little.

DAY 3

Kevin drops the newspaper and two overstuffed bags of groceries on the counter in Vale's kitchen. Vale unpacks them. She piles up cans of soup and stacks boxes of pasta, crackers, and cookies. She takes out smoked sausages and other dried meats, cans of fruit juice, a jug of bottled water, and arranges them on the counter. At the bottom of each bag are single-serving boxes of breakfast cereal.

Vale holds up a box of Apple Jacks. "My favorite."

"I grabbed a bunch of those," Kevin says. "It's not all that much, but it's the best I could do."

"It's wonderful." Vale smiles at him. "Thank you so much. I could last for weeks on all this. I'm sure I won't need it all."

"I don't know. This thing is so messed up it might be a while before we can get to the store again. The shelves are pretty much picked bare. Lewis said deliveries to all the Food Wizards in town have been canceled for the week. There's still plenty of stuff in the stock room at the main store, though. I called in a favor and Lewis let me in the back door to do my shopping. Got a bunch of stuff for Aunt Dee and Uncle Jerry too. I'll drop it off on my way home."

"Can't you stay with me tonight and drop it off tomorrow?" Vale asks. "We should stick this out together."

"I can't leave Dee and Jerry hanging." Kevin glances at his watch. "I talked to Dee this morning. They're kind of freaking out. Locked up tight, and haven't been out since the day before this started. I need to make sure they're okay. I wouldn't want them to starve to death while I was kicking it back a few blocks away."

"I'll go with you. I haven't seen them in awhile. It would cheer them up," Vale says. "We'll come back here after."

"No way do I want you out there. I can get around okay on my own, but it's not exactly safe. There are more of those things every time I go out. They have a way of creeping up on you so you don't even notice them until they're close. When they catch someone... No, Vale. It's a stupid risk. I don't want you to get hurt. The dead aren't the only thing to worry about, either. People are fighting each other over fuel and food. Some of them are armed. I stuck to the back streets, but I was lucky to make it here. It'll only be worse after dark."

"I'm worried about you," Vale says. "Promise me you'll come back tomorrow and stay with me?"

Kevin walks around the counter and embraces Vale.

"I promise. First thing tomorrow morning. We'll have breakfast together. Save me some Apple Jacks."

Vale cups the back of Kevin's head and kisses him. Afterward she asks, "Do you have to leave right away?"

Kevin smiles. "I have a little time."

He kisses Vale back and then she leads him into her bedroom. The room is stuffy and bright from the afternoon sun streaming through the window, but later, when Kevin goes, the light is dimmer, the air cooler, and he leaves without looking back.

DAY 5 AND 6

Vale hides.

The reporters on what seems like every radio station and television channel warn people to lock themselves indoors and stay there except in case of emergency, so Vale does. She fills her bathtub with fresh water, checks the batteries in her flashlights and radio, and gathers candles. She rations the food Kevin brought her, locks her door and windows, and keeps the shades down and the curtains drawn. Her tidy apartment becomes a comfortable bunker, where she waits for the nightmare outside to end. She keeps in touch with her parents across town and Kevin two neighborhoods away via phone, e-mail, and text. By the morning after he dropped off the groceries, the streets were too thick with the dead for Kevin to return; Vale spent most of that day looking out her window and saw not one living person on her street. She hasn't let it upset her. If she follows the instructions from the news reports, if she waits things out, then the horror will pass, and then she and Kevin will be together.

Vale leaves the television news on even when she sleeps, but it doesn't help make sense of what's happening. Reports and video air from around the world, all documenting the same things: chaos, death, and horror. Vale watches the world fall apart on TV, while outside, the living dead take over the streets of Actsburg. No one mocks them anymore. Once the walking death was everywhere and ordinary people started rising in the streets, humor no longer kept the fear at bay. Vale looks out her window at her block filled with wandering corpses and sees three dead children chase down a living woman, rip her apart, and eat her in the street. It's beyond understanding.

There are moments when they seem unreal to Vale, as if looking out her window is like watching television, but she can't switch off what she sees outside. When she hears low moans and heavy footsteps scuffing along the hallway outside her apartment, she locks herself in her bathroom and ignores the sounds until they stop. She pretends this is no different than staying home because of a blizzard or a hurricane, but she can't think of a time bad weather kept her shut in for so long, and she doesn't remember so many people ever dying from a storm.

She sticks to a routine of sorts. She calls her boss at the tax preparation office every morning at 9 a.m. to tell him she won't be coming in that day. For the last two days, his voicemail answered even though he's always at his desk by 8:30. This morning she leaves her usual message then tries some of her coworkers, but no one picks up, and Vale thinks the office must be closed until things are safe again. It's strange no one called to tell her.

Mid-morning she checks in on her mother and father.

"It's bad out there, honey, very bad." This is the first thing her mother says every morning; her father never gets on the phone. Vale sometimes hears him bumping around and grumbling in the background. As of yesterday, Vale's mother has lost contact with her sister in North Carolina, one of her cousins in Florida, and an elderly uncle in the next town. "I'm glad you're still safe, dear. Do you have enough food? It was so nice of Kevin to take care of you. You won't go out, right? Promise me you won't go outside until this is all over. Stay home, stay safe. Promise?"

This morning, like every morning, Vale promises.

In the afternoon she talks to Kevin.

"You doing okay?" he asks.

"I miss you, but I'm all right," Vale tells him. "How about you?"

"Miss you too." Kevin's voice sounds like he's in the next room. "Wish I could be there with you, but it's getting worse over here. The dead are everywhere. About forty of them are hanging around right now on the corner. I'd never make it past them."

"I know. It's bad here, too," Vale says. She wishes there was an underground tunnel between their buildings so they could go safely between each other's apartments. "They're killing people out there."

"Did you see it? Were you looking out the windows?" Kevin says. "You don't need to watch that stuff. I told you to stay away from the windows. You should board them up."

"I'm on the fourth floor," Vale says.

"It doesn't matter. If they see you, they'll find a way into your building. I watched them break into a house across the street. Took them twelve hours to crack the door, but they did, and then a mob of them pushed right in and pulled out the family living there. You have to be smart. You have to hold on. A few more days and someone will figure out how to fix this. You can hold on a few more days, right?"

"Sure," Vale says. "Only I miss you."

"I miss you too," Kevin says.

They have variations of the same conversation every day, sometimes twice a day. One time Vale asked Kevin what he thought caused the dead to rise. After a long pause he said he had to go and then hung up without answering her question. Sometimes they talk about days they spent at the park, the beach, or hiking, and what they'll do when the crisis is over, but they never talk about those things for long. Kevin doesn't like to be on the phone, but he always writes back to Vale on e-mail. That afternoon, while they talk, Vale thinks she hears a woman whisper on Kevin's end of the line; she thinks it might be Erica, a neighbor from Kevin's building, a pretty, blonde who was two years behind Vale in school. Vale asks him if she's there with him, but Kevin says he's alone.

That evening Kevin doesn't answer when Vale calls. She tries him three times, but only his voicemail picks up. Texts and e-mails go unanswered. For a moment, Vale allows herself to hope that Kevin has found a safe way to travel through the city and he's coming to her. Her heart leaps before she talks herself down from her hope. She doesn't want to sit there waiting only for Kevin to never show up. She knows what his silence probably means, but there are other reasons he might not answer the phone, most of them bad, but few of them as awful as the dead having gotten him. She tries him every hour until she falls asleep around 4 a.m. She calls again when she wakes up in the morning. Still no answer. No replies on e-mail, either. She calls the police to have them check in on him. A recording comes on and directs her to stay indoors and take precautions or move to a shelter if she's phoning from an outdoor location. It plays twice then disconnects.

Vale calls her mother and tells her she's lost touch with Kevin. Her mother sighs, and says, "You know its bad out there, right, honey? It's really very bad. These crazy people are everywhere, and they're giving a hard time to anyone who goes outside. Promise me you won't go out, okay? Stay safe in your apartment. Don't go looking for Kevin. Promise me."

Vale promises.

After she hangs up the phone, she cries.

It's the first time she's cried since the dead plague began; it lasts a long time and leaves her feeling like the husk of a plant left too long in the sun without water. When Vale's tears end, she mutes the television, sits by the window, and watches the dead wander her block. The setting sun makes everything look dipped in bronze, and there's not a cloud in the sky. Nothing is in the sky at all. The police and news helicopters that circled the city for days are gone. Where a steady stream of airbuses and 747s and small-engine aircraft once streamed across the horizon from the airport outside the city limits, there is only emptiness. Once last summer, Vale saw a yellow-and-orange hot air balloon out there on a cloudless day. The memory seems like a dream.

DAY 9

Vale lets the phone ring twenty times then hangs up and dials again, but still, her mother doesn't answer. Her parents have no voicemail, no answering machine. Vale tries her boss at work and gets his voicemail after three rings, proving there's no problem with the phone lines. Her boss's voice is weirdly reassuring. Vale wonders who would answer if she called him at home. Maybe no one. She doesn't make the call, because she doesn't really want to know. Instead she presses her ear to the front door and listens. The hallway on the other side sounds empty.

She wants to open the door and take a look.

But it isn't safe out there. It can't be. The only safe place is her apartment.

She picks up the phone and dials her parents' number again. It rings a long time. Vale thinks of other people she can call:

Kristy and Sara, who sit in the cubicles next to her at work; Peter, her trainer from the gym; Donna, an old school friend she sometimes meets to go shopping. Her only real friend, who she's known since the second grade, is Ebbie, but she moved to Seattle last month and since the dead plague began, she hasn't answered her phone once when Vale called. She tries again today—still no answer and none from any of the others either.

Vale drops the phone in its base and listens at her door again. She holds her breath and hears nothing. She touches the doorknob with her fingertips. A few minutes later she withdraws into her apartment, to the TV, and the romance novels on her bookshelves, and the albums and boxes of photos she dragged down from her closet. She looks at pictures of all the people she can no longer talk to, and for the rest of that day, she stays away from the windows.

DAY 12

Vale sees no one through the peephole in her door. The corridor seems quiet. She puts the chain on, cracks the door, and looks out. In her mind Kevin is yelling at her to *close the door, go back, don't be stupid, don't risk it*, and she hears herself promising her mother over and over not to leave her apartment, but Kevin and her parents aren't there for her now, and another voice drifts around theirs in her thoughts—the whispers of a woman. Kevin's neighbor. The more Vale thinks about it, the more certain she is that Erica was there with him, which explains why Kevin didn't go to see his aunt and uncle first so that he could have stayed with Vale the last time she saw him. This realization, even more than him not answering his phone, drives home for Vale that she's lost Kevin. She thought they were going through this together despite being apart, but she's been on her own since before the dead plague began.

The hallway looks clear.

Vale closes her door, removes the chain, and then opens the door again and steps out of her apartment. The building is quiet, except for Vale's television and sounds drifting in from outside: bird calls, insect noises, the moans of the dead. Vale studies her neighbors' doors. All three look shut tight. She knocks on the first. No one answers. She knocks again and then tries the knob. The door opens onto a dark apartment.

Vale hesitates, unprepared for this.

She leans into the opening. "Hello?"

She hardly knows her neighbors. The people in her building keep to themselves. They nod and smile when they pass on the way to the elevator, hold doors for one another, and trade fast greetings without ever learning each other's names. She knows a middle-aged man lives here, a police officer, she thinks, because he keeps odd hours, and once she saw him with a gun on his belt.

"Is anyone here?" Vale says.

Vale takes two steps into the apartment and listens. She hears nothing. Three more steps and she realizes how far away the open door seems and how much farther than that it is to her apartment. She left her door open wide. Anyone could wander into her place. But who would? No one's around. Taking a deep breath, she walks through her neighbor's home. The lights are off, but daylight trickles in through the shaded windows. There's no one in the bathroom, kitchen, or living room, but the wall behind the couch is covered with framed photographs. She switches on a lamp to see them. Her neighbor in a police uniform. Women and children. Vale guesses they must be his family. In one her neighbor holds a fishing rod at the side of a lake; in another he wears military gear. A framed set of medals hangs at the center of the photo display, but Vale doesn't know what they mean. Except for this one wall, everything in the apartment seems so neat, ordinary, and expected that Vale feels like she's wandered into a furniture store display.

She switches off the light and moves through the apartment. At the end of a short corridor, the bedroom door is closed. Vale forces herself to grip the doorknob. There's no one here, she tells herself. He must've left days ago, probably called on duty to respond to the crisis. Who could possibly be in there? If her neighbor was home he would have answered when she called out. Her fingers tighten around the knob. She gives it a quarter turn, and then she hears something bump on the other side. Something thumps the wall. She feels it in her fingers and yanks her hand back from the door. She waits for the noise to reoccur, but it doesn't. It could've been something outside, she could've imagined it, or it could've come from another part of the apartment. She studies the gloom behind her. The apartment seems tiny and confining now, the path out of it long and shadowed, and all at once, Vale feels like an intruder. An urgent sense that she doesn't belong there—*that something doesn't want her there*—drives her out. She runs, tugging the front door shut behind her.

She slumps against the opposite wall in the hallway and waits for her nerves to settle and her breathing to calm. Only then does it occur to her that maybe her neighbor was in his bedroom, sick or injured, too weak to call out for help, that the bump might have been a signal. Vale hopes not, because the thought of going back into the apartment terrifies her.

When her legs are steady again, she goes to the second door and knocks. No one answers, but Vale hears movement inside. There's no mistaking the sound. She knocks again and presses her ear to the door. A chair scuffs. Footsteps. Voices, faint and familiar. A television, tuned into the same channel Vale left hers on. It creates a strange, out-of-sync echo. The footsteps shuffle closer to the door, until someone is standing right on the other side. Vale knocks once more. A lock clicks, and the door inches open. A chain sags across the narrow opening. Behind it looms an old woman's face, a deflated moon pitted with wrinkles and yellowed teeth.

"What do you want?" she asks.

"Hi," Vale says. "We've never really met. I'm your neighbor from across the hall. I'm Vale."

"I didn't ask you that. I already know that. I asked you what you want."

"I'm not...I'm not sure. I guess I wanted to know if anyone else was here. I haven't been out of my apartment since...the dead started rising. I thought it would blow over or someone would figure out a way to stop it by now, but no one has, at least not that I know of. I can't reach my family on the phone anymore or my boyfriend, not even on text. I'm alone, and I thought maybe you needed some help. I checked one of the other apartments. It looks empty, but I heard something bumping in there. Anyway, do you need food or anything? I have extra."

The old woman squints then clears her throat and spits into a tissue she pulls from the sleeve of her housecoat. She coughs with a deep, shivering motion that quakes her body. She wipes her mouth with the tissue and stuffs it back in her sleeve.

"You got any cigarettes?" she says.

"I don't smoke," Vale says.

"I'll take that as a no."

"Yes. That's a no."

"Then listen up, girlie, because I don't like to repeat myself. I've been living here for going on thirty years, and I ain't planning to leave anytime soon. You've been living over across the hall, how long? Four years? Yeah, that's about right. Not once in those four years did you ever come over here and ask an old lady if she needed anything. You didn't even so much as introduce yourself. Did you ever bother to learn my name? No, you did not. It's Harriet. And now that there's dead people walking and you're all alone, you suddenly grow a neighborly conscience? How nice for you. But I've been living alone a long time. I like it that way, and I can take care of myself."

The woman opens the door to the limit of the security chain, exposing a shotgun, angled loosely in Vale's direction.

Vale gasps.

"This happy horseshit going on out there, the dead and all that, don't matter much to me. Won't be long before I'm one of 'em, and I don't give a rat's ass what happens to my body after that 'cause I won't be using it anymore. So you come across any ciggies, I'll be glad to take 'em off your hands, especially seeing as how you don't smoke. Otherwise stay out of my door, stay out of my face, and when I die, leave my body wherever the hell it lands. If I need anything from the likes of you before then, I'll be sure to let you know."

The woman jerks the door shut and jams the deadbolt in place. Vale trembles. She doesn't want to cry, but the tears spill down her cheeks anyway. She steps back from the door and takes a deep breath. For the second time since she left her apartment, she fights to regain her composure. When she does, she's embarrassed and drained, but she forces herself to move to the third door. It looks no different than the others, or even her own, except for the number below the peephole. She raises her hand to knock, but before she does, she glances at the other two doors. They seem like megalithic stones, enormous markers over fresh graves. Voices from Vale's television carry on, making it sound like there are people in her apartment, like there's a quiet party going on.

Vale drops her hand to her side.

She turns on her heels and retreats to her place, slamming the door behind her.

DAY 14

On her thirtieth lap, with ten more to go, Vale walks a circuit of every room but the bathroom. The loop is part of her daily routine to keep her muscles from atrophying and burn off the nervous energy that spoils her sleep. Most of the TV channels are blank now. The few still on the air broadcast emergency information and tedious discussions of what the walking dead mean for the future of the world. The last remaining TV pundits and analysts are obsessed with the eyes of the dead, the out-of-place eyeballs popping up all over and even in the internal organs of the reanimated corpses. No one knows what they mean, but the TV people struggle to make sense of it. Vale finds their unease much funnier than the late-night comedians ever were.

She doesn't know what to do with herself. She wants to read a newspaper, but she hasn't seen one since the day Kevin came, and no one updates the online news anymore. The only fresh information comes from blogs and message boards, from Facebook, YouTube, and Twitter, and even those sources have dwindled to a fraction of what they were a week ago. Sometimes Vale tries to read one of the novels on her bookshelf, but she's read them all before, and she loses interest after a few pages. Music only makes her miss Kevin and her family. Her mountain bike hangs in a closet next to her bathroom; she wonders if she'll ever use it again. She misses the long rides she used to take, often with Kevin, when she explored the city or nearby parks. She has to be careful about how much she eats because now the food Kevin brought seems like too little to carry her through the crisis. She's already run out of milk. She ate the last box of Apple Jacks dry this morning, thinking with each bite that she might never see another.

She wishes she could go to sleep and wake up to find everything back to normal; she wants to go the gym then to work then come home and watch real TV, have dinner with Kevin or visit her parents, spend the weekend hiking or at the beach or in bed at Kevin's place. Except for her apartment and her TV, all the things that shaped her life are gone. She makes her fortieth lap and keeps going. TV voices rise and fall as she moves from room to room. Vale closes her eyes and pretends she's in the park, listening to people on the benches talk, but it doesn't work. There's no sun or breeze touching her skin, no scent of trees and grass or car exhaust or fresh fertilizer filling her nose.

She makes another lap then another, and then she jogs a few, and soon she's running, tracing an awkward path through her apartment, dodging her furniture, panting and moving as fast as she can manage, her body kicking into high gear, as if she can outrun all the bad things around her. She runs until she wears down, and then she trips on the leg of her sofa. She crashes to the floor, cracking her elbow, smacking her nose, and slamming her chest hard enough to knock the wind out of her. Pain immobilizes her; she lies on the floor for a long time until it wanes. When she gets up again, she grabs a quilt from the back of the sofa, wraps it around her, and flops onto the cushions, her eyes glued to the TV screen across the room.

A little while later, she falls asleep.

A clap of thunder awakens her. It's dark out and rain rattles against the windows. The television paints the room with a cold, blue, electric flame. Men and women on the screen argue over what brought the dead back to life. Every one of them seems so certain, so insistent, yet no one knows the reason. Vale tunes them out, renders them background noise, until fifteen minutes later, she realizes she's heard all this talk before, and she saw this program last week.

It's a rerun.

A goddamn rerun.

Vale grabs the remote and cycles through the channels.

The few still broadcasting are all running taped shows or government emergency announcements. The videos and reports from around the world are gone, but the smarmy reporters, the strident woman from the CDC, and even the early videos are back, along with all the pundits and would-be prophets, who were so confident they had all the answers. A senator from Massachusetts, with a Boston accent stretching his words, predicts that a bio-research lab in his state for which he secured $1 billion in federal funding will have the answer in three days' time, and then the dead will stay dead again.

His message filled Vale with hope the first time she heard it more than a week ago.

The live broadcasts are over.

A reservoir of rage and despair bursts from Vale before she can control it. She hurls the remote control across the room, smashing it against the wall. Then she screams, loud and long, hoping her voice frightens Harriet next door, not caring if the dead things in the street hear and come for her. And when her first scream dies out, she sucks in air and screams again, and keeps screaming until her chest is tight and her head is spinning, and she's falling sideways onto the sofa...

...and everything goes black.

DAY 15

By morning, the prerecorded shows are gone, and all the channels are blue blanks or gray and white static. Vale can't even hope that something only killed her cable signal, because she still has her Internet, which comes through the same line. There's nothing online, though, except stale news and dead blogs and a scattered, few recently posted videos full of blood and violence that tell her nothing new. Vale's last connection to the world is gone. As long as television kept broadcasting, Vale had faith she would be safe and the world would return to normal. Now the priests of her belief are dead, their divine light extinguished, their prophecies unfulfilled. She looks out at the street. Through the stormy gloom, everything looks almost as it should. People walk along the sidewalk in the teeming rain, but no one rushes and no one carries an umbrella, because the dead are indifferent to the downpour. Vale can't recall the last time she saw anyone alive out there.

The world has become a wasteland, unimaginable from two weeks ago.

Except, Vale thinks, *what's really different for me?*

She's still sitting in her apartment, focused on everything her parents and Kevin wanted her to do—staying home, locked up safe and sound where nothing can touch her. Even now that they're gone, Vale can't shake free of the promises she made them and her hope that she'll see them again. The only real difference in her life is that she hasn't gone to work, but she doesn't miss it. She worked for a paycheck and a way to spend eight hours a day she would've otherwise spent alone. Like she's alone now. Like she was even when she was with Kevin no matter how he made it seem. She doesn't even have the people on TV anymore.

Everything in the world is different now.

Everything except for Vale.

Pathetic, she thinks. The living dead overrun the world, you lose the only people you care about, and the thing that finally sets you off screaming is when TV goes off the air. *Pathetic. And awful.* You don't belong in here; you belong out there with the dead, because even the old lady across the hall has more life in her than you do. Why did you listen to Mom and Dad all the time? What were you so afraid of if you made decisions they didn't like? Why did you ever trust Kevin? The only things between the two of you were habit, biology, and convenience. You tried to be what they wanted, but you never knew what you wanted, and now you may never get a chance to find out.

Fucking pathetic.

Pathetic. Lame. And stupid.

This apartment is your coffin.

You may as well be dead.

Like everyone else.

Dead and too dumb to lie down and rot.

Except you're not *dead.*

The thought catches Vale off guard, rising from a long-quiet part of her. *Not all the way, anyway. You walked into the police-*

man's apartment, didn't you? You faced Harriet. You looked for people.

You tried to make a connection.

You failed—but you tried.

You've still got life left in you.

You're alive.

Yes.

Vale rises from the couch and throws the quilt on the floor. She pulls her front door wide and props it open. Then she yanks her flat-screen television from its stand, ripping the cable and electrical cords from the wall. She carries it into the hallway, almost dropping its awkward weight, going down on one knee to regain her balance. Footsteps patter behind Harriet's door; shadows shift in the thin gap above the saddle. Aiming for the peephole, Vale flashes a wide smile and flips Harriet her middle finger.

"Smoke 'em if you got 'em, Harriet," she says.

Vale tightens her grip on the TV set and marches down the hallway to the stairs. She kicks open the door and sets her foot on the first step. The TV makes it hard to climb the narrow stairway, but Vale makes it to the fifth floor landing before she trips again and almost falls, catching the TV inches from the ground.

"No way. Not yet," she says.

She shifts the weight of the TV and continues, passing the sixth and seventh floor landing, walking until she reaches the roof door. It's latched. Vale balances the TV on the top step while she undoes the bolt then pushes the door open. Rain and gray light stream in, coating her face with moisture, forcing her to squint. Vale takes the TV to the edge of the roof that overlooks the view from her apartment and places it on top of the low wall along the roof's perimeter. Breathing heavily, she sits down to watch the street below. Seven stories down, the dead are everywhere. Vale gets up and walks to each side of the roof. On every street, on every block, the dead fill the city. She spots Kevin's apartment building poking up into the ashy haze of the storm and stares at it for a long time, trying to recall the good days she spent there, but those memories of Kevin flee and hide, driven away by her memory of a woman's whispers overheard on the phone. Soon, Vale is soaked from head to toe, her hair and clothes clinging to her like a second skin, and she doesn't know how much of the water running down her face is rain and how much is tears.

She runs across the roof, splashing puddles. Bracing herself, she grabs her TV, lifts it as high as she can, and then, with a long, furious scream, hurls the TV out over the street. The black rectangle tumbles as it plunges to the ground. It smashes on the curb with an eruption of glass, plastic, and water. One piece shoots to the sidewalk across the street, skipping twice on a puddle. The broken box rocks to a stop. Its shattered screen reflects the mottled gray sky, rippled by drops of rain splashing onto it. When Vale's scream dies out, she feels like she's bled a poison from her body, like she can breathe again. She drops to her knees. Her chest heaves and her hands tremble. Then she peers over the edge of the wall and sees the dead staring up. Even as the rain pools in their unblinking eyes, they're looking at her. Their moans make a forlorn undercurrent to the static of the storm, and all the living corpses in sight turn and draw together, all of them scuffing toward the entrance to Vale's building.

"Oh, shit," Vale says.

She lurches to her feet and scrambles back to her apartment. If she's fast, if she doesn't stop to think about it, maybe she can grab what she needs...maybe she can beat them...maybe the dead won't be in the alley behind the building....

DAY 16

Getting around by bicycle gives Vale an edge. She can go places a car can't, and she can dodge the dead faster than they can react. As long as she finds somewhere safe to hide before nightfall, she thinks she'll be okay. She spent the first night hiding in a shed, sleepless beneath the rattle of a steady rain, worried that every bump and creak heralded a gang of dead people breaking down the door. A little after dawn this morning, she goes to Kevin's apartment. The front door is open. She carries her bicycle up the stairs and brings it inside. No one's there. A bookshelf lies broken on the carpet, its books scattered like fallen birds. Streaks of dried blood crisscross the kitchen floor and cabinets. There's a hole in the sheetrock wall by the front door. It's as big as Vale's head, its edges smeared red and black. Everywhere Vale looks there are hardened patches and spatters of blood. Furniture is out of place, curtains half torn from their rods. In the bathroom, a woman's severed finger lies in the bathtub, wriggling around the drain like a worm. Its long nail is bright with pink polish. Vale picks it up in a tissue and throws it out the window. In the bedroom the pillows and blankets of Kevin's bed are disheveled on both sides, and a woman's silk nightgown lies on the floor. A discard pair of pink thong panties lies askew in the corner.

"Bastard," Vale whispers.

She raids the cabinets for food, stuffing Kevin's favorite energy bars into her backpack. She replenishes her water bottles and takes four bottles of Gatorade. Then she locks herself in and sleeps on the couch for five hours.

Later, after the storm passes, thin steam rises from the road where the sun cooks the wet pavement. Vale pedals around the deep puddles, bicycle tires hissing water spray. The dead watch her when she passes, but she's always out of reach before they come after her. When there are too many in the road, she goes on the sidewalk or cuts across lawns, schoolyards, parking lots, or storefront patios. Yesterday, her legs ached, but today, she feels powerful and tireless, her lungs expansive, her muscles electrified from exertion. She rides to the house where she grew up.

Her parents' block is mostly empty. A few of the dead are down at the other end, their backs turned to Vale. She coasts along the curb, cuts up her parent's driveway, and comes to a sharp stop by the side stoop, landing one foot on the bricks of the bottom step, and dismounting her bike in a fluid motion. She made that maneuver a thousand times or more when she was a child. It means she's home. Her hands shake as she opens the side door and enters the house. The air inside is rotten, but underneath its stink are the familiar scents of her childhood. They fill her with sadness. Everything looks normal but abandoned as if her parents were doing okay then simply got up and left like they were going to the store. Vale checks upstairs and finds her old room, unchanged; her parents' bedroom is clean, bed made, and her father's office is organized, his computer on, a screensaver rainbow spinning across the dark bed of the monitor.

A floorboard creaks.

Vale freezes.

Another creak.

Then a footstep.

Someone's in the attic. Vale walks to the end of the hall, to the door of the narrow attic stairway between the bathroom and the linen closet. She listens. More footsteps, creaking but slow, irregular, dragging along the attic floor.

Vale calls them through the door. "Mom? Dad? You up there?"

The footsteps stop.

Vale grabs the doorknob. "Mom? It's Vale."

A low moan replies.

The footsteps resume, faster, firmer, and something thumps down the attic stairs, growling and moaning as it comes. Vale throws her weight against the door even as the thing on the other side slams into it, jolting it in its frame. She pushes back hard. The knob jiggles. The door bounces open an inch, cracking Vale's shin, but she shoves it closed. It bounces out again, wider. Vale holds it back, but she can't for long. On the next thrust, she yanks the door open and flattens herself to the wall as two dead things crash past her and topple onto the floor. Vale glimpses a pair of dirty moccasin slippers she bought for her mother, a robe she gave her last Christmas, and her father's familiar plaid pajama bottoms but she doesn't let herself look at the dead people, doesn't see them as anything more than dark shapes scrabbling on the floor. She runs past them, ignoring their faces. Fingers scratch her leg as a hand almost grabs her. The grunts and moans of the dead things chase her down the stairs. Then Vale is in the driveway, mounting her bike, pushing off the stoop, pedaling as hard as her legs will pump, the breeze pulling the tears away from her eyes.

Beyond the trees and houses to the west, the sun hangs low on the horizon, a blob of fire casting deep shadows. Vale rides to a neighbor's house and breaks in through a basement window.

The family, friends of her parents, were on vacation when the dead plague started, and they never made it home. Vale checks every room in the house twice, and when she's sure she's alone, she lies down on a bed to sleep, but the thoughts racing through her mind keep her awake.

Kevin is gone. Her parents are gone. The office where she worked will never open for business again. She thinks she will never return to her apartment and all the things she left behind. Part of her is relieved. She is no longer the person those lost things defined. If she tries to be then she really will be like one of the dead. The world is new, and she must become something new to survive. It seems odd, unfair, and slightly blasphemous for her to feel reborn as everyone around her dies, but it's the thought of getting to know her new self that finally calms her enough to fall asleep.

DAY 21

Vale passes around some of Kevin's energy bars while she sits beside the fire in a courtyard surrounded by the empty classrooms of an elementary school. Mac slips the energy bar into his pocket and stokes the fire with a length of pipe. The rifle strapped across his back rises and falls with each idle thrust of his arm. In the amber glow of the flames, his wiry gray hair resembles a tangle of electrified light bulb filaments. Andrea and George rip the wrappers off their bars and bite into them.

"Thank you," Andrea says.

"Yeah, man, thanks a million," George says.

Keeping one for herself, Vale zips up the pocket in her backpack holding the rest of the energy bars. "Sure. I've got plenty for now."

Across the fire, Mac raises an eyebrow. "*Man?* Son, I know you're young, but surely you've learned the difference between a man and a lady by now. Or is it a vision disorder that afflicts you?"

George blushes. "I know. I just meant it like *dude*, you know?"

"No, I don't know. *Dude* is hardly a more appropriate description of our new friend than *man*," Mac says.

"Whatever, old man. Just 'cause you worked in a library doesn't mean you know everything." George nods to Vale with the energy bar. "Vale, thanks."

"Yes. Very nice of you to share," Mac says. "Not a lot of that going on the past few weeks, although now there's more *stuff* than the few of us left alive could ever use in three lifetimes, it's been less of an issue. It won't last, of course. Most of the useful things will rot and spoil. The bounty will decay. Plenty of SUVs and iPads to go around, but I'm afraid you'll find they disagree with your stomach. Can't help but wonder if we'd been better at helping each other before all this horror maybe the dead plague never would've come."

"What?" Vale says. "Like we're being punished for not being nice to each other?"

Mac shrugs. "It's as good an explanation as any."

"It's no explanation at all," Andrea says. "There's a scientific reason for what's happened. It's some kind of bacteria or chemical pollution or a parallel universe bleeding in, something like that. Has to be because all that spiritual karma nonsense doesn't make a dead body get up and move around."

"Telling you, it's a genetically engineered death virus," George says. "I read it online before the Internet flatlined. There was a fire in a secret lab in Texas, and the virus was released into the air. It started there."

"An entertaining idea, but a dubious one at best," Mac says. "What do you think caused the dead plague, Vale?"

Vale tosses the wrapper from her energy bar into the flames and stretches back as the foil curls and blackens. "Does it really matter?"

The others exchange glances, and then each falls to staring into the fire. Mac uses the pipe to toy with the embers. No one speaks for a while.

A few minutes later, Mac says, "No, I suppose it does not. What matters now is our survival."

An abrupt darkness falls after the words pass Mac's lips. Illumination from the school's lights, and the nearby streetlamps, and the school parking lot lights blinks out, leaving only the light of the fire and the stars. In tandem, the silence seems to thicken around them, broken only by the crackling flame.

"Shit," George says. "There goes the power."

"It's a marvel it lasted as long as it did," Mac says. "We'll be fine tonight. We're safely enclosed here. We can stick close to the fire, stick together."

"We should tell Vale," Andrea says.

"Yeah," George covers his mouth to mute a burp. "She shared with us. She's cool. She should know. Especially now. The nights will be rough without power."

"Tell me about what?" Vale says.

"The airport." Mac's face looks solemn and aged in the dancing glow of the flame. "That once glorious testament to humankind's ingenuity and insatiable need to reach what lies across mountain and ocean alike, in other words, to be as free as the birds."

"Free to be groped and irradiated by government rent-a-cops," George says, but then stifles his laughter when Andrea elbows him in the gut.

"I haven't seen a plane in the air for more than a week. What's at the airport?" Vale asks.

"Safe haven," Andrea says.

Mac tugs a folded piece of paper from his shirt pocket and hands it to Vale. She opens the stark, black-and-white flier, printed in all capital letters, promising safety and supplies, summoning anyone who finds it to take shelter in the airport. It's signed by Captain Jack Davis and Captain William Elder, pilots for JetAm Airlines.

"This for real?" Vale says.

"We believe so." Mac retrieves the flier from Vale and replaces it in his pocket.

"We've found stacks of them in different places, some in places we know there weren't any the day before," Andrea says. "People are out there, seeding these around the city."

"They're trying to bring everyone together," George says. "It's probably to make an army to fight back against the dead."

"This isn't a video game," Andrea says.

"Whatever."

"Are you going there?" Vale asks.

"That's our plan, put on hold by our chance meeting with you this afternoon," Mac says. "We thought we ought to size you up before telling you."

"If I wasn't the right size? Then what? Leave in the middle of the night while I'm sleeping so I can't follow you?" Vale says.

Mac shrugs. "Not a bad plan. Much easier than killing you. I like how you think."

Vale laughs. "So this means I get to go?"

"As long as you pony up an energy bar now and then, you're in," George says.

Andrea eats the last bit of her energy bar and drops the wrapper in the fire like Vale did. "We thought we'd head out there in the morning after a supply run. If we're leaving the city, we ought to have some more water, maybe some medicine, and other stuff too."

"All right, count me in," Vale says. "But don't think I haven't been sizing up all of you this whole time, too."

"Of course, duly noted, we'd be disappointed in you if you hadn't," Mac says. "But bear in mind we promise nothing about what we'll find out upon the tarmac. This airport scenario might be a dead end. Or even a trap."

George groans. "For the millionth time, old dude, it's not a freaking trap. They're assembling an army against the dead. It's the only thing that makes any sense."

DAY 22

Vale's head feels like it's going to crack open from the pounding of her pulse, a throbbing beat so strong it almost erases the shrill sound of Mac's screams. The dead are all around them. Every second, more come creeping from the shops and abandoned cars that fill the strip mall parking lot. Vale's first instinct is to run back to her bike and flee, but Mac is screaming and Andrea and George are cut off, and they're calling for her help. She can't leave them. She doesn't want to fail; she doesn't want to give up.

In her hand is the pipe Mac gave her for a weapon when they left the school. She raises it and charges at the dead things ripping into Mac's body. One of them is biting into his leg, tearing away scraps of flesh and muscle. Three yellow, rheumy eyes look out from its back. The other straddles him, trying to sink his teeth into his face, but Mac fights it. Caught by surprise when the two dead men clambered out from the back of a pick-up truck, Mac stumbled and fell. The dead were on him before he could recover. Vale swings the pipe against the first dead man's head, but the corpse holds tight to Mac's torso. She swings again and crushes part of its skull then kicks it in the chest, forcing it to the ground. It rolls over and works clumsily to right itself. Vale attacks the one gnawing on Mac's leg, breaking its jaw and knocking it loose with her first blow. Mac tries to scramble free, but his leg is a wreck, blood pouring out of it, bone showing at the bottom of deep bite marks visible through his shredded pants. He can barely move. Vale grabs him by the shoulders and drags him away from the dead, but there's nowhere she can take him, nowhere she can run before they come back. Hiding in one of the cars would be a death trap. As she searches for anyplace else to go, she realizes Mac's screams have faded and he's saying her name.

"What? What is it?" Vale says.

"Take...the rifle." Mac struggles to slip the gun's strap from around his torso. "Take the gun. Go help George and Andrea. Get them...to the airport. If you leave me, you can make it."

Vale meets Mac's eyes, flooded with tears and filled with horror, and she wants to refuse him. She wants to tell him not to die, to scream at him to hang on because there's another way. *She can save him. No one's going to die on her watch.* The words are right on the tip of her tongue, a reflex that springs from all the times she's heard something like it on television or in the movies; she thinks that's how people are supposed to act in situations like this. A glance around her tells her something very different.

She kneels down and looses the rifle from Mac's body. Then she kisses him on the forehead.

"Thank you, Mac. You're a good, brave man. I won't ever forget you," she says.

Mac closes his eyes, and says, "*Go...just go.*"

Carrying the rifle, Vale jogs around the two corpses already creeping back to Mac and heads for Andrea and George. They are caught outside a coffeehouse, on a patio encircled by a chest-high, picket fence draped with artificial ivy. A group of the dead from the card shop next door comes at them from one side, while another group rounds the corner of the building and comes from the other. More dead approach from the parking lot, drawing closer every second.

There's no way Vale can reach them.

Behind her, Mac starts screaming again.

Andrea and George jam the café entrances with tables and chairs, but the wobbly, decorative fence won't hold for long. Vale checks the street. There's a clear line to her bicycle and a path to the corner, away from the dead and into the city. She isn't strong enough to fight off all the walking corpses surrounding the café; she'll die if she tries. The weight of the rifle grows in her hands. Guns frighten her. A dead man appears on the far side of the street, moving in a line toward Vale's bicycle. A dead woman follows him, a line of jerking shadows behind her. More dead come, moving into Vale's escape route.

She's ready to run, to forget Andrea and George, when a voice cuts through the tumult of her thoughts, and says: *Be alive. Don't fail.*

Vale stares at the rifle then braces it against her shoulder as she's seen people do on television. She doesn't know how to use the sights, so she watches the tip of the barrel and points it toward the first dead thing trying to push its way into the café patio. She yanks the trigger.

The rifle stock bites her shoulder, pushing her sideways.

The report slams her ears.

The scent of spent gunpowder stings her nose.

Power fills the air around her, transferring from the gun to her body then back again, filling Vale with excitement and determination.

Her shot strikes the dead man in the throat and blows out the other side with a spray of blood and flesh, but it doesn't stop him. Vale steadies the gun and fires again. Nothing happens. She looks at the trigger, at the bolt, at the safety, but nothing looks wrong. She smacks the side with her hand then tries again. Nothing. She lowers it, grabs the bolt, and jiggles it. It shifts in her hand and moves. She slides it back. An empty shell casing ejects from the chamber, and then Vale jams the bolt back into position. Her next shot rips through the dead man's head, blowing a quarter of it away, but it doesn't stop him. She fires again and the trigger sticks again before she remembers to work the bolt. Her next shot goes into the dead man's hip and knocks him down.

"Yes!" Vale shouts.

She works the bolt faster now, feeling the rhythm of the metal sliding over metal. She relishes the explosive punch that spreads through her when she fires, the power it shares with her body. She catches the next dead man in the knee and sends him to the ground. In five more shots, she takes down three more of the dead, buying Andrea and George enough space to flee the patio. They rush to Vale's side, and then the three of them dash across the parking lot, Andrea and George each clutching plastic bags full of bottled water, bandages, antibiotic ointment, and other medical supplies. The dead are closing in on Vale's bike. She stops to fire. Her first shot misses. Her second takes the closest corpse down with a hit to the pelvis, and her third drops the one behind him with a shot to its right ankle. Then, even though Vale works the bolt, the gun won't fire.

She works the bolt again. Nothing.

"You're out of ammo," George tells her.

"Shit." She never thought to take ammunition, and now Mac is gone under a mass of feeding dead things.

"In the strap." George touches one of the pouches sewn onto the rifle strap. "Check there."

Vale opens the pouch and finds bullets inside. "I have no idea how to reload."

"Yeah, right, you shoot like a Special Forces sniper," George says. "*Badass.*"

"No, seriously, I don't know," Vale tells him. "This is the first time I've ever even held a gun."

"Cut the shit, Vale, no way," George says. "Nobody shoots like that first time out of the gate."

"Well, I guess I do." Vale's voice rises. "Do you know how to reload this thing or not, dammit?"

"Yeah, of course, it's easy," George says. "You pop out the magazine, put in more bullets, and pop it back."

"You'll have to do it later," Andrea says. "We need to go now or we're going nowhere. The road is almost closed off by the dead."

"Come on," Vale says.

The three of them run to the bike. Vale slings the rifle across her back like Mac wore it and jumps on the seat.

"Andrea, behind me," she says. "George, on the handlebars. Keep your balance and hope this works."

The bike wobbles as it rolls, straightening out as it picks up speed along a slope in the road. Vale hasn't ridden two or three on a bike since she was a child, and it's a lot different with adults. Her muscles sting from pushing the extra weight. Her body breaks out in a thick sweat, and she feels like they're going to fall with every little bump and pit in the road. But the voice in her head tells her *don't worry, be alive, don't give up, keep going.* She doesn't know where it's coming from or why, but she doesn't care. She likes what it has to say. She grips the handlebars tighter, pedals harder, and when George cries out in triumph as they speed past the thickest lines of the slow-moving dead, Vale cheers with him.

They ride until they're clear of the shopping center, and then Vale turns down a street where the dead are few. She stops at the curb. Andrea and George jump off.

Vale hands the gun to George. "Reload this."

"Let's all agree now," Andrea says, "no more foraging in big shopping centers, no matter what we need." She moves the medical supplies into her backpack. One of the plastic bags, emptied, blows away and rolls down the street.

"Don't worry." George knuckles fifteen bullets into the magazine. "Things get out of hand, Vale will save us again."

"I didn't save you," Vale says. "Mac did."

Andrea shudders and starts to cry.

"Shit," George says. "Mac."

He finishes reloading the gun in silence.

DAY 30

Vale awakens to nearby conversation.

She sits up and stretches, stiff from sleeping across three chairs in the Gate 7 departure lounge. A large group of the others is down the concourse, gathered at McGrady's, the bar that's become their town square. Captain Jack is there, introducing them all to a barrel-chested man with shoulder-length, salt-and-pepper hair and cold blue eyes. Three other men stand behind him. All of them look hardened and drained, dressed in muscle T-shirts and camouflage pants or jeans and football jerseys, each with a weapon in hand and one or two more on his belt. Vale puts on her shoes and walks to the bar.

"I've offered Mr. Morgan and his crew the exact same hospitality Bill and I have shown everyone else here," the captain says. He grins, enjoying playing host. "For as long as they want to stay, they're part of our group, and I know you'll all treat them that way."

"Thank you so much, really, thank you, all of you," Morgan says. "Way things are these days we all got to stick together for survival. I don't have to tell anyone who's lasted this long that it's hard as hell out there for a man by himself or even a few working together. My guys and me, we been out there running the whole time, lost a few along the way, and we've seen some pretty brutal things go down. We're truly grateful for you sharing what you've got here, and we'll pitch in any way we can. These fellows with me are Malloy, Estevez, and Norris. Good men, the kind you want watching your back in a fight, and that's what we're all doing these days, fighting for our lives."

It bothers Vale how the crowd eats up Morgan's words, but she's not surprised. The airport people are starved for leadership. Despite Jack and Bill setting up a sanctuary and bringing people together, they don't want to hold the lives of strangers in their hands. Everyone here is free to come and go as they please. It's live and let live as long as they all follow the rules that keep the dead away and respect the others living there. The lack of purpose, though, leaves a void that hangs over everyone, a gaping need for direction—because nobody wants to spend the rest of their life in an airport, waiting to die.

That, Vale thinks, *is why no one walks away while this blowhard, Morgan, keeps talking, why even Captain Jack smiles as he listens. He wants a leader as much as the rest of them.* But Morgan gives Vale a queasy feeling. There are wheels turning behind his eyes, hidden meanings in his words, and Vale thinks he must see the same weakness she did the day she arrived. He looks shrewd enough to know a good thing when he sees it. Maybe he's already working out how to make this place his. Her reaction to Morgan is a gut instinct—a natural revulsion like the kind that springs up when you stumble upon a snake or a bloated, nasty spider. Vale zips up her jacket and goes outside. She's the only one who leaves while Morgan is speaking.

She walks out behind Hangar One, where there's a makeshift shooting range used to train new arrivals who don't know how to handle a firearm. Vale spends a lot of time there, picking up tips from the experienced shooters in the group. She hardly ever misses now, and the few men there who really know what to do with a gun treat her with respect she doesn't fully understand. Most of the others are simply uneasy around her. Or excited like George. She walks up to him where he's loading a shotgun for Carlie, a stocky woman in her early forties.

"Some army, huh?" Vale says.

George smiles. "We got the guns, but they got the numbers."

He hands the loaded weapon to Carlie, instructs her on how to hold and fire it, and then points her toward the target. He steps back and pulls the ear covers hanging around his neck into place. Vale covers hers with her hands. Carlie fires. The gun blast jerks her arms upward. She screams, stumbles back, and falls flat on her ass, accidentally firing the gun a second time, straight into the air. After a stunned moment, she laughs and picks herself up.

"That's how it's done, folks," Carlie says. "Put one in front of me and one behind me, and I'll give you a two-fer every time."

"Hey, Carlie, watch yourself, now," Tom calls from another shooting station. "We got impressionable youth present." Tom, a grizzled man in his sixties, laughs like bark cracking as he walks down to help Carlie find a better grip on her shotgun.

Vale and George wander away from the shooting stations, and George slides his ear covers back around his neck.

"Bad news showed up this morning," Vale tells him.

"Like what?" George says. "Things are pretty good here."

"I thought you were upset we're not building an army to fight the dead."

"Who says we're not? We got plenty of good weapons. A lot are police issue, from the sheriff's and TSA stockpiles in the airport, and that guy Tom showed up here with half the inventory from his gun shop. All we need is some more people to bulk up our numbers, then a strategy, some kind of communication systems, maybe walkie-talkies, and then we take this world back, baby. The living on the march. More people come here all the time. Once we get enough, you won't be able to stop them fighting back. It'll be Left4Dead, real life. Trust me. It's all coming together, exactly like—"

Vale touches her index finger to her lips. "George, hush."

George's face blanks. "What?"

"Remember when we got here, and I said this place was like a vat of gasoline waiting to go up? Some new guys showed up this morning. They're the matches."

"Oh, okay," George says. "Wait, what are you talking about?"

"Things are going to change here soon. We may not like the way they go. Get ready. Stock up on whatever you can't live without and hide it. Make sure you've got a weapon handy all the time. If things get hairy, don't get caught up in it. You got me?"

"Yeah, I guess. Not really. Who's here?"

"A man named Morgan and his friends. I hope I'm wrong about them, but I got a strong feeling they're trouble."

"You should tell Jack and Bill."

"I don't think they'll listen."

"They might. They're pretty fair."

"How many people have showed up here since we did?"

"I don't know. Maybe twenty, twenty-five."

"Plus four more this morning."

"So?"

"More than sixty people are here now, and you're right, more will come. That many people in one place will want someone to be in charge. They'll *need* it. And even if they don't, someone will put himself on top to run things, because there's too much at stake, too much to be gained not to. Jack and Bill could do it. I wish they would, because I don't think they'd hurt anybody, but they'd rather run things like a bed and breakfast."

"You think it will be this new guy?"

"Yeah, I do."

"You don't like him."

Vale shakes her head.

"Should we leave?" George asks

"I'd rather not. But let's see how it goes."

"What does Andrea think?"

"I haven't talked to her yet. I will soon as I see her. Let's keep this among the three of us for now. Whatever happens here, we'll be all right as long as we prepare and stick together."

"You trying to scare me?"

"You shouldn't ever stop being scared," Vale says. "Life is different now. I know it's obvious and everyone says it, but not everyone really gets *how different* things have become. They're trying to live like they used to. It's easy to see what's changed on the surface, but what matters more is what's changed underneath. Mac was a kind man. He helped you and Andrea. He helped me. We're alive today because of him. Most people aren't like Mac. People aren't who they were before the dead plague. For better or worse, we've all seen parts of ourselves we never knew existed, and you can't trust the way anyone seems to be anymore."

The report of Carlie's shotgun blasts the air, cutting Vale off. Then it fades and gives way to Carlie and Tom's laughter. When that dies down, the morning falls quiet. George looks like he might ask another question, but he doesn't.

"I trust you, Vale." George looks Vale in the eye. "And you can trust me."

"I know. I do."

George nods then walks back to his shooting station and packs up his gear. Vale watches him and wonders where he finds his courage and his optimism. She wishes she shared them. From the open field behind Hangar One come the moans of the nearby dead, and Vale thinks, *George deserves better than this.*

DAY 51

Campbell enters the observation and control room of the air traffic control tower. Vale ignores him. Her gaze roams the fields around the airport, where scattered dead people walk—bloated, rotting, and speckled with glassy, unnatural eyes.

"Hey, Vale," Campbell says.

"Shut up," Vale says.

"Hey, come on, I need to—"

The crack of Vale's rifle silences Campbell. A couple hundred yards out in the field, a dead man flops sideways to the ground and wriggles like a pinned worm, a chunk of his spine blown out his back. The men working along the fence stop, cup their hands over their eyes, and stare into the field. Whenever Vale takes a shot, they pause laying down coils of barbed wire and reinforcing the gate to look for her target. One of them spots the dead body twisting in the dirt and points it out to the others. Another flashes Vale the okay sign.

Campbell rubs his ears. "Give a guy some warning next time, will you?"

"I see a few more dead out there every day." Vale removes her earplugs. "They're getting the idea that we're here. We'll probably see a lot more of them in the next couple weeks."

"Okay, so, that's what the fortifications and barriers are for," Campbell says. "We didn't drag those materials down here from the construction site for exercise."

Vale glares at Campbell. "What do you need?"

"I have to take you to Morgan. He wants your help."

"I'm busy."

"Duncan's on his way here to cover your station."

"You think Duncan could make that shot?" Vale says.

"No. But that's who Morgan sent." Campbell shrugs. "You going with me or not?"

"You do everything Morgan tells you? Like everyone else? No questions asked? That's all there is to it?" Vale extracts her gun from its shooting position, sets the safety, and slings it onto her back. "*Morgan knows what he's doing. Morgan hasn't steered us wrong yet. Morgan's protecting us. Let's do what Morgan says and everything will be a-okay.* You really buy into all that?"

"Vale, listen—"

"Don't make the mistake of thinking he has our best interests at heart. He's only out for himself."

"Stop. I know." Campbell grips Vale's arm. The two lock stares and stop talking until he lets go of her. "I don't trust Morgan anymore than you do, but I don't go around telling everyone about it either or making a point of contradicting him. If you'd keep your mouth shut, he'd stop making an example of you."

"Two people," Vale says. "I told two people I trusted with my life. One of them stabbed me in the back."

"She didn't know what she was doing."

"Don't defend her. She didn't have to know. All she had to do was keep her mouth shut."

She pushes past Campbell out of the room and starts the descent to ground level. Campbell follows her, jogging at times to keep up. Duncan comes in as Vale leaves the tower, but she passes without greeting him. She stalks across the weedy field to the terminal, a long walk, with Campbell at her heels, letting him catch up only when she reaches the entrance.

"Dial it down, Vale, okay? You aren't alone," Campbell whispers as he reaches past Vale to open the door. "Pick your battles. Morgan can't ride this wave forever."

Vale enters through the door Campbell holds for her then waits for him to lead the way. He takes her to Morgan's command center in the duty-free shop. Maps and open liquor bottles cover the counters, and half a dozen men stand around while Marcus, their helicopter pilot, marks a location on one of the maps. Malloy and Estevez cast dirty glances at Vale as she enters; she knows what they'll do to her if they ever catch her alone. They've been watching her like hungry rats since she caught them in one of the hangar offices with a dead woman. Her legs were amputated, her head strapped down, her blouse pulled off. Only the barest spotting of decay marked her throat and shoulders. Malloy and Estevez were there with their pants around their ankles, taking turns. Morgan only laughed when she told him, and Vale thought, *so, this is how we live now.*

Marcus draws a red circle on the map. "I saw it at this junction, halfway off the road, but it looked intact. Might run okay if you get it straightened out."

"Well done," Morgan says. "Hell of a lot closer than town, and sure as hell, we could use the supplies. This is so close, it's practically home delivery."

"There are people with it," Marcus says.

"How many?" Morgan asks.

"I saw three men, one woman, but there could be more," the pilot says. "Looked like they were living out of the backs of a couple of pick-up trucks. But it was weird, they didn't signal me. I hovered there about two minutes. Thought about setting down. They stared at me. Didn't wave or anything."

"Why would they? Probably, they got a good thing going, living on the highway, truck full of food. They want to keep it all to themselves," Morgan says.

"Maybe they're there because the truck won't run," Malloy says. He grabs a bottle of single malt from the counter, pours some into a crystal tumbler from McGrady's, and downs it. "They're camping out where the food is."

"Good point. We'll take trucks to haul food back in case the big rig won't run." Morgan folds and stacks the maps, leaving open only the one Marcus marked up. "Whatever the situation, I can't stand by and allow folks to hoard more food and supplies than they'll ever use, not when we got hungry people here. No more finders-keepers. People got a responsibility to share what they got whether they like it or not. We'll drive out there tomorrow morning and—one way or another—we'll bring those people and that food back here."

"What if they don't want to come?" Vale says.

"Vale." Morgan greets her with an ugly smile. "Glad you came. I want you with us for this. You're our insurance policy against any dead who wander too close and any living morons who give us a hard time. Consider it a chance to get back on my good side."

"Not interested," Vale says.

"Then do it to get your boyfriend back on my good side."

"George isn't my boyfriend."

"Know what? I don't care," Morgan says. "Do it because we need food. If you don't do it then I'll make sure everyone knows you refused to do your part getting us that food."

"How do you know there's food in the truck?"

"It's a Food Wizard truck," Marcus says.

"What else would be in it?" Morgan says.

"Could've been sitting there for weeks," Vale says.

"True." Morgan nods once then rubs his chin. "Some stuff might have spoiled. But it's a big truck. I bet we'll find something edible in there even if it's just crackers and canned peaches. If it was all bad, those folks wouldn't be hanging around it like flies on shit."

Vale glances at Campbell, whose face is a blank.

If Morgan's right, she thinks, *scavenging a truckload of food will make him more popular and more powerful—and that will make him more dangerous.* He's building barriers to keep out the dead, but they work as well to keep in the living; the airport feels like a prison in progress. No one comes or goes without Morgan's approval. Jack and Bill keep to themselves in their quarters most of the time now, and Vale thinks they're afraid. She doesn't like the idea of helping Morgan. Yet supplies really are running low, and people still trickle in a couple of times a week. Without new sources of food, things will only go from bad to worse, with or without Morgan.

"Who's going?" Vale asks.

"Me, Malloy, Estevez, Marcus, Campbell, Green, and a few others," Morgan says. "Dawson, too, in case we need him to fix the truck."

Vale nods. "All right. We need the food. I'll go."

She risks another glance at Campbell and thinks she sees approval in his eyes, but she isn't sure. She wonders if he understands what he's dealing with in Morgan, if they can protect each other through this, and if they do, she asks herself, what might come after?

DAY 52

Morgan leads them. They take three trucks, including a tow truck to pull the Food Wizard vehicle back to the airport if it won't run. Marcus directs them to the junction on the outskirts of the city, and when the trucks roll up and stop, six people emerge to meet them. The Food Wizard truck is unmistakable with its giant red-and-purple logo painted on the side of the trailer: a smiling wizard's face topped with a cone-shaped hat speckled not with stars and moons, but with drumsticks and hot dogs, apples and bananas. The truck, an eighteen-wheeler, sits at an angle partly off the road, but it looks fine, not stuck like Marcus described, and Vale guesses that from the air maybe it looked as if the truck ran off the road into a ditch.

Morgan talks to the truck people. He offers them an invitation to come live at the airport and trade their food for security and company. Malloy and Estevez stand behind him, and although Morgan's words are soft and civil, the armed men backing him up make it clear that refusal is a bad option. Vale sits in the bed of the third truck, her rifle ready in her hands; she studies the spaces along either side of the highway, seeking the dead. There's no one out there as far as the horizon. It's odd how clean the area is. Even though the airport is miles from the city with mostly open land in between, the dead have been a constant, low-level, but growing, presence all around the area. But then, Vale figures, there's not much reason for them to go roaming along an empty highway.

She glances at the truck people. They look sick.

They're pale, sweaty, and thin, with bags under their eyes, lips stretched back over their teeth, and a strange sheen to their skin. Their hair is stringy and matted with grime, and their eyes seem wild and cold. Four are men, two women. They listen to what Morgan says; they notice the guns all around them. Vale sees it in their expressions when they recognize the unspoken threat. When Morgan stops talking, they move off to the shadow of the truck to confer.

Vale yawns and scans the sides of the highway through her riflescope. She spots one of the dead, well outside the range of her weapon, too far to be dangerous. A few more appear at about the same distance, but none worth taking a shot. Campbell is in one of the other trucks. Vale tries to draw his attention, but he's too engrossed in watching, waiting. She wonders what he'll do if the truck people refuse Morgan's offer and Morgan tries to take their truck by violence. Vale decided last night she won't fire a shot against any living person who isn't attacking her.

It doesn't come to that. The truck people agree.

Better yet, the Food Wizard truck runs.

Its motor growls like a snorting dragon.

Malloy rides shotgun with two of the truck people.

An hour later, Morgan's pick up is at the front of a caravan barreling through the airport gates. One of the truck people blasts the eighteen-wheeler's big horn as the truck speeds inside the fence, and in minutes, almost everyone is gathered outside, stunned, excited, watching the trucks roll up and stop. Green hits the gas in Morgan's pick-up and cuts tight circles before the crowd. Standing in the truck bed clutching the roll bar with one hand and holding his gun over his head with the other, Morgan whoops and hollers. Then his truck parks alongside the Food Wizard truck, making a backdrop of its colorful logo.

Morgan jumps down and walks behind the eighteen-wheeler. Malloy and Estevez meet him there, bringing two of the truck people with them. Morgan starts to talk, giving his bastardized version of the welcome speech Jack and Bill used to deliver, but there's little hospitality left in it. Morgan's version is all about the fight against the dead, the duty everyone has to make sacrifices for the greater good, and how he can only bear the burden of keeping the airport running and safe if everyone does their part. Beneath it all Morgan is playing people's fears and desires with virtuoso precision.

Vale tunes him out.

She finds a shady place by the terminal and sits on the edge of a concrete barrier. She sights Morgan in the scope of her rifle, holds him there while she imagines firing, and then sets the gun down beside her. She spots Campbell, hanging back with Duncan and Chambliss by the tow truck. Campbell notices her watching and nods. Vale wonders if maybe he's right about keeping a low profile and waiting for Morgan to trip himself up, but that seems a long way off now that he's riding the wave of excitement about the truck. Maybe she should forgive Andrea for telling Morgan she was planning to leave. Andrea didn't understand the situation; she didn't know how Morgan would react, that he wouldn't allow Vale to go. She thought she was helping. The celebratory mood is sinking into her, and Vale can't remember the last time she felt good like this. Maybe she should go along with it, call this a win, and enjoy the moment. Her stomach is grumbling as much as anyone else's to see what's in the truck.

Morgan winds down his speech and asks the two truck people to open the back of the trailer. They unlock it and lift the door. Inside, in the dark space where everyone expects boxes of food piled to the ceiling, waiting to be grabbed and passed around, there waits instead a snarling mob of the walking dead. They move slowly into the light that pours onto them, unsure at first of what the open door means. Then they see the crowd of living people. In seconds, they flow from the truck in a tangled, tumbling mass of dead limbs, gray flesh, and gnashing teeth. There are more of them than anyone is prepared for. At the same time, one of the truck people grabs Morgan from behind and slits his throat with a knife. Blood gushes out. Morgan's body drops to the ground when the man releases it. Cheers turn into screams. Gunshots crackle in the air. But the dead keep coming, pouring from the truck.

Vale jumps to her feet, grabs her rifle, and runs toward the crowd, searching for Andrea and George, but Andrea who was standing up front is already gone, being torn apart by the dead, beyond even screaming. George is on the far side of the field, firing a rifle, trying to cover people rushing back to the terminal for shelter. The walking dead close around him, and Vale thinks of the day she saved Andrea and George from the outdoor café. This time there are too many of the dead, and they're too close. In seconds, there's nowhere for George to run. Even if Vale could shoot them all at once, it wouldn't be enough. She looks away as George disappears beneath the horde.

She spies Campbell in the thick of the fighting, pauses, and fires two shots into the dead things coming up behind him. Both fall down, and Campbell moves on without realizing the danger he avoided. Next Vale finds some of the truck people and freezes with the rifle halfway to her shoulder.

The truck people eat their victims.

They are spattered with blood, their faces smeared red with it, and they're running around the field, screeching and shouting, killing anyone they get their hands on and then cutting off pieces of them and devouring them. Some of them are even eating parts of the walking dead when they fall. Vale notices then how many of the dead are missing hands or arms or pieces of their torso or even parts of their legs. The area where they found the truck seemed so empty of the dead, and the truck people are so pale, sickly, and strange looking—and then she understands how they were surviving out on the barren roadway. Her stomach clenches. She wants to scream but holds it in. She feels like she's going to vomit, but then she overcomes her disgust and starts shooting.

She hits most of the truck people in the head, putting them down, but not for long.

Morgan, the first killed, rises.

Vale finds him in her sights.

All around her are screams of fear and pain, savage growls and shouts, and the plaintive voices of the dead spreading fast. It is chaos and horror; it's the undoing of all that they've built. Campbell was right about Morgan but wrong too. Vale never would've guessed he would bring them this low. The bastard is only the first of many to fall and rise that day, and Vale grants him no mercy.

Let him walk, she thinks. *Let him rot.*

She finds another target and pulls the trigger.

TEARS OF BLOOD
ONE

Something stank.

Vale roused from unconsciousness and found she was lying in a warm puddle inside the pen. Beyond the bars, three lamps burned, replacements for those smashed during the incident with Duncan and Burnett. Outside the range of the lights, someone moved in the darkness, and the hangar shell made weird echoes of the person's footsteps.

Vale sat up and checked herself.

The stink came from her legs.

Someone had pissed on her while she was out, leaving stains up and down her pants and feet. She gagged, fought down the urge to throw up, and then wobbled onto her feet. She slid out of her soiled socks and pants and tossed them into a corner, leaving her wearing only panties and a long-sleeved T-shirt.

"How long have I been out?" she asked the dark. "Where are my guns?"

No answer.

"What time is it?"

A man snickered.

"Don't you understand what's coming? We're all dead meat if the stranger is right."

"Dead meat, anyway," the man said.

She recognized the voice: Estevez.

That explained the urine. She must've really pissed off Campbell for him to let Estevez guard her.

"Tell Campbell I'm sorry. I didn't want to hurt him, but I couldn't let him do it," she said. "I only wanted to protect the stranger."

"Putting a tourist ahead of one of our own," Estevez said. "Stupid move."

"The stranger might be our only chance to survive."

"Not anymore," Estevez said. "The holy man's gone."

"Holy man?" Vale said.

"The stranger. He ran away." A metal joint creaked as Estevez swiveled a work light up and cast its illumination toward the ceiling. "And Campbell isn't in charge anymore. Right, Campbell?"

The lamplight revealed Campbell, hanging fifteen feet in the air, suspended by chains wrapped crosswise under his arms and around his chest, strung up from the overhead pulley system like a carcass waiting to be butchered. Blood ran from a cut along his forehead and trickled in steady *plink-plink* of drops from the tip of his nose. Vale felt a flood of relief when she saw his chest move even though it was faint. She looked at the gunshot wound she'd given him. The singed hole in the wet cloth gaped like a burrow into muddy soil. Nothing had been done to dress the wound or stop the bleeding. Blood drizzled down from Campbell's soaked pants.

"Who's leader now?" Vale said in a whisper.

"Malloy."

"Fucking idiot," Vale said. "The others won't follow him. Do they know what he's done to Campbell?"

"No." Estevez laughed. "After Campbell passed out, Malloy told everyone he was taking him away for Farley to fix him up, but he brought him here instead. Never let Farley touch him."

"Get him down before he bleeds to death."

Estevez stepped into the light and shook his head. "No can do. Not that I like it. Campbell was all right by me, but this is how Malloy called it. I take my orders from him."

"The plan doesn't work without Campbell."

"The plan is history. Malloy says we ain't going. Head out come spring maybe. Maybe not. If you were so hot on Campbell's stupid plan, you shouldn't have shot him. Dumb move, bitch."

"I wanted to protect the stranger. Didn't you hear what he said about all the wormfeeders coming here? At least with Campbell's plan, we'd have somewhere to run to before they get here."

Estevez cleared his throat then spat a wad of phlegm into the shadows. "That's a pile of crap. Like that fucker is really some kind of saint. Give me a break. Fucking holy man, my ass. Just another crazy shit-kicker like the rest of us. Gordon's just a goddamn loon."

"What are you talking about?"

"You missed it because we had to violently subdue your ass. Gordon says the stranger is some guy called the Pale Saint. She saw his body at St. Regis's Cathedral in Dover before the dead plague. He's some big deal American saint or something. Worked with the poor. Did miracles. Even had that thing where your hands and feet bleed for no fucking reason. Gordon says because of all that, his body didn't rot when he died, even after thirty years. She says his corpse used to cry tears of blood when bad shit happened in the world, and the blood's supposed to smell like perfume or honey. She thinks he was resurrected like all the other dead people, but different because of who he was, and that's why he looks alive. It's a bunch of flaming bullshit. Gordon snapped."

Vale thought of how the stranger's presence made her feel, how his gaze invited her to accept that whatever harm the world might bring her way could never truly touch her if only she believed it couldn't—if only she believed in him.

"The stranger's a saint? A walking dead saint?"

"Aw, shit, you're not another Jesus-freak like Gordon, are you? Thinks this is the end of days or some shit? It's obvious there ain't no fucking God."

"Was Gordon sure?"

"Gordon's a fucking idiot, and her story's a steaming load. That shit about the stranger crossing the meadow through the corpse orchard, keeping Reading and Burnett from rising?

Nobody believes it! Burnett's body wasn't even here when we came for it. Probably got up and walked off. Don't know what kind of crap you were up to but it's over. Malloy says you can have your guns back if you stick with us. He's grateful for you taking out Campbell, and you shoot real good, so you got a place here if you want." Estevez leered through the metal cage, casting an eye toward Vale's bare legs. "Of course, you're going to have to prove your loyalty first."

"Fuck off." Vale slammed her open palms against the bars of the pen through a gap in the razor wire. "Malloy will get us all killed. Hope you enjoy life as a walking corpse."

"I don't know about that." Estevez made an obscene gesture. "But I know I'll enjoy it when you're one."

The hangar door crashed open, and the noise reverberated through the building. Estevez backed off from the pen. In the darkness, Vale couldn't see who had entered, but she knew by his booming, obnoxious laugh that one was Malloy. Then she recognized the voice of Dawson, their mechanic. When they reached the light, Vale saw Dawson had no idea what he'd walked into. His face jumped when he saw Campbell. He took three steps away from Malloy, inspiring a fresh bout of laughter.

"Pussy," Malloy said. "What are you afraid of?"

"What the fuck is this?" Dawson said. "Get Campbell down from there. He needs help."

"Hey, man, Campbell is old news. Fucker's spilled half his blood all over the floor by now. Only thing he needs is a hole in the ground. But if you're so eager to see him up and running, hang around awhile. I'm sure he'll start kicking again real soon."

"Shit, I've been working on the trucks for months. We're supposed to start the trip in a week or two. Campbell is the only one who knows the route."

"Well, then, let me put your mind at ease. Forget the trip. We're not going. But we still need the trucks so you've got your job, mechanic, if you want it."

"What do you need them for?"

"Gotta keep foraging."

"For what? And where? Actsburg is thick with the dead and almost picked clean," Dawson said.

"We'll find enough there to get us through winter. We spent the time fortifying this place, why should we ditch it for the open road and some godforsaken wreck in the middle of nowhere that for all we know is overrun by the dead?"

Vale called out from her cell, "Because this place is going to be Hell on Earth by tomorrow night."

"Shut your mouth, Vale," Malloy said. "You got no say in this, unless you want to put your shooting and your ass to good use for me. Otherwise, you're going to die right there in the pen. That offer goes for everyone else, too. No more *sides*. Everyone's on *my* side. They do what *I* say. If not, then they're gone like Campbell. I'm betting Dawson here is smart enough to know which end of that deal he ought to be on."

"Hey, man, listen," Dawson said. "I do what I do, all right? It's all I'm good at. You keep us warm and safe, keep our bellies full, I'll keep the machines running."

Malloy grinned. "You drive a hard bargain, Mr. Dawson, but you got yourself a deal."

Vale wanted to despise Dawson, but she couldn't. Defying Malloy would only get him killed, and these days everyone did what was necessary to survive.

Others came, one by one, escorted by Malloy, anyone with key responsibilities or skills like Farley and the woman, Gallegos, who'd been an architect and could build just about anything. He offered them all the same choice: Campbell's fate, the pen, or follow him as leader. They all turned, and Vale watched horror blossom inside each one of them as they did so. It was the product of their fear that refusal would force Malloy to make a painful example of them combined with the knowledge that whatever Malloy had in mind could only ruin them all. Still, they added their names in allegiance to Malloy, alongside thugs like Estevez and his dirty pal Green, the kind of men Malloy knew well how to exploit. By dusk, it was all over.

The dream of leaving the airport and the rotting city, of finding a new life elsewhere lay raped and shattered. Hanging deathly still in the air, Campbell looked down on its remains with broken, unseeing eyes. The pool of blood beneath him spread and coagulated. Vale didn't want to see it when Campbell rose;

she didn't want to be trapped in the pen when the wormfeeders invaded the camp tomorrow.

Estevez had removed everything she might use as a weapon except her belt still laced through the loops of her discarded pants. She wondered if the belt would be enough to choke herself to death when the wormfeeders arrived, when they were close enough she could see the maggots crawling in their eternally raw wounds. She'd probably pass out and let up the pressure before she died, but at least she wouldn't know it when they tore her apart.

Around midnight Green relieved Estevez. He perched opposite the pen, sullen and silent, and stared at Vale, tightlipped, his rifle resting across his lap. He could stay like that for hours. For someone so dumb, Green possessed amazing powers of concentration, which he now focused on Vale's mostly naked lower body. Vale hated Green. So, she felt no sympathy for him when an axe handle split the darkness and cracked against the back of his skull. She watched him topple, his face white with shock as he tried to recover, and then he fell under the handle as it connected a second time with a bone-splitting snap.

Gordon, Farley, and Dawson waded out of the shadows.

"Hit that bastard once more," Vale said.

"Don't want him dead," Dawson said. "He'll just get back up and try to eat us."

"We couldn't let them do this to you and Campbell. It isn't right." Gordon walked up to the pen and handed Vale a pair of clean pants, a jacket, and boots along with her rifle and automatics. "Malloy left them in the armory. I stole them back," she told Vale. "Dawson said you needed clothes."

"Thank you," Vale said.

Farley knelt down and took Green's guns from their holsters and his keys from the ring on his belt. Dawson worked the control board for the pulley system and lowered Campbell. When they released Vale with Green's keys, Vale dressed and then relished the heft of her guns back in her hands, her rifle strapped across her back. She felt their power flow into her.

Dawson laid Campbell out on the cement floor. Though his chest stirred almost imperceptibly, his skin was ashen and cold. Farley gauged the tacky wash of blood all around him.

"He's bled too much. Nothing I can do for him without equipment and a blood supply," Farley said. "I'm sorry."

"What do we do?" Gordon said.

"We should burn him, so he doesn't rise," Dawson said.

"Shit, he's not dead yet," Farley said.

"He will be soon," Gordon said. "Maybe St. Bianco could bless him."

"St. Bianco?" Vale said.

Gordon looked away. "The stranger. The Pale Saint. I'm sorry, Vale. I didn't want to believe it was him when I saw him."

"What would his blessing do?" Vale said.

"Stop him from rising," Gordon said.

"We can't wait around for him to die," Dawson said. "Malloy or anyone else could walk in here any second."

"Leave him," Vale said.

The others fell silent and stared at her.

"Let him die, let him rise," Vale said. "Let him be here waiting when Malloy comes back."

"No," Gordon said.

"That's not...I won't...no...," Farley said. "No. We can't let him rise. He wouldn't let it happen to us."

"Yes, he would," Vale said. "To avoid putting people at risk, to save lives, he'd do it. That's our situation. If any shred of hope existed that we could help Campbell, I'd drag him across this airport to protect him, but it doesn't. He's as good as dead."

And I killed him, Vale thought.

She had put the bullet in his leg. She had torn open his flesh and veins. She had freed the blood that bled away his life. She had meant only to stop him with a minor flesh wound that could've been closed and healed with a simple bandage or a few stitches from Farley. Malloy had prevented that. The next time Vale saw Malloy, she meant to kill him.

TWO

Outside the hangar, Dawson led them along a neglected walkway toward a row of abandoned boarding gates, a secondary wing that branched from the main pavilion. It had been cleared out and closed down after the fiasco with the Food Wizard truck so no one would have to guard unoccupied living space. Gordon stuck close to Vale as they walked.

"You made the right choice," she said.

Vale only nodded.

"Campbell was a good man. No matter what happens to his body, something better than this life is waiting for him," Gordon said.

"Maybe," Vale said. "Don't count on it."

"I get your skepticism. I really do," Gordon said. "I never much believed in God or the afterlife either. My grandparents did, though. Used to take me to church with them every Sunday, whether I liked it or not. When I was in junior high, they took me to see St. Bianco's relics and body at St. Regis's Cathedral. My grandmother prayed to him almost every day, so the trip was a pilgrimage for her, but I didn't expect much. I figured at best we'd see something like a mummy, at worst a pile of bones in a cassock. The body was displayed in a glass-and-bronze coffin in a chapel beneath the cathedral, and I have to admit it shocked me. It was so weird to see this dead guy who looked like he might just wake up and start talking. He'd been that way for at least a couple of decades then, and other than looking dehydrated, hardly anything seemed wrong with him. It rattled me. It made me wonder if something like that was possible, what else might be, you know? But I closed the door on that as soon as I got back home to life as usual. That was the closest I ever came to having real faith—faith like my grandparents had, anyway. I was too scared then to let myself believe, so I backed away from it. But after St. Bianco walked through the door last night, I realized how wrong I've been."

"You should've warned Campbell and me when we came in," Vale said.

"Yeah, I know, and I'm sorry I didn't. I didn't want to believe it was him at first, but the longer I was around him, the more I *felt* him. It felt the way it did that day at St. Regis's, only stronger. He gets inside you, under your skin, into your thoughts, and he makes you feel safe and terrified at the same time. Do you know what I mean?"

Vale hesitated then said, "Yes. That's the only reason I'm listening to you. Get to the point."

"St. Bianco is a patron saint of the lost and the ill. I don't think anyone these days is sicker or more lost than we are. He came to us for a reason."

"He came to warn us," Vale said.

"Sure, but why *us*?" Gordon said. "We can't be the only living people left. There must be others in the path of this crowd of dead people coming our way, other people out there he could help, but he came here."

"I don't know why," Vale said.

"It's because he sees something in us that we can't see ourselves."

Vale glared at Gordon. "Like what? You mean we're special? We're chosen? No. We're not. There's nothing special about us, except we're still alive. We've lost so many people, made so many mistakes, been at each other's throats."

"Maybe that's why he chose us."

"Because we're failures?"

"Because we've made sacrifices. We've paid a price to stay alive. Maybe we are failures, but at least we've tried to do better, to be good."

"No," Vale said. "Forget it."

"It can't be only coincidence. Hear me out. St. Bianco was born Jacopo Bianco, the only son of Italian immigrants. His family was poor but their faith was strong, and Jacopo lived a simple life. He had nothing and no prospects for a future, yet as a boy he was moved by suffering. So, he fed stray animals. He made friends with lonely and sick children at school. He did chores for his elderly neighbors. He'd been born with one leg shorter than the other, so he limped and had a hard time running. When he was sixteen, he had an epiphany. His father died that year in a construction accident, and six weeks later, he appeared to Jacopo in a dream and showed his son two aspects of himself—one violently beating the other with a cracked bone. Jacopo couldn't tell them apart, until he noticed that his violent aspect moved with ease while the peaceful one shared his limp because his opponent was repeatedly breaking his bones. After that, Jacopo understood that his dark side was crippling him. If he learned how to subdue it and heal himself, then maybe he could teach others to do so too. The next year he entered a religious order. He spent thirteen years in seclusion, praying for insight and strength to control the violence and sin in his spirit. When he emerged, his legs were equal in length, and he'd lost his limp. No doctor could explain it. That was his first miracle."

Dawson signaled everyone to stop. He surveyed the dark expanse between them and the nearest corner of the terminal wing. The group fell silent. For several seconds, there was nothing but the constant, chilling lullaby of the moaning dead. Then they heard voices and footsteps, men running, somewhere around the corner of the terminal. They waited until the voices faded.

"That sounded like Duncan and Green," Dawson said. "From here, we'll be in the open until we reach the terminal. Move fast and be careful, and Gordon, keep your voice down."

"Will do, but Vale needs to know before we get there," Gordon said.

"Agreed, but speak softly."

"Know what?" Vale asked.

"About St. Bianco," Gordon said, as the group resumed walking. "After coming out of seclusion, he traveled to places torn by conflict. Northern Ireland. The Middle East. Eastern Europe. Half a dozen nations in Africa. He lived with people on all sides of a disagreement and tried to understand them and urge them all toward peace. There were reports that he healed the sick, that people in his presence went unscathed when bombs exploded near them. Some people saw him in one place when his physical person was in another location far away. People who believed were already calling him the Pale Saint years before he died because "Bianco" means "white" in Italian and he was so fair-skinned. No one from the church ran an official investigation at the time, but among his devoted, the stories are taken for fact. Other than healing his leg, though, he's credited with two other miracles, which qualified him for sainthood.

"Once he led rescuers in the Philippines to an eight-year-old girl trapped beneath the rubble of a school destroyed by a mud slide. The girl was buried thirty-two feet down and never would've been found before she died. Workers freed her and she survived. Another time, during a cholera outbreak in Ethiopia, he visited a hospital where the worst cases were treated. He blessed twelve people there, and the next day all of them were recovered and in better health than they had been before they got sick.

"When he got old he became fully ordained and settled down in a poor parish outside Actsburg. He'd lived with the stigmata for five years by then, and it lasted until he died exactly five years later. His body didn't decay. It didn't rot. It remained almost unchanged. And it wept sweet-smelling tears of blood whenever Bianco sensed that the world was on the verge of sinking into darkness."

"You believe this?" Vale asked.

"The dead plague showed me the world isn't how I thought it was," Gordon said. "There's more to life than only physical existence."

"The dead plague showed everyone that. But it doesn't mean those stories are true," Vale said. "It only means we didn't have the all answers we thought we did. So we adjust, we adapt, and we go on living."

"Except this isn't living, not really, is it? It's only survival. At the end of the day, we can't control much of what happens to us."

"We never could," Vale said.

"I guess not, but now we have help from St. Bianco."

"He warned us. What more can he do?"

"He's opened a better way for us," Gordon said. "Yes, he's dead, but he's not the same as the others. He's full of light and goodness. He can help us escape. The dead are the dark side of the living, crippling us, and we're all fighting our dark selves like St. Bianco did. He came to help heal the darkness inside us, around us, like he did for himself. With his help, we can beat death. We can beat our darkness. And if we do that then we'll be whole again and we can reach the other side after we die. We won't rise."

"There's no other side," Vale said. "Nothing is waiting for us when we die. The only escape we have is leaving this airport."

"I don't believe that. I don't think you do, either, not really. I know it's hard to accept," Gordon said. "But I hope you'll see when the time comes."

"Time for what?" Vale asked.

Gordon looked away and didn't speak for the rest of the walk, and Vale let her question hang in the air. When the group reached the terminal, they mounted a mobile boarding staircase to a jetway door that had been left jimmied open and stepped into a passage that connected to the main corridor of empty flight departure lounges. There they dashed past the windows and hurried into what had been the Gold Card Flyers Club. Others were there: Corrigan, Gallegos, and Hutchins. And one more: the stranger, St. Bianco. He sat on a lounge chair with the others on the floor around him, cross-legged in a loose semi-circle—praying. They broke off when Dawson's group entered.

St. Bianco stood. He radiated confidence. "I'm very sorry for your loss. Mr. Campbell was a good man," he said.

Vale studied the odd light in the holy man's dusky eyes, maybe an inner light or maybe a reflection of the brightening dawn. His stare dampened the pyre of grief and rage that burned inside her. It promised that he knew and understood all her pain, sorrow, and anger, in the same way that he knew everything would be all right in the end. The image of Campbell's body filled Vale's mind. She wanted to grieve, to let anguish flood out of her, to cleanse herself of fury. Warm tears trickled from her eyes. St. Bianco's expression was an invitation for Vale to become part of something greater than herself, something that seemed right and true, and Vale tasted stark temptation to accept, but the same voice that had warned her not to shoot the stranger now warned her not to trust him. He had come here to help them, but when she remembered what he'd said—*some are meant to die; some are always meant to die*—she wasn't sure he could, or *would*, help them all. She wiped her tears from her cheeks.

Voice cracking, Vale asked, "You said they'd arrive today. How long?"

"They're close. Moving slower than they were, but coming, inexorable."

"An hour? Three? How long do we have? Tell me!"

Hutchins jumped to his feet. "Lower your voice," he said. "Show some respect."

"Let her be. She means no harm," St. Bianco said. "You'll have most of the day, Vale, probably until late afternoon or early evening, but you'll see them sooner swelling the ranks outside this house, for it has been marked."

"Marked? How?" Vale said.

"Marked to play its appointed role," the stranger said. "All of us—the living and the dead—have a part in what's occurring. All are accounted for. None go overlooked, no matter how much it seems otherwise. There is no greater purpose than to surrender to your fate."

"I don't have time for this." Vale turned to Dawson and Gordon. "Let's go now. We can take the trucks, fight our way inland, try to get around the horde before the rest of it arrives. Then we can drive back roads south and find Campbell's farm or somewhere else safe."

"It's pointless," Hutchins said. "You'd only be running from something you can't escape. The dead are everywhere. You'll have to fight thousands to get across Actsburg. What about food and gas? What about sleeping? You'll never rest again, even when they finally kill you, because then you'll be one of them."

"You'd rather sit here, waiting to die?" Vale asked.

"Everyone dies. We're waiting for salvation. St. Bianco will bless us so we don't rise," Hutchins said. "You've seen him do it. With his blessing, our corpses will never walk the Earth. We'll be free. We'll escape damnation."

"You promised them this?" Vale asked St. Bianco.

"I would do this for any who ask," he said. "I've done it for two of your friends, as you witnessed. Or do you not believe what your eyes showed you? After I fled during the violence, I went to Mr. Burnett's body, took it from the cage, and buried it properly. I cared for him as I care for all of you. You're all free to go if that's your choice, but for those who stay, I'll see to it their bodies find peace in death, that the dead will not take their blessed flesh for their own. Their souls will find their final home."

"And where's that? Where will they go after they die? What will they find there?" Vale said. "What's waiting for them? Heaven? Hell?"

Saint Bianco said nothing.

"Or is it nothing at all?" Vale said. "Nowhere and nothing. They won't be saved. They'll simply be gone from existence. That's it, isn't it? If I'm wrong, then tell us where they'll go."

The stranger's expression reminded Vale of a television talking head, speaking endlessly, assuming authority out of arrogance, claiming expertise where none existed, acting like they knew the whole story and had all the answers, when they'd only glimpsed some small, disturbing part of the truth. They'd been as ignorant and terrified as everyone else, but most of them refused to show it.

"You don't know, do you?" Vale said.

"*We know,*" Hutchins said. "We know what we're doing. It's the only way to get free from this hell. And when we die, we'll go on to eternal life rather than endless rot and suffering."

"He didn't say that," Vale said. "He only said he'd stop your bodies from rising."

"He doesn't have to say it. We believe it." Hutchins walked to the window and peered through his reflection in the glass at the lightening sky. "That's faith. That's enough."

"Enough to make you surrender like sheep? To let the world devour you? You're taking the word of a man you believe is dead. Are you sure he isn't lying? What if he has other reasons for keeping you here? Why not just cut your own throats, now, and be done with it," Vale said. "You fucking cowards! You're worse than Malloy. At least he's too damn dense to know he's committing suicide."

Hutchins turned from the window, trembling. "You're the frightened one, Vale. You hide behind your guns because you're too scared to put your faith in anything you can't see or touch. You're afraid of life, of being close to anyone. I bet you hid from it every chance you had before the dead plague. I bet you lived in a safe, little cocoon. It was always you who told us to give up on ever understanding why the dead walk, you who said to forget about ever rebuilding the world how it was. You like things the way they are. It thrills you up there in the tower, shooting dead people. All there is in you, Vale, is death and hopelessness."

"You're right." Vale released a long breath and rubbed her eyes. "I did hide from life in the old world. I took the easy way out anytime I could. I let other people tell me what to do. I tried to be what they wanted me to be, to believe what they wanted me to believe. But no more. And I do have hope. And faith. But it's faith in myself. I won't ever go back to being like I was before the dead plague. And neither will the world. It can't. No matter what happens, no matter how good things might be one day, they can never be like they were. You don't like that, do you? So, who's really the one running and hiding?"

Looking around to Dawson, Farley, and Gordon—all of them so uncertain—Hutchins said, "You told us she'd understand. You said she'd want to join us."

"She shot Campbell to save St. Bianco," Farley said. "I thought she knew what she was doing."

"I thought she wanted what we want," Gordon said.

"All I wanted was to know what information he had," Vale said. "Campbell was going to cut his head off. What else could I do?"

"We risked everything to save you. If Malloy knew we were acting against him, he'd kill us all, and who knows what he'd do to St. Bianco?" Dawson said. "Maybe you should leave, Vale. That's what you want, anyway, isn't it?"

"Yes," Vale said. "I want one of the trucks, so I can be far away from here when all this comes down."

Dawson shook his head. "You'll never make it across the meadow without a gunner."

"Honestly, Dawson, what difference can it possibly make to you, now?" she said.

"All right, all right. I got nothing against you. You want it, you got it. Come down to the garage with me and I'll set you up. No skin off my nose. You aren't our prisoner or anything."

"I'll come, too," Gordon said. "Better not walk around without someone to watch your back. Malloy's going to be pissed when he finds Vale gone."

"Be quick," Farley said. "We should all be together when the end comes."

Dawson nodded. The trio moved to the door then paused when the holy man gripped Vale's shoulder.

"You were the first here to sense what I am, Vale, even though you didn't understand and you still don't," he said. "I felt your eyes on me, looking down from your high tower, tracking me with your gun. So many times you could've shot me but didn't. You must have asked yourself why. You must have wondered what you see in me that stays your hand, how it is you feel the power within me and yet you can resist it. Have you found an answer?"

"If I have," Vale said, "it's none of your damned business." Then she strode out the door with Gordon and Dawson following her.

THREE

Traveling the grounds in secret was riskier with daylight spreading. There were too many open spaces to traverse, too many windows gaping toward the bronze sun cresting the horizon. Vale, Dawson, and Gordon rounded the far side of the terminal and scrambled down a concrete slope toward the motor pool building. They kept low to the ground and moved fast. Distant gunfire sounded from the direction of the hangar. A tendril of smoke rose through the morning sky. More soon joined it, and then came the scent of burning wood and plastic, of hot metal, of scorched earth. The trio hunkered down along a concrete barrier and paused to listen.

"Guess they found Campbell," Vale said.

"Which means they know you escaped," Dawson said.

"Maybe it'll keep them busy for awhile," Gordon said.

After awhile, no more gunshots came, and the three stood and rushed to the back entrance of the garage.

There were five trucks. Three, waiting to be cleaned, were encrusted with dried blood and scabs of necrotic flesh left from recent foraging runs. Vale accepted the small delivery truck Dawson recommended, the second to last one he had rigged out and the most solid. He had cleaned and prepped it for a run into the city. Its fuel tank was full. He gathered up half a dozen empty gasoline canisters, filled them from the main tank, and stored them in the truck. Next they laid in equipment and tools, spare tires, and other parts. Dawson collected all the weapons and ammunition he had stashed in the shop and gave them to Vale. For food they raided supplies from Campbell's last foraging run. The cases of water and canned goods had not yet been unloaded.

They moved them to Vale's truck. Then, finished, they stood back and surveyed the vehicle Vale hoped would carry her away from the airport forever. Her preparations would be futile if she didn't make it across the meadow, and she hadn't yet figured out how she would pull that off.

She thought Dawson might be right about needing a gunner, but she didn't care. She would take her chances, and if she died today, she meant to die fighting for her life, something unthinkable to her before the dead plague. Vale climbed into the driver's seat, checked the dashboard, and adjusted the wheel. She hopped out and hugged Dawson.

"Thank you," she said.

"You're welcome. Where will you go?"

Vale shrugged. "Campbell's farm, I guess."

"How can you find it?"

"He told me how to get there, in case something happened to him. He... trusted me."

Dawson nodded. "Well, be careful. And go easy on the clutch. Treat her like a virgin, she appreciates a gentle touch."

Vale smiled then lifted herself back into the truck.

"Wait!" Gordon said, grabbing Dawson's arm. "What if Vale's right? What if we're giving up for no good reason? Why shouldn't we try to keep living? What kind of God would want us to roll over and die?"

Dawson backed off, his face wrinkled with confusion. "You told me last night you couldn't go on anymore, living like scared rats in a cage, that you couldn't handle the fear and despair," Dawson said. "You said the way we're living now isn't even living."

"I was frightened," Gordon said. "I thought Vale knew who St. Bianco was. I thought she protected him to save us all. But what if she's right about what comes after death? I mean, St. Bianco didn't answer her when she asked. Why wouldn't he? With everything going on around us, why wouldn't he tell us the truth?"

"Well, fuck me on Christmas," Dawson said. "The idiot lot of us getting ready to kill each other half because of you and you're running scared."

"I only said what I knew. Then everyone went crazy. Hutchins, Farley, the rest of them—they're looking for answers.

They want out, no matter what. I never told anyone what to do. I just said what I knew."

"What the hell are you telling me here?" Dawson asked.

Gordon stepped up close to him, placed her fingertips on his cheeks as she looked into his eyes, and said, "Let's go with Vale. I don't want to die hiding here. I don't want to die at all."

"I thought you had faith in St. Bianco."

"Faith, maybe..." Gordon said.

"Not mindless obedience," Vale said. "Our minds, our personalities, even our souls, if they really exist, are what separate us from the dead. Give them up, stop thinking for yourself then whether or not Saint Bianco blesses your body, you may as well be out there with the dead."

Dawson ran a hand along the rough fender of the truck. A loose nut in a plate of metal attached to the front grill caught his eye. Almost without thinking he reached out and tightened it with a wrench from the workbench.

"Are you serious?" he said.

Gordon nodded. "Maybe we'll find something better. Maybe we won't. For now it's enough to believe we will."

"You're a better driver than me, Dawson," Vale said. "If I can concentrate on shooting, we might actually get out of here."

Gordon pulled Dawson to her and kissed him deeply, then stepped back, and said, "We stay here, we know what's coming. Out there, with Vale—who knows what we can do?"

Dawson extended an open palm toward Vale. She dropped the truck keys into it, and he closed his fingers around them. "Ladies, you do the shooting, and I promise we'll make it at least as far as the city limits. Everything I know went into this truck, and if it can't get us where we're going, then fuck it all. I was getting tired of waiting at this goddamned airport, anyway."

FOUR

The odor of smoke poured in when Dawson rolled back the garage doors. Far across the grounds, flames consumed Hangar Four. Malloy's men scurried around outside it, waving guns and firing into the air. Vale studied them through binoculars. They must have found Hutchins' group, she thought, and dragged them out from the terminal. All of them were lined up on their knees outside the burning hangar, with their hands bound behind their backs, and at the end of the row knelt Saint Bianco. Vale shifted around to survey the exit gates. All of them looked thick and overrun by wormfeeders, except for the gate beyond Hangar Four. There the crowd of the dead was a little sparser. Short of tearing down part of the fence and barbed wire perimeter, that would be their best way out. At least it was to the west. They'd have the rising sun at their backs as they approached. Vale hoped it would give them an edge.

"Shit, Malloy found them," Dawson said. "We have to help them."

"There's nothing we can do," Vale said. "Count yourself lucky you left with me."

"We can't just leave them to Malloy," Gordon said.

"Why not?" Vale said. "If we cut north past the terminal and come at the gate from the other side, no one will spot us until it's too late for anyone to interfere. Besides, Malloy has seven men to our three."

"Those are our friends," Gordon said.

"All of whom were planning to commit communal suicide today. What's the difference if Malloy does it for them?"

"Malloy won't let St. Bianco bless them. They'll rise as wormfeeders," Gordon said. "That isn't what they wanted."

"If we rescue them, what then?" Vale asked. "We don't have room in the truck for everyone."

"Son of a bitch," Dawson said. "We're wasting time. They can't come with us, no argument, but I don't like leaving them to Malloy. I say we take out Malloy and his men and leave the others to live or die as they please. They change their minds about bugging out of here, there are four other trucks. They can follow our dust."

"Fine. Let's get it over with," Vale said. "Bring us south into the shadow of the tower then cut west along the runway. If you get us within a couple hundred yards before they see us, I'll nail at least two of them before they know we're coming. That'll even the odds."

Gordon and Vale climbed into the back of the truck and crouched among the supplies that crowded the two shooting posts. Vale swapped the mounted automatic over to Gordon's post and replaced it with her rifle. It was hot and stuffy inside the truck, and a film of sweat formed on Vale's face. She took a deep breath then knocked on the small window at the back of the cab to signal Dawson that she was ready.

"Vale," Gordon said. "Thank you."

Vale frowned. "If you want to thank me, shoot Malloy. The others will crumble without him."

The truck rolled from the garage then turned and picked up speed as Dawson guided it along the tarmac. When they came within range of the burning hangar, Vale banged on the window, and Dawson braked. Vale's side of the truck stood exposed to the group by the hangar but hidden in shadow. Farther across the empty turf and cracked tarmac, the wormfeeders massed together against the fence. The front rows of the crowd were shredding themselves on the barbed wire, ravenous at the sight of so many living people in the open by daylight.

Vale slipped her rifle through the gun slit and sighted through her scope. She hunted for Malloy, but she didn't see him.

Soon, the rising sun would steal their shadowy camouflage. Vale waited as long as she dared, then chose Estevez and squeezed off two quick shots. One lanced through his gut and into his spine; the other ripped open the top of his skull. He twisted around, arms flailing, and fell. She took Green next and put a bullet through his throat. He clutched the wound as he crumpled. After he fell, Vale sent another bullet into his pelvis. It was the first time she'd ever shot to kill, and it wasn't like shooting the dead. Vale quivered and felt as if she might vomit. Then she thought of the things she'd seen Estevez and Malloy do with the dead, how Green had leered at her, how they'd let Campbell die, and that Estevez had pissed on her in the cage. This was self-defense, a fight for survival. It didn't make the killing easier, but it steadied her hands and calmed her stomach.

By the hangar, Duncan, and Schutt erupted into panic then hit the ground for cover and fired back. Dawson floored the gas, sending the truck toward them. Gordon fired the automatic; her bullets gouged chunks of tarmac and ripped up a dotted line of debris. Bullets pinged off the truck's exterior. Dawson zigzagged to avoid the gunfire. He slammed on the brakes and cut right around a turn in the runway then slowed to a crawl and held the truck in a straight line. Vale caught Schutt in her sight and shot him in the eye. He flopped into a ditch alongside the tarmac. When the wild motion of the truck resumed, Vale pulled her weapon back inside.

She wondered where Malloy was. Unless he was in the terminal, he had to have heard the firefight. The gunfire cut through the steady murmur of the moaning dead like thunder. Vale searched for him through her binoculars. Nothing. She checked each of the prisoners, most of whom had dropped and kept their heads down during the crossfire. Corrigan rose first and struggled to free his wrists from the ropes tied around them. He was working at the knots when a quarter of his skull vanished in a puff of blood and spattered flesh, bone, and hair.

"No!" Gordon screamed.

At first, Vale thought Gordon had hit him with a stray shot, but Gordon hadn't been firing. Hutchins died next, spinning over onto his back from the force of a gunshot. Vale scanned the area around the hangar. Malloy and Tomaselli were rounding the back of the building. Malloy gripped a rifle against his shoulder. He stopped, took a third shot at the captives, missing this time, and then he resumed jogging toward them. Tomaselli lurched along behind him, struggling to keep up under the weight of the flame thrower strapped to his back. Vale guessed they'd used it to incinerate Campbell's reanimated corpse and let the fire get out of control and spread to the entire hangar.

Dawson slammed the brakes and the truck skidded to a rough stop, jolting Vale and Gordon off balance. Vale recovered, slid her rifle through the gun slot, and fired twice. The first bullet grazed Malloy's face. The second bit through his upper right arm. He tumbled to the ground, fumbling his rifle. It skittered out of reach. He stood a moment later, waving an automatic with his uninjured arm, and firing at the captives. He pegged Farley in the chest. The medic bucked, rolled over, and went still.

"Get us closer!" Vale cried. "Now, goddammit!"

Dawson drove and the truck barreled over the strip of gravel and scrub between runways. Duncan hurried to meet Malloy and

Tomaselli. The truck crested a low rise, and its tires squealed as they gripped the pavement outside the burning hangar. Dawson stamped the brakes. The vehicle shuddered and jumped as it halted. The sudden change slammed Vale and Gordon against the sides and toppled boxes of supplies. Vale scrambled back to position and sighted Malloy through her scope. Her finger grazed the trigger—and then Malloy fell out of sight, taking cover behind the corpses of his victims. Vale let out a short, angry scream then chose another target and fired. Duncan jerked sideways, struck in the chest, and fell. Vale's next round turned Tomaselli's right knee into a crimson puff of blood and bone. Another cracked through his clavicle. He went down hard with the weight of the flamethrower tank and struggled to roll off his back.

Malloy screamed.

His voice carried through the air.

Dawson slowly circled to put Vale in position.

All around Malloy the dead began to rise. Estevez, with a severed spine, wriggled across the ground toward his former boss, while Green jerked upright and shambled after the last of the live meat. Soon Hutchins joined him, then Corrigan, and lastly Duncan, Farley, and Tomaselli. Malloy leapt to his feet. He yanked Gallegos back on her knees then drew Saint Bianco up next to her. Both were still tied up. Gallegos closed her eyes and sobbed. Ignoring the wormfeeders closing on him, Malloy pressed his gun against the back of Saint Bianco's skull and fired. The bullet ripped outward through the holy man's left eye, and drove him forward. He fell against Gallegos, slid down her, and then landed, smacking his face on the ground.

Malloy shifted his gun to Gallegos.

He didn't shoot. The figure of St. Bianco appeared beside him and grabbed his gun arm, halting him. Yet even as he did so, the stranger's wounded body also lay bleeding on the tarmac. Malloy stared at the man gripping his arm, at the body of the man he'd shot, the two indistinguishable except for the head wound, and then he opened his fingers and dropped his gun. He released Gallegos. St. Bianco rolled over on the ground and climbed back onto his feet. His bonds fell away as if they'd never been tied, and then with no sign of how it occurred, there was only one of him, standing straight and powerful how Vale had first seen him, reaching for Malloy with a strange gentleness. Malloy froze, transfixed by what he saw in the dead man's face. The saint smeared blood from his ruptured eye onto his fingers then he pressed his hand to Malloy's wounded face and anointed him with it. He sketched a cross on Malloy's forehead and streaked a line beneath each of his eyes like tear tracks. Malloy peered around him at the ruins of the airport, the litter of flesh and corpses, the stinging smoke and fire, and the masses of the dead that filled the landscape to the horizon. He looked at it all as if seeing it for the first time—and understanding it in a way he never before could.

He dropped to his hands and knees and kissed the feet of St. Bianco. He sobbed. Tears streamed from his eyes. They mixed with the blood the stranger had smeared there and ran red streams over Malloy's skin. He was like a lost child greeting his rescuer.

Green grabbed Malloy's ankles and dragged him away, burying his teeth in the man's flesh with greedy enthusiasm. Malloy simply wept. He offered no resistance, not even when Green chewed his ear away from the side of his head. The others came. Together they feasted on Malloy's body and blood.

Saint Bianco knelt beside Gallegos and undid her bonds. Her clothing dripped with bloodstains from his shattered face. He whispered in her ear and then pushed her off in the direction of the truck. Crying, she stumbled, regained her balance, and then ran. She never looked back.

Gordon cleared space in the truck for Gallegos, kicked the back door open, and helped her in, locking up fast behind her. Vale watched the stranger, the holy man, the so-called Pale Saint. He cut a noble figure and gazed at them—perceiving them, Vale sensed—even through the metal and dirty glass of the truck. A chill raced through Vale, a premonition of a vast emptiness and a powerful, unending misery, of a churning sea of chaos and pain swirling around an island of peace. Then Saint Bianco raised his bloody hand and blessed them with the sign of the cross. Fresh blood pooled beneath his eyes, one a devastated ruin, the other clean and clear. The blood poured down his face.

"Oh my god," Gordon said. "Do you smell that?"

Vale looked at Gallegos. The woman smelled like a field of flowers after a fresh rain, like fine perfume, like sugar, and honey, and the richness of skin scrubbed raw with lavender-scented soap.

"It's her shirt," Gordon said. "His blood's on it."

The truck lurched. Dawson drove them to the gate and parked. Vale and Gordon helped Gallegos out of her bloody clothing. The pungent scent of saccharine viscera clung to their skin, embedded itself in their nostrils. They cleared out a plastic cooler and placed the clothing inside, handling it with care. Gordon found a clean rag and wiped away the blood that had soaked through to Gallegos' chest and abdomen then put the rag with the shirt in the cooler. Afterward Vale looked back once at the scene of destruction by the hangar. She saw no one left standing but the wormfeeders. And no sign of the stranger.

She reloaded her rifle.

Vale and Gordon jumped from the truck, ran to roll open the exit, and then scrambled back, slamming the truck door behind them. The wormfeeders came like floodwaters, the eyes of their bodies coldly focused on the truck. Vale fired into them and Gordon backed her up. The going was slow, but Dawson knew how to drive, knew all the tricks and rough spots of the ground ahead of him. Vale and Gordon sent bullets out to shatter the wormfeeders' joints, and one after another fell. Their bodies popped and bounced off the battering ram, crunched under the truck's tires, bounced off the sheets of airplane fuselage armor.

Once, peering out through the gun aperture, Vale saw Saint Bianco standing among the masses. He stared back at her, his wound a dry eruption of dead blood, his face a bisected nightmare clothed in an aura of peacefulness. He stood among the dead, one of them, but not like them, a stranger among his own kind as much as among the living. He was part light, part darkness. Vale thought of the person she had once been and the person she was now, the person she'd become. The smell of St. Bianco's blood thickened in her nostrils. She scented something sour intermingled with the sweetness, something faint yet toxic, something rotten under the lush clean aroma. She leveled her gun, caught St. Bianco in her crosshairs, and as her finger brushed the trigger…

…he vanished.

A flash of anger burned through Vale.

She put all her rage into shooting. Her body became a blur of precise movements as she took aim and fired round after round, reloaded, and continued while Dawson drove forward foot by foot and Gordon blasted scattershot with the automatic. They reached the edge of the meadow, where the ranks of the dead thinned out. The truck lurched from open ground onto paved highway, and Dawson took them north toward a junction with another road that would lead them inland to the route they would take south. The truck crested the peak of a high overpass. There were no dead around. Dawson stopped for a moment to let out the tense breath he'd been holding in and stretch his arms. Vale turned her binoculars on the airport. The hangar fire burned with the intensity of a furnace, a shining, smoking beacon for the sea of rotting atrocities that stretched out from the airport for as far as the eye could see. The pilgrimage of the dead had arrived.

Vale asked Gallegos, "What did he say to you before you ran to the truck?"

Gallegos sniffled and wiped her eyes.

"Tell me what he said." The hardness in Vale's voice surprised her.

Gordon gave her an alarmed look.

"He said…" Gallegos told them, "He said 'Blessed are the dead.'"

Vale gazed farther now, past the ruin of the makeshift home they'd abandoned, peering into the space beyond it where the earth itself seemed alive and crawling with the deep, dreary colors of the dead masses, and beyond them was only the gray palimpsest of the ocean. She imagined more dead on their way, an infinite procession, an army of rot and corruption out to claim the world. She set down the binoculars and signaled to Dawson.

The truck rolled onward. Vale hoped she would remember how to get to Campbell's farm; he had only told her the way once, on the night they spent together, when he whispered to her of his secret, safe place. But Vale doubted any place would ever be safe again, and she expected the idea of Campbell's farm would turn out to be no more real and satisfying than the peace St. Bianco had offered.

DEAD-END STREET

The moment in Christopher's life when the concept of death became a real thing didn't occur the day the dead began to walk. The living dead only made the idea of death weirder and less certain. He had never seen a dead person before then, but dead things weren't supposed to move or eat, and the rotting corpses that overran the town did both. Whenever Christopher saw them—only ever from a distance thanks to his parents— they looked like characters from a movie, or a video game, or a Halloween haunted house. Even when they killed people and ate them, even with blood smeared on their hands and faces, they still seemed somehow unreal, like a tragedy that could never happen to him or his family.

Christopher knew, of course, it could but only like he knew that dinosaurs had once walked the earth or that racecars drove more than 200 mph.

He never felt it in his bones.

At least not until after the day Dad came home alone.

That day Christopher sat watch in the attic's south gable, rifle in hand, head tilted back in the shadows of the late afternoon sun when Dad came running alone across a lawn at the corner of their dead-end block.

Christopher's first thought: *Where's Mike?*

It took at least two people to survive on the streets, and Mike and Dad always stuck close together when they went "shopping." They had ventured into town a dozen times or more since the dead forced everything to shut down, but they foraged with care and they knew their way. Seeing them round the corner at the end of the day, rifles slung, arms full of supplies, always filled Christopher with joy; when Mike and Dad came home, it signaled time to go downstairs and find out what they'd brought. Always they returned with staples like food, batteries, and medicine, but sometimes they grabbed new Hot Wheels cars or comic books for Christopher too.

This time, though, Dad carried nothing but his gun.

His torn shirt flapped with the wind, and streaks and smears of blood painted him red.

He hustled as fast as Christopher had ever seen him move.

Christopher poked the tip of his rifle through an empty windowpane and took position to cover his dad. A handful of Hot Wheels cars, lined up on the window ledge by Christopher, flanked the barrel. One, red with yellow racing stripes, the "Speed Demon," rolled off and fell to the floor. Christopher let it go and squinted at the street. He pulled the stock tight against his shoulder, letting his finger brush the trigger the way Mike had showed him, but he didn't fire when a dead man rounded the corner. Two more followed, then a woman, and still more came. They moved too slow to catch Dad, though, and Mike had made it clear he should never shoot unless he had no other choice.

Mike! Where's Mike?

The question made his heart race.

He searched every part of the street he could see but caught no sign of his big brother.

Halfway down the block, Dad paused to fire a few shots at the dead, knocking down two of them. After that, he ran straight for home. He passed the white garden fence along the edge of the lawn and moved from Christopher's sight up the front walk. Christopher withdrew his rifle then flipped down the wooden cover rigged above the open windowpane. He grabbed his cars and stuffed them into his pockets. Then he bolted down the attic stairs.

While he raced along the upstairs hallway, he heard the front door open. Mom yelled for Dad to get inside. A moment later the door slammed shut and all the locks and braces clicked into place one after another. Halfway down the next flight of stairs, Christopher heard the dead crash against the reinforced entrance. They pounded on the hurricane shutters over the windows, closed since the first corpse had been sighted on their street. The clatter rattled loud even through the boards nailed over windows on the inside.

The noise startled Christopher. He leapt the last three steps to the first floor.

Mom and Dad sat in the living room. His father panted and held onto Mom to steady himself as he wiped blood from his face with a towel she'd handed him.

"Dad! Are you okay?" Christopher asked. "Where's Mike?"

"Hush," Mom told him.

She opened Dad's torn shirt and exposed a shallow, red gash from his left shoulder to the center of his chest. She dabbed at it with the shirttail, but then Dad grabbed her hand.

"Leave it…" he said. He breathed heavily and struggled to speak. "It's only… a cut."

"Dad, where's Mike?" Christopher asked. "Why isn't he with you?"

"Chris… I'm so sorry…" Dad said. "There were half a dozen of them… cooped up in the manager's office in Walgreens… Caught Mike by surprise…. Nothing I could do…. One second he was there… then they were *all over him*… I'm so sorry…. Almost got me too… one of them scratched me…"

Dad glanced down at his wound and winced. He let go of Mom's hand, and as if his touch had been the only thing keeping her on her feet, she slumped to the floor and sobbed. Dad knelt beside her and wrapped his arms around her. They cried, pressed tight together, shaking, and tried to comfort each other. Christopher felt uncomfortable watching them. He didn't understand what had happened. Dad had lost track of Mike in Walgreens, but then where did Mike go after that? He walked to the front door, raised the cover on the block glass spy window his father had made, and stared out.

The dead roamed everywhere on the block. It had happened before, dead mobs crowding the street, trapping them in the house, once for seven straight days until the herd dispersed. To pass the time they'd played cards and board games, and Mike had even helped Christopher win a few hands of poker. Even more of the dead filled the block now. Christopher rarely saw so many so close. He thought their faces looked like rubber masks, and it made his skin crawl to see the strange eyes staring out from their necks and hands, from their arms and shoulders, backs, chests, from all over their bodies. He didn't like to look at them, but he couldn't leave the window, couldn't stop watching the corner, hoping to see Mike running hard, fighting his way through the dead to reach home. If he didn't make it soon he'd have to find a place to hide for the night.

Granddad's footsteps shuffled in the front hallway, paused by the entrance to the living room, and then resumed until he stood close enough to touch Christopher's shoulder.

"Mike didn't come home, huh?" he said, wheezing between his words.

Christopher shook his head.

"You looking for him out there?"

"Yes," Christopher said.

"What'll you do if you see him?"

"Open the door." Christopher patted his rifle. "Give him cover."

Granddad shook his head. "If you see him—out there with them, with the dead—you know that's not Mike anymore, right? You can't let him in. You know that?"

Christopher shrugged.

"I know it's hard to understand, but those things aren't alive like us. They aren't people. Same goes for Mike, me, even your Mom or Dad, even you, if any of us ever die and come back. That happens, we're already gone, okay? You get as far away from us as you can. Mike's gone now. You see Mike again, it's not the real Mike unless you meet him in Heaven, and God willing that won't be for a long time to come."

Christopher didn't answer; he resumed looking out the window.

A burst of sobbing came from the living room. Dad said the same thing over and over: "I'm sorry, I'm so sorry."

Granddad took Christopher's rifle and slung it on his shoulder. "You got all your cars?"

"No," Christopher said. "I left one in the attic."

"You want to go get it?"

"I can get it tomorrow."

"Okay, come downstairs with me for a while. Let your folks be. They need some time."

In the basement, Christopher and his grandfather played checkers and cards until Mom called them up for dinner. Her eyes glistened red from crying. Dad wore fresh clothes and had cleaned the blood from his face, but red spots seeped through the bandages on his chest and shoulder. His pale hands trembled.

For a time, they sat in silence. Christopher and Granddad ate, but Dad only pushed food around on his dish, and Mom left her plate empty. Dad spoke first. He told about last week when Mike saved him from three of the dead; they'd come out of an abandoned minivan and crept to within a few feet of him before Mike opened fire on the closest one, buying him time to run clear. Next, Mom talked about how Mike always rushed to help her carry in the groceries or took out the garbage without being asked. Granddad remembered practicing baseball with Mike when he still played Little League. Christopher told about the time Mike took him to a monster truck show last summer.

"Maybe we can go see the trucks again next summer when the dead people go away and the show comes around. I'd really like that," he said. "Because Mike's so fast and tough he's probably okay. I mean, if Dad couldn't *see* what happened to him, maybe he got away. Maybe he hasn't come home yet cause of all the dead guys on the block. He has to hide until they leave."

After that, the silence returned. Then Mom went into the kitchen and cried.

When they finished dinner and cleared the table, they locked themselves in the basement as they did every night, settled into sleeping bags on mattresses laid on the floor, and went to sleep.

A few days passed.

Mike didn't come home.

Mom and Dad spent a lot of time talking to Christopher about what had happened to Mike and reassuring him that they'd keep him safe. Christopher didn't doubt them; but he didn't think Mike was really gone either. He believed his big brother much too smart and quick to let the dumb, slow dead things get him. Even the ones outside only bumped and groped at the house until they seemed to forget what they wanted and pretty soon they wandered off and the crowd on the block thinned out. Only half a dozen still wandered the street when the army trucks rolled through town.

The rumble of the vehicles shook the ground, and staccato gunshots cracked the air. Christopher heard the reports from blocks away. When the trucks reached his street, he saw through the spy window that the men riding in the truck beds fired machine guns. Some of the trucks sported armor and had treads; others had heavy tires and open beds; and a few shaded the men under canvas covers. The line of them slowed at his corner, and the soldiers opened fire on all the dead, spraying them with bullets, shooting their legs out from under them. The corpses fell then lay in the road and twitched. Soldiers in torn, dirty uniforms leapt out of the trucks with machetes and axes and approached the bodies. Many of the men's rank insignia had been torn away. Out of all the soldiers, Christopher counted only three with American flag patches on their uniforms.

While the soldiers moved in the street, Dad made everyone go downstairs then locked the door behind them. They sat in the basement with their guns in their hands and waited until the trucks rumbled away and quiet descended again before they went upstairs and looked. The army men had hacked the bodies to pieces and then piled them in the middle of the road and lit them on fire. A column of oily smoke swirled up to the sky.

"Maybe they could've helped us," Mom said. "Maybe they know a safe place."

"They wouldn't have helped us," Dad said. "They looked lawless. We're as safe here as anywhere. Safer, even. It's only when we go out there…"

Dad's voice trailed off, silenced, Christopher guessed, by thoughts of Mike, out there on his own, surviving by his wits, like a hero in one of his comic books.

Maybe Mike would hook up with the soldiers.

Maybe he would save them from a dead attack, and then they'd owe him one and have to help him, like Mom said. They'd have to protect them.

A few days later, the time came to go into town for food.

Only so much could be brought home on foot, but Dad refused to risk driving because the first time he'd tried it, the car noise had attracted the dead, and he'd had to turn back before he reached town. Another time, he and Mike had wheeled home loaded shopping carts, but the squeaky wheels and rattling metal cages caused the same problem.

With Mike missing, Dad wanted Christopher to come with him, but Mom said no, he was too young, and Granddad was too old, so it had to be her. Dad didn't want her to leave the house, but going without someone to watch your back meant dying. The dead walked so quietly sometimes they could sneak right up on you. Christopher sat watch in the attic while his parents walked up the street and out of sight around the corner. Then he lined his cars up on the ledge, retrieving the one he'd dropped and adding it to the row. He hadn't been in the attic since the day they "lost" Mike. Christopher had gotten lost downtown once when he was five and wandered off on a street he didn't know. Every turn took him deeper into unfamiliar places. He was gone twenty minutes before his parents found him, and they'd been almost as teary-eyed and upset then as they were about Mike.

Maybe, Christopher thought, *they'll find Mike like they did me and bring him home.*

The attic stairs creaked.

Christopher stopped playing with his cars.

Granddad pulled himself into the attic then settled in a rocking chair in the corner and smiled at Christopher.

"Why'd you come all the way up here, Granddad?" Christopher said. "Don't the stairs hurt your knees?"

Granddad wheezed. "I didn't want you to be alone."

"I've got my rifle and my cars," Christopher said. "But it's better with you here. Thanks, Granddad."

"Your mom and dad will be fine, you know." Granddad settled back and rocked a little. "Your dad's a smart man. Smarter than

I gave him credit for when I first met him. I remember then I worried that my daughter would marry an electrician instead of a doctor or a lawyer, but he's good to her, and to you. And he's taken good care of us through this crazy thing. What happened to Mike wasn't his fault. They were caught by surprise. Could've happened to anyone. There's always risk. You understand, Christopher? In life, there is *always* risk. Risk is part of survival. If you take no risks then you're like those things outside—you're still moving around, but you're dead. The trick is to take smart risks. Try to put the odds in your favor, only take risks when there's something worthwhile to be gained, and know exactly what you're risking. Mike was good at that. He had a knack for sizing up a situation and making it work for him. But sometimes even if we do our best things go against us. That's part of life too."

"Yeah, I guess," Christopher said.

"Don't guess. Be sure," Granddad said. "Be sure of yourself, of what you know, of what you choose to do, and who you do it with. Doubt will only kill you."

"How can doubt kill me?"

"It can make you hesitate when you should act. It can make you second-guess yourself. It can cloud your judgment." Granddad rubbed his eyes and coughed for a minute. "Huh, climbing up here really took it out of me. Let me rest my eyes a bit then we'll talk more."

Granddad shut his eyes and nodded off. His chair stopped rocking.

Christopher turned back to the window and listened to him wheezing while he fiddled with his cars. Through the trees and the narrow slivers between houses, he glimpsed things moving on the nearby blocks and in neighboring yards. The dead, he figured, but he never saw them clear enough to be sure. He only knew it wasn't Mike because Mike would've come straight home if he could've, especially if he was that close.

No doubt about it. Christopher was *sure*, like Granddad said.

The old man snored.

Christopher felt a little sleepy himself, but nervous energy kept his eyes open, and anyway he wasn't supposed to sleep on watch. He had to be ready whenever Mom and Dad came home.

Besides, maybe the army guys would come back, and he'd get a better view of them.

Or maybe Mike would come walking around the corner.

Instead, only the dead came.

A scattered group of them staggered down the street.

Christopher lined them up in his sights, practicing his aim, but he didn't fire. The dead things were too stupid to look up and see him in the window. No point in giving himself away. He began to worry when more and more of them wandered onto the block. They kept coming, spreading out among the abandoned houses. If they didn't leave before dark, Mom and Dad would be cut off. Now and then a few left the street, but more came to replace them. Christopher tried to count them all but lost track after twenty; they were moving around too much. Then something familiar caught his eye—a flash of red and yellow and a patch of blue. A shirt and shorts on one of the dead people. The crowd obscured his view, but he knew who the clothes belonged to. The dead shifted, and he glimpsed his brother's face.

"Mike!" he shouted.

He pulled his rifle in, slung it, and then shook Granddad twice before he scrambled down the attic stairs, shouting, "It's Mike, Granddad! Mike's home!"

Christopher was already topping the next flight of stairs when his granddad shouted for him to stop and wait. He kept going. He ignored his granddad's heavy footfalls on the attic steps and his pleas for him to wait. He ignored the muted noises of the dead coming from outside, the moaning and rattling of empty throats, the scuffling of dozens of feet, the noises always louder on the second floor. He ran as fast as he could down the stairs and to the front door, threw open the spy window, and pressed his eye up against it.

Mike mounted the curb. He stepped onto the strip of lawn along the sidewalk and crept forward until he reached the gate and the top of the front walk. He stopped. His gun was gone, his clothes were torn, and the left side of his neck was shredded to ribbons and coated with a dry, black crust. Wounds peppered his body.

He stared at the house as if struggling to remember it.

Christopher placed his hand on the top lock.

"Mike!" he shouted.

If Mike or any of the dead heard him, he couldn't tell.

His fingers twisted the lock half way.

Mike took two steps.

Christopher yelled his brother's name again.

Mike took another step and turned away. He stumbled back down the curb and let the dead crowd swallow him. Christopher's fingers dropped from the lock.

He wanted to open the door, rush out, and drag Mike inside, but he was listening to the echo of Granddad's words: *You see Mike again, it's not the real Mike....*

"Mike...?" he said.

The thing outside looked like Mike, and it wore Mike's clothes—but Mike would never have forgotten his home, never would've walked away when he was so close.

That wasn't Mike.

Granddad came thumping downstairs, wheezing louder than ever, shouting at Christopher to get away from the door, to leave it closed, but when he reached the front entrance, Christopher was nowhere near the door and all the locks and braces were secure.

"Thank... God..." Granddad said.

He leaned over and steadied himself on his knees, gasping for air, and then broke into a fit of shallow coughing. Christopher waited until Granddad's coughing subsided then pointed at the spy window.

"Look."

Granddad pressed his face to the window.

"Is he still there?" Christopher asked.

Granddad nodded. He crossed the little foyer and hugged Christopher against him.

Christopher shivered. He breathed in the scent of his Granddad's old clothes, old skin, old breath, and hugged him back.

"Mike didn't know he was home," Christopher said. "He looked right at our house and then he walked away."

"That isn't Mike," Granddad said. "It isn't him."

"I know," Christopher said. "I know. Mike's gone."

"Yes, yes," Granddad said. "But we're still here."

The tears Christopher had denied for days broke free then and washed over his cheeks.

Granddad hugged him tighter and helped him into the living room. They sat down on the couch. Christopher balanced his rifle across his knees and eyed the bloodstains his Dad's wound had left in the carpet. Granddad kept his arm around his shoulder. The voices of the dead carried on outside, reminding Christopher how the world used to sound when his neighbors had barbecues and backyard parties. Those days were gone. Riding his bike, gone; school, and going to the movies and the library, and visiting his cousins on the other side of town, all gone. Like Mike was gone. Christopher shoved his hands in his pockets, pulled out his cars, and counted them. All there. Even the one he'd dropped. The sight of them soothed him a little. His crying subsided. Granddad nodded off, wheezing as usual, and Christopher sat and listened to the sounds of the new world outside.

His tears had stopped coming. He didn't know how much time had passed when he heard the deep, distant rumbling of trucks.

He shimmied loose from Granddad's arm and looked out the spy window.

The dead still filled the street. They cast long shadows in the low sun. Mom and Dad should've been back by now, and Christopher began to fear they might've been lost as Mike had been. The growl of the truck engines grew louder, and soon one of the armored vehicles on treads Christopher had seen the other day appeared at the corner. It crossed the intersection and stopped on the other side. An open truck pulled up behind it and blocked the street. Another armored truck stopped behind that one. Soldiers hopped down from all three. Some of them stopped to help a couple from the middle one.

Mom and Dad. They held hands as the soldiers directed them down the street. They had no packages and no guns.

The dead gravitated toward them, but the soldiers cut them down with machine gun fire.

A flash of light stung Christopher's eyes—a flamethrower lancing into the crowd of the dead. The walking corpses burned and fell over.

The soldiers advanced, bringing Mom and Dad with them, moving straight for the house.

They're coming to help, Christopher thought.

He reached to open the first lock but hesitated. His parents had told him he was never to open the door to anyone but his family and his family *alone*. He wondered where his parents' had lost their guns and why they were surrounded by soldiers. His father hadn't trusted the military men, and Christopher knew things weren't always what they seemed. Like Mike, who was dead but still moving around, looking like his brother, but not him, not anymore. Death changed the living as much as the dead, maybe even more, and he didn't understand why the soldiers were coming to his house.

Were they brining Mom and Dad home?

Coming for him and Granddad?

He ran to the living room and called Granddad. The old man slept on the sofa. Christopher shook him, but he didn't wake up. Going up and down the stairs after Christopher had exhausted him.

Outside, machine gun fire rattled.

Christopher darted back to the window. Soldiers approached up the front walk. Mom and Dad stood at the curb. Christopher had never thought of his parents as being old, but they looked so now—old and tired and frightened. The dead strayed all around held back only by the soldier's weapons.

The lead soldier, a bald man with a thick mustache, pounded on the door.

Christopher jolted back.

"Hello," the soldier called. "You in there? Open up. It's not safe out here."

Christopher crept back to the window and studied his parents' faces. What did they want him to do? Why didn't they come to the door? Why weren't they speaking?

The soldier hit the door again. "We've got your parents here. Open up and let us in."

Christopher saw loose threads and rips in the cloth of the man's uniform where his rank insignia and a nametag should've been. He didn't want to open the door. But Mom and Dad were there. Except why wouldn't the soldiers let them to the door? Why didn't they say anything?

The solider knocked with the butt of his rifle. The sound echoed through the house; it hammered Christopher's ears. Granddad said he shouldn't guess, he shouldn't doubt, but he didn't know what to do. He only knew that the longer he left his parents out there with the dead, the more likely something bad would happen to them.

The solider pounded on the door. "Open up already!"

Christopher reached up and undid the top lock then glanced out the window.

The soldier stepped back from the door.

Mom and Dad waited at the curb, both so pale.

Christopher opened the rest of the locks and removed the braces, leaving only the door's original deadbolt slid home. Once he turned that, he could open the door.

The living room sofa creaked. Granddad shuffled into the foyer.

"There are soldiers here with Mom and Dad," Christopher told him. "They're out there with a lot of the dead things. I don't know what to do. Should we let them in?"

Granddad moved to the spy window, but he didn't look through it.

"Granddad, what should I do?" Christopher asked.

Granddad gave no answer, didn't even wheeze.

Christopher looked at him and screamed.

Granddad's face was ashen and drawn. His mouth hung open as if his jaw was broken, and his eyes were glassy and dark. An eye had sprouted open on his neck. It stared at Christopher with what that felt like hate. Christopher swung his rifle off his shoulder, but Granddad lurched too close for him to use it, trapping Christopher in the foyer with only one way to go. He flipped the deadbolt, grabbed the knob, and opened the door.

He tripped out onto the front steps and stumbled to the walkway.

Granddad came after him.

Mom and Dad screamed as the old man emerged from the house. Dad tried to run to Christopher, but one of the soldiers hit him in the side of the head with the stock of his gun, and he dropped to his knees. Another grabbed Mom's arms, yanked them behind her back, and pulled her into the street. The soldier with the mustache raised his rifle and fired a barrage of shots into Granddad, forcing him back into the house.

Christopher ran through the yard, but everywhere he turned the dead waited for him. They were too close for him to take a shot. He used his rifle to beat them back and moved fast to avoid their hands until one of the dead grabbed his gun away from him. Off balance, Christopher fell on his neighbor's lawn. The dead converged on him, their stench so repulsive Christopher thought he might throw up. He scrambled away, nowhere left to go.

Only the soldiers saved him. They swept in with flame throwers and machine guns to repel the dead and then grabbed Christopher and rushed him clear.

They all ran back down the street, Christopher carried in the bald soldier's arms, Mom and Dad herded by the other men. The trucks cruised down the block to meet them. The soldier threw Christopher into the back of the open truck where more soldiers dragged him down out of their line of fire.

Christopher pulled himself up and peered over the side of the truck.

The dead had overrun three of the soldiers and Dad. The other soldiers fired on them, ripping them apart with bullets. His dad twisted then collapsed. More soldiers were running into the house and coming out with the food and supplies Dad and Mike had gathered. On a neighbor's lawn, the dead cut off Mom with two soldiers. Among them was Mike. Christopher watched Mom go to him, arms open, tears pouring down her face; he watched Mike bite into her neck and drag her to the ground. Then fire spewed from one of the flamethrowers, igniting mother and son, igniting the dead around them, and even the soldiers they'd attacked.

Christopher knew that wasn't his mom anymore, or his dad lying on the street with dead things chewing on his limbs. His granddad was not his granddad. The soldiers weren't soldiers.

No more than he was the boy he'd once been.

Even the cars in his pockets had changed—no longer treasured toys but mementos of a life that no longer existed. He didn't understand how everything had transformed, but he knew it would never go back to the way it was. The sense of it churned, impossible to absorb in so little time. This was death; this was grief, emptiness, and finality. Death could claim the living as well as the dead—unless the living found a way to carry on. Of that Christopher had no doubt.

He had to be. Or he was dead.

Granddad was right

When the little convoy fled from his block, Christopher hunkered down in the truck bed.

Smoke from burning corpses spilled into the sky, smoke from his mother's corpse, and his brother's, but not his father's, who would rise with the dead. He stared at it and ignored the questions the soldiers asked him and the taunts they directed at him. He said nothing when they told him how they would put him to work until he grew old enough to fight. He showed no reaction when they joked about how his mom and dad died or how they'd cut his granddad's corpse to ribbons with machine guns and left him in the living room.

He only waited until the trucks rolled past the park on the edge of town.

Then he took a risk.

He leapt so quickly, he hit the ground before the soldiers realized what he'd done. He hit hard, the speed of the truck spinning him over the rough earth of the shoulder.

A blast of pain exploded in his left leg. It filled up his body, blinding him for a moment. Then he moved, limping but running as best he could into the nearby trees. He dashed out of sight before the first gunshots came, and none of them hit him as they ripped leaves and chipped bark from the trees all around him. The soldiers came after him. He reached the crest of a hill he'd climbed many times before the dead came back to life, threw himself over the side of it, and rolled, tumbling, bouncing off of stones and tree branches. More pain came. He threw his arms over his head and face to protect them. The soldier's voices faded. Christopher struck the bottom of the hill, rolled under a fallen tree, and hid in the shadows.

The soldiers never came down the hill.

After a while, they left.

Afraid to stay in one place through the night, Christopher limped along, using a tree branch to hold himself up. He found a trail and traced it through the woods to an old road on the far side of town. There the pain overwhelmed him. He fell by the side of the road, too exhausted, in too much agony to get up again.

He wrapped his hand around the red-and-yellow "Speed Demon" he'd dropped the day they lost Mike. The last thing he heard before he blacked out was the sound of an engine approaching. He prayed it wouldn't be another truck full of soldiers.

A ZOMBIE ATE MY BOARDING PASS

FLIGHT DELAYS

After publication of an early version of "The Dead Bear Witness" in *The Dead Walk* (2004), an anthology editor contacted me about writing a piece for a book of new zombie stories. We hadn't worked together before, and I didn't know him, but he'd read and liked "The Dead Bear Witness." I was flattered that he'd taken the time to find me and e-mail me, so I agreed to do a story. I requested the guidelines, and those I received were pretty loose—too loose as it turned out (at least with regard to acceptable story length). But I didn't know that when I began writing what has become *Tears of Blood*. If I had, I don't know if it would've made much difference in what I wrote; I was too excited to revisit the *Corpse Fauna* world.

The moment I finished writing the first version of *The Dead Bear Witness* (the first *Corpse Fauna* story), I knew there were more stories to be told in this cycle. If for no other reasons because I liked Cornell too much not to spend more time with him and the end of *TDBW* is very much the beginning of another story—one told in *The Dead, in Their Masses*, volume three of this series. But I also wanted to meet some of the other survivors of the dead plague and explore the world beyond Cornell's experiences. In creating my *Corpse Fauna* dead, I'd changed one popular convention of zombie fiction—how the dead can be destroyed—and given them a unique feature—the strange eyes that appear on and in their bodies. I wanted to see where those elements might lead me.

As I thought about where to go next, a few things fell into place.

The first was the setting: an airport.

George Romero's living dead movies were among the inspirations for *Corpse Fauna*, and in Romero's movies, the setting is much more than simply where the action happens; it's an essential part of the story. The farmhouse in *Night of the Living Dead*. The shopping mall in *Dawn of the Dead*. The underground military base in *Day of the Dead*. The luxury housing complex in *Land of the Dead*. The RV in *Diary of the Dead*. The island in *Survivors of the Dead*. All of these places add depth and layers to the story. They help shape the themes. They further the satirical and social commentary that I consider an important part of what defines modern zombie fiction. Many other monsters have their favorite haunts seen time and again in film and fiction: werewolves in the woods; ghosts in empty old houses; slashers stalking campsites and lonely cabins; vampires hanging out in castles, crypts, and Goth nightclubs. Locations are no less important for the walking dead, but they have more options. Any setting will do for them so long as it adds weight to the story.

The idea of a group of survivors living trapped in a place meant for transients appealed to me. Anyone who's flown even only a handful of times has likely experienced a late or canceled flight. No one likes hanging around the airport; no one enjoys sitting hours on a plane, waiting for it to take off. No one enjoys the stasis of epic air travel fail. That's how I saw Actsburg Airport fitting into *Tears of Blood*. The people in this story would go anywhere in the world to get away from the living dead, if only there was anywhere safe to go. They have the means to travel, but instead, they are reduced to cannibalizing airplanes for armor, forced into a sort of living death almost as final as that of the living dead. Even more enticing, this meshed well with the protagonist I had in mind: Vale.

DEADEYE VALE

Vale rose from a simple idea: No matter how bad things seem in a crisis or a disaster, there's almost always someone who benefits rather than suffers. Maybe it's the guy who makes up his mind to buy a new car the day before a hurricane drops a tree on his old one and nets him a nice check from the insurance company. Maybe it's the woman whose abusive husband drowns in a flash flood. It could even be someone whose brush with tragedy reminds him or her of what life's really about. Looking at the dead plague this way, I came up with Vale.

Vale's life before the dead plague was the definition of ordinary.

Pleasant, controlled, prefabricated—but empty and devoid of challenge.

I asked myself how someone living that life might react to her entire world being stripped away and destroyed. Would she break down? Would she go insane? Would she die a victim? Or would the horror and loss surrounding her stir the strength sleeping inside her and bring her fully to life for the first time? If you're reading this book in the right order, you already know the answer.

When the world changes, some people pine for the old ways.

A few walk forward and never look back, no matter how hard, ugly, or shocking the new reality may be. This sets them apart from the masses of humanity; it separates the living from the dead, literally in Tears of Blood, figuratively in the real world.

Vale's talent as a shooter reflects that reality.

It's the one thing she's truly gifted with, the thing she does best, the thing she was meant to do. It defines her. And she never would've known it if not for the dead plague because her old world had no use for it.

On a side note: I wrote the first draft of "Crying Tears of Blood, Sweet Like Honey," many months before the release of Romero's *Land of the Dead*, which also features a character with an uncanny talent for shooting. It was pure coincidence. I considered scrapping that element of the story out of deference to the master and to avoid unwarranted comparisons. However, after some deliberation, I concluded that the characters and their roles in their respective stories are vastly different and so I chose to leave things as they were.

BLESSED ARE THE DEAD

Before Vale there was Saint Bianco.

Or Saint Pacifica, in the original version of this story.

This was another of those first few things that fell into place for *Tears of Blood*. It came from wondering what would happen if a corpse that wasn't rotting—a corpse that *couldn't* rot—became one of the living dead. There are many stories of saints and other holy men and women whose bodies don't decay after death. Their purity and holiness, it is said, were so great that they defied putrefaction. And if their bodies, then why not their minds, and perhaps even their souls?

It was only after writing the story that I realized what a linchpin this idea would become in the Corpse Fauna cycle—and that I hadn't seen the last of Saint Bianco. (The name change came about because "Pacifica" seemed too unlikely and facetious to me when I revisited the story.)

This idea and the others were already knocking around my mind when I received the e-mail that started me writing the story. When I was done "Crying Tears of Blood, Sweet Like Honey" existed in much the form in which it was first published.

That publication, however, was not in the anthology for which it was written.

Because the anthology guidelines gave no limit on length, only a minimum, I'd written the story on the long side, roughly in the same range as the original version of "The Dead Bear Witness." Since the editor had cited that story as his reason for contacting me, I assumed the length would be acceptable. I turned it in before my deadline and waited. After a short time, the editor declined to use it due to the length. I offered to make cuts, of course, but he had already received more stories than he needed, so that didn't make sense. A simple misunderstanding had bumped me from the book.

Yet, it worked out okay for me.

I soon sold the story to Kevin Donihe, who loves zombies and published it in issue nine of *Bare Bone* magazine in 2006. The anthology for which it was first written—to the best of my knowledge—has never been published.

With this new publication, Tears of Blood is almost three times its original length, extended mainly by the addition of a new section, "Vale's Dark Days," and with deeper characterization and more details about the events of the story.

I hope you have enjoyed it.

—James Chambers
January 2012
Resurrected / August 2019

THE DEAD IN THEIR MASSES

FOR BILL, WHO REHEARSED
SO ENTHUSIASTICALLY
FOR THE ZOMBIE MOVIE THAT NEVER WAS.

Whitley 2019

THE DEAD IN THEIR MASSES

ONE

Turned out Lohatchie was a long way off, and the road there a hard bastard with a chip on its shoulder. It got rough the second we broke out of Warden Lane Grove's prison, but even so, none of us would've ever willingly gone back inside. Della, Mason, and I took the only way left open to us: out into the dark and dying world. So we fought past the living dead things that came for us. We beat them back, and we cut them down, and we left them lying broken in the mud and grass. And we ran. Until stitches of pain laced our sides and we panted for breath, we ran. And when the crowds of the dead that crammed against the prison walls thinned out and fell behind us, we pushed ourselves harder still, stopping to fight only when the wormfeeders came too close or swarmed us too deep to go around them. We crossed the wooded hills by sparse moonlight, chipping away step by step at the twelve-mile stretch between the prison and Mason's house. We fled from hundreds of the dead, put down three dozen or more, and took our fair share of scrapes and bruises along the way. Mason got the worst of it when he slipped down a hill onto a pile of deadfall that gouged a six-inch gash in his leg. Della dressed it tight with a handkerchief, and we kept moving. The dead lurked everywhere, and the night seemed endless—but at least we were free. That thought kept me moving all night until, in the hour before dawn, we reached Mason's house.

We approached the back door through a yard overgrown with neglected grass and tangled weeds. A child's play set shone dully in the morning twilight. On the edge of a half-finished patio stood a barbecue grill draped in canvas spotted with bird droppings. Behind it lay a pile of bricks beside a rusty wheelbarrow. It all seemed so ordinary, so quiet except for the moans of the wormfeeders carrying through the air. But for a blessed moment, there wasn't a dead thing anywhere in sight, so we seized the chance to scramble into the house unobserved.

After we locked up tight and covered the windows, Mason lived up to the promise he'd made before we left and fed us. We ate only canned food and powdered drinks made with bottled water, but my first meal as a free man since I'd been arrested and gone inside tasted like a feast. Later, our bellies full, we took turns showering while the sun came up. Afterward, Mason gave me some of his old clothes to change into so I could shuck my orange prison suit. He let Della pick what she wanted from his wife's wardrobe. Then we slept for twelve hours straight and awoke after dark.

Only we three out of the group that had planned the prison break made it out alive. Before the dead plague, Della had been a nurse in the prison infirmary and Mason a guard. They'd known each other since high school, not friends exactly, but a hell of lot better than either of them knew me. I'd only been on the inside for few months—one of them spent in solitary—when the dead began to rise and the world went to shit. I wondered how they felt having to put their trust in a bank robber, a killer, and now, I suppose, a fugitive too. Not that anyone remained to hunt me down. And anyone who tried would have to make their way past all the living dead folks roaming around outside, same as we did. The same as we'd have to do all over again when we set out for my place in Lohatchie.

Mason's house offered us food and comfort, sure, but not safety.

The dead filled his street and more kept coming from the east, from the direction of the prison, where thousands of them remained only a few hours walk away. They'd seen us pass by in the night and come looking for us. They sensed us hiding—fresh, live meat for them to sniff out like pigs rooting for truffles. They searched for us with cloudy, dead eyes and the incongruously bright eyes that gazed out from the wrinkled slits on the backs of their hands, on their necks and shoulders, and their chests and legs where clothes had rotted away. Those terrifying and inexplicable eyes where none should be. None of us understood them or what they meant, but the dead didn't care what we thought. They simply stalked the block, waiting for some sign of our hiding spot, and though we made sure not to give ourselves away, the longer we stayed at Mason's the more likely our luck would run out like luck always did.

If we'd stuck to my plan, we would've packed Mason's car with food and gear that night and gone on our way the next morning before more of the dead moved into the neighborhood. But right around midnight Mason collapsed. One minute he stood by the picture window, spying through the blinds at half a dozen wormfeeders struggling along the street, and the next, he staggered, gasped, and then folded to the floor. I lifted him onto the couch so Della could tend to him. He burned fiery with fever, and sweat soaked his clothes. We undressed him. The skin around the bloody furrow in his leg flared crimson and pus crusted the wound. Infection had set in, and Mason had bled much more than we realized. I knew then it'd be a while before we went anywhere.

Fortunately for Mason, Della was a damn good nurse, and she had brought along a variety of antibiotics, which she fed to Mason and made sure he swallowed. It still took three days of care to get him back on his feet. We spent most of that time in the living room, Mason on the couch, each of us afraid to leave his side, to leave each other alone. While Della nursed him, I saw the sparks of a deeper bond forming between them, and I figured that no matter how much I helped them, no matter how long we stuck together or how close the three of us might get in the coming days, the time would come when I'd be the odd man out.

I came from a different place than Mason and Della, and it didn't matter that the entire world had fallen into chaos. Except for the dead not staying that way, the rules of nature hadn't changed. Like would still gravitate to like. On one hand, Mason, rugged and all-star handsome, a man with a clean record, a gentle touch, and a fearless light burning in his eyes, and on the other hand, me—a smartass killer wanted in nine states before the FBI locked me up. The kind of man Della had spent her life despising, the kind Mason had worked to keep behind bars. I had become the savior they were counting on to guide them to a safe home, but once I'd done that—maybe they'd turn on me, maybe not. But they'd never consider me one of them.

That's all it took for there to be *us* and *them.*

I tried to put it out of my mind while we waited for Mason to heal.

I felt sorry for him, suffering in a house full of reminders of what he'd lost in the dead plague. Framed photos of his family. A spilled basket of Transformers figures and Hot Wheels cars. Women's magazines left open on the kitchen table, never picked up again. Della told me about the last time Mason had seen his family alive: They'd come to the prison, his wife and two boys, with a busload of refugees begging protection behind the walls. Not only did that son of a bitch Grove turn them away, claiming it was God's will they were on the outside when the dead plague began, but he ordered his guards to fire on them. His idea of mercy. The ones who died got up and killed the rest. And Grove made Mason watch.

That marked the real difference between me and Mason.

He'd bought into the game, played by the rules, and worked hard for everything he had, but when it mattered most the rules of the game changed and stole all the things he valued. Pretty much how it always goes when you're dealing with authority. Those with power may treat you right when times are good and they're feeling generous, but they never let too much slack in your leash. They like to keep you close and controlled. I'd never given a damn for all that happy good citizen bullshit. What Mason lost had been taken from him. Everything I'd ever had, I'd taken for myself, and when I lost it all, I lost it myself too. I got Evelyn and our unborn child killed during the last bank job we pulled. I shot the bank manager who killed her to death, along with the two guards backing him up. Then I ate a life sentence like a sap because I thought I didn't deserve any better. But I'd left all that back inside the prison walls and made my peace with it. I wanted my freedom again, and that's why Della and Mason would never fully trust me. We simply didn't play by the same rules.

Understanding that got me thinking more than once while Mason healed and the dead gathered around us that I should take the car and light out on my own. I couldn't do it, though. Even if some day down the line they did toss me away like garbage, I couldn't leave Della and Mason trapped to die; I could be driven to kill but I wasn't a killer by nature. I only hoped Mason would heal fast so we could be on our way before it became impossible to drive a car down the street.

As it turned out, we cut it damn close. The same day Mason finally got back up on his feet long enough to move around, a couple of wormfeeders camped out in his yard. Their rotting, hungry faces stared at the front door like they saw right through it. Eyes on their foreheads and cheeks, on their arms and abdomens watched and waited. Three more arrived by twilight, another four before midnight, zeroing in on us, and we noticed then how they seemed to be hardening, their flesh turning leathery, the spread of rot arrested, as if they were toughening up, hardening into some final form, another mystery none of us knew how to explain. That night we packed the car, a black Toyota Camry with nearly a full tank of gas, in Mason's attached garage and prepared for our trip to Lohatchie, to my cabin there in the Everglades, far and away from anything like civilization or what little remained of it, a place so isolated we hoped we might be able live in peace there.

The next morning, we hit the road.

TWO

The dead chased us down the street. They flooded out from the yards and houses, forming a gray wedge of walking decay that clamored after us as Mason floored it to the corner, cut the wheel, and sent us barreling down the road toward town. Under different circumstances, the sight of those dumb corpses stumbling and tripping over each other as they shrank into the distance behind us might have been comical, but I didn't feel much like laughing. We'd cut it a lot closer than I'd liked.

Another day—hell, even a few more hours—and the dead would've been too dense to drive past without slowing down and fighting our way through them, and how the world worked now, speed and motion equaled life, while death waited for the slow or timid.

Mason's car held up well despite the beating it took from bad roads and sudden impacts with occasional wormfeeders too clumsy to get out of the way. As we drove out of town with the roar of the engine thundering in the quiet, I thought about how we were running down the new American dream: living long enough to reach a three-room swamp shack where no one would ever come knocking, hoping we could live there free from the smothering crush of the dead, and maybe when we died, not get back up again. After our first day of driving, though, I got the idea the road itself was dead set against us. Things worsened the closer we drove toward town, but they didn't get horrendous until we tried to take the highway. All six lanes, north and south, resembled a scrap yard patrolled by the dead instead of junk-yard dogs. I'd expected it to be bad, but when Mason stopped the car at the top of the entrance ramp, more than a hundred wormfeeders turned and stared at us from the rows of immobile cars, their attention drawn by our presence. As far as I could see in both directions along the highway, more of the dead wandered. The stench coming off the road made me nauseous. I rolled up the window as Mason threw the car into reverse and guided us toward the back roads, the only ones left passable.

Houses and stores rolled by, and Mason asked me, "How long did you figure the drive would take?"

"North Carolina to South Florida? About fifteen hours driving straight through, so I figured two or three days things being what they are," I said. "But I sure as hell didn't count on that."

Della leaned between us from the back seat. "Better accept it's going to be a long trip, boys."

"Shit." The word left my lips on a long breath.

Della proved right. It got no easier as we headed south. The longer we traveled broken roads populated only by the rotting dead, the more I felt like a helpless pariah trapped between a killing field and an infinite and hating sky. The total absence of aerial clutter and mechanical noise—of any human life other than our own—hammered home our utter isolation. I've always considered myself a loner, except where Evelyn was concerned, but even I felt like we no longer belonged in this world. The new world cast us as aberrations, throwbacks with no place left for us.

Still, we drove, even when we could only go in circles until a path forward became clear, but no road we traveled was ever really clean of the dead. A few here and there often turned into a hungry mob with an insatiable appetite for living flesh when we drove too slow or idled too long. That fear kept us moving even on those bone-weary nights when we all wanted to curl up in our fatigue and sleep all the way through the next day. Instead, we took turns napping in the car and stopped only during daylight to scrounge for supplies, food, and fuel, wherever we could find them. We were warm-blooded ghosts haunting an abandoned maze choked with ruined vehicles and burnt-out ghost towns populated by hordes of the dead. They forced us to double back almost every day, sometimes more than once, sometimes a hundred miles or more, to find another way south. We lost days at a time.

A week passed, and we hadn't reached Florida yet. Della became a sullen shadow lurking in the back seat. She did her share of the driving and rooted around for supplies when we stopped, but she kept her distance from me and Mason and seemed jumpy much of the time. Mostly she said nothing nonessential. I credited the change in her to fear and depression, but I didn't understand the edge to it, not until on one of those backtracking detours, Della opened up about what had really been on her mind.

"You know, before all this crap with the dead, I was married and divorced twice?" she said.

Mason and I eyed her, surprised, unsure of her point.

"That's right. Both those bastards beat on me and cheated on me, and I put the second one in a coma with a crowbar the last time he came at me with a belt in his and anger in his eyes. Even holier-than-thou Warden Grove made a pass at me in that damn prison. So I've been riding here this whole time wondering which one of you was going to come at me first to demand a pound of flesh, and neither of you has so much as laid a finger on me or given me a sideways look, and just now, I mean right then when we made the turn, I started wondering if it was *me*. Am I not your type? Am I losing my looks? How damn crazy is that?" She laughed and covered her mouth with the back of her hand. "You two just aren't like that, are you? Like so many other men. Now I actually hope we might live through this, which I didn't back at the prison. I prayed then that every single one of you crazy fools pushing each other around, playing power games, and mind-fucking each other would be wiped off the earth with the damned wormfeeders. You two have treated me well enough, though, so I suppose all is not lost. There's still some light left in the world. We shall go on somehow."

Mason and I took that as a compliment. In fact, we started laughing so hard at the idea that the two of us had restored Della's faith in the future of humanity that Mason pulled the car over. All three of us got out by the side of the road and gasped for air until the uproar died down to a chuckle. Before then, it had never crossed my mind that there might be more to Della than what she showed on her surface. She saw the humor in what she'd said as clear as we did, and for the first time I felt the three of us all really moving together in the same direction, and I felt pretty good about it. Felt almost like the old days of me and Evelyn blazing a trail of robbery from state to state, making headlines, and scribing a big "fuck you" to the law.

Miles further down the road, though, embraced in the quiet that often chases such moments, I thought about Della's time trapped in the prison after the dead began to walk, one of three women among hundreds of convicts. Maybe Warden Grove had lived up to his high ideals, warped as they were, and protected her and the other ladies stuck inside with us. But even if he had, he couldn't have shielded Della every hour of every day. The weight of that sank into me and deepened my appreciation for Della's toughness. She'd lost as much as me or Mason, and she was a survivor. I decided then that if she wound up with Mason, if that's what she wanted, I'd do nothing to stand in their way. Not that I relished the idea of winding up on my own, but I wanted to repay her trust. And when it came right down to it, I was no stranger to being alone.

THREE

A day later, finally across the Florida state line, we pulled into a gas station in some pisswater town where the post office and the firehouse shared a building—a day's drive off our route seeking a way around a worm feeder-infested rest stop on the main highway. The town looked empty of the dead as well as the living, but like I said, no town ever gets really free of the wormfeeders. While Della and I worked the gas pumps, Mason broke into a police cruiser parked outside the garage. He checked the trunk for guns and gear but found the remains of a legless, hungry corpse.

The legless thing hoisted itself on its hands and lunged onto Mason. It dripped a trail of ripe intestines and tacky viscera, while its liver dropped out the bottom of its torso like a black, bloated egg. The dead thing dug its cracked teeth into Mason's cheek and bit down. Mason yelled for help and started shooting. Five rounds punched craters of putrid flesh and blood out the thing's back, but it held on tight.

Mason hopped around and tried to shake it free while Della and I ran to help. Della tugged on the corpse by the ragged end of its filthy shirt, but the cloth tore away in her hands. I planted my shotgun between Mason's chest and the wormfeeder's neck and fired. Mason howled at the noise and concussion, though none of the shot hit him. The dead body broke apart and fell to the concrete. It flopped around on flapping arms, launching gobs of bloody sludge from the stump of its neck. The head held on tight, though, way too close to Mason for me to risk another shot from the scattergun. Instead I pounded on it with the stock, hoping to rupture it like a pumpkin. A patch of bone the size of coffee can lid cracked loose and pin-wheeled away, exposing a dark slick of rotten gray matter.

That's when an eye popped open in the folds of the thing's brain and glared at me past the jagged edges of its busted skull. Pure white with an iris the color of sand. An eye where none should be. It blinked from between folds of necrotic brain tissue, watching me the way a wounded fox might watch a wolf. Its gaze crawled over me, made me queasy; the stare of those damned eyes was the most repulsive thing I'd ever experienced. I drew my automatic and poked the barrel into its pupil. Then I pushed the head away from Mason and fired. The skull burst in a splash of black and red.

Mason screamed. He swatted and clawed at the viscous blowback splattered onto his face, wiping away chunks of bone and meat. He dropped to his hands and knees and heaved until his stomach hit empty. Then he fell over on his back, chest pumping as he caught his breath. Blood dribbled from his wounded cheek. Della knelt beside him to treat the bleeding with a clean cloth from her kit; she sanitized the wound and then packed it with gauze. Bad as it looked, it wasn't deep, and it sure didn't dampen Mason's spirit. He shouted some downright nasty phrases whenever Della's nursing stung.

I picked up a stick lying in the grass and used it to sift through the quivering remnants of the head. The largest chunk of brain splatter on the pavement shimmied and then sprouted another cold eye, a twin of the one I'd shot. Its gaze hit me like a cold breath and left me feeling kind of sick and poisoned. I drove the tip of the stick into the pupil, burst it, and then flicked the whole mess into the tall weeds beyond the edge of the parking lot.

Della's screams snapped me back.

Things shouldn't have happened how they did then, but strained past our breaking points and worn down from running day and night, we didn't realize the toll it had taken on us or how badly the sight of those awful, dead eyes rattled us.

No excuses, though. We got sloppy.

It was too late before I turned around.

We'd forgotten to destroy the torso. It crept up beside Della and shoved her aside. Its cracked ribcage leaked a tail of dead organs as the thing clamped flylike onto Mason and drove one of its splintery hands into his chest. The corpse dug in deep, ripping cords of flesh and cracking ribs as it excavated Mason's heart and raised it toward a phantom head. It acted on the instinct to feed even though feeding was now impossible for it. My eyes fixed on Mason's living heart, crimson and fat, pumping uselessly in the wormfeeder's gray, rotten fingers. It glistened in the morning sun and washed the concrete with its steaming blood. Mason screamed until his voice died with him.

I gathered Della and her kit and rushed us back to the car. A wormfeeder appeared across the street, a group of them down the block, all headed our way. No point staying. Nothing we could do for Mason, and we had enough gas to carry us for a good while. But we had to get clear fast. Seemed obvious to me it was the right move, but that didn't stop Della from swearing me up and down and calling me a coward or from punching me hard enough to leave bruises. I weathered her storm until we made it outside of town, and then, afraid to lose control of the car, I pulled over on the grassy shoulder. Wormfeeders stood a couple hundred yards down the road, moving slow but eyeing us. They headed our way the second the car stopped.

Della jumped out and slammed the door.

Give her a few minutes, let her work it out, I thought.

I hoped she'd see things how they'd been, otherwise, this hard patch could get tricky fast. If she harbored some illusion that we could've saved Mason after his heart had been torn out—that I'd dragged her away, left him to die when we could've helped him— it would put a fine crack between us, and she might wind up wondering if I might run off on her to save my own skin. I massaged the aches in my bruised arm and waited out her rage, keeping an eye on the dead down the road as they drifted closer.

Della shook as she sobbed. I watched her in the rearview mirror, one hand planted on the trunk holding herself up, her tangled, black hair draping her face. She spun around, screamed some more, kicked something in the road, then after a little while, she rubbed her tears away on the back of her hand and got back in the car. The stark redness in her eyes frightened me.

"I'm sorry," she said.

"Yeah. Me too."

"We both know that didn't have to happen."

"No, it didn't," I said. "We fucked up. We let Mason down, and now he's gone, and I feel like hell about it. At the end of the day, he was nothing but good to us. But it ain't gonna do us any better to break down. I'm not saying we shouldn't mourn him. He was our friend and a good one. But let's take this experience as an object lesson about letting circumstances get the best of us."

Della looked wired, ready to fly off the handle again, to go on working out her anger by hitting me some more, but instead she sucked down a few deep breaths and settled into her seat.

"You're right," she said. "There are wormfeeders up the road. Let's get out of here. Fast."

"You got it."

I let out a little sigh of relief. Then I gunned the engine and we drove in silence.

The road rolled away beneath our wheels, and a harsh sun marked our passage.

Couple miles later, Della said, "Shit, Cornell, we have to go back and burn him. I can't stand the idea of him becoming a wormfeeder."

"No can do. We go back, we'll wind up dead like Mason, and all three of us will rise," I said. "All that commotion and spilled blood probably pricked up the senses of every hungry corpse for five miles. Besides it's not Mason getting up, only his body. Mason's dead and gone now and free of all this bullshit."

Della sniffled. "You think that's true? You think our souls go free when we die?"

I hadn't exactly said that so I didn't answer. I'd never wondered much if souls even existed let alone what happened to them after death. Figured everyone learns that when their time comes, so why waste effort on idle speculation? Better to live in the moment, do what you needed to get by. But whatever the truth, I didn't want to believe there could be any human part left in the nightmares that plagued us.

"I'm gonna miss him," Della said.

"Me too," I told her.

Neither of us mentioned Mason again for several days. The wound needed time to scab over. I tried to find meaning in Mason's death, but there wasn't any. He had been a good man. He should've had a better life and a better death, but then these days what *should be* and what *is* were like a pair of bitter ex-lovers. Cold as it may seem to think of such things after losing a good friend, I knew from the moment Della got back in the car that she and I were going to wind up much closer than we ever would've if Mason had lived. It didn't feel right to me then but I knew it would be okay later. Maybe if I'd saved Mason nothing would've ever flared up between us. That would've been all right, I suppose. Least then we might've avoided that lonely detour into some of the worst business I've ever witnessed among the living or the dead.

So much for learning our lesson.

FOUR

My fear of losing Della tripped us up.

Time was I had a good woman at my side and not a shred of doubt in my heart, back when the world was still a place for the living. Evelyn had been one of a kind, and in no way did Della a substitute for a past love. Had Evelyn lived, with my child growing inside her, maybe we would've married, maybe even gone straight before we were caught. Who knows? My life would've followed one different path or another—but I might never have become the kind of man who could survive in a world overrun by the dead. Or maybe I'd always been that kind. I don't know. I'd made my peace with Evelyn's ghost the night we broke out of prison, so she and I were square as far as I was concerned. Aside from a passing resemblance in the right light, Della and Evelyn had little in common, and what I felt for Della was a different thing altogether than what I'd felt for Evelyn.

I'd never once felt an urge to shelter Evelyn from the violence and danger around us. Hell, half the time she was the one looking out for me on a job. Our relationship was a true marriage of equals. With Della, we were equals in another way, but something in her character made me want to shield her. Not that she needed it. She was smart, tough, and dangerous when she had to be, but that didn't change how I felt. It didn't help that Della went along with it to humor me, I guess, or maybe because she liked to have a protector or because it helped her feel a little bit normal again to be playing boy meets girl like in the old days before the dead plague.

Whatever the explanation, that feeling is why I made her wait in the car while I raided the police station in a godforsaken suburb west of Jacksonville. I searched for ammunition and equipment, not expecting much since part of the place was burned down and the rest looked pretty well looted. Figured I'd be in and out, ten minutes tops. Della and I had foraged together like that dozens of times, and I had no real reason to keep her out of it that morning.

Except for what had happened the night before.

A while after Mason died, things boiled over between me and Della. The night before Della and I reached Baker County and the burned out police station, we camped in a roadside stop abandoned while under construction. The place seemed free of the dead, maybe because no one living had been there when the dead plague started, but I knew if we stayed long enough, they'd come. We nested in a back storeroom with cinderblock walls, high small windows, and a solid, metal door, a place we could secure long enough to get some shut-eye. Sleep had been our plan, but sitting there in the silver moonlight, tension flowing out of us for the first time in days, we tumbled together as if drawn by gravity. Our lips grasped in long kisses that sent shivers through my body. We spread some blankets on the floor, stripped, placed our clothes on top of them to pad the icy tiles, and then we eased into the furnace of each other's heat.

Della felt firm and smooth. I relished her touch.

The pure silence that surrounded us was extraordinary, broken only by the rush of our breath, the whisper of our skin rubbing together, and our half-voiced moans of joy. We lasted quite awhile, each of us sparking the other through the ebb and flow of desire. We had a strange chemistry, the excitement of our first time together blended with the comfort of familiarity. Knowing death waited on every inch of ground we had to cover, in every second we had to live, bred intensity too; that plus our conviction we might be the last living man and woman in the world. I had never expected to experience anything like that. I don't think Della had either. If that had marked our last night alive, neither one of us would have been wholly dissatisfied.

The effect was powerful. It opened my eyes to the prospect of something more than a never-ending struggle to take another breath, travel another mile, and see another sunrise. I saw Della in a different light after that. The singular dread of the wormfeeders I'd lived with for so long now had company: my fear of letting down Della, like I had Evelyn and Mason.

So I made her wait in the car.

That's why the breath whooshed out of me and my blood froze when I came back empty-handed from the police station and saw she was gone.

FIVE

The sight of the empty passenger seat in Mason's car ran a spike of fear through me. I sprinted across the street and shouted Della's name. The car was clean; the doors were closed. Della's shotgun was gone. Hope flickered inside me. I clambered onto the front hood for a better view of the street and searched in every direction.

Nothing.

A dry breeze swept trash and debris along the vacant street. I waited for the noise of it rustling to die down then listened. Distant, shouting voices and the faint grumbling of a car engine came from the distance. *Sounds of living people.* My heart raced. A shotgun blast reverberated among the abandoned streets, booming as if its echoes alone might bring the buildings crumbling down around me.

I leapt from the car and bolted toward the nearest intersection in the direction of the gunshot. Around the corner and halfway down the next block Della stood on the steps of a cathedral, shotgun raised to her shoulder, a patch of silver smoke spreading from its barrels. The shadow of the steeple hid her target, but as I ran closer I saw two bodies: a man, dead but not yet reanimated, sprawled atop one of the walking dead, a woman, on the cathedral's granite steps. The man embraced the dead woman in a lifeless grip. Blood gushed from his neck, making islands of the scattered bits of his head on the stairs. The dead man's pants bunched down around his ankles, and the pale flesh of his rear stuck up in the air. He had managed to strap a gag around the mouth of the dead woman and tie her arms behind her back so he could get down to business.

"Sick bastard," I said.

Della snapped alert at the sound of my voice and waved her gun my way before she recognized me and lowered it.

"You all right?" I asked.

"I heard him howling," she said, trembling, her voice rising. "Kind of cheering, whooping it up. It's been so long since we saw anyone else living I wanted to check it out. I wanted to see another living person again. *This* is what I find! Damn it, months go by, we don't see another living soul, and then this is the shit I have to come out here and see!"

She screamed, her voice full of anger and horror.

I wrapped my arm around her shoulder and pressed her face to my neck. We held each other a moment and then I started walking, steering us away before the dead man came back.

"You did the right thing," I told her. "No telling what he might've done. Man like that can't be right in the head. Know what I mean? He's better off dead. You did him a favor."

Halfway down the block, I looked back and saw the dead man jolt upright, the skin of his face hanging inside-out over his chest like a soiled bib. His wormfeeder partner got up, too, hands behind her back. They played out a pitiful, clumsy bump and grind, working clear of each other and then shuffled after us, their desires of the flesh finally aligned.

"Time to go," I said, picking up the pace. "The police station was a bust, but we're not alone either. I heard voices and a car while I was looking for you."

We hustled back to the Camry to leave town, eager to avoid any other living people nearby, afraid the ones I heard might prove as sick as the man on the church steps. That's when something sharp and fast gouged a chunk of pavement out of the road three feet ahead of us and a gunshot cracked the air. Della and I crouched and dashed for the car as another shot buzzed between us and chipped the curb outside the police station. A third grazed Della across the shoulder, tearing her shirt and streaking a line of blood along her skin.

I spun and fired five shots in the direction of the sniper, buying us time to reach the car. Faint static crackled on a distant walkie-talkie. A man laughed through the heavy stillness and a second voice joined in, maybe two more after that. The shotgun blast had drawn whoever I had heard to come looking for us.

Della and I scrambled into the car and blasted off along the road. Our planned route called for us to double back toward the highway, a route now closed by the sniper, so we sped toward the other side of town, relieved when we left the buildings behind us and hopeful when we turned down that broken, desolate road, thinking it would lead us away from the madness. The road stretched ahead like a ribbon of concrete snakeskin; its barrenness should've been more than ample warning to steer clear, but I was too intent on getting out of town to notice.

About two miles along the way, we reached the blockade: a jumble of wrecked cars shoved into the road and crushed together under a telephone pole. From a hundred yards away I saw the shadows of men with guns moving on the other side of it. I hit the brakes, cut the wheel, and spun the car around, driving hard. We made it a quarter mile back the way we came before two pick-up trucks rolled into view, side-by-side, blocking the road, each one bearing an armed man mounted behind the cab, at least one of whom had sniped on us in the city, I guessed.

Right then I felt the presence of a nasty old friend of mine slinking back to my side, an unwelcome harbinger with dank, familiar breath that burned against the back of my neck; the hot, carrion air of the one I'd thought I'd left behind with memories of Evelyn and the madness of men who killed to rule over an empire of rot and dust.

My damn jackal returned, and I could smell his anticipation for whatever trouble now lay ahead of me.

SIX

I'm not a social person. People are too easy to manipulate, too ready to be misled, taken advantage of, and ridden herd, complacent so long as their basic needs are met, and willing to pay much more than required for the privilege. So the arrival of organized and armed men who'd tracked us out of town, discouraged me more than a little. Della and I held our guns out of sight on our laps and wondered if it might be better to hold tight and see what developed or burst out shooting and end this thing fast and clean. Going out in a blaze of glory would not have been a tragedy.

For a little while, no one made a move. Roadside pines swayed in the fast wind and dead maple leaves tumbled across the pavement. Horsehair clouds drifted above us. The faint aroma of the woods filled my nose, and time felt frozen, even as cold sweat dripped down my back.

A barrel-chested man jumped down from the closest truck, paused to adjust his belt, and then strolled halfway to our car. He knelt and set his rifle down on the double-yellow line, showed us a handgun he pulled from the back of his belt, and then placed it beside the first weapon.

He resumed walking.

I rolled down my window.

"That'll do," I called. "We can hear each other fine."

He stopped and smiled in the shade of his Marlins cap, his eyes hidden behind mirrored shades. "Well, listen to you giving orders," he said. "In case you hadn't noticed, friend, armed or not, my men and I got the upper hand here."

"Oh, is that how you see it?" I asked.

His smile faltered.

"Listen, we don't want any trouble with you and we don't intend to hurt you. Fact is we're kind of happy to see some other living folks. Been too long staring at the same faces down at our camp. We thought everyone else in these parts was dead and gone, that we were the only ones who survived."

"Oh, yeah? So, what, you and your snipers aimed to keep it that way?"

"No, no. It's not like that at all. We're real sorry about that. The shooting was uncalled for. A mistake. See, that was one of ours, a fellow named Cutter, your girlfriend shotgunned back by St. Pete's," he said.

"You saw what he was doing with that wormfeeder?"

The man nodded. His jaw tightened into a grimace.

"I did. That's why you two aren't dead. Probably would've done the same myself if I'd found him first. I suspected Cutter wasn't all right in the head, but he was cagey. We're better off without him poisoning the rest of us. If he's capable of that, who knows what he might do to one of our women or children."

I held my tongue.

"It's a harder world now than it's ever been," the man said. "Sometimes you have to kill the corruption before it spreads. I apologize for my snipers firing on you. Couple of the guys got a little overexcited before word went round who it was the lady shot and why. They had a good laugh afterward, though. Boys had a pool on how long that maggot would last." The man paused. A shadow of a grin bent his lips. "Big Mike won."

"Ain't that a joy for Big Mike," I said. "What the hell do you want with us?"

"Seeing as how we got off on the wrong foot here, let me introduce myself," he said. "Name's Tom Weichert, and despite what this looks like, I'm pleased to meet you."

"All right, then, Mr. Weichert. Let's chalk this up to a misunderstanding. Apology accepted. Been nice chatting with you, but now if you'll move your trucks, I think we'll head back the way we came and be on our way," I said.

"I wouldn't recommend that."

"Why's that?"

"You're heading south, planning to take the interstate, right?"

"What difference does it make to you?"

"None, really. But, see, I know you didn't come from the south, so I figure that's the way you're traveling. And about fifty miles along that way here there's a cluster of the dead. Got to be a hundred thousand or more crammed together around a little town down there called Baxton. They're all gathered there like it's some kind of party. Been hanging around six weeks or so, standing around decaying, as best we can tell. Waiting for fresh meat to show up, I guess. That's what you're heading into if you keep going."

I saw in Della's eyes that she believed Weichert's story. So did I. We had no reason to trust the man, other than the honest resonance in his voice and his unwavering eyes; the prospect of what he described chilled me. I'd never seen that many dead in one place. They tended to spread out and go wandering unless live humans attracted them to one place or another.

"Tell you what, here's my offer," Weichert said. "We got a place a little ways down this road, hidden, fortified, about a hundred and sixty of us living there. We keep the area clean by hunting scarecrows every day. We call the dead ones *scarecrows*. You want to spend some time with us, you're welcome. You prefer to take your chances on the road, that's your call and it's been nice meeting you. I wish you good luck."

Weichert gestured to the men behind him. Engines coughed to life and each truck pulled onto the shoulder, leaving the route clear.

I didn't hesitate in slamming my foot down on the gas, rocketing by so fast that Della squealed. Weichert flinched, grabbed onto his hat, and leapt backward. We shot between the trucks and blazed up the road, and no one fired a shot or so much as made a move to follow us. In the rearview I glimpsed the shock on Weichert's face and his men's puzzled expressions. Would've been easy enough for them to squeeze off a few pot-shots at us, try to cripple our car, but none of them even lifted a gun. No one tried to chase us. They simply stood there and watched.

I eased up on the accelerator and rolled to a stop.

"What's wrong?" asked Della.

"Think a minute," I said. "If what he says is true maybe we ought to hole up here a while and figure a better way to get south."

"Cornell, we don't need them," she said.

"No, we don't, I suppose, but we could use them to catch our breath, see if anyone knows what the hell is going on out there," I said. "If we have to wade through an army of wormfeeders to make it home, I'd like to have as much information as possible ahead of time."

Della considered it, her expression hardened by apprehension.

"I'm not sure I want anything to do with whatever it is they've got going on," she said.

"Thing is we need some real rest. We lost Mason because of a stupid mistake. I almost lost you this morning because of another one, leaving you alone like that, and then we drove down this dead-end road and got ourselves trapped. We aren't thinking clearly anymore," I said. "I'm no more excited than you are to meet the fucking neighbors, but we've got to stop moving for awhile and sleep more than a few hours here and there. We need to get our heads together and recuperate a little. Otherwise we got no chance at all getting through that many wormfeeders down the road."

"All right," Della said, but I could tell she didn't like it. "But we don't tell them where we're going, where we've been, or who we are. This is nothing long term for us. We're only visiting."

"Agreed," I said.

I turned the car around and drove back, noting the confused faces of the men as we rolled between the pick-up trucks and stopped beside Weichert. I cut the motor and stepped out.

"What the hell was that about?" he asked.

"Making sure your offer was sincere." I extended my hand and Weichert shook it. "We'd like to take you up on it. Name's Cornell and this is my wife, Della."

I don't know why I called Della my wife. Instinct took over and the words came out, but when I saw the subtle shift in Weichert's expression and felt his grip tighten around my fingers, I knew I'd done the right thing on that count. Up close and exposed something didn't feel right to me now. Della's warning jangled in my head. *We've been doing fine without these losers,* I told myself, but it wasn't true. We were on the edge. We needed a respite, and we couldn't be choosy about how we got it. Still, that didn't soften the hard rocky feeling in my gut telling me I'd just made my third dumb mistake that day and that this might be the big one. The jackal's laughing bark came rolling through my head, and I sensed his presence at my side, his muzzle so near my hand, I could almost feel the steam in his breath.

SEVEN

Weichert's pick-up led us down the road, me and Della following, the other truck bringing up the rear. The land around us bristled with overgrown honeysuckle twisting amidst sugar maple and blackhaw trees and tall pines, all of it shielded by waist-high grass growing along the shoulder. Here and there bits of glass and metal sparkled in the sunlight, the remnants of debris where wrecked cars had been hauled away to clear the road.

Out this way offered only wilderness. No stores, houses, gas stations, or farms, nothing but sun-cracked concrete and wild vegetation, probably infested with mosquitoes by the billions. I wondered what kind of encampment awaited us down the road and imagined a pathetic collection of faded tents and beat-up RVs. The farther we drove from town, the quieter Della got. I knew how she felt. We were weak prey if Weichert's men decided to jump us, but I didn't think that would happen. They could have done it right where they first stopped us, and Weichert seemed too straitlaced for that kind of shit.

Man liked his rules and kept his word. Saw that much in his eyes. No doubt that's how he got to be head of the pack with this simmering bunch that included a freak like Cutter. Weichert's men were all clean-shaven, wearing fresh clothes without stains or tears, good shoes, and carrying well-maintained weapons. They put on a nice, civilized show, but I smelled secrets scratching beneath its surface, and I wondered what Tom Weichert kept hushed up, waiting for a chance to air out or be buried for good.

The pavement ended at a three-foot drop down to soft ground, but Weichert's pick-up cut right and moved along a gravel trail hidden by brush. I followed. The car lurched and the tires spun when we hit a sharp incline, but then the treads caught and trundled us upward into a hollow of high pines and mottled shade. Six armed men, three along either side of the path, watched us. Della shrunk down in her seat.

"You still think we did the right thing?" she asked.

I didn't know, so I kept quiet.

Around a crook in the road stood a twelve-foot black bear carved from a pine trunk but looking fierce and alive in the dusty shaft of sunlight that angled down onto it. Twice the size any black bear ought to be and sporting a mean snarl, it startled me. A sign mounted at its feet read: Cady's Indian Museum and Nature Outpost.

We crested a hill and a cluster of six buildings came into sight. A sprawling brick mansion stood flanked by a cottage, a long garage, two large cinderblock and cement longhouses at the rear, and a brick station at the edge of a weed-pocked parking lot. Fifteen cars cooked in the sun, lined up in the spaces, all of them clean and looking ready to roll. People roamed the grounds out in the open as if the dead couldn't walk up and take a bite out of them any time. That disturbed me for its arrogance and foolishness—or maybe my subconscious only wanted to piss on the first rays of hope I'd felt in a long time.

I pulled in beside Weichert's truck. Della and I got out. The noontime breeze chilled my back where sweat had matted my T-shirt to my skin.

"Welcome to Camp Cady," Weichert said as he left the truck. "Not much but it's home." He laughed and slapped me on the back, flashing a smile better suited to an insurance salesman or a cocaine dealer.

"You folks are awful comfortable moving around in the open," I said.

Grinning, Weichert shook his head.

"Naw, we're safe here," he said. "We send hunting parties out daily to pick off any scarecrow comes within a few miles of the place. Long as they don't make it down here to the camp, they don't know we're here, and that keeps their numbers down and manageable. They're kind of like ants. Kill the scouts, the others go looking for food elsewhere. Being off the beaten path works in our favor in more ways than one. Couple months ago, an army troop came through town. They burned and foraged and mowed down scarecrows like twelve year olds at a shooting gallery. Fine enough, except then they came across a dozen or so living folks hiding out in the basement of an apartment building. They cleared them out. Killed half the men, took all the women, set the children loose, and kept on their way like a pack of coyotes following the scent of carrion. We watched from a distance. They never knew we were here. We took in a couple of the survivors afterward, those that wanted to go with us."

"The army's still online?" I asked.

Weichert shrugged. "Doubt it. These fellows looked rogue, maybe not even real army. Had the patches and insignia ripped off their uniforms. If they weren't on their own then I guess they have orders to survive and damn the civilians. Either way, it's all the same to us: no help there."

"What about Cady? He don't mind you setting up camp here?"

"If he does, he's not going to say much about it. Cady died about a month before the dead rose up. He was my friend, which is how I knew about his place. He was fixing to turn this into a tourist attraction. Developers planned for a shopping mall and hotel complex about two miles back up the road. Cady's family owned this land going back more than a hundred-and-fifty years. He figured the time had come to cash in. Built those longhouses and started up his collection of genuine Indian artifacts and museum-quality taxidermy displays. Got a hundred acres of nature trails out there, too. I'll give you and your wife the dollar tour later. Right now, though, let's get you checked in."

We crossed the parking lot with Weichert. Della stuck close and held my hand. Weichert ushered us into the squat building on the edge of the blacktop. Inside, three men sat behind desks piled with stacks of papers. They looked up in unison as Weichert introduced us.

"Figure on them being with us more than a few days," he said, and then he glanced at me over his shoulder, and asked, "Right?"

"Don't know," I said. "We're not looking to impose."

"No imposition," he said. "This isn't a free ride. We'll get files started for each of you, get you in the registry, and then interview you about what kind of skills you have. Depending on what we need done, these men will assign you work detail. Once that's set, they'll fix you up with quarters and you can start working tomorrow. Earn your keep fair and square and take your turns in the hunting rotation. That's how we do things around here."

"What kind of work?" Della asked.

Weichert winked at her. "Well, that's up to you, isn't it? What kind of skills you got, ma'am?"

Della glanced at me, waited for my slight nod.

"I'm a nurse," she said.

Weichert laughed. "That sure is welcome news. You'll be working over in the infirmary. See how easy it is? This is no tent city. The world we knew may be gone, but we're not savages. We've got to keep the building blocks of society alive, or else how will we rebuild? We have to preserve something to go back to when all this ends."

"What makes you think it ever will?" I asked.

"The dead got to rot away to nothing sooner or later."

"We've seen plenty look like they stopped decaying and started toughening up. If you're planning to wait this out, you may be rebuilding society from behind a walker."

"Heard rumors about that, reports from the hunting parties," Weichert said. "Well, we'll see, won't we? We're working on it. Meantime, you get yourselves all official and then get acquainted with some of the folks. You're permitted one weapon apiece in case any of the dead find their way here. Whatever else you're carrying goes in the armory."

"Fuck that," I said. "You're not taking our guns or anything else we own."

All affability fled Weichert's expression as it soured and tightened, and his face flushed sunburn red.

"Excuse me, Mr. Cornell, but I doubt you actually *own* any single item you're carrying. If you got receipts to prove it then fine, keep it. I understand people need to do what they can to survive, but that doesn't mean stealing and looting is condoned. It's only a necessary evil. We got a civilized community here and if you're with us then you're going to follow our laws. Someday the world will get back on track one way or another, and we're all going to have reckon for what we've done and taken. You got that?"

Two of Weichert's men dropped hands beneath their desks. I didn't have to strain to figure they were wrapped around guns.

I nodded, slow and deliberate, feigning resignation.

"Your camp, your laws," I said.

"Fine. Mind you something else. Got a good number of kids running around here, so we don't allow swearing in public. Do it again and you'll spend some time in the 'swear jar,' a small, dark place you won't like very much," he said. "Now that's out of the way, I'm happy to have helped you out today. I want us to be friends, but for now, maybe you'd better to think of me like most of the others do. I'm not some high-minded volunteer. I'm a duly authorized officer of the law for the great state of Florida, and until we get to know each other better, you can call me sheriff."

Weichert flipped back his jacket and revealed a bronze badge pinned to his shirt. Fuck my stupidity and fear and lack of confidence in finding a way for Della and I to weather whatever hell awaited us further down the road. I'd had enough of lawmen to last me until my hair turned white and my balls shriveled up back inside my body. It took a lot of willpower to stand my ground when I wanted to bust Weichert's nose then grab Della by the hand and run, but I knew we'd never make it down that winding gravel road, never reach the highway or the barricade before somebody squeezed off a lucky round to take us down. Della and I exchanged a quick glance, realizing in the same moment that we'd have to bide our time. And right then we started hating every fucking second of it.

EIGHT

They put us up on the third floor of the mansion, in a tiny clean room furnished with a nice bed. In the morning, sunlight streamed in through the windows. Married couples stayed together, which made me grateful for my improvised lie. Otherwise single women got the second floor and one of the longhouses, where Cady's museum displays had been cleared out and cubicles and cots had been set up; men took the other longhouse or roughed it in tents or under open sky. Weichert asked about our absent wedding rings, and I told him a group that jumped us back in Georgia had stolen them. That seemed to satisfy his curiosity.

Della's work in the infirmary made her feel good, and she telegraphed it in her face, in her walk, in how she smiled once in a while after going so long without smiling at all. The routine helped. So did getting a good night's sleep and having a safe place to be alone together. Mostly, though, I think that helping the injured nurtured Della's spirit; it gave her a way to fight back against the death and horror around us and reminded her that good things could still be done in the world and she could be part of them.

Weichert kept his word. He dumped most everything we had into "community ownership" for use as needed for the good of everyone at Camp Cady. They took our guns, some of our camping equipment and other supplies, but left us our clothes and personal belongings. I managed at least to hide the spare set of keys for the car. After that first day Weichert left us alone. We became two more faces among the crowd, two more names on a roster he needed to feed, shelter, and protect, of no special concern to him so long as we played by his rules. Few folks we met liked Weichert, but no one argued with his results keeping

Camp Cady organized and secure. The ones rankled by the rules vented their frustration on the daily scarecrow-hunting expeditions. I appreciated Weichert's cunning in giving folks a way to work out their anger by putting it to good use. Have to admit the man had a knack for leading the sheep and what he did wasn't all bad, either.

Della and I actually enjoyed ourselves there. We ate good meals together like normal people and hiked along the trails around camp in our off time. At night, cozy in our little room with the door locked and the windows open to the breeze, Della and I made love, moving like we had that first time, rediscovering the energy and passion that had drawn us together. Our bodies fit like they'd been tailor-made for each other, designed by fate. I cherished the scent of Della's hair, the texture of her skin, the taste of her on my lips, and the secret desires she whispered in my ears. Even when we lay side-by-side, spent, with the dawn creaking through the trees, we pressed our bodies together like parting would be a form of amputation.

Those first few days felt wonderful, but at the same time it chafed to remember what living—really living instead of concentrating on not dying—was all about, because I knew one day this too would end. Didn't matter how good or safe life was if it was living on someone else's terms, spending each day on a leash, no matter how slack or invisible. And that I wouldn't do anymore. With the world going to hell and death hiding in every shadow, that kind of life offered us little to be gained and everything to lose.

Della felt likewise. Most mornings she woke up before me, and I stayed in bed to watch her dress, savoring the way her taut body moved through the hazy sunlight in a muscular perfection of lines, curves, and shadows. Her skin gleamed, and when she breathed her chest rose and fell in measured time that hinted at her growing confidence. She became more meticulous in her habits, more reserved in her choice of clothing as she slipped back into a professional state of mind. The change worried me a little. I wondered if maybe she liked things at Camp Cady too much, but she always put my mind at ease without even trying with how she said things like "when we leave here" or "when we get down to your place in Lohatchie." She said things like that often and I took them to heart.

At the infirmary they mostly dealt with injuries—cuts, scrapes, sprains, and the like. Nothing too serious. Almost no one came in ill, which Della chalked off to the good weather, hard work, and the absence of pollutants in the air. The other infirmary workers told her they hadn't seen a patient with a cough, cold, or infection in months.

"I do feel bad for this one boy, though," Della told me one morning.

She sat brushing her hair in front of the mirror, dressed in only a pair of faded blue panties with her back half-turned to me while I reclined propped up on pillows.

"He's been in a bed since he got here about two months ago," she said. "Only twelve years old and he's on his own. Lost his family and everyone he had to wormfeeders. He got away but he broke his leg jumping out of a moving truck. Lucky someone found him out on the road and brought him here, but it was a bad break. He ought to be able to start walking again any day now, though. His name's Christopher. You can see in his eyes what he's been through. The way he stares off into space sometimes makes me think maybe it's even worse than the things you and I've seen, like it's aged him and there's an old man living inside him now."

I thought about the eyes growing from the brain of the wormfeeder that had killed Mason and the man Della shot on the cathedral steps, and I wondered what worse things the boy could've seen.

"Good thing, then, he's got you to care for him," I said. "You wait and see, get him up on his feet again and he'll be running around like a normal, healthy boy in no time, playing football, dreaming about girls. I promise."

"You should come visit him," Della said. "Not a lot of men come by the infirmary unless they're hurt, and I think he's getting tired of being mothered."

"Stuck in bed with a bunch of good-looking sympathetic women to wait on him hand and foot? The boy doesn't know how good he's got it," I said. "Give him another two years, he'll change his tune."

"Still, wouldn't hurt if you stopped by."

"I'll make a point of it," I said. "But mainly cause it'll give me an excuse to come by and harass your sexy ass. Drop by this afternoon, all right?"

Della smiled. She put her brush down then crawled back into bed and kissed my neck. Another minute and she was under the covers with me, slipping out of her panties, and we picked up where we'd left off only a few hours ago.

That's how it went most days, the two of us indulging in the luxury of not having to look over our shoulders every minute or put all our energy into keeping alive. Got so goddamn comfortable sometimes I started worrying I might be the one who'd want to stay at Camp Cady.

Lucky for me, though, I had Weichert and his cronies to make sure I never forgot what was going on in the world or where was the safest place for me and Della to plant our roots. They assigned me to work the greenhouse with a man named Birch, an ex-military scientist no one liked. I guess I brought it on myself to some extent. I didn't want Weichert to know what I'd really done in the past, so I'd told his people that I'd worked as a janitor. Thus, as a new guy with no special skills, I pulled duty as Birch's assistant. They joked when they told me where to go that they expected me to last no more than a day or two.

Birch's lab stood in a meadow a short hike through the woods, fixed up in an old greenhouse of glass and steel hidden from the compound's main grounds by overgrown orange groves. Most of the botanical supplies had been dismantled and set aside, replaced with Birch's equipment. My first day there I saw why everyone else avoided him. When he saw me coming, he stepped out from the greenhouse and greeted me by flipping me the bird.

"Hey, asshole, did Weichert send you down here to keep tabs on me?" he said. "Where does that hollow-headed mouth-breather think I'm going to run off to?"

"I'm supposed to assist you," I said.

"Piss off. I don't need assistance."

"Not that simple. I got a job to do, and I guess I ought to do it or risk the wrath of Sheriff Shithead." I pushed past Birch into the greenhouse. "Where do I start?"

Birch and I sized each other up. The dusty Special Forces insignia tattooed on his forearm gave me ample warning to not pick a stupid fight. At least we seemed to share an opinion of Weichert. I hoped that gave us enough common ground to get along. If Birch's grating personality had been the only thing driving people away, I could've toughed it out easily at the greenhouse, but that didn't tell the whole story. Birch also had the Wall, and that got under my skin. Birch gave me no warning about it. He let me go to work cleaning up, and I put in a good half-day's effort sweeping and getting piles of supplies organized before I reached that part of the greenhouse.

The Wall.

Where the body parts were hung.

Mixed in with ivy growing in the shadows in the back corner. Legs and arms. Hands. A pair of lungs. Several hearts. A head with no eyes, ears, or nose. Six loose eyeballs, wide and staring. And a selection of organs rotted beyond identification—all pinned up like a butterfly collection. You hardly noticed them when they kept still, but when the wind carried the scent of the living through cracked panes of greenhouse glass it set them all to stirring so the Wall came to life like a blanket of wriggling critters and insects.

Worst part was the eyes. Not the ones staked there for observation, but the ones that sprouted from the other specimens, the ones that stared out from lung tissue or rolled and blinked in withered cardiac muscle, the ones that watched me from the stump of a severed hand. They tracked me from beneath an oily film of putrescence. As Birch and I worked in the lab, the eyes marked our progress, silent, accusatory, their gaze palpable even to my turned back. My skin never stopped crawling in the greenhouse. That's the real reason no one wanted to work with Birch—that sensation of constant surveillance. No one wanted the dead watching them all day long.

Didn't seem to bother Birch, though.

Maybe he'd been pushed past the point of caring. Wherever he went, his eyes flickered like Christmas tree lights in the rain, and his scrub of gray hair clung to his skull like dried heather as if he hadn't thought to comb it for a week. He moved in fits and starts, standing stock still, lost in thought for minutes at a time before rushing to one part of his lab or another, fumbling with some inexplicable mechanism or some assortment of glass containers filled with sloshing fluids. He hardly ever glanced at the specimens or the eyes on the Wall except to take tissue samples. And he hardly ever spoke to me.

Birch gave me nothing but shit work and the silent treatment for a week, but I stuck it out because I enjoyed the solitude of the greenhouse, even if it meant working around Birch's dead specimens. Also, I figured if anyone at Camp Cady could tell me something I didn't already know about the dead it was Birch. Things between us brightened when I found his personal library on a back shelf. Not much, but it included Faulkner, Hemingway, O'Connor, even Jim Thompson, all in a small treasure trove of tattered paperbacks. I had never put much stock in school and all its bullshit, but reading kept my mind sharp. Half of what had put me three steps ahead of the cops and the feds during my days robbing banks I'd learned from books, and I'd even tried my hand at writing now and then. I asked Birch if I could borrow a couple novels. He nodded, and the next day, we started talking books. That stabilized things between us; it gave us a basis for communication.

One day I told Birch about the eyes I'd seen in the brain of the dead man who'd killed Mason as well as the eyes I'd seen in other wormfeeders.

"Happens all the time," he told me. "I've been studying it since the beginning. I keep hoping it'll lead me to some answers, but I only wind up with more questions. The hunting parties keep me supplied with plenty of test subjects, but I hang on to the bits and pieces that grow eyes the longest. Burn the rest when I'm done with them."

"Weichert says you're working on 'a cure for not dying when you die,'" I said.

Birch laughed. "There's no cure. Weichert is a man whose mind works in two modes: black and white. His world fits together like a crossword puzzle, and he thinks if he plugs in all the right letters, everything will make sense and order will be restored. In his mind, everything happens for a reason, and I don't mean that in a pussy 'oh, it was meant to be' kind of way.

With Weichert, there's a bump in the night, it's because someone knocked. You get what I'm saying?"

"Yeah, he's the original problem solver," I said. "No mysteries. Find the cause, you find the cure."

"Exactly. Catch is, there's no cause," Birch said. "At least nothing scientific like Weichert thinks. There ought to be, sure. He's right as far as that goes. And I can tell you with an unfortunate degree of certainty that I've come closer than anyone alive to finding it. So close, in fact, that I know it simply isn't there to be found. I can describe some of the mechanics involved. I can tell you some of how the dead are walking but not the why. It's like understanding that people need lungs to breathe air but not knowing what oxygen is or how it transfers to your blood or why we even have lungs to begin with."

"You did all that here?" I said.

"No." Birch grinned without humor. "I used to be VP for research at Vanguard Biotech, a company with a shitload of military contracts and the direct attention of the president. When the dead plague started, they sent a tank brigade to our facility to protect us so I could keep working. Got as far as identifying a mutated tetanus virus as the key mechanism involved with muscular function in the dead before the worm-feeders drove us out of there. Now, I'm doing my best with what I've got here, but the only way I can describe what's happening is that time stands still for the dead on a cellular level. Decay slows almost to the point of cessation. But as for what's keeping them moving, making them feed off the living, I'm stumped."

"So? Seals don't ask sharks why they want to eat them," I said. "By now the dead must outnumber the living, anyway. This world is more theirs than ours."

Birch stared at me for several seconds, seeming to slip into some mental tar pit, but then he climbed back out of it and nodded. "Yeah, it is." He went back to work and didn't speak another word the rest of the day.

On my two-week anniversary, Birch told me no one else had worked with him that long, then declared it time for a celebration. He slapped me on the back and steered me to the far side of the greenhouse and a cabinet from which he produced a bottle of Johnnie Walker Black and two glasses. We sat in wide-backed wicker chairs, surrounded by ferns, and Birch poured.

"Glad to have you around," he said

He threw back half his drink.

"I appreciate the work," I said, following suit.

"Tell me something," Birch said. "Weichert pick you up on the road near town?"

"Yeah." I told him the story of how Della and I came to Camp Cady.

"Most folks knew Cutter would need putting down sooner or later," he said. "But listen, some free advice. Don't get too comfortable here if you value your principles or your sanity. This isn't 'Cady's Indian Museum and Nature Outpost' anymore. It's 'Tom Town.' That's what I call it since Tom Weichert's started running it like a tin tyrant. You got anyplace else to go, do yourself a favor and go there. Clean sheets and hot food have their appeal, but things will boil over here sooner or later. Leaving before then will make your life a lot easier in the long run, especially if you can look out for yourself out there."

"A comfortable prison is still a prison," I said.

"There it is in a nutshell."

"Yeah, that's about my sense of things," I said. "Trouble is I don't know if the good sheriff is ready to let us go. My wife's a hell of a nurse. Word is she's been a godsend in the infirmary. Besides, we were heading south."

Birch frowned.

"The first problem I might be able to help you with, but if you're heading south, well, then maybe you don't have anywhere else to go. Forty, fifty miles south the dead are gathering. Something big brewing down at Deadtown, a place called Baxton. The damned scarecrows are shambling in by the thousands."

"I heard. What's it all about?"

"Damned if I know, but don't tell Weichert. He thinks I'm working it all out so I can hand him a big fat report three weeks from Tuesday."

We drank again, and I enjoyed the soft burn of good liquor. A light drizzle fell and pattered against the glass and the leaves overhead. It turned the air damp and chilly. Whiskey warmth filled me, and I didn't object when Birch refilled our glasses before he put the half-full bottle away. I stared through the glass ceiling where smoky, furrowed clouds swept over swaying treetops.

"Tell me for real," I said. "What's with the eyes?"

Birch cleared his throat. "What do you mean?"

I straightened up and studied his craggy face, its lines deepened by the afternoon gloom. He knew more than he wanted to tell. I'd suspected it for a few days, but seeing his face then, I knew it. He hid it well, but my survival and my livelihood used to depend on solid snap judgments of people. It helped to know whether or not an assistant manager was lying about not being able to open a bank vault before you pushed a gun in his face to persuade him to do so.

"I mean," I said, "what makes those eyes pop up like that?"

Birch's gaze drifted toward the trails of rainwater snaking down the outside walls.

"Magic," he said.

"Is that so?"

I walked over to the Wall. It bothered me the way Birch had everything strung up, mounted, and spread out over an eight-foot span. The limbs and bits of flesh resembled a man pulled apart alive, only I knew nothing living hung there, only mute and mindless scraps of what had once been life.

"Acid works," Birch said. "To destroy them, I mean. So does fire. Lye. Anything that causes irreparable cellular damage. Microwaves work. Dries them right up. Shooting them or cutting them slows them, makes it hard for them to function. Told Weichert what he needs are flamethrowers or some pesticide tanks filled with acid, but he's holding out for a panacea. Thinks he can get his hands on some crop dusters and spray a miracle cure far and wide. Man's got visions of reclaiming the entire Panhandle and running it like his own little kingdom."

The Wall repulsed me, yeah, but it drew me in too with its constellations of eyes, their glistening pupils growing and shrinking with the light, dead flesh straining to blink. I couldn't imagine how they could see without a brain to process the image, but I sure as hell felt seen.

Birch laughed. "You got some balls to get that close."

"Don't worry. I'm well acquainted with this sort of bullshit," I said. "Tell me about magic."

A thick chuckle rolled out of Birch's throat.

"I mean it," I said. "What? Like ghosts? Voodoo?"

Birch's face adopted the bone-weariness that until then had only been apparent in the cast of his shoulders and the tepid resignation in his voice.

"Nothing like that. I've got some theories. None that'll solve Weichert's problem. I've worked on the why long and hard and I've come to the conclusion that it's a matter beyond science," he said. "Unless you want to believe the basic laws of physics and biology can be broken or made to change on an individual basis."

"I don't follow," I said.

"It's like I told you. Time is standing still for the dead, so they're not rotting. You've heard of relativity? Imagine ten seconds go by. Ten seconds pass in the world while maybe one, or one-tenth, or one-one-hundredth, or one-one-thousandth of a second passes for these dead fuckers up walking around and making our lives miserable," Birch told me. "Can you explain that? I sure as hell can't. That doesn't even touch on why they're ambulatory or need to eat live flesh. I'm trained to look at the world in a rational way, to seek the underlying reason things are how they are, the mechanisms that drive reality. But as far as I can tell, what's happening with the dead is a cosmic whim or the result of some fundamental alteration in the nature of existence. *Magic.*"

I gestured to Birch's equipment on the greenhouse tables. "You can tell all that from this little kitchen chemistry set you got here?"

"You haven't seen downstairs," Birch said. "I've got all the equipment I need plus two generators Weichert endlessly bitches about keeping fueled to run it all. Took most of it from my old lab. Before the dead rose up I was working on the highest profile stuff, my friend. Things the mainstream would say were fifty, sixty years out, all top secret, all rather dire and revolutionary, and one or two patently illegal under international laws, but hey, I never let that stop me cashing my big, fat paycheck. Before all that, I did things in the Special Forces—*saw* things— before I went back to school and got into the lab. That all gave me a rather finely tuned set of instincts for sorting fact from horseshit. So, believe me when I tell you that if there's a biological reason for the dead to be walking, I'm the man who would've found it."

"So what's the sticking point? You said you had some theories."

Birch scowled and hunched forward.

"You really want to know? I think there's *no* scientific reason. The dead come back to life because, for lack of a better word, God—whatever he, she, or it may be—*willed it so*. The universe is dying on the vine. This is all part of its great, last gasp. You and I are nothing but pallbearers who've overstayed our welcome at the funeral, nothing but carrion crawlers and dung beetles surviving on the remains. Corpse fauna. If we're lucky the Almighty won't forsake us altogether when he finishes with all his killing and resurrecting. In fact, I think despite appearances he's not even close to done with us yet."

The scientist sipped from his glass and sank back into his chair. I set my drink on the table and rubbed my eyes.

"How do you know you're right? Take it on faith?"

"I don't have any faith," he said. "I've seen this—out there in the ranks of the dead, in here when I look into their eyes, and their flesh, and into their cells. I've seen it in my dreams. I've seen and heard things I don't think any man was ever intended to know. Maybe I'm fucking nuts. Maybe I'm plain wrong. But if I'm not, then about fifty miles south of here where the dead are gathering in their masses, they're getting ready to write the epitaph for an entire world and maybe countless others beyond. It's some fucked up shit, believe me, but you asked, and now you know why I'm leading Weichert along and keeping this to myself. I don't want to make poor Tom's head explode."

I smirked. "I'd like to see that."

"Me, too, now that I think about it."

Neither of us laughed, though.

No matter where I went, I wound up with the law to my left and God to my right, and true to form neither side was playing nice with the other. Once again I found myself caught between the slavering jaws of the same beast that I'd thought I'd left behind in prison. I pined for the road, to be alone with

Della, barreling down the ruins of highways no one cared about anymore, the sky and the earth our own to do with as we pleased, and no one to get in our way. Birch called earth dead; I thought maybe it could be the Garden of Eden. And right then I started planning how Della and I were going to make it back to paradise.

NINE

Weichert volunteered me for a hunting party. All the men took turns in rotation, but he bumped me to the head of the list after I lasted two weeks with Birch. My hitting it off with the scientist irked him, and he wanted to remind me who was in charge. Della hated the idea of me going into the woods with Weichert's men. She didn't trust them or Weichert, and she worried I might never come back, leaving her stranded at Camp Cady.

We'd been talking about leaving in another week, maybe two, and our plans had gotten more complicated. Della wanted to bring Christopher. The kid reminded her of her dead brother, and he talked to no one but her about his experiences. She wouldn't tell me what he said. I didn't press it.

I hung out with Christopher now and then. We shot the breeze about rock music, and the walking dead, and how he wanted to grow up and race cars, and though it seemed impossible he'd ever get the chance, I liked that he still had a dream. He was a skinny, picture-perfect kid with fine, unruly hair, the kind of boy I could picture swinging off a long rope into a cool lake on a July afternoon, the kind girls would be all over when he was old enough. A smart kid, too, and I liked him, but I didn't see the upside to him hitting the road with Della and me. Chances were good not all of us would live to see Lohatchie, and Christopher would probably do better staying put. I was enough of a realist to accept that; Della wasn't. Except where Weichert's intentions toward me were concerned, she clung to her optimism.

Despite her worries, though, I saw no way out of my going on the hunt.

I tried to ease Della's mind by pointing out that sending me off to the woods to be killed wasn't Weichert's style. He wanted to break me. The man was a prick but not a cold-blooded killer. Everyone at Cady's lived in Weichert's shadow, and he liked it that way. It showed in their guarded expressions and furtive conversations, in their efficiency and conformity calculated to keep them off Weichert's radar. I saw how unhappy most of them were, except Weichert's inner circle of "trusted deputies." That's what he called the men who kept the rest of us in line. Life at Camp Cady was so well ordered and polite, folks hardly hollered when they stubbed a toe, and Weichert had to know that with the strings pulled that tight, a revolt could erupt any time.

So I didn't expect him to pull something clumsy like staging a hunting accident to get rid of me. I hadn't challenged him openly, but he understood what kind of threat I might be to his rule now some of the others had started to look up to Della and me. Della had bandaged up a lot of injured folks, and my lasting so long with Birch amazed people. They thought I worked hard every day to find a cure. Weichert watched us, gauged our influence, our potential to challenge him, and he wanted to smack me down. I could eat that if it bought us time to make our escape.

The morning of the hunt, sun poured down from a pristine sky and baked my skin. Three days of rain had broken in the night, leaving the ground soft and the air damp with the perfume of pines and wet loam. The heat would dry it soon enough. Six of us trekked out, led by a deputy named Wrigley, driving a pick-up as far into the woods as the terrain permitted, and from there we continued on foot. Each of us carried a handgun, a rifle, ammunition, a machete, and a day's worth of food and water. One man led two mutts on long leashes, our early alert system: Canine noses would smell the wormfeeders long before we could and dogs got skittish around the dead.

Trudging single file through the mud we marched a couple of hours over grassy slopes and fields until we reached the bank of a marsh. An odor of rot wafted off the stagnant water, and the air buzzed with a haze of flies and gnats. We circled to the far side, swatting insects the whole way, and then picked up the trail, which ran narrower and rougher on the other side of the marsh. By then we'd traveled twelve or fifteen miles from the compound, moving in burdensome silence and sweating under the high sun.

Our concentration turned razor sharp for signs of movement in the brush, for the dogs to bark or whine, for the telltale stink of the dead. And when it came it hit like a gale coming off a sun-cooked landfill.

The hounds dug in and refused another step down the trail. Bared their teeth and growled so loud their keeper trotted them back the way we came before they gave away our position. The rest of us crept forward to where the path widened through a stand of pines and led toward cottony brightness and shadows filled with movement among the tree trunks.

"There's a meadow on the other side of those pines," Wrigley whispered. "We scatter, move up, weapons ready. Hunker down just this side of the trees. Fire on my order. Cripple them and then we go in close for the hack-and-burn work. Everyone got it?"

We crept through the dead stench that billowed around us thick as smoke from a tire fire. A chorus of moans cried out from lifeless throats, rising and falling in a way that reminded me of the losing team's fans at a football game. A buzzing current underpinned it, white noise like electrical lines humming on a rainy day. The men swapped anxious glances, everyone edgy but too uncertain to speak up. Good thing I wasn't.

I gripped Wrigley's shoulder and said, "Wait."

The deputy snapped around, surprised, jittery. He glared at me. I dropped my hand, gave him some distance.

"Cut the crap, Cornell. You got your orders."

"Use your head," I said. "Smell that? Hear that? A few strays wandering by don't put up that much stink and noise. Got to be a mob of them, dozens, maybe more. You want to walk right into that?"

"Can't be a mob. We never get that many scarecrows back here. No reason for them to come this way," he said.

A man named Farmer inched forward and spoke. "You're right, Deputy, but so is Cornell. Okay? We've all been on enough of these hunts to know something's different, here. Damn stink is making my eyes water. You ever see the dogs tense up that way before?"

Wrigley flashed me a "see what you started" kind of look, but then he wandered a few feet farther down the trail, dropped to his haunches, and listened. Languid wind shook the pine needles and a bird called from somewhere far away, a delicate musical sound against the groaning of the dead.

Wrigley returned with a hard expression, and said, "You best be right, Cornell, or Tom will hear about your insubordination."

The threat rang hollow, words to keep face even if he knew they were bullshit.

"I can live with that," I said.

"All right, then, here's how we do it," Wrigley said. "We creep up to the tree line, stick to the shadows, hang fire, and see what we're dealing with. Y'all can handle that? Y'all feel better this way? Bunch of tired, fucking pussies I got backing me up."

I smirked and said, "Language, Deputy. What would Sheriff Weichert think hearing you swear like that?"

Farmer and the others chuckled, and the tension eased, but Wrigley sneered at me before he led us down to the edge of the trail. We crouched on hands and knees, nestled into the high grass encroaching from the field, concealed behind a jumble of deadfall. Past the pines the dirt trail cut into a deep, concave meadow. Grass bleached dry and pale by sunlight practically glowed as it swayed in the breeze, flitting back and forth like the golden tongues of a million snakes. Through it shambled an unbroken line of corpses, their rag clothing flapping from their decomposing bodies, their flesh gray, black, and purple in the searing daylight, their wounds that would never heal rippling with maggots and flies. The noise of a billion carrion crawlers hummed among the moans of the dead. The fresher corpses still resembled men and women, but most had deteriorated beyond distinguishing features although the filthy ruins of a necktie or a bra strap or a nametag provided an occasional clue. Children stood out, but nobody wanted to look at them. The line shuffled along, a thread of guided chaos, eight or ten bodies wide, stamping the grass flat, killing it as they followed a well-worn route. They moved slow and steady, shuffling and lurching, their shriveled eyes and empty skull sockets fixed on an unknown point to the south. Wrigley took a pair of field glasses from his belt and gazed northward in the direction of the column's source.

"Shit and piss in a blender," he said.

He passed the glasses to Farmer, who stared through them for several seconds and then handed them to me. I raised them and looked. On and on walked the dead, coming from as far as the eye could see, a distance of maybe a couple miles with every indication that the line reached much farther than that, stretching toward a hidden source maybe fifty miles, maybe a thousand to the north. The corpses passed out of sight south of us. This forced march of the damned, this measured torrent of rot and decay, this scar upon the quiet earth—the sight of it drove home what Birch had said about the living being like carrion bugs infesting nature's new order. We were six living men against an irresistible wall of moving dead flesh, and I didn't need to see the others' faces to know how small each and every one of us felt in its presence.

Some of the wormfeeders slowed down as they passed our position. Those trailing them bumped into them. They danced clumsy circles for a few minutes, tangled up in one another, until one of them fell over and broke the clog. The others stomped along, crushing his twitching body into the soil, but more came and got hung up right there in front of us, distracted from their journey. It was clear our presence threw them off. They sensed us.

As silent as we'd come, we retreated up the trail, hoping we hadn't lingered long enough for them to follow. Past the marsh the path rose to a low hill and we dug in there for a couple of hours to make sure the dead wouldn't track us back to Camp Cady. None of them came up the trail, though, and when we felt sure none would, we hurried back to the pick-up, jogging every other mile to reach it before dusk.

The whole ride home Wrigley rambled on, without really saying anything, asking himself all sorts of pointless questions as he tried to find some explanation for what we'd seen. The rest of us kept quiet, sifting the murk of our own thoughts. No one wanted to voice it but the meaning loomed clear. Baxton, where the dead gathered, stood to the south. We hadn't stumbled upon a random migration but a pilgrimage with a known destination. That meant something no one had yet guessed—that meant the rotting scarecrows, the mindless dead, the stinking, fucking wormfeeders walked with a purpose.

TEN

Credit where credit is due: Weichert played the hand dealt him as well as anyone could once my hunting party returned with news of what we'd seen. He met with his deputies then ordered them to spread word to the others a few small groups at a time so as to put everyone on guard without sparking a panic. He organized eight armed groups, four men each, to camp at posts three miles outside the complex and stand guard in the direction of the dead march. A rotation of scouts placed deeper in the woods kept watch on the walking corpses. They did their best to protect us, no doubt, but they guarded the wrong place. Three days after my hunting party gave its report, my initial fears about Camp Cady being so open and exposed proved right on the money.

A wormfeeder wandered into camp, but it came from the direction of the highway not the deep woods and the dead march. Most likely it crossed the parking lot, strolled by the cars, and stumbled over the rough ground there before it trudged up to the front door of the mansion. It came in the early morning, and no one saw it. Posting so many men to the west left the eastern perimeter vulnerable. A woman, Nancy Morris, leaving the mansion must have walked head on into the thing, and judging by the state she turned up in later, the wormfeeder tore open her throat before it dragged her to the ground and started gnawing into her stomach. It fed for a while, leaving a pile of organ scraps we found and burned later, slurping down what it could until three children turned up the walk and disturbed it. They took one look, screamed, and fled. Smart kids. Too bad they didn't have a decent weapon among them to end things before they really got started. The wormfeeder chased after them, leaving its fresh kill to clamber onto her feet a couple minutes later and wander to the infirmary, dragging her guts through the dirt.

The children evaded the first corpse, and a little later it wandered by the old gazebo where Chester Lang was making repairs. The carpenter fought back with a hammer, caved in the wormfeeder's skull, smashed its brain, and then chopped the thing down to manageable bits with a hatchet, coming away with a dozen or so nasty bite wounds and a gash along his abdomen—but he lived.

Across the compound dead Nancy Morris got as far as the open grass outside the women's longhouse, which housed the infirmary. Della saw her first. While everyone else scrambled to lock the place down, she stepped outside with her gun drawn and put two rounds through dead Nancy's head. That took her off her feet long enough for Della to pin her down with an ax then go to work with a scalpel and a hacksaw, concluding poor Ms. Morris' existence as a mobile flesh-eating corpse. Della took her apart the way she'd done so many others back when she pulled disposal duty in the prison infirmary. That should've ended it, but all the activity over the intrusion meant no one noticed three more wormfeeders coming from the east, proving my rule that nowhere ever stands really free of the dead.

Rotted down to little more than bone and ligaments in places, they crawled out of the woods and crossed the camp like giant beetles clacking for prey. They found their way to the garage where each one killed a man. Of course, their victims rose, driven by a sudden hunger for flesh, and so six wormfeeders roved into the heart of Camp Cady. A lot of people died before the sheriff put the lid back on, and yeah, we can call that a loss and a big, bad day for Tom Weichert and his almighty rule of law. It took Weichert's men two hours to round up all the dead ones and when the last had been put down and burned, the body count numbered twenty-three residents, including four killed by stray shots fired by Weichert's deputies. A riot almost broke out then and there, but it had been so long since most folks at Camp Cady had seen a wormfeeder that shock trumped outrage. That wouldn't last long, though. The illusion of happy life at Cady's lay shattered.

Down at the greenhouse, hard at work in the cellar, Birch and I missed the ruckus. I only heard about it later from Della. That night we decided we ought to leave in another day or two, three at most.

"Camp Cady is not a safe haven anymore," she said. "What's the point in hanging around? Besides, Christopher is ready to travel now."

I wrapped my arms around her, reveling in the flush of having made love and not wanting to talk about such stuff but knowing Della was right.

I said, "It's a good idea. The dead march isn't that far from us. Only a matter of time before some of them wander this way and the secret about this place gets out. Only thing is Birch has been up to something new, and I'm curious to find out what. He hasn't been this intense about anything since I met him."

"Well, tell him to hurry it up. I've been swiping supplies from the infirmary, putting together a little stockpile," she said.

"Like old times."

Della laughed. "We'll need some food, too, and our camping gear and stuff, and weapons."

"The car," I said. "Got to figure a way to load up and sneak out of here without getting shot. Birch said he might be able to help us with that. I'll talk to him tomorrow."

"You think he ought to come with us?"

I shook my head. "Doubt he would. And, anyway, I like him, but I'm not sure his deck is full anymore."

"That woman who died today," said Della. "She sprouted eyes everywhere when I started cutting her up. Every time I took off one of her limbs an eye blinked back at me. It made me feel like cold beetles were crawling under my skin. Whatever's behind those hated me. I felt it, no doubt in my mind. Cold, stony hate. I sliced the eyes to stop them from looking at me, but more kept popping up, in all the wormfeeders. It's getting worse than it ever was."

I told her about the Wall and some of Birch's ideas. She listened, her quiet body warming me, her gentle breath brushing my neck, her heartbeat thudding against my chest.

"I don't care what they are or what they want. I only want to get away from them," she said. "Promise me, all right? That we'll go away from here, away from all this horror, and find our own, safe place? Okay?"

"I promise," I said.

I kissed her and slid my hand along her body, feeling her heat. She welcomed my touch.

The next morning I made Della wake up early and after a stop by the infirmary to pick up Christopher, I took her and the boy into the woods to the place where Weichert had dumped all of Cady's taxidermy displays when he'd had the longhouses cleared out for housing. Cady had been a real enthusiast and so the three of us stood amidst animals from six different continents, each one expertly preserved though now soiled and frayed from being left outdoors, torn and punctured from being used for target practice. Among them were two black bears; an array of big cats that included a leopard, a tiger, and some cougars; an alligator and a crocodile; three spider monkeys; two wolverines; a group of raccoons; a wolf, a dingo, and one other to which I felt a special attachment: a jackal.

It looked exactly like the one in my head.

With their fur matted down, paws spattered with mud, and dry leaves clinging to them, the animals looked all the more lifelike. I expected them to come to life like the dead, but they never did. Every so often, I glanced over my shoulder at the jackal and could've sworn I felt him looking back. Della didn't know about the jackal, and I didn't tell her. Sharing that kind of secret can change how people think of you, not often for the better. Besides, we had work to do. Birch had given me a set of hunting knives. I handed one each to Della and Christopher and showed them how to use it. Science wasn't all Birch and I had been up to down at the greenhouse.

"He doesn't like to talk about it, but Birch was in the Special Forces," I said. "He adapted his military, hand-to-hand combat training to fight the dead close up. He made a system of cutting them so their joints are left useless but you don't have to sever their limbs. We learned the hard way a legless body can still drag itself across the ground and bite you. A severed hand or arm can still claw you. Just like with Mason. Birch says you sever the spine to burden them with their own dead weight. Then you clip the shoulders and hips the right way, and you got a trunk straddled with limbs like a plastic doll whose rubber bands have snapped. Takes them right down. Since they're half dried out already, you can slice into them a lot deeper than you'd be able to cut a living person."

I showed them what Birch had taught me: the proper way to hold the knife, how to thrust, to slice, where to place the blade, how to keep moving so they couldn't grab you. Then we practiced the motions.

"Don't cut too deep. You might get your blade stuck or cut the limb all the way off," I said.

"I'm not that strong," said Della.

"Strength's not the only factor. A lot of the dead are rotten inside," I said. "Five blows is a lot, I know, but the wormfeeders are slow. It works if you keep your head and stick to the pattern."

"What if there are too many?" Christopher asked.

"Run," I said. "Nothing else you can do."

"Why don't we just shoot the fuckers?"

Della smacked the boy in the back of the head. "What'd I tell you about watching your mouth?"

"Give me a break," Christopher said. "We're out here learning how to slice up living corpses in five easy steps, and you get on my case about swear words?"

I grinned and said, "Little fucker's got a point."

Della scowled at me for a moment, then turned away to hide the smile creeping into her face. "You boys must be closer in age than I thought."

"You know how to use a gun?" I asked Christopher.

"My brother taught me. I'm a good shot."

"All your family could handle one?"

"Sure. We learned after the dead started walking."

"How many wormfeeders were there the last time you saw all your family alive?" "Cornell, don't," Della said.

"It's all right," I said. "I need to make a point about thinking a gun in your hands is a magic wand that's going to solve all your problems. They got in close, right? Overran you. You couldn't get in a good crippling shot, and one bullet, even at point blank range, doesn't do much to them does it? Maybe you ran out of ammo, no time or room to reload, and then all you had was a club, something blunt they could grab, two or three of them latching on to pull it away from you. Did it happen something like that?"

The exuberance left Christopher's face. His stony glare made it clear I'd struck a nerve. His mussed, sandy hair twitched in the breeze, and he looked more like a child in that moment than any other time I laid eyes on him. He looked little and lost. His eyes welled up a bit, but he squelched his tears.

"Guess a knife is a handy thing," Christopher said, his voice a hair above a whisper.

"Save your life, maybe," I said.

Christopher stepped toward me. "Show me that last move again, okay?"

After that we practiced a while longer. Della never uttered another word about what I'd said to Christopher. The two of them caught on quick. Our blades flashed through the shadows and sunlight time and again until they knew the pattern as well as I did. When we finished, I turned and hurled my knife into the jackal, landing it dead in the side of the thing's neck. A puff of dust spewed out but the jackal didn't come to life or snarl as I saw it in my mind. Its glass eyes bored through me, stale, indifferent, staring straight into forever as if nothing in the world could ever kill their owner. I'd never seen a real, living jackal, but I couldn't imagine there would be any more life in its eyes than I saw in this one's.

ELEVEN

Weichert held it together for two days before he showed up at the greenhouse, bright and early, stepping through the door while Birch and I spiked our coffee with a touch of Johnnie Walker. The mood at Camp Cady remained bleak. The sheriff waited inside the door for a minute, watching us through the lattice of morning shadows. Then he glanced once at the Wall and shivered before averting his gaze to a row of African violets Birch cultivated. He eyeballed Birch's gadgets and experiments in progress spread out all over the long plant tables as he approached us.

"Time for a talk, fellows," he said.

Weichert's tone bore a touch less antipathy and a few degrees less arrogance than usual, undoubtedly due to the humbling security breakdown, maybe even an aftereffect of Wrigley reporting how I'd helped the hunting party stay alive. I think Birch sensed it too, because he refrained from the usual verbal lashing he saved up special for Weichert. Or maybe he mellowed only because he hadn't had his coffee yet. Either way, I suppose it's true: troubling times bring folks closer together, at least where their instincts for self-preservation converge.

"All right," Birch said. "Want some coffee?"

He filled another mug from the pot and then tipped the whiskey bottle over its rim, pausing a moment to see if Weichert would object, then letting the honey-colored liquor splash into the dark brown brew. That emptied the bottle.

He handed the mug to the sheriff, and said, "Let's talk in the lab."

Birch had spent more and more time in the greenhouse cellar over the past week, and it gave him a home field advantage. He hadn't lied about his equipment. I couldn't name half his machines and gadgets, but Birch worked them like a virtuoso, setting them up, priming them, letting them run, and making sense of the results. He recorded his data on three laptop computers and a dozen notebooks scattered around, each one dedicated to a different research path. I'd tried reading them but Birch's tech jargon and calculations only got jumbled up in my head. As best I understood, Birch resumed looking for a viral or bacteriological factor, re-treading work he'd done months ago in hopes of spotting some overlooked detail or finding new inspiration. He fixated on the idea of bacteria already present in human cells but only activated when its host expired, perhaps even by some other bacteria that thrived in decaying human tissue. Not that he had changed his views on what really fueled the resurrection, but he seemed driven by sheer intellectual curiosity. Birch the man might not have needed answers, but Birch the scientist couldn't stop asking questions. Despite his beliefs, he tortured himself working every angle that might unlock the secret of the reanimated dead, and I believed him when he said if there was a reason to be found under a microscope or in a test tube that he would've found it by then. A man like that—who's exhausted all rational options, who's sweated blood working to prove himself wrong—well, when he tells you there's only one answer to be had, no matter how much you hate the idea of what he's saying, you know odds are he's right. A man like Weichert, on the other hand, a man hell-bent on reconstructing an impossible way of life—he won't accept anything that doesn't fit his crystal clear, box-framed picture of the world no matter how bold the evidence. Put the two together and there's nothing to do but sit back and wait for the shouting to die down. At least things started off calm.

"We lost good people the other day. I let everyone down. Did my best, but I still let them down. I'm man enough to admit my best didn't cut it," Weichert said. "Now everyone's scared, and I need some answers, fast, to keep things from falling apart."

Weichert's humility surprised me. Birch, too, I think, because he hesitated before he answered, and when he did, he spoke with genuine regret.

"I'm sorry, Tom. I'm really sorry that I can't help you more, that I've got no good answers for you. But I don't have enough information to know anything for sure and you don't like my theories," Birch said.

Honest, yeah, but not what Weichert wanted to hear.

Weichert had put himself at Birch's mercy. Maybe he thought Birch was holding out on him, keeping back information out of spite, and if he only admitted how much he needed Birch's help then the scientist would grant it. For Weichert, humility and desperation made for uncomfortable companions. His face reddened, he snapped at Birch, and then the conversation tensed up fast. Their verbal artillery escalated, and in minutes, their shouting filled the room. Each man jabbed at the other's insecurities and fears; neither gave an inch. Though they had known each other less than six months, they argued like old men who've been taking each other to task decade after decade until they don't know any other way to communicate but to fight. They wanted to help each other, sort of, in a strange way. Birch would've given Weichert answers if they were his to give, and Weichert wanted to believe that a man in a lab with clever machines and tremendous knowledge at his disposal could solve any problem. I almost wished Birch would make something up or tell Weichert the things he'd told me, if only to kill the argument and buy some quiet. Instead, the shouting carried on and on— until I'd had enough of it. That's when I stepped between them and slammed my coffee mug on the hard countertop, hard enough to slosh out a splash of coffee and crack the pale ceramic.

"Shut up, both of you," I said. "Shut the hell up."

I spoke with the tone of voice I'd once relied on to send terrified bank employees and their customers into fits of trembling before I even drew my weapon. Birch and Weichert listened.

"It's real simple," I told them. "Two of you standing here hashing words with each other gets no one anywhere. No agreement is gonna come from this. Hear me? You want to keep people alive? You want to know what's going on down in Baxton, why the dead are marching south, what it is that's keeping them on their feet? Go to the damn source. Go to Deadtown. Go and see for yourself."

Damn me and my big, dumb mouth.

After the shock faded from Birch and Weichert's faces, I saw in their eyes they agreed. They'd already made their decision: We had to go. I'd spoken without thinking, and I couldn't back down from my words. From down in the recesses of my mind, animal laughter bubbled up, high-pitched and shrill, only it wasn't laughter but the cackling bark of my hated, constant companion, that savvy fucker who knew the day I was fated to die but would never tell me. I wouldn't ever be free of the jackal till I was free of the world.

TWELVE

That night I tried to convince Della that going to Baxton would be a good chance to scout the lay of the land between Camp Cady and Lohatchie, that I'd go, come back, and then we'd sneak ourselves away for good. Guess I wanted to convince myself too. Della said nothing for a long time then she asked to go with me. We both knew Weichert wouldn't allow it, and I knew she didn't really want to leave the compound without Christopher, but I loved her for saying it.

I told her to stay and get things ready for our departure. Christopher grew stronger every day, and I saw how it made sense for him to come with us, another set of good hands, another pair of sharp eyes. Though I didn't say it to Della, Christopher would help keep her mind off the horror all around us. She needed to take care of him and make sure he gathered his strength for the journey. We chewed over the argument until we had nothing left to say, and then we spent the small, black hours of the night cocooned in our room, wrapped tightly together. Della held onto me like she needed to imprint the sensation of my body against hers, trapping the heat and pulse of my life in all her senses. We fell asleep entangled, glued together with sweat, but Della woke before the sun rose and slipped away without waking me. She didn't want to say goodbye, and I didn't go looking for her. That way it felt like any other day. In case I didn't make it back, I left the spare car keys hidden where I knew she'd find them, inside a little box she used to keep her odds and ends, and then I went to meet Weichert at the greenhouse.

The sheriff had gathered a dozen men, including me, him, and Birch, to make the trip. Our plan was to take three jeeps down the highway as near to Baxton as was safe then hike across the open wilderness and come at the town from the northeast to avoid the dead line. By the time I finished packing and got to the greenhouse, Weichert and his group were ready to go and waiting on me and Birch.

"Nice of you to join us," he said.

"Where's Birch?" I asked.

"Downstairs getting some equipment."

Morning spread through the trees, telegraphing the sweltering day ahead of us, but I was grateful to see clear sky in every direction. Weichert's men milled around, unhappy and jittery. I didn't hold a case of nerves against them. No one, including me, wanted to make this trip.

"What do you think we'll find down there?" I asked Weichert.

"Bunch of stinking, rotting dead people," he said. "Doing what stinking, rotting dead people do. If we're lucky, we'll see why they're doing it and how we can stop the bastards."

"What if there is no *why*?" I said. "What if it's just one of those things that *is*, you know? No reason, no logic, only nature."

Weichert turned to me with a stony glare. "You're talking Birch's brand of superstitious bullshit. There's a reason. There has to be a reason. That's how the world works. There's a reason for everything."

Birch appeared, pulling an oversized backpack across his shoulders as he exited the greenhouse. He paused to straighten it then spat a wad of phlegm into the dirt.

"You need to check your makeup again or you ready to go now, princess?" Weichert asked.

"Fuck you, Tom," Birch said, with the kind of cheer he might've used to say *good morning.* "If you're feeling like an eager beaver, you can go on ahead without me. I'll catch up after I finish my coffee and the morning paper."

Weichert shook his head, ignoring the laughter that rippled through his men. He stalked up the trail to the parking lot. The others followed in a loose group. Birch and I fell in at the rear. As we left the clearing behind and stepped onto the narrow trail, a distant bird cawed, a lingering, porcelain sound like a lonely dirge echoing under a vaulted ceiling. We planned to be gone three, four days tops, but I wondered if I would ever see Camp Cady or Della again.

THIRTEEN

We covered thirty-five miles that day, traveling the desolate road out of Camp Cady and through the deserted town, picking up the highway then leaving it behind two exits above the one for Baxton. Or "Deadtown," as everyone called it since Birch's pet name for the place stuck. It was slow going once we left the near stretches where Weichert's men had cleared away old wrecks and dead cars. We encountered fewer dead as we headed south but the road worsened, clogged with massive jams of immobilized cars crammed together like racers waiting for a start flag that would never fly. We passed the remnants of old accidents, too, moments of violent, kinetic chaos preserved in 3-D freeze frames. Corpses occupied many of the wrecks, the remains of folks trapped in bent or crushed cars who died where they sat. Chewed-up arms and half-eaten faces hung out of broken windows. Some hunched behind broken steering wheels or under caved in roofs or framed by shattered glass webs. They stirred as we passed, tried to wiggle loose to get at the fresh meat. We gave them a wide berth and kept moving.

Where the road turned impassable, we drove along the shoulders, and a couple times we forced a path, eight or nine of us straining and pushing to clear cars off the pavement while the others kept watch. Traveling back roads brought little improvement, but it was easier to get around things with open fields, parking lots, and lawns alongside the road. We stopped fifteen miles away from Baxton, and there, with the sun hanging low, we made camp at an abandoned lumberyard. We pulled the trucks into an old warehouse, closed up the place as best we could, and settled in for the night amidst the smell of old wood. With dusk barely behind us, we collapsed, exhausted. In the morning we'd hike across back roads, fields, and rough ground, following a man named Grant, who knew a route to Deadtown that would keep us off the main streets.

Birch and I crashed in a corner, apart from the others. Birch frightened some of them, and none of them much liked him. A few had been lobbing hostile remarks toward me and Birch throughout the day, blaming us for getting their sorry asses dragged along on the expedition. Way I saw it, as long as Birch and I were right there with them to do the dirty work, they could shove their complaints where the sun don't shine. But imagine telling that to a gang of nervous armed men who disagree, and that's why Birch and I kept to ourselves.

Sometime after midnight, Birch shook me awake. I shot upright and reached for my gun, settling down only when I felt his hand pushing on my chest and saw his haunted face staring at me from the dimness. He sat cross-legged atop his rumpled sleeping bag, his eyes two pale smudges in the gloom. The smell of stale sawdust and forgotten oak and pine filled my nose.

"Shit, you scared the hell out of me," I whispered. "What is it, goddamn it?"

"Keep your voice down." Birch touched a finger to his lips and nodded in the direction of the three men on guard outside while we slept. His nylon sleeping bag whispered under him. "I got a bad feeling about Baxton."

"Hundred thousand or more walking dead hanging out there? So do I," I told him. "You woke me up to tell me that?"

Birch slid up against the wall and leaned back. "No."

"Then what?"

"Remember I told you about my dreams?"

"Yeah."

"I had one. It woke me up," he said. "They used to hit me once a week, or so, but lately I've been having them two or three times a night some nights. Wake up screaming and sweating bullets most times."

"They're only nightmares," I told him.

"It'd be nice if you were right." Birch yawned and rubbed his eyes. "What we'll find in Baxton, well, I think we're not going to like it. In fact, I got such a black fog over my thoughts right now, I'd bet you most of us won't leave Deadtown alive."

"Should we turn back?"

"No," he said. "That's the screwy part. I think we're doing the right thing going there, but I'm sure it's going to get ugly."

"Shit, man, what'd you dream tonight?"

"It's not what I dreamt so much as it is how I felt dreaming it," he said. "I was standing in the heart of a gray desert like the surface of the moon, thick dust all around me but clear air. I gazed up at a night brimming with stars, more than I'd ever seen in my life, and then one-by-one they winked out, going dark. I thought how each one might be a sun, and how maybe their worlds froze or flash-burned to ash, everything on them dying in an instant as their star exploded or went dead and black. I wondered how long before our sun burned out. But then the stars changed, became an infinite number of eyes, looking down from the abyss of space. As each one blinked, it vanished. I felt something drawing closer from behind them, a kind of raw energy, vast but lacking purpose. Like the fury of a nuclear bomb when that smoking, glowing dome of destruction goes on spreading, eating up everything in its path with light and fire and wind—except this was the opposite of heat and light. Behind me, someone laughed. It echoed through the air. Then I woke up."

"Damn. You had that one before?"

"No. Not exactly. Something similar with the stars and the eyes and blood once, but never a thing coming out of the darkness. Never felt anything like it before. Felt like a waterfall of pure hate. Mostly I dream about the dead, that they're all around me, going about business as usual as if they hadn't died.

Then they realize I'm alive, and it's like that scene out of *Invasion of the Body Snatchers* when all the pod people shriek at the real people. Remember that? Screw me. I watched too many horror movies growing up. Stuff gets all wound up in your subconscious and comes farting back out when you least expect it."

"Guess so," I said.

Quiet seconds ticked by, marked only by the sounds of men snoring or shifting in their sleep and the creaks of tired boards as the warehouse swayed in the stiff wind. A howling gust kicked up and sent the nearby trees rustling with a noise like rain pattering down. Our guards passed by outside. Their feet crunched the earth.

"I had a dream like that one time," I said. "Everyone in the world was dead except me. Probably a lot of people dreaming that dream. Probably hard not to."

"You might be right," Birch said. "Except sometimes there's someone on the other end of my dreams."

"How's that?"

"Someone sends them to me. He watches me through them. Maybe he's watching all of us now."

"C'mon, you serious?"

"It's someone I know. I'm not sure who." Birch shut his eyes for a moment. "It's someone I killed."

I knew Birch's background, knew he'd almost certainly done violence in the past, so what he said shouldn't have surprised me—but it did.

Birch rubbed his hands together. "It's not a guilty conscience, and I'm not losing my mind. I met him in person before I came to Camp Cady. He fucked me over as bad as he could, did some very nasty things to the people with me, to a woman I loved, and he's been lingering on the edge of my thoughts ever since. He fades in and out, but he's been there almost since the dead plague began. Worst part is he's dead."

Birch studied my face, waited for my reaction.

"How the hell is that possible?" I said.

"I got some ideas," Birch shrugged. "Told you there was more to this than I can explain. There's no question he's dead, but he's no dumb corpse. He has power. He can..." Birch hesitated. "If I tell you this, it stays between you and me. Understand?"

I nodded and mimed zipping my lips shut.

"He can put the dead down with a touch," Birch told me. "No idea how he does it. It's like magic, like he blesses them, and then—it's over, they don't move anymore. I watched him walk through a field after a battle between the living and the dead, and he was putting the broken and crippled corpses to peace. He touched their eyes, and their bodies stopped moving. He did it even to limbs that were no longer attached. And he can travel anywhere he wants. Now he's playing cat-and-mouse with me again."

I opened my mouth to tell Birch how crazy he sounded but then stopped when I thought of the jackal hovering over my shoulder. My longtime companion, who came and went and loved to stand by my side, laughing whenever my chips were down—and as real to me as anything else in life. Maybe Birch and I had more in common than I'd realized.

"You think we could learn how he does that to the dead?"

"No. I think it's something beyond the living. That's why I've kept it a secret. If Weichert found out, he'd think I was a lunatic or he'd never stop hounding me about figuring it out," Birch said. "Remember this and everything I told you, everything we talked about, okay? It's important. Someone needs to keep it alive. The other men will follow Weichert, even the ones who can think for themselves, because when push comes to shove security, company, and what's safe and expedient will win out over what's hard and best. Except you're not built that way. You've got a chance of surviving the long haul. I know he doesn't mean to, but Weichert's going to get a lot of people killed. Not his fault, really. The world changed; he didn't. He's done his best, but it's inevitable. I feel it coming. Maybe you can save some folks, maybe not. Stupid, fucking thing to come waltzing down here into the middle of a town full of walking corpses. Kicker is, though, you're absolutely right. It's the only way to find out what's going on."

"Well, I hope you're dead wrong," I said. "I'd like us all to get back to Camp Cady to put whatever we learn to good use."

Birch didn't register my words.

"Think about this," he said. "When was the last time you got sick? When was the last time you met someone who was sick?

Since the dead rose up, you hear about anyone dying from AIDS or cancer or diabetes or pneumonia? No. Only accidents, infections, gunshots, and being killed by the dead or each other."

"I knew a guy had the flu or something," I said. "Killed him and he became a wormfeeder, but that was weeks ago."

"Hunh," Birch said. "Exception that proves the rule, I suppose. Back at Vanguard I had a corpse that didn't rise—rotted out like it was supposed to. Still can't figure that one out."

"What are you getting at?"

"The new tests I ran compared living cells with dead ones," Birch said. "I started with my own then moved onto samples from some of the others around camp. Told them I was using live cells to find a cure."

"That's not what you were doing?"

"It was a new path to follow," he said. "Bottom line is you do everything you can to keep from getting hurt tomorrow, all right? If I die here someone has to bear the truth forward. Understand me? Maybe it's a small thing but it matters. Someone should live to tell whoever's left alive how important living is now. You know where all my work is. You can figure out enough of it to make it useful. You're smarter than you think."

"Man, no matter how smart you think I am, I don't understand a quarter of what you scribble down. I don't know what to tell anyone, and even if I did, who the hell is there to listen? So hit me with the plain English, and tell me what you're talking about."

"All right." Birch took a deep breath then let it out. "Time hasn't slowed down only for the cells of the dead but for the living, too. Aging, disease, deterioration, all of it has slowed to a crawl. Not for everyone, maybe, but for most folks. We heal at a normal rate, which has me puzzled, and we can still die as we saw the other day. But barring violence, mishap, or suicide, keep yourself intact, and you might live forever."

"You're fucking crazy. Anyone ever tell you that?"

"First thing I say to myself every morning, but being crazy doesn't make me wrong."

"You tell me this shit now?"

"I want to make sure you're careful tomorrow. Don't do anything stupid. Don't be a hero," Birch said. "I never told you but some of the stuff that's come to pass these last few months, that's stuff I dreamt ahead of time. The people I lost, I dreamt that before it happened. I knew I'd be leaving Camp Cady on an expedition like this. I knew a man like you'd be part of it. If I'm right you've got a bigger part to play in what's happening than you realize. I got a bad feeling about myself for what's coming tomorrow. I think the dead see something inside us we can't see ourselves, like they're passing judgment on our sins. I've done a lot of bad shit in my life, you know? Ah, fuck it. I'm nothing but a 'mad scientist.' Go get me a lab coat and a Tor Johnson look-alike, while I practice my hysterical laughter. Anyway, you play it safe tomorrow, so you can go back and tell them what they need to hear. Tell them about my dreams."

"I haven't been inside your head. I haven't dreamt your dreams."

"Yeah, well, I got a feeling you might." Birch lowered himself into the shadows and drifted toward slumber. "Get some sleep, now. You'll need it."

"Fuck you, how am I gonna sleep after that?"

Birch didn't answer. He only commenced snoring.

I closed my eyes, but too many thoughts spun through my mind. Maybe the living and the dead shared some deeper connection than that of predator and prey. Maybe living people still had a shot at a future. I wondered what Della was doing— lying awake in our bed, thinking of me, or glancing out the window at the high quarter moon in the misty sky and listening to the murmur of the woods, I hoped. I tried to summon her face in my memory, but Birch's words consumed me. I considered waking him up and making him talk, but he never said more than his piece. So I lay awake, running scenarios through my head, looking for the single perfect backup plan to guarantee I made it back to Della in one piece and still breathing.

I came up empty.

Not many situations I couldn't find a way to control or manipulate, but this was too big and chaotic, too much un-known, and I only hoped to hell I could roll with whatever punches came in Deadtown.

Later the sun rose and probed the cracks in the walls with blades of dusty light. A strange sensation came on the morning air like an electric fog on my skin, and I thought of the blind energy Birch had described. It made me despondent, made me want to go out and smash something, hurt someone, find all the wormfeeders and hack away at them until my muscles grew too weak to lift a blade. I wanted it all over and done with. I wanted nothing more to do with any of it.

I toyed with the idea of slipping out before the others woke up, going back for Della, and leaving this all behind. But I couldn't. I had to face the fact that part of me wanted to be here, wanted to know. All that had happened, all that I'd seen, everything stretched out ahead of me with Della at my side compelled me to stick it out. Running, hiding, and hoping the dead never caught up or caught us off guard would only ever take us so far, and the time would come when there'd be nothing to do but make a stand.

That's how life goes.

And it's always better to know what you're standing against.

I got up and walked out into the damp yard to take a leak. If I had to meet the coming darkness head on and hold my ground in the face of Birch's nightmare, I wanted to be prepared. If what Birch said about the living was true then everything I'd ever done and said in the name of immediacy, every stolen, breathless moment of passion that had ever fueled me seemed now to amount to little more than a hot puddle of piss. Above the trees, the apricot sky lightened. I finished and walked away.

The day began, and I felt like I used to on the morning of a bank job.

A cold calm settled over me.

FOURTEEN

The dead came for us on the outskirts of Baxton. They poured from every street and alley, every front porch and storefront, a gushing stream of lifeless flesh wrapped in a ripe miasma of putrescence. Rot and dry sores blemished their mottled gray flesh. Their tattered clothes crinkled and flaked with matted dirt and crusted bodily fluids. They looked fake in the direct daylight, like movie props or animatronic amusement park monsters. Remnants of life clung to them in bits of jewelry and identification badges, in shredded uniforms and the ruins of once-fine suits, in T-shirts emblazoned with rock band logos and bicycle shorts that sagged over withered flesh. Yet all their faces bore the same hungry, hollow-eyed, thoughtless death mask. Greedy mouths hung wide on broken jaws. Eager hands grasped with awkward, splintered fingers, gesturing for more, always more, telegraphing their lust for warm flesh. Their dead eyes stared at us, popping open from every part of them, gelid and white in the sun's brightness.

Weichert shouted.

Everyone heeled around and started to run back the way we'd come only to stop short a moment later.

The dead spilled out from the spaces behind us, too, on all sides of us, clogging the road and drawing into a circle that tightened with every shaky step they took. A billowy cloud crossed the sun, throwing down a shadow like the fist of heaven rising to smash us.

We opened fire, throwing round after round into the crowd of lifeless meat, but the dead only shuffled closer. We tightened together, a dozen men paralyzed at the center of a lonely intersection on the cusp of a town that had once been for the living but now stood less hospitable to us than a desert on Mars. Everywhere I looked I saw empty eye sockets on ravaged faces, the eternal grins of skulls stripped of flesh, the sheen of organs bloated with decomposition. Words I'd said to Birch the first week we met came back to me, and I knew I'd been right: This world existed for the dead now. At best the living were feedstock, and at worst, intruders, an infection, an invasive species.

The dead must have known we were coming, maybe through Birch's connection with the mysterious dead man who haunted him. They had laid a trap that left us nowhere to run, no way to fight back. We'd been wading through their stink all morning, listening to their distant, mournful chatter, but that was no less than we expected on the approach to Deadtown. Now, ineffective gunshots popped all around us, but neither Birch nor I drew our weapons. No point. The dread in Birch's eyes told me that some part of his premonition had already come true.

An explosion ripped the air then.

An abrupt gust of heat and a bone-jarring concussion knocked me to my knees. A line opened in the wall of the dead. Men rushed past me, through the thin smoke, to reach it. Someone had thrown a bomb into the mob. I guessed Weichert must've been holding out on us when it came to munitions, and I prayed he had another dozen of whatever the hell he'd used.

I jumped to my feet and Birch and I hauled ass with the others. We ran farther into town, deeper into the masses of the dead, the only direction we could go. Pavement underfoot gave way to grass, grass to dirt and then gravel as we rounded the corner of an auto garage and turned toward a high, chain-link fence in the distance. Behind it across an open field stood a towering water tank, its lofty catwalk accessible only by a single staircase winding up around one of its support columns.

Wormfeeders swept in from all sides, closing ranks like a giant, arthritic hand. Two of our party, Coogan and Daniels, stumbled and screamed. It happened so fast, we couldn't help them. Their bodies twisted as gray arms lifted them, and then they crowd-surfed a tide of clutching, dead fingers, kicking hard and wailing for help. The rest of us kept running. The dead drew so close, an inconceivable number of them. Stopping—even slowing for half a second—would equal suicide. I glimpsed splashes of red as the dead split open Coogan's or Daniel's skin like orange rind, and then the men disappeared beneath a patchwork of rotting bodies.

Three more men—Janson, Libby, and Tanner—fell along the way. They fired blast after meaningless blast into the arms of the fetid things swarming over them. After seeing what had happened to Coogan and Daniels, though, they didn't wait to be picked apart. At the absolute point of no return, each one turned his weapon on himself and cheated the final horror of being eaten alive. Made no difference to the dead. They still divvied up the warm bodies like lazy butchers.

The forward men were scrambling up the fence now, flipping themselves over, and dropping to the clear ground beyond it. Birch and I pumped our legs harder, driven by the cold wave of death tickling our asses. At the fence Weichert shouted for everyone to hustle as he shoved his men up and over then waved like a lunatic for me and Birch to pick up the pace. We did. Our fingers wrapped around rough aluminum and our feet left the ground. Chain link rattled and shook. A sudden weight struck below us. I grabbed for my gun before I realized it was Weichert bringing up the rear. I climbed faster as he closed on me. Weichert, Birch, and I—we all hit the top rail of the ten-foot fence as the dead slammed into the mesh and jolted the whole structure. My fingers slipped loose, but then I was over, the last to clear the fence. Tumbling then slamming against hard ground. Rolling, crawling, scraping to get back on my feet. No question the weight of the dead would bring the fence down; it was only a matter of whether or not we'd reach the water tank ladder before that happened. We had nowhere else to run.

Seven of us had survived the gauntlet. Four were already out of sight overhead, climbing higher and higher toward the catwalk. Again Weichert brought up the rear. I felt an unexpected burst of gratitude and admiration for the sheriff. As much of a hardcase as he was, he was no coward holding onto his authority like a crutch, but a granite-minded man doing what he believed necessary. He was looking out for every man still alive. Birch and I mounted the narrow metal risers. Weichert followed. We were twenty feet up when the fence folded like cardboard under the press of the dead. A swarm of black figures rambled over it, piling up a jumble of flailing corpses as the frontrunners toppled into the tangle of aluminum poles, chain link, and cold flesh. Their clumsiness bought us precious seconds, enough for the men up top to find positions and start shooting the first wormfeeders to reach the stairs. In their excitement to catch us, the ranks surged forward, mashing their fallen into the ground. I pounded the last steps upward, hit the catwalk, turned back, and pulled Weichert up the rest of the way.

All around the base of the tower the wormfeeders churned in a festering, unbroken wave of dead flesh that blanketed the earth. They filled every street and open space, every stretch of ground, stood on every rooftop, every car and truck, and way off in the distance at the limit of our sight, more ambled into the crowd. The noise of them, and the buzzing and clicking of the bugs that came with them could've drowned out the roar of the ocean on a stormy day. I'd never even seen so many living people in one place and of one mind, let alone such hordes of the dead. Estimates of a hundred thousand at Baxton were pitiful. Had to be a half a million. Had to be more. At least that's what it looked like, and I thought, *they must have started gathering here the day the dead plague began.*

Round after round snapped through the air as Weichert and the others dropped a shower of lead to cover the stairs. It didn't take much for good shots to tip a womrfeeder off balance. They always stood up again, yeah, but you could knock them right back down. We'd be safe as long as our ammo held out, which wouldn't be long at the rate of fire it took to keep the stairs clear. Then the dead would climb up to us and force us to fight hand-to-hand.

Birch grabbed my arm and pointed to the center of Deadtown. "Look."

A red light shone bright despite the late morning sun. It rose from the town's distant avenues.

"It's coming this way," Birch said.

The brightness shimmered as it crept through the low canyons of the Deadtown streets.

"Is that fire?" I asked.

Birch shrugged and then called Weichert to come look. The sheriff's face kind of twitched when he saw the glow, and he swore under his breath.

"You got any more of whatever it was you blew up back there?" I asked him.

"One," he said, lifting the edge of his jacket to reveal a hand grenade clipped to his belt. "Scavenged them after that army troop passed us by months back. Wish I had a hundred more. Figure all this one is good for is taking along as many of these scarecrows as I can when I go."

A volley of shots crackled.

The guns fell silent.

I feared everyone had run out of ammunition but they were only waiting for the next wormfeeder to hit the stairs—except the corpses had given up. A smashed pile of them lay wriggling in the shadow of the tower. None of the others approached. They stood still in the soft wind, their heads craned upward in our direction, and everywhere in their soft gray flesh I saw eyes. They stared out from dry blisters and scabby excavations, from cracks in smashed skulls, from dangling stumps of broken fingers, from black gashes in dead skin, from arms, legs, necks, torsos, and shoulders. One wormfeeder missing its lower jaw unfurled a swollen, rotting tongue, and an eye prodded from its tip.

"Would someone tell me already what the fuck is this crazy shit with all the eyes?" Weichert shouted. He slammed the heel of his hand against the steel guardrail. "Dammit, shit, and hell!"

"Language, Sheriff," I said. "When we get back to Camp Cady, you'll be doing time in the swear jar."

Weichert heeled around and tried to glare at me, but a grin cracked his face. He couldn't dampen his laughter. He doubled over as he let loose big-voiced guffaws. Some of the others laughed with him, letting off a little of their tension; the rest—tear-streaked and coated with sweat—gaped at Weichert like he'd lost his mind.

"Hell, that's a good one," Weichert said, when his laughter faded. "Get back to Camp Cady. Heh. Yeah, right. Then I'll open an ice cream shop and retire. Son of bitch, that tickles my funny bone. I should be angry as hell at you, Mr. Cornell, for suggesting we come down here, but never in a million years would I have imagined this many dead could be in one place. Forget the damn swear jar, because we are well and truly fucked. What the hell are we going to do now?"

"We wait," Birch said.

"For what?" Weichert asked.

Birch pointed to the red light moving through town. "That," he said. "We came here looking for answers. I think they're coming to us."

We watched the red glow creep our way, painting the streets with a pale pink luminescence as it came. The dead crowds let it pass, rippling like confetti making way for the wind. It reached the main road beneath the tower and then emerged from behind a house on the corner. It came from a gaunt dead man, his flesh scaled with modest decay, wearing only a pair of tattered blue jeans and dirty boots. The red light radiated from his body. He crossed the street then the field and then ambled over the fallen chain link fence. He stood below us, looking up—and all the dead turned with him, mimicking his gaze like an army of robots, turning thousands of corpse faces toward us, and with them the countless pallid specks of eyes peering. The sight reminded me of the stars from Birch's dream.

The Red Man raised a hand, flashed us a grim smile, and then waved a two-fingered peace symbol.

He started up the stairs.

Weapons ready, we watched him climb. His aura faded until it blinked out altogether when he crested the last step onto the catwalk and faced us. His skin looked pasted onto his bones, etched into the spaces between his ribs, glued to muscle and tendon, and ligament. Two black pits scarred his face—one above his left eye, the other through his right cheek. I looked for the telltale rise and fall of his chest, but he stood as still as the dead.

"Welcome to Deadtown," he said. "Been expecting you."

His voice rattled like a rat scratching inside a metal pipe; it rolled and crackled like his teeth were falling out and rattling around his mouth; it popped and sizzled like frying meat; it escaped him like coffin dust floating from an unearthed grave. Every syllable he spoke cut like razors.

"Stay where you are," Weichert said. "Don't come any closer."

We readied our weapons.

Birch grabbed my arm hard enough to hurt. His face turned pure white, and he struggled for words and air, trying to speak. Then a gunshot drowned out whatever he wanted to say. One of the men, Owens, had shot the Red Man, and now the man looked down at his chest, fingering a dry, fresh wound to the left of his sternum. The bullet had passed through him as if he were paper. Too fast for any of us to react, the Red Man grabbed Owens and seized his gun. He tossed the weapon aside; it skittered along the catwalk before it dropped over the edge. Then, lifting Owens by the waist, the Red Man raised him up and hurled him over the railing. Owens screamed as he plummeted into the hungry horde below us. As they dug into him, the sounds of his flesh tearing and his joints snapping mingled with their hungry groans.

"There's no need for violence. I have business with some of you," the Red Man said. "But if you want to be stupid about it, go ahead. I don't mind adding to my flock. You're all bound there sooner or later. You all died when you came to Deadtown. You died the moment you were born."

"Who the hell are you?" Weichert asked.

The Red Man gestured to the ranks of the dead extended in every direction, and said, "The Lord of the Dead, I am, yet, only a humble shepherd. Witness ye my sheep."

A vein in Weichert's forehead throbbed, and he ground his teeth together. "What's your name?" he said. "How can you be dead and still talk?"

"I'm dead because that man there killed me." The Red Man pointed at Birch. "Why don't you ask him who I am?"

Everyone looked at Birch.

The scientist trembled. Perspiration coated his face. He tightened his hands into fists and pushed ahead of us.

"You're right. I killed you," he said to the Red Man. "*I fucking killed you years ago.* There's no way you can be here. *No damn way.*"

"Now, finally, you remember me," the Red Man said. "Took you long enough. I knew you would sooner or later, especially after all the time I've spent in your head. I thought it would come to you the day I killed your woman, but I don't think you were ready to face the fact that you made me. Could've told you who I am anytime, could've showed you, but I wanted it to come back to you on its own, so it meant more. Do you remember what you said before you shot me?"

Birch swayed and looked as if his knees might buckle. He gripped the rail to steady himself.

The Red Man said, "I remember it."

"How can you be here?" Birch asked. "You died before the dead plague started."

"Did I? Are you sure? How do you know when the dead plague began? Because you saw it on TV and read it on the Internet corpse they told you what to think? Well, then that must be true. Can't question the good old idiot box. Can't doubt the online chatter. All the talking heads and government officials and people in uniform, all your priests, rabbis, and ministers, all your wizened sages who claim to own the truth. Well, you sure can't doubt them, can you? " The Red Man laughed. "I'm here because I am, and that's all that matters. Do you remember what you said to me or not?"

Birch nodded. "I told you that you weren't God and if you wanted to meet God, here he was in my hand. Then I showed you my gun."

"That's right. Then I said, 'Wishing doesn't make it so.'" The Red Man's voice cracked and grated like a long transmission over a dying radio. "After that you squeezed the trigger so that I could hear your God speak and feel his awful, burning touch."

Napoli, standing behind Birch, slipped his automatic from his pocket, keeping it low and out of sight, planning a shot on the Red Man. It was a mistake, but I had no time to warn him. The Red Man moved too fast. He darted toward the water tank, reached around Birch, and grabbed Napoli's hand. I had never seen one of the dead move so fast. He dragged Napoli in front of everyone then forced his wrist back until the gun barrel touched Napoli's forehead. He squeezed the trigger with his other hand. The shot echoed off the metal tank, a close thunder. The slug pinged into the sky. Napoli's head erupted onto the faded blue paint. The Red Man caught his body as it fell, lifted it up, and threw it down to the hungry dead.

"One more for me and mine," he said. "Who's next?"

No one moved. Birch stared at the glistening splatter on the tank, peppered with bits of bone, hair, and brains, dripping down the side.

"You still think you're God," he said.

The Red Man approached him.

"I came back from the dead, didn't I? I can send you visions. I can control the dead. Aren't those traits of the divine?" The Red Man shook his head. "But you're wrong. I *know* I'm not God. I have you to thank for that. You sent me to where God ought to be—and he wasn't there. The truth is God is dead and gone. He left a long, long time ago. The living taught me that, taught all the dead that, and that's why we've come back: to help you all find your way to the cold light of the universe. Death is the only God there is and death is a perfect God because one day everyone, no matter what they believe or how they live their lives, will become death's eternal disciple."

"Birch," Weichert said.

Birch didn't respond. He gripped the railing, trembling, seemingly unable to turn his eyes away from the Red Man.

"Birch, dammit!" The sheriff raised his voice. "Who is this freak?"

Without loosening his grip on the railing, Birch said, "His name was Darrell Philip Stradley."

"Never heard of him," Weichert said.

"No, you wouldn't have. He's the man who sends me my dreams. I've seen him in them," Birch said. "He killed my friends. He let me live to suffer. And he can kill the dead."

"What the hell are you talking about?" Weichert asked.

Birch said only to me: "He sends me dreams. He watches me. You understand?"

"I'm trying," I said.

"Understand what?" Weichert said. "What do you mean he can kill the dead? How? Make some damn sense already."

"Let me help with that," the Red Man said. "Let me send you all on a little daydream."

The red light flared and shimmered out of the Red Man's body. It emanated from him, enveloped us, and cast the world in a reddish tint, like looking at Christmas lights through blood smeared on a pane of glass. It brightened until it hurt my eyes; it flared with a silent eruption of energy. My skin crawled. My hair stood on end. I felt like I had to piss, like I might throw up, like my skull might crack apart. My mouth dried out. The red light consumed everything but us and the Red Man. Then it flickered and sparked out, leaving us in darkness, my eyes struggling with the gloom of night, under an open sky, outside on a summer night...

FIFTEEN

...in the dank, littered space behind a strip mall convenience store. A sliver of moon hangs over us. The odor of trash rides the breeze. A young man emerges from the store's back door, dragging three big bags of trash behind him. A fat woman in a green-and-white uniform leans out of the open doorway, shouts at him, then slams the door shut. The man pulls the garbage along to a dumpster placed against a chain link fence. Beyond it stand

trees, a slight hill, and then yards and houses, where television lights dance in the windows. One of the bags tears open and spills out the remains of food, wet paper, and other debris. A stink rises from it. The man swears and kicks the broken bag, spilling more trash. He takes the other bags to the dumpster, shoves the lid up then crams them inside.

It's difficult to see, but the resemblance is there: the man is Stradley.

Younger.

Alive.

He kneels to clean the trash spill. Then he coughs and his body jerks like someone pulled on strings tied around his shoulders. His eyes roll back in their sockets, and his head tilts toward the sky. He slips into a trance, his attention turned to the night.

"If you want to know who I am, you need to understand who I was. A minimum wage slave who could barely hold a job on the convenience store night shift," the Red Man says.

I stand in the alley beside the Red Man and Birch. The others stand with us, all of us apart from what's happening, like we've invaded Stradley's dream—or his memories. Blank patches and gray areas hang in mid air, holes in reality. Trees, boxes, litter, and other things come and go or change. I feel solid ground under my feet, but I'm a foot above the earth. Kneeling beside the trash, Stradley's young self shimmers, then separates into two of himself, one a ghostly duplicate of the other. The faded double approaches us.

"I was a big fat failure," he says. There's a gray cast to his face. Light and shadow seep through him. He wipes his garbage-stained hands on the front of his green-and-white work shirt. "I had no friends. My family wanted nothing to do with me. I wasn't even a junkie or a criminal or a head case they could rally around and try to save. I was one hundred percent pure loser. That busted garbage bag I'm cleaning up is full of wilted vegetables from the salad bar and magazines some kid threw up on. That's the smell of no life. You know what I was thinking about while I was doing that? Going home after work to masturbate in front of the TV. That was my goal. Except even that didn't work out for me, because this was the night I finally decided to give in and listen to the damn Voice."

Ghostly Stradley bends over his double and feigns whispering in his ear.

"Yadda, yadda, yadda," he says. "The Voice popped into my head one night, and it wouldn't go away. I ignored it for days, weeks, months but it kept talking, telling me to do things, to say things that I refused to do—until this night. After that bitch boss of mine screamed at me about the damn trash one too many times, I finally agreed. Knee deep in trash and kid vomit, I figured what the hell did I have to lose? If I was going crazy, I may as well enjoy it. And that was the end of this dumb loser."

Stradley kicks his double in the back, knocking him facedown into the spilled garbage. He kicks him again, and the double rolls into a ball. Stradley erupts into a rage, shouting and spitting, kicking and hitting the body until it bleeds and stops moving. His appearance changes, jumps between that of his younger self and the dead Red Man who stands less than three feet away from me. He gives a final kick.

The red light fills my eyes. The world vanishes into it. I feel dizzy and sick, flush with clinging warmth, and when the light dies, I stand with the others in the convenience store stockroom, where young Stradley beats his boss. Their green-and-white uniforms hang torn and disheveled. He slaps her face, shoves her, knocks her into stacks of boxes. He yells at her, calls her a bitch, shouts that he won't take her shit anymore, and if she doesn't like it, he'll do worse, much worse, he promises. Violence ripples off of him like heat. I've seen scenes like this before; he'll kill her if she pushes him. I want to grab him and make him stop, but I'm paralyzed.

"I felt good when I did what the Voice told me to do," the Red Man says. "First thing it said was to beat the shit out of my dumb bitch boss. She never nagged me again. It was easy after that. When I did what the Voice said, people listened to me. They respected me, some of them at least. And I didn't give a fuck about the rest. They feared me, and that was even better."

The Red Man stands beside his younger self, watching himself hit the woman, and every time she flinches or cries out, his dead smile deepens.

"That was a good night," he says.

The red light flashes, filling my gut with nausea, and the Red Man's dream—or whatever the hell he's dragged us into— becomes a red-and-black swirl of violence and chaos. Flashes of his life play out around us. In a smoke-filled nightclub, Stradley beats a man in a corner, both of them moving in jump-cut motions as strobe lights flash around them. A group of people watches, cheering him on. There's a gleam of joy in Stradley's eyes. The red light flashes. Stradley sits on a tall grave marker in a cemetery at night, speaking to a dozen people, many of the same faces from the cheering crowd at the nightclub. Most hold bottles of beer or liquor or plastic cups. Stradley's words mesmerize them. The red light flashes. Stradley leads a group down a dark street. Armed with baseball bats, boards, and pipes, they're hunting one of the women from his crowd of followers. When they find her, she vanishes beneath Stradley's gang, lost in a flurry of striking weapons. The red light flashes, and when it fades this time, I notice the others look as sick as I feel every time it comes and goes. It leaves us pale and wobbly, and the sights of Stradley's life do nothing to soothe us. Now he's in a room with three women, all of them naked, and Stradley goes at them in turn with short bursts of angry thrusting, while a dead man lies in the corner, blood dripping from his cut throat. Again, the red flashes. Stradley speaks to a crowd crammed into the living room of a rundown house, and I see it now, in their expressions, in their body language, how these people don't simply follow Stradley—they idolize him. He has a hold over them. The red light flashes. Stradley stands on the front porch of an old farmhouse, his face matured, all traces of doubt and weakness expunged by confidence and arrogance, by hatred, meanness, and lust. He shouts to a crowd of fifty people or more gathered on the lawn. More come from cars parked on the street, all of them enrapt by Stradley's words. Standing there with the Red Man is almost like being there, but the sound is muffled, and the scenery is broken and disjointed, and there's a stiffness about the people, a plastic tension in their faces, as if they're afraid to show Stradley any emotion other than joy. Stradley erupts into frenzy. He stamps back and forth along the porch, waves his arms; the crowd cheers. He shouts and points to a man near the middle of the group, and like a single organism, the crowd turns on the man and swallows him with abrupt violence.

"What the hell did you say to them?" I ask.

"Only what they wanted to hear," the Red Man says. "I told them what the Voice told me. I told them they were living their lives all wrong. I showed them how to liberate themselves from the preconceptions and rules that made them miserable. I taught them it was okay to take what they wanted, to enjoy it, to be happy, to put themselves ahead of anyone else, to play by their rules and no one else's. To live...well, kind of like you do, now that I think about it."

"I never lived like this," I say. "I only stole money. I never hurt anyone for no reason. The only man I ever killed was the man who shot my woman."

"And the two sorry bastards standing behind him. Forget about them?"

"No."

The Red Man shrugs. "But so what? Right? You were justified and that makes you better than me, better than the people who followed me? Is that how you see it? I know you tell yourself you live for freedom, but you're a slave to the shitty remains of living society, beholden to an old-fashioned ideal of playing house with your best gal. You've got no concept of what real freedom is or how free you could really be."

"How do you..." I say. "How do you...know about me?"

The Red Man makes guns of his dead fingers and mimes shooting some invisible target. He smiles.

The red light flashes. I'm frozen again, behind the farmhouse where acres of fallow land sprawl. Stradley's people plant it and build rough cottages. The group grows. Many people younger than Stradley arrive as well as some older, but all of them lost, angry, and disillusioned. I see it in how they avoid each other's eyes, in how they throw themselves into their work, and how Stradley electrifies them—like they all want to avoid ever again thinking about where they came from. They worship Stradley, stop and stare at him when he passes, act without hesitation when he speaks. Stradley walks the grounds like a king. At night people sit around bonfires, waiting until he comes, and when he does, brutal revelry breaks out. Wild dancing, and drinking, and *fighting, and fucking by the firelight, and Stradley observes it all with approval before he chooses his entertainment for the night. Some nights he picks a man or a woman and tortures them by the bonfire. Other nights he takes a woman or two or more into the shadows and orders them to please him. The red light flashes...*

Rows of cages in the woods, half buried in the earth, filled with those who've lost Stradley's favor as well those whom he favors most.

The red light flashes...

People tied high up on trees, naked, left for days without food or water and some of them, it's horrible to realize, are grateful to be there.

The red light flashes...

Someone butchers a body in the light of a bonfire, slicing pieces of it away and passing it around, heated over the flames then devoured by Stradley's followers.

The red light flashes...

Deep in the woods on a sunny morning, Stradley kneels beside a corpse, touches its forehead, and its eyes flutter open, dead white, before its mouth cracks wide and howls.

The red light flashes...

Daylight. Two police officers stand on the farmhouse porch by the front door with a sickly woman propped between them. Two of Stradley's followers greet them from the shadows of the entrance, their faces as bruised and cut as the woman's, but their wounds are older, healed over. The woman tries to go inside, but the cops hold her back, until Stradley emerges from behind his people. He shimmers and sprouts another ghostly double, who walks down the steps to meet me and the others on the front lawn.

"Cops showed up here a lot. Those bastards never paid me the proper respect," he says. "They brought home our strays, the ones who wandered off to the hospital in town when things got too rough for them. Low-dose strychnine poisoning or a few teeth cracked off above the gums. Acid burns or patches of missing skin that wouldn't heal. My true believers bore those burdens like badges of honor, but not the weak ones. It didn't matter. The cops questioned us every time. Not one of my people ever talked, though. They knew how bad it would be for them if they did. And whatever excuse we gave, I had a dozen or more people

ready to back it up, to tell the police the injuries were accidents or self-inflicted."

The red light flashes...

The farm brims with more people than it can handle. Groups have set up camps in the fields where they sleep in tents or under open sky. Some never leave the bonfires. Sick, wounded, tired, naked, filthy, lost, they sleep where they fall when each night's revelry ends.

The red light flashes...

Stradley stores weapons in the barn. Machetes. Pitchforks. Handguns. Shotguns. Semi-automatic rifles. Explosives. Enough for every person living on the farm.

More than enough.

The red light flashes...

Stradley mortifies his flesh with a cat o' nine tails and his faithful follow.

Stradley purges his soul on the flesh of his followers and his faithful follow.

Stradley fasts for a week and his faithful follow.

The red light brightens, dims...

None of Stradley's faithful match his fervor; none attain his heights of transcendence. He enters a trance and floats off the ground. He heals his followers with the touch of his right hand, maims them with his left. He makes the sun and the moon stand still in the sky, and he turns the waters of a stream to blood. He makes the fire dance and spark. A red aura embraces him in a full-body halo. Yet while his power grows, the outside world keeps pressing in. Suspicions never die. The police come around more often. They watch who comes and who goes from the property; and they monitor the bonfires at night. Stradley sees to it that every man and woman on the farm has a gun, plenty of ammunition, and a knife, a machete, or a hatchet. In Stradley's mind, he's already won. The cops won't risk a stand-off, and as long he keeps his people's activities contained to his land and out of sight, there's nothing they can do.

The red light carries us forward...

New faithful arrive, and Stradley takes their money. He holds it, accumulates it, builds a fortune, until he hits the big time the day a manic-depressive millionaire, aging into dementia, rolls up in his limousine. The rich man signs everything he owns over to Stradley and joins the people at the farm. Stradley turns the wealth he's collected toward a stockpile of death: black market nerve gasses and disease specimens. He stows them in the barn, in the woods, in the basement of the house.

The red light flashes...

The men come on a cold, clear night with the lights of their vehicles turned off; they give no warning, no chance for Stradley to arrange a stand-off. FBI agents and local police with special military support swarm onto the farm, cutting the dark with precision and determination, free to kill anyone who resists too much. The operation is a secret; a cover story about a right-wing militia is already floating around the fringes of the media in case things go wrong. The firefight turns heavy fast, casualties on both sides, but more among Stradley's people, whose bodies litter the ground. They run in groups against the intruders, almost mindless, their eyes brimming with rage and a hunger for flesh and blood. They look like the dead, the illusion only broken when one of them falls or dies and doesn't rise. The farm complex burns, the cottages, shacks, and tents go up fast, engulfed in flames carried by the wind. Columns of smoke rise toward the stars.

The red light flashes...

Now Birch stands before us.

Younger, fitter, his hair darker, and a hard light in his eyes. A trained killer's stare. He wears a black uniform devoid of insignia, a belt laden with equipment, and an automatic rifle strapped to his back. He clutches a black forty-five in his hand. He chases Stradley through the farmhouse, into the cellar, where Stradley works at opening a canister of nerve gas, but Birch arrives too fast. He knocks the canister from Stradley's hands and kicks him to the floor.

He shows him his weapon.

They exchange words about God.

The red light flashes...

Three shots: two through Stradley's head, one through his right lung.

The red light...

SIXTEEN

...faded away, dispelled by daylight flooding my eyes.

Fifteen years later Stradley's corpse still bore its fatal wounds.

He touched each one, and I heard the echo of Birch's gunshots in the recesses of my mind. The Red Man laughed. A sick feeling came over me. I clutched my stomach, doubled over, and dry heaved. Weichert and Birch did the same. Lee and Ferring hung their heads over the railing and retched into the air.

When I recovered, I said to Birch, "After fifteen years, he should be rotted away to bones and dust. How the hell did he rise?"

"I don't know," Birch said.

"It's true. I shouldn't be here," the Red Man said, and for that one moment his voice sounded normal, human, and living, as if the last dying scrap of his soul recalled what life had been like and wanted to wish away all the bad things Stradley had done and seen—but that moment passed fast. Then the Red Man's monstrous voice returned. "I learned things after I died. Where I'd been right and wrong in life, what the Voice was trying to tell me, and where it came from. Everything my faithful ever said I did was true. I can still do all those miracles and magicks. The world condemned us for how we lived, but there was holiness in it. And purity, too. Not any polite kind, no, but our pain and deprivation opened our souls. We lived like mad monks in the wilderness, scorning the needs of the flesh, beating our bodies down so that the spirit might thrive, and no one's spirit thrived more than mine. I believed in everything we did. Oh, *how* I *believed*—more than anyone else ever could. I became the saint of sinners, a shaman, a dark bodhisattva, a holy man with the powers of Heaven and Hell in my touch and a direct line to the divine."

The Red Man surveyed the dead gathered in Baxton. A few at the base of the tower still dripped blood from feeding on Owen and Napoli. The Red Man smiled, skeletal and reptilian, like a split in the bottom of the earth.

"Holy men don't rot when they die. Our bodies remain incorrupt. Crack a history book if you don't know what I'm talking about. My assassins buried me in a pauper's grave, where I lay dead as a stone for years, a relic till my body rose and walked again. What I saw in death, what I came back knowing...." The Red Man shook his head as if recalling the awe of his experiences. "Chaotic multitudes of souls swirled around me like grains of sand spinning in a whirlwind. An endless stream of raw energy flowing through the void. A storm of anger, bitterness, and isolation. Billions of dead crying out for the afterlife, for the Word, for anything that might fill their emptiness and tell them what to do—and hearing only silence in reply.

"I found others like me beyond death. Souls who remembered and knew the dead were abandoned. But they were weaker than me. They forgot who they were. Like all the others, they became only whatever it was they'd felt when they died, and for a lot of people—*for so many people*—that was either pure, burning rage at dying or icy fear at what comes next. Those souls wanted only one thing: to *live* again. Sure, a few voices of love and mercy cried out amidst the din, but they were faint. And easily silenced. When the needs of the dead hit a fever pitch, I was there to answer. *We* were there. The saints and the holy men. The magicians, the shamans, and the devils. And speaking with one voice, we said, *'Rise!'* And the dead did listen."

The Red Man's horrible voice faded into the wind.

Then the wind died, stranding us in silence.

Birch hung his head. Weichert panted through gritted teeth. Lee and Ferring clutched their guns, talismans to protect them.

"A God once existed to tend all souls, that much is true," the Red Man said. "But he died, or went away, or we killed him with our perversions, or our indifference, or maybe he abandoned us out of disgust or boredom or because he had better things to do. Who can know the mind of God? Who cares? What matters is what he left behind: nothing. A void to contain the souls of the dead. With nowhere to go and with the help of those of us who hold the secrets of life and death, they turned back to the flesh that once served them. But they found their flesh rotten and decayed and no good to accommodate so many righteous, angry ghosts. Where could the ones whose bodies had burned or disintegrated or been broken beyond recognition go? The ones whose corporeal homes had been pulled apart and divvied up among the living? They could only shelter in what bodies remained, many souls dwelling as one."

The Red Man raised his arms above his head. Smoky, crimson light streamed out of him. His flesh bubbled and coruscated like an infestation of bugs writhed beneath it. A hundred or more bloody seams creased his skin then snapped open with liquid rents that jetted sprays of blood and revealed eyes covering every part of his body. They blinked against the brightness of the sun.

"Many souls dwell in me for my corpse is strong," the Red Man said. "The souls of the dead demand what was once theirs: living flesh."

He grabbed Grant, our guide, by the scalp, tugged him up close, and bit hard into his arm, gnawing, working the joint until the limb popped loose. Weakened, sickened, and shocked, none of us could stop him. Grant didn't fight back, didn't utter a sound, when the Red Man threw him over the railing to the corpses below, keeping back his arm. Blood spilled down the Red Man's mouth and chest as he sucked on the torn limb. Blood ran into the eyes of his flesh.

"The dead came back to...*eat* the living because somehow, some way, we killed God?" I said. "What the hell? What about all you dead sons-of-bitches who lived and died before us? Weren't you the ones who did the killing?"

"Don't believe him," Birch said. "He was insane when he lived. A con man, a pervert, and a megalomaniac. There's more to this, Cornell. I've seen it in my dreams. He's not telling everything. He's not as strong as he thinks. The world isn't done with the living yet."

The Red Man spat a hunk of gristle onto the catwalk. "Shut up, Birch. No one cares what you say. Murderer."

He dipped a finger into the stump of Grant's arm then reached out faster than I could follow and smeared blood onto my forehead. His touch lasted only a moment, but it chased the heat and strength right out of my body. I shuddered. My knees bent, and I nearly fell.

"The dead know no mercy," he told me. "Death to the flesh to free the spirit, death to the spirit to free the flesh."

He crushed his thumb against Birch's forehead the same way, daubing an "X" on his skin, leaving Birch and me leaning against the water tank to keep on our feet. He shoved by us to get at the others. He ripped out Lee's throat. He gutted Ferring and then dropped them on the catwalk. He reached for Weichert, but the sheriff jabbed a knife into an eye on the Red Man's chest. It popped like a blister. The Red Man shrieked, but without pain, without fear; joy filled his voice. He welcomed whatever injury Weichert gave; he ate it up and waited for more. Weichert stabbed another then another. For every eye Weichert blinded, a new one popped open to replace it.

A little energy returned to my body. I felt steadier. I drew my knife from its sheathe on my belt, and then mustering everything I had in me, I crept behind the Red Man, the eyes on his back and shoulders lighting my nerves on fire with their stare. Then I sliced my blade into the side of his neck, dug in, and twisted. I brought the cutting edge down exactly how Birch had showed me, biting into the Red Man's spine. Something snapped. His head drooped. He took two steps then punched Weichert in the chest, sending up a little burst of red light as he cracked bones and slammed the sheriff backward. Then he crushed me against the water tank. A crimson haze filled my eyes, and I thought we might flash away again to another time and place. Then the Red Man let go of me and touched the dry wound at the back of his neck. It glowed for several seconds and when he lifted his fingers, his wound was healed.

He looked at me and shrugged. "You tried."

He hefted Lee's corpse over the railing then caught Ferring, who emptied his gun into the Red Man and kicked to get away. It did no good. The Red Man tossed him over. Weichert caught my attention. His chest heaved as he struggled to breathe. His pale face dripped sweat as he lifted the flap of his coat to show me the grenade still clipped to his belt. I took the hint and nodded.

When the Red Man came for him, Weichert—still choking and gasping for air—spat blood and saliva into the dead man's face. I scrambled away, a sharp pain in my chest telling me I probably had at least one bruised or broken rib, but I ignored it. I grabbed Birch and hurried him toward the far side of the tower.

The grenade blew too soon.

The catwalk bucked and the tower shook. I tumbled into the air, lost my grip on Birch, and came down rough, smashing my face against coarse metal. Iron scraps darted around me, clanging against the catwalk and its railing. A jet spray of water followed and hit my legs, shoving me toward the catwalk edge. The spray surged, and a river gushed from the tank. I grabbed on to the platform, digging my fingers into the sharp grooves of the metal mesh. Water swamped me in a flash flood. It cascaded onto the dead below.

Something jabbed my arm.

Straining, I saw Birch hanging over the side of the catwalk, clutching the edge with one hand, digging into my side with the other.

"Remember my dreams," Birch shouted over the roar of the water. "Remember everything I told you."

I grabbed his hand, but his wet fingers slipped loose and the raging water carried him away. I hollered his name. A flash of red sparkled below me. I closed my eyes and focused on holding tight. It felt like hours that the water flowed, icy, hammering at my legs, filling my ears with thunder, as it pushed and pulled, trying to drag me over the side. The world became a roiling, wet spiral hell-bent on punishing me. My hands ached and cramped. Pain lanced my wrists. The edges of the metal grooves sliced my fingertips. My body teetered on the brink of exhaustion. When I thought I couldn't hold on any longer, when I felt my feet creeping over the catwalk edge and dangling in empty air, the gusher died. The pressure dropped. The flow of water slowed to a feeble stream.

I flopped over on my back and sucked air.

After a while I forced myself to sit up. A gaping hole full of darkness faced me from the ruptured water tank. No sign of Weichert or the Red Man. I looked over the catwalk edge and saw the dead down there scattered and busted up by the fallen water. They wiggled like ants caught in a sudden downpour. An enormous puddle spread out from the tower, and a steady stream of water drops rained from the catwalk. It pattered like ice melting off the edge of a frozen roof.

I sat alone.

I screamed, loud and harsh, straining my voice to its limits, venting my anger to the open sky, shouting my horror and frustration to an indifferent world, until my voice cracked and faltered.

After that my mind blanked for a time.

Metal bit into my back. The dead would come for me sooner or later. I should've gotten up and ran. But I was too washed out to fight half a dozen wormfeeders let alone a hundred thousand. I rolled onto my side and watched the trees on the edge of town dance in the blustery afternoon, wishing I'd been able to keep my last promise to Della.

The jackal sat by my side, licking his paws.

Not laughing now.

Strange as it might sound, I was grateful for his presence. I mistook his silence for sympathy, his restraint for comfort, but I should've known better that no kindness dwelled in him, that the dead world and its scavengers were far from done with me. I think the jackal sat so quietly by my side because the fate he foresaw for me horrified even him. But I didn't think that then. I was only glad not to be by myself. After all, a dying man grasps at whatever lifeline comes within reach.

I blacked out and fell into nothingness.

I dreamed of the red and the black, of voices and stars, of the dead, and swarms of eyes, of a universe whose existence depended what those eyes saw.

When I woke stars glittered in the night sky like ice crystals on a blanket of black, virgin glass. I waited for them to snuff out like they had in Birch's dream, but they kept twinkling. The moans of the dead rose from beneath the tower. I shivered in cold air that turned my sopping clothes to a shroud of ice. I drifted back into unconsciousness.

In the morning, stiff and aching from lying so long on hard metal, shaking from the chill that had seeped into my bones, I opened my eyes and crept to the edge of the catwalk. Every move ignited firecrackers of pain. No sign of Birch or the Red

Man or any of the others. Only the dead remained, holding vigil. I wondered why they hadn't come for me in the night.

I waited an hour, but they ignored me.

"Enough of this shit," I said.

I stood up, limped to the stairs, and descended.

SEVENTEEN

The dead refused to touch me.

When I set foot on the ground I braced for them to rush me, but not one of them did. I walked right up to them, shouted, and cracked one of them in the face with the stock of a shotgun I'd retrieved from the mud.

Nothing.

Gangly and frail like scarecrows, dappled with black stains of rot, they watched me. Something about Weichert's preferred name for them seemed right to me then.

Scarecrows.

"What the fuck's wrong with you?" I shouted.

Silent eyes regarded me.

To my left stood a dead man in a brown courier's uniform, his face mashed beyond recognition. From a muddle of crusted wounds peered stark, rheumy eyes. I put my shotgun in his face and blew his head off.

Nothing.

He only fell over and crawled away, headless, through the mud.

The rest of the wormfeeders—the *scarecrows* did nothing.

Like I didn't even exist.

Wherever I walked, the dead let me pass.

Down among them the stench of decay became almost suffocating, and to my horror I realized I'd gotten a little bit used to it. I tore off a patch of my shirt and tied it over my mouth and nose to take the edge off the stink. I couldn't stop their groaning and gurgling. I crossed the muddy field, passed the auto shop, headed toward the street where the dead had ambushed us yesterday, and found the road out of town. I passed the crater Weichert's first grenade had left. I moved into the shade of the trees and kept going. As much as I didn't want to, it proved impossible not to stare at the death surrounding me in all its strange and savage glory. Bodies ripped open. Limbs hanging by threads of drying ligaments. Dead faces mottled purple and gray. Eyeless skulls. Organs poking out of flesh split open like old leather. Scraps of metal and wood broken off and still protruding from rotted meat. And always, the eyes. Those damn, dead eyes, tracking me wherever I went.

After a while I stared right back at them.

Trying to ignore them made it worse. Something had shifted around in my mind and changed how I saw them. It rose out of disgust and frustration but settled into anger. I glared at every one of the eyes I saw as I walked through the mob. I flashed them the stare that had earned me the fear and respect of lawmen who'd hunted me and thousands in loose cash from the hands of terrified bankers.

An unexpected thing happened then: those dead, white eyes blinked.

The longer I looked back at them, the more of them that blinked, twitching odd folds of flesh. I stared back at least as good as I got, and a lot of them dropped their gaze to the ground, looked off to the side, or closed up. I stared down the dead. My stride grew more confident. Maybe Birch pegged it, and the world still needed the living. I didn't understand it, didn't see what role other than food we might yet have, but I suspected that the dead did, and that's why they didn't take me. That and because the Red Man had smeared his sign on my forehead.

A hundred yards more and the dead fell behind me. A hundred thousand, a half a million, however many they were, I was leaving them and Deadtown, and the dead let me go. I walked out from their shadow. The road lay open, only the empty earth, and the far horizon, and the path home free and clear ahead of me, and not a dead thing in sight.

I didn't look back.

Not once.

I walked until my legs ached and my body screamed for water, and then I forced myself to keep moving, pushing one foot ahead of the other, grinding for every inch of ground, staggering north until the dark made it impossible to go any farther. With the day's sun a memory I found an office without windows in the back of a grocery store, blocked the door with boxes, and then I slept.

EIGHTEEN

I woke during the night, my body a rolling wave of pain. Three wormfeeders stood over me, swaying like drunks, a rotten stench pouring off them. Maggots crawled over their pitted flesh, and flies buzzed in the dregs of their clothing. One wore a hunter's cap, the second a police hat, and the third was bald with the top of his skull caved in like a soft-boiled egg. The eyes of their bodies glowed in the dimness. I reached for my gun but by the time I brought it around, they'd lost interest and shuffled away.

I leapt up, slammed the door behind them, and then barricaded it with more boxes and office furniture. I sat up for a time, expecting others to come, but nothing stirred in the corridor. I dozed back to sleep, but it brought me no rest. Instead, my mind came alive to visions of a sweeping darkness filled with the eyes of the dead. They rolled on a black wave like flotsam on a stormy ocean. I hunted for safe shelter. A dry, granular rain pelted my skin and peppered me with sooty smears; in the distance a pillar of light lanced into the night. Showers of brightness erupted from it like fireworks. I ran toward it, drawn by the voices coming from its glow—all dead, meaningless voices. I reached the light and saw it came from the light of countless souls ascending out from an infinite field of graves and pouring upward into the sable sky. As each reached the pinnacle of its ascent, it flared and flickered then snuffed out. The flashes of light lit the ruins that surrounded me. The remnants of bright buildings cast long shadows, and enormous, glassy eyes with blue, green, and yellow irises stared up from beneath the ash and soil. I sensed a black line of annihilation crossing the infinite space behind me. Everything it touched withered, and behind it lurked a wicked, faceless will. Malicious. Greedy. Bloated with dread and despair. A brazen, irresistible, hollow with an endless hunger aching to be filled.

I woke up in a cold sweat from my dreams—*Birch's dreams*—and I understood what had been behind the haunted look I'd so often seen in his eyes.

The dream had been as real as anything I'd ever experienced. I felt the presence Birch had described, like something hiding behind a curtain or waiting in the next room. It had reached into my head. I felt the echoes of its touch. Maybe the Red Man. Maybe something else. I shook it off as best I could then relieved myself in the back corner and headed out into the morning.

I needed to find Della and Christopher; it was the only thing I wanted. The Red Man had known we were coming, so I figured he must have known about Camp Cady. The dead line ran so close by, maybe he had used them to spy on us. Maybe he had even sent the dead that had wandered in and attacked us. Anything could've happened at the camp while I was gone. I needed to know that Della and Christopher were all right.

I crept along the back of the grocery store, checking each cluttered aisle I passed. Almost nothing left but junk and spoiled food but hunger drove me to search the debris anyway. I turned up an unopened bag of marshmallows hidden under a pile of dented pots and pans and broken glassware. I tore it open and shoved three into my mouth.

Sweet and fluffy.

Marshmallows never go bad.

Up front past the cash registers, the glass windows were smashed. Something there bumped then crashed.

I shoved the marshmallows into my shirt, grabbed my shotgun, and eased down the produce aisle. A man stumbled through the wreckage of the front entrance. The sun at his back made him a shadow, but he didn't move like the dead.

I wrapped my finger around the trigger. "Something I can help you with, champ?"

Startled, the man jerked forward, stumbled, and fell to his knees, grunting, waving his hands. He inched out of the brightness, and as my eyes adjusted, I recognized Birch. Blood-smeared clothes and wild eyes, his forehead tagged with a daub of blood like the one on me. He looked like he'd aged ten years overnight. I couldn't imagine how he'd survived falling off the water tower. He gestured to his open mouth, spitting, sort of snarling a little. A trickle of blood dribbled over his lips. His tongue was gone.

"Sonofabitch, Birch," I said. "I'm glad you're alive, but what the fuck happened to you?"

I hooked my arm under his and helped him to his feet. We stepped outside into the morning light. It wasn't easy, but Birch made it clear that the Red Man had mutilated him and that the dead had led him here in the night and left him for me to find. There was more to the story, but he didn't have it in him to tell me then. All the time I'd slept on the water tower and hiked away from Deadtown, Birch had been with the Red Man, a man he'd killed, a dead man who was more than a man now. I tried not to think about what else the Red Man might have done to him.

Birch and I traced the remaining path back to our lumber-yard camp and reached it by early afternoon. We took one of the jeeps and drove north. Birch nodded off right away, and I sank into a loneliness deeper than any other I've ever known. We passed the dead along the side of the highway, more now than we'd seen on our way down. Maybe drifting away from Baxton now that all the excitement was over or maybe arriving late to the party. They roamed along the road and picked through wrecked cars for food. Sometimes they turned and chased us, but I hit the gas and let them grow small and vanish in the rearview mirror.

I kept the pedal to the floor whenever I could. The world became a place of streaks and blurs, punctuated by snapshots of scenery when road conditions forced me to slow down. Ruined cars formed a slalom run on some stretches, but no matter how much the jeep jerked and swerved, Birch slept through it. The speedometer needle quivered and the hum of the engine drilled into my head. I rammed some of the dead along the way. They fell beneath the wheels or burst in a mess of viscera that spattered the windshield. I didn't care. I told myself to slow down but I couldn't. No matter how I tried, I couldn't bring myself to ease up. My leg locked tight, my foot hugged the accelerator. My arms stayed riveted to the steering wheel, my back welded to my seat. I couldn't stop before I found Della.

Close to evening I saw an oncoming car across a clear stretch of road, and finally the spell broke.

The other driver noticed us about the same time. Our vehicles screeched to a stop, maybe a quarter mile between us and separated by a grassy ditch between the lanes. None of the dead lingered nearby, but we'd passed half a dozen a couple hundred yards back, and I wasn't happy to be sitting still. I tried to see the other driver, but the setting sun glancing off the car's windshield made it impossible. Then I recognized its familiar shape and blue paint: Mason's car. I prayed that meant what I hoped it did, but in case it didn't I made sure to load the gun I'd found in the jeep before I got out.

A second passed as I approached. Ten. Twenty. Then the driver's side door of the blue car flew open.

Della leapt out.

She raced toward me.

The sight of her destroyed my loneliness.

Della jumped into my arms and wrapped herself around my torso. We clung to each other and kissed, holding on, afraid to separate. We might've stood there forever if Christopher hadn't poked his head out from the passenger side window and shouted, "Get a room, losers."

I laughed.

The sound shocked me.

I hadn't thought I still had it in me, but seeing Della alive, Christopher with her, and the old car that had carried us so far raised my spirits.

"I thought I might never see you again," Della said.

I stroked her hair. "I promised."

"I know." Della tensed. "I wasn't sure Christopher and I would make it."

"What happened?" I said.

"Got bad after Weichert left," she said. "People grabbed weapons and equipment without asking. I acted fast. Christopher and I gathered what we could, packed the car full of food, gear, and guns. No one hassled us. I'd helped most of them, one time or another. Then the dead came, from the direction of the dead line. Dozens poured out of the woods. All our guards we'd sent out to watch came with them. They overran the camp. We took the car and bolted. Some of the others made it out too. They all headed north together. We came south to look for you. Shit, it was like when Mason died. There was nothing left to do but run to stay alive."

"Lucky you found me," I said.

"I had to try." Della's eyes glistened. She wiped them with the back of her hand, and then licked her thumb and scrubbed my forehead with it. "You got some blood on your face. It won't come off."

I eased her hand away. "Worry about it later. I've got a lot to tell you."

We woke Birch and helped him to Mason's car. The jeep would've been a good choice, but with gas so scarce we opted for higher mileage. Besides, Mason's car had served us well and it was already packed. Birch and Christopher squeezed into the back seat with packages and boxes. Della, remembering what I'd told her about Birch's research, had grabbed some of his computers and notebooks, whatever fit into two boxes. Birch stared at it for a long time, and then he dug out a pen and a mostly empty notebook and started scribbling. I slipped behind the wheel with Della riding shotgun and turned the ignition key. The engine growled. I let it idle for a minute, then shut it off and rubbed my eyes.

Della took my hand. "What is it?"

"Where the hell are we going?" I said. "Nothing but the dead in every direction."

"Maybe," Della said. "But one way or another we're going home."

As if the word still meant something.

I was free again. Free of Weichert and his rules, free of giving a shit how other people thought I should live, but I didn't feel free. Instead I felt the Red Man's mark dried onto my skin; I remembered his frigid touch.

I started the engine again, put the car in drive, and roared off south, planning to speed past the Deadtown exit without so much as slowing down. The Red Man had made the other side of death sound a whole lot like life, maybe even worse, maybe even more pointless and punishing, and if that was so, then living forever, like Birch thought we might, didn't sound bad at all. Way I saw it, whatever the Red Man or the dead wanted, none of the living owed them so much as a stray tear or a handful of dirt. I wanted no more to do with any of them. I planned to drive us to Lohatchie, nonstop if I could. But I knew it was a fantasy.

I could never outrun the mark on my head.

And my four-legged friend hadn't abandoned me. The jackal had stayed with me every second since Deadtown. His cackling bark echoed out of every shadow we passed, and his hot breath came on every breeze that rushed by. It tickled the back of my neck. Wouldn't be long, now, I thought, before he let me in on his secrets.

PASSENGERS

ONE

Show the rich bastard what he wants to see, and he'll put the world at your feet.

The voice murmured inside Darrell Philip Stradley's head, unceasing, never silent, his guide and guardian angel since the day he first listened to it. Darrell nodded in agreement as he greeted the black limousine idling at the curb. The engine shut off, pinging as it cooled, and then a chauffeur emerged and rounded the vehicle to open the rear door for his passenger. An old man in a tailored, navy blue suit and a dark red tie leaned on the driver's arm as he rose from the car. His silver hair twitched in the breeze. He clutched a black briefcase by its handle as he swayed and trembled like a sapling in a hurricane.

Stradley watched the man squint with displeasure at the raggedy, overgrown front lawn speckled by tall dandelions and the saw-toothed weeds that sprang from every crack in the walk that led to the farmhouse. The man shaded his eyes from the sun as they took in the many odd faces peering from the house's grimy windows. Other faces spied from the front porch and the sides of the house, from behind untrimmed hedges in the neglected yard, from rows of garbage cans ripe with rotting trash, even from behind an old pickup truck left rusting on four flat tires. Stradley's people, watching his back. He felt their presence and relished it.

The old man's shoulders slumped as he finished his survey. "What a shithole."

Stradley chuckled and reached out to shake the man's hand. "Only a façade, Mr. Nelson, only a façade. You'll like it much better in the Garden, I have no doubt."

Nelson glared at Stradley's hand but didn't shake it.

He doesn't deserve better, doesn't deserve your touch. Show him your fists instead. Bare your teeth. Teach him respect.

Stradley lowered his outstretched hand. "So, how was your trip?"

"I'm here, aren't I?" Nelson coughed, then cupped a handkerchief to his mouth. He spit, then tucked the cloth away in his pocket, but not before exposing a patch of wet crimson. "Now listen, I don't like amusement parks."

"Uh, what's that, sir?"

"You heard me. I'm done with the midway madness. Don't put me in the bumper cars and tell *me* how to drive, understand?"

Stradley eyed Nelson's chauffeur for a clue to the joke, but the man's expression signaled only relief to hand off his burden, as if saying, *He's your problem now, buddy.*

"I'll keep that in mind," Stradley said. "What I meant is we let appearances run down out front to intimidate the locals and keep away prying eyes. The heart of what we do, what we've built, the Garden, is out of sight of the road, of course, but no point making outsiders feel welcome, right? So, you go ahead and drive your bumper car any way you want."

"What the hell are you talking about? Didn't I just tell you I hate amusement parks? Get the wax out of your ears, boyo. Quit pissing away my time, and what say we get to business?"

"I'd say you read my mind."

Stradley reached to help Nelson with his briefcase. The old man swatted his hand away.

"I'm not an invalid, dammit. You'll get *this* when I give it to you."

"Of course. Whatever you say, sir."

Nelson tottered along behind Stradley, taking his time on the steps to the front porch. As Stradley opened the front door for him, the limo growled, and its tires crunched grit as it rolled away. The two men walked to a back room where a picture window framed a view of the farmland that sprawled behind it. Five hundred acres of Central Florida far from the reach of strip malls and beaches. From an unseen fire beyond the soft hills and brush rose a lonely tendril of smoke. A trail wound toward it, past makeshift huts and sheds of corrugated steel, vinyl tarps, and wood and drywall scraps that hinted at more buildings out beyond the tree line. Nelson eased himself into an old leather, high-backed chair and propped the briefcase on his knees. He stared out the window. His jaw loosened, and his mouth drooped at an awkward, aimless tilt.

"I can feel it," the old man whispered.

Stradley grinned. "Good, that's good."

Let him soak in the energy. Let him take a taste. Bait this bastard and then set the hook.

Stradley, his attention fixated on the briefcase, sat in a chair beside Nelson.

Faces appeared at the window. Pallid onlookers gaped at the visitor. Bruises and scars blemished many of them, some wounds gleaming with fresh blood or wet scabs, a few with hair pulled out and blood matted in what remained. Nelson grimaced, but then looked past them at the smoke rising from a fire that seemed to burn in his honor. Without taking his gaze from it, he said, "You greedy creep. You're more interested in what's in my briefcase than anything else."

"I'm most interested in what's in here." Stradley tapped his chest above his heart. "And what's up there." He gestured generically toward the sky. "What you have in that case is a means to an end, nothing more. I'll get where I'm going one way or another, but your help will sure get me there faster."

"I don't give a dog's dump about your ends and means," Nelson said. "I'm dying, you heartless fucker. *Dying.* I want to know where we go after we die. You say you can show me—*really* show me? Then do it so I can die in peace. Then this and much more is all yours."

Nelson popped the clasps on the briefcase and raised the lid to exhibit tight stacks of hundred-dollar bills packed solid inside. A letter-size manila envelope lay atop them.

Every one of those money packets buys a dozen deaths.

"A dozen deaths," Stradley said under his breath.

"Huh, what's that?" Nelson said.

"Just a little prayer of hope."

Faces gathered at the room's entrance. Half a dozen more at the back door. Dirty, torn clothes and bruised, scabby flesh. They eyed the old man and the money with flat curiosity.

"Five million, as agreed."

"Bless you for it, Mr. Nelson."

"Shove your blessing up your ass, Stradley. I'm not here for that. *Show me.* Understand? I don't 'pays my money and takes my chances' anymore. I don't watch the pretty lady while you pick my pocket clean. I buy results. I didn't survive six decades in business gambling with my resources. Dammit, if I can't buy doctors who can save me, who can even relieve my pain and depression, then I want to know what's waiting for me."

"I hear you, Mr. Nelson. You won't be disappointed."

"What the fuck do you know about my disappointment? I'm *always* disappointed. Every goddamn morning when I wake up, every second my eyes are open. Sitting here talking to you right now. *Disappointed.* But, hell, I've gone everywhere in this world, tried everything to find my answer, so I may as well give you a turn. What's one more chance to win the brass ring in a long line of cons and failures? So, when can we start?"

Show him your fists! Show him! Show him NOW!

Stradley's grin widened into a smile that showed his teeth. He rose from his chair. Without so much as a moment's warning, he punched Nelson square in the face.

The old man's nose crumpled under Stradley's knuckles. His head snapped back. Blood gushed from his nostrils. The briefcase spilled from his lap, disgorging money onto the floor. Nelson slumped sideways in his chair, grabbing the armrests to stop himself from sliding out of it. He gasped for breath and gaped at Stradley—who punched him again, pummeling his head back against the chair.

"We can start right now, Mr. Nelson."

Onlookers rushed in, grabbed up the envelope and bundles of cash. Some tried to stuff it back in the briefcase while others ran off with handfuls of money. In moments, they carried it all out of sight. Nelson righted himself. Blood stained his fine clothing, and tears poured from his eyes. He trembled. Then he laughed, deep, hearty, directed at himself. In that moment, Stradley saw into Nelson's soul, saw him for an old, frail, needy man, shaking, a man on the threshold of a new world slamming the door after him on the one he left behind.

Let's show him everything he ever wanted to see. Let's take from him everything we need to set the world right. But before you show him heaven, show him your fists.

"Set the world right," Stradley muttered as he tensed his arm to throw another punch.

As Stradley's fist sped toward his face yet again, Nelson croaked, "Start right now, yes, yes, good, why... wait?" Then he laughed until Stradley's knuckles crushed his lips against his teeth.

TWO

Indeed, what Stradley had to show in the Garden did not disappoint.

Nelson regained his senses several hours later and discovered himself lying in a fetal ball on the damp earth, dressed only in his underclothes. His tremors, uncontrollable as he came alert, diminished as he gained some control of himself.

Screaming voices had dragged him awake from the recesses to which Stradley's beating had banished him. Now firelight stabbed at his eyes. He cupped a hand over them for shade and tried to make sense of what he saw. Black bars cut his view. He lay in a cage sunken a few feet into the ground on a gently sloping hill above the center of what Stradley had named his Garden. A low wall of earth surrounded half the cage, but the front portion remained clear, providing Nelson with an unobscured view down the slope to where a mob rampaged around a behemoth bonfire that shouldered back the night. Men and women chanted, shrieked, and moaned. Some wielded short whips with which they lashed their own backs. Others crawled on hands and knees, wailing whenever someone stamped on their fingers and legs. One swung a hammer at the elbows of anyone foolish enough to approach him. None of them wore more than rags, and most wore nothing, letting bloody red streaks and smears, created by their wounds, paint their flesh. Small groups joined each other in tumultuous, wrestling masses of twisting, stretching bodies, then separated and rushed back to the melee. Now and then voices hollered, alone or in unison, "Death of the flesh to free the spirit, death of the spirit to free the flesh!"

Nelson thought at first that his mind had cracked and summoned a nightmare out of a medievalist's sketchbook. But the harsh ground beneath him and the air rich with smoke and the tang of blood persuaded him he witnessed something real. Next, he guessed that Stradley had mounted a show to intimidate or impress him, but that comfort soon fled too. The wounds looked too real, and some of the bodies hit the ground in awkward, uncomfortable positions and didn't get up again. Finally, he accepted what his aged eyes showed him. Acceptance brought him no more understanding than his fantasy explanations had. The tableau weighed him down with the all-too-familiar weight of unfulfilled hopes. He had seen such things before, mad rushes to pleasures and torments of the flesh, witnessed them in many forms in many places around the world. Yet no matter what meaning people gave them these acts never penetrated more than skin deep.

I'm back on the damn bumper cars, he thought.

Then he wept, fulsome disappointment overwhelming him.

Soon a crimson glow caught his eye and drew his gaze higher.

He might rationalize and dismiss the feral orgy that unfolded around the fire, but he could not process how Stradley floated above it and looked down upon the violent ecstasy.

Beatific, in a horrible way, and limned with red light, Stradley levitated.

Twenty, thirty feet off the ground.

A hovering angel of madness.

A monster.

A man with power Nelson had never witnessed but only dreamt he might one day touch.

Now it lay within his reach. He sensed it through the space between them like the rolling concussion of a distant explosion, the air tainted by a battery-acid sharpness.

The old man scurried back until he pressed against the bars on the far side of his cage. He curled down onto himself, wrapped his arms around his knees, and wished for warmth.

As if answering a prayer, Stradley's glimmering and teary red eyes opened and flashed in his direction. A splinter of fire rushed at Nelson.

It grew until its light filled his vision, then his mind. Heat flooded him, burning off some part of him from the inside out, consuming his disappointment, carrying it away, leaving only troubled awe. Then he succumbed again to the depths of insensibility, the yawning darkness on the far side of consciousness, which he now knew Stradley himself ruled.

THREE

Beyond the bars of Nelson's cage, Stradley's acolytes worked to clear the debris left by the last night's ritual. They dragged the bodies of a man and a woman out of sight behind one of the sheds. What they did with them after that, Nelson didn't know. He watched people drift out from huts and sheds into the circle at the heart of Stradley's Garden, the ring of the bonfire pit. Judging by the height of the sun, he'd slept into early afternoon, a restless, sweaty slumber in the open brightness that had left his skin reddened and sore.

So calm in the light, so ordinary and meek, dressed in everyday clothes as if doing yard work, people set about preparing the grounds, Nelson guessed, for another night of perversions and wonders. He grasped now what Stradley held over them. The vicious guru promised his followers a way through the corrupted flesh to the pure spirit, to raw power. Judging by their unmistakable ecstasy the night before, he certainly seemed to deliver. Like Pentecostalists speaking in tongues or voodoo faithful ridden by the Loa. Yet feral, suffused with unbridled energy, and awash in blood that most ordinary people of faith preferred remain symbolic.

Not so here where the literal ruin of the flesh reigned.

A woman roused in a sunken cage neighboring Nelson's, one of a dozen or more around the Garden. She dragged herself upright. Her naked chest heaved as she coughed and then spat out bloody phlegm. Scars laced her body. Graying hair sprang from her scalp in matted tendrils that formed a dirty halo. How long had she been here, Nelson wondered. What sacrileges and miracles had she witnessed?

The woman rubbed her eyes, and then, noticing Nelson's gaze, glared at him. He looked away when she stepped out of sight behind the ground cupping the rear of her cage.

A process. Preparation and contemplation. Mortification of the flesh. Destruction of self-consciousness. Severing one's earthbound connection to free one's spirit. Exposure of one's awareness to peer behind reality's curtain and observe the truth. These things Nelson had sought for so long, only to find unfulfilled promises from spiritualists and sages, physicists and chemists alike. They all promised miracles but delivered only sleights of hand.

"What did it get me?" Nelson's voice cracked with dryness. "*Fuck all*, that's what."

"That's all anyone gets," the woman in the next cage said.

She stood at the side nearest Nelson, still half-hidden by the earth, her arms through the bars, idly scratching at the dirt. Several broken teeth rendered her smile reptilian.

Nelson pressed against his cage and reached through the bars. His fingertips came within six inches of the woman's. She flicked a pebble at him, and it bounced off the back of his hand.

"When 'fuck all' is all you got, Mr. Stradley offers real answers."

"He's a huckster like the rest. Carnival barker. Pay your money, ride the wheel. Whee!"

"They all are, though, aren't they? You trust anyone outside this place, they only fill you up with lies. Play their game to get their prizes, right? Church, the cops, the doctors, my parents. They all lied to me about who I am and where I belong in this damn world. My husband was the worst." The woman showed Nelson the underside of her forearm, dotted with small round burn scars amidst crisscrosses of long, thin keloids; it resembled a tic-tac-toe game. "See that?"

"Your husband did that to you?"

"The cigarette burns, yeah. Woke me up that way when I overslept or just for shits and giggles. The other scars? Whenever he burned me, I cut myself to mask the pain he caused with pain I created. At least I owned the hurt then. Right?" The woman pulled herself up on the bars, immodest in her nakedness, and stuck her feet through, with her shoulders pressed against the top of the cage. A mesh of scars covered her body. "Kept it up whether he burned me, cut me, beat me, or treated me like shit. Did it so long and so hard, I started to see things after I made the cuts. Thought they were hallucinations until I learned how to hurt myself so I could see what I wanted. Any time I didn't know what to do I cut myself and the answer appeared. Crazy, right? They all told me so. 'Oh, Virginia, you're off your rocker.' 'Oh, Virginia, you're going too far.' My fuckwit husband sided with them, of course. Tried to have me committed so he could shack up with a cashier from Food Wizard. That's where we met. I used to work there too. The damn checkout, me wondering who the handsome man with such good taste in beer was, looking at my future of bruises, burns, and insults, and thinking I'd found true love at last. So, we all pay our money and then ride the wheel, I guess."

Virginia hopped down from her perch.

"Why are you here?" she said.

"I want to know where we go when we die before I die."

Nelson drew his unsteady arms back into his cage. Solar heat beat down, searing and relentless. He wiped the sweat from his eyes with his quivering hands.

"We all want to know that."

"You think Stradley can show me?"

"Oh, honey, he wants to show *that* to everyone. Death of the flesh to free the spirit, death of the spirit to free the flesh."

"What does that mean?"

Virginia chuckled, exposing her rotted, fence-post teeth. Blood filled the spaces among them and pooled by her gums.

"You'll find out soon enough, sweetie."

Nelson opened his mouth to reply but coughed instead, a fit that lasted nearly a minute and culminated in him spitting out a bright, bloody gob of the rot inside his lungs.

FOUR

Night dropped around the compound like a parachute buoyed on the bonfire thermals.

People crept from the sheds and huts, came from the wild dark of the grounds, and from the farmhouse. So many more people than last night or at least more than Nelson had realized were there in his rattled state of mind. Certainly, more than Nelson expected a man like Stradley to attract, but when Stradley arrived for the revelry, even Nelson felt the tug of his native magnetism. Unavoidable. Irresistible. Charisma that devoured the self, shredded the individual will, and left only the many—and Stradley.

Firelight painted the man red at the center of the compound. His sweating skin glistened with the flickering. His bare torso displayed bruises, scars, and layers of wounds, a testament legible to those who shared its language. As he roamed among his congregation, he touched each one he passed on the fore-head. Each, in turn, quivered and lit up with joy, then one by one they leapt into a brewing revelry. Soon a line of people danced a circle around the edge of the fire. Singing broke out. It calmed Nelson's shakes for a moment even as it chilled him to his core.

"Death of the flesh to free the spirit, death of the spirit to free the flesh," many sang.

Stradley approached Nelson's cage. The old man's heart leapt with unexpected hope. For mercy and relief, for an end to suffering. Despite the warmth in the air, a chill had settled deep in his old, ill bones, and his stomach raged for nourish-ment, his throat for water. Every motion sent waves of vertigo through his head and flocks of black bubbles across his vision. His chest ached. His skin throbbed with sunburn. His body trembled. He stayed upright by leaning on the bars of his cage. Stradley could release him from his torment. He possessed the power.

If only he unlocked the cage.

Let him out. Fed him. Clothed him.

Showed the barest touch of mercy.

Instead, Stradley passed him by and went to Virginia's cage.

"No," Nelson said. "Please. I want to see and be done with it."

Stradley unlocked *her* door. She grasped his helping hand and clambered out.

"Please," Nelson said.

Holding her head with his fingertips, Stradley leaned close to Virginia's face and spoke words inaudible to Nelson. They lit a fire in the scarred woman. She stamped her feet, grinned wide until Stradley released her, and then rushed downhill to the revelry. Seizing a softball-sized rock as she ran, she hurled it at the crowd. The stone struck a man on the ear. He folded to his knees with blood pouring down the side of his head and neck. Virginia leapt on him, punched him, scrabbled to undo his raggedy pants and pull them down. A group parted from the circle to surround her and her victim. They blocked Nelson's view, but through brief gaps, he witnessed Virginia, bloody mouth full of broken teeth, naked legs straddling the man as she choked him—and then the man smashed his elbow into her face. She reeled and spit out a tooth. Smiling, she threw herself at him again with her fingers raised like claws. Then the crowd blocked the view again.

Nelson heard the rest. Grunts and shrieks mingled with the crowd's cheers and gasps.

From the wider circle came chanting and singing. Somewhere Stradley laughed, unseen.

When the commotion around Virginia ended, the crowd fell back into the circle. Virginia didn't reappear. Nelson couldn't see her or the man she'd attacked, didn't know if they'd gone into one of the sheds, or joined the blur and shadows of the circle.

Stradley reappeared at the center of the ring.

A red aura outlined his figure. His eyes burned with a reflected flame.

A group followed him. Men and women carrying whips, which they cracked in the air, and iron brands, which they set to heat in the fire. Stradley gestured at a man in the crowd; one of his followers lashed his whip along the man's side. He yelped, staggered, resumed dancing, but another lash set him stumbling. When he fell, Stradley and his people set upon him and dragged him into the center of the circle where they tied him to a wooden post, his arms stretched so high, he stood on tiptoes.

"Oh, thank you, thank you, thank you," the man chanted. "Death of the flesh to free the spirit, death of the spirit to free the flesh! Bless me!"

"You are blessed, my friend," Stradley said. "You will show us the way."

"Yes, let me show the way, let me serve. Thank you!"

Stradley placed his right hand on the man's forehead. His red aura intensified.

The circle erupted in fresh fervor. The ones with whips and glowing red brands put them to work. Screams filled the night. Nelson couldn't tell those of pain from those of ecstasy.

Stradley's red light grew to encompass the man tied to the post.

Its energy crackled. It prickled across Nelson's flesh, summoned goosebumps, and set his hair on end. Power gathered in a rising wave poised to break on them all and release the torrent of an ocean of infinite malevolence. Nelson sensed it on the other side of what he saw, the spirit beyond the flesh. What awaited the dead beyond this life existed within their reach, its entry livid in the energy Stradley controlled.

Nelson dropped to his knees. His body shook so badly it blurred his vision.

Still, he saw well enough when Stradley retreated from the bound man, and two of the dancers came with long knives, sliced him open from throat to waist, then folded back his skin. An angelic expression of fulfillment came over him. He cried out, but his words drowned in the roar of the circle, and Nelson never heard them.

Stradley raised his arms and cheered. The huckster showing his ugly face.

Nelson understood then how he used that as a tool to control his followers. But past the façade, all Stradley's claims and offerings promised to provide Nelson with the long-sought truth. Even miracles, as attested by the eviscerated man, alive and blissful as his organs spilled out from him.

Nelson wept and watched through tears as Stradley levitated above the Garden.

The cut-open man lived long after he should've expired.

Stradley's red aura melded with the vibrancy of the flames, a brightness that owned the night, and rendered everything beyond dead black as if nothing at all existed outside of the reach of Stradley's power.

FIVE

"Death of the flesh to free the spirit, death of the spirit to free the flesh."

Stradley's voice came to Nelson as he trembled on the earthen floor of his cage. Sunlight baked him, sweaty and burned red despite shivering like a man dragged in from the icy cold. His eyelids split, and he cringed against the light. He saw Stradley staring down at him and then roused himself, dug his hands into the earth, and tried to push himself onto his feet.

"Look at you trying to stand when you should kneel for me. You disappointed yet, Mr. Nelson?" Stradley said.

"Can't say it hasn't been...," A coughing fit interrupted the old man at the end of which he gagged out a spray of blood. "...hasn't been a wild ride."

Stradley leaned forward on a walking stick. "Better than bumper cars?"

"Fucking bumper cars, fucking amusement parks is all there was, every place I looked, the same heartbreaking songs and dances, but here..." Nelson seemed at a loss.

"Here it's real. You've tasted what I can provide those who join me."

Nelson nodded.

"Want to see some more?"

Lifting his head, the old man met Stradley's confident stare. Nelson recalled himself sixty years younger and full of the youthful self-assurance and entitlement that had set him on the path to incredible wealth. He had believed then that money bought all things only to learn as he aged and saw the end of his life on the horizon that it didn't buy the things he truly wanted, things that Stradley possessed. Seemed, in fact, to have pulled out of thin air. Nelson wanted to know how.

"You've already got my nickel. Show me the rest of the damn freak show."

"Good." Stradley produced a key with which he unlocked Nelson's cage. He helped him up and out and then led him, limping, to the rim of the massive firepit. "What do you see around you?"

Nelson surveyed the sheds and huts, the tools of torture abandoned on the ground, the ashes of the bonfire, and the countless muddled footprints in the dirt and matted grass. They looked different here than from his cage. Momentous yet ephemeral, a contradiction he couldn't explain, as if they only marked the surface of something subterranean and each held within it the key to a hidden door. The little buildings shifted in his bleary eyes. They became eyeless heads with doors for mouths from which dark power overflowed. The ashes looked like a pool of milky bone powder into which he could dive and never stop sinking.

"I don't know how to describe what I see," Nelson said.

"Excellent. When you see only things you know, you gain nothing new." Stradley offered him the walking stick. "Here. You'll need this. You don't deserve it, but you'll need it."

Nelson accepted it. "Okay."

"The power wants me to break your teeth off at the gums and shove them down your throat. It wants me to yank your hair out at the roots. Right now. But I know you're not ready. Suffering has to come in the right measure and sequence."

"The power wants you to... do things?"

"Oh, yes, the power has a voice, and I've heard it all my life. When I finally listened to it, I saw so many things I couldn't describe. I found it placed the world at my feet. Come with me."

They departed the bonfire circle, the huts and sheds, and walked into the overgrown wild of the fallow farmland. Rough tracks cut through the worst of the foliage, but vines grew across their path, and branches clutched and scratched at them. Nelson strode with hesitant steps, head down, eyes focused on each next one. When he looked around, he saw an unrecognizable world full of abysses and lacuna, of flowing black lines like oil streaking the air, of gray-and-red specks that darted and swarmed like insects. He kept his eyes on his feet. The walking stick kept him steady. Every fifty yards or so, Stradley stopped and waited for him to catch up. When he heard sobbing from the trees ahead of them, Nelson planted the walking stick and raised his head.

"Someone's crying," he said.

"Isn't there always?" Stradley said.

"Who is it?"

"One of the people I want you to meet. Come on."

They rounded the curve of the track and entered a grove of Southern Live Oaks, old trees with massive roots rippling in the ground. Strung from their high branches hung another type of cage. Giant birdcages. Of the ten within sight, seven contained people. The sobbing rose from one of them, a man who looked as if he hadn't eaten in weeks. He pulled tufts of hair from his head as he wept.

Stradley approached him.

"Take comfort, brother," he said. "Death of the flesh to free the spirit, death of the spirit to free the flesh."

Stradley's voice livened the man, but he managed to say only, "Death to... the flesh...," before he collapsed back into sobbing.

The other caged people stared at Nelson with unyielding eyes, unashamed of their naked, filthy bodies, arms and legs dangling through the bars, their skin rich with bruises, cuts, and the red welts of insect bites. A stench hovered in the grove's air, rising from bodily wastes expelled onto the ground. Through his skewed perceptions, Nelson watched lines of orange insects he feared did not exist crawl on the cages and their prisoners, on the tree, on the ground. The cages appeared to stretch and drip pieces of themselves in the breeze.

"You're a torturer," Nelson said.

"No. I didn't put these people here, and I take no joy in their misery. They asked for this. I have a list thirty long of others who want the same thing, but I don't allow it if they're not ready. That's what matters. Preparing the flesh and refining the spirit. In that, I find joy. What they become when they emerge from the cage, transformed and opened to my gifts." Stradley seized the walking stick from Nelson, who lurched to keep his balance. He banged on the cages with it. "Hello! Is anyone here against their will? Would anyone like to be set free? Say the word. I'll lower your cage and let you out right now."

No one answered. They only stared at Nelson, the interloper, the doubter.

Stradley returned the cane to him, and they continued along the track. Next, they passed a place where people buried to their necks glared up at them from the ground. In another grove, people tied to the trunks of wide trees struggled to lift their heads, one on either side of a trunk, ropes digging into flesh, arms stretched around the circumference, fingers within a hair's breadth of touching. A third held several of Stradley's followers in stocks, and the fourth led to the door of a long outbuilding, like a small hangar. Nelson viewed it all through his damaged eyes, the world alive and swirling like skies in an impressionist painting, but ugly, threatening.

"All of them?" he said while Stradley unlocked the door.

"What's that?"

"All of them? Do that willingly?"

"They beg me for it once they understand what I offer. You must be ready in both flesh and spirit, or you might wind up, well, *disappointed*."

"What if I asked? Am I ready?"

Stradley considered the question. He stepped back from Nelson and gauged the frail man. A trickle of blood ran from the corner of Nelson's lips. He hadn't even noticed it. Only the walking stick kept him vertical.

"You needy bastard, who do you think you are? The power tells me to beat you deaf just for asking," Stradley said. "But I know better. You asked me that very question just by coming here, and, Mr. Nelson, you are so close to ready. All the pieces are there awaiting your full understanding to shuffle them into place." Stradley opened the door and ushered Nelson into the building. "Once you have that, then I can show you what you want to see."

They passed through a small anteroom and then into a large storage area full of weapons. Rows of racks and shelves held a motley collection of handguns, rifles, machetes, clubs, land mines, grenades, knives, and other mechanisms of killing. Stradley guided him through the room to the far end without comment. The contents of the room conveyed everything that needed saying. This was a stockpile of death awaiting delivery.

They came to another door and stepped into a side chamber.

A cube made of plastic sheeting—a room within a room—occupied the central space. Wires and tubes connected it to various machines and a ventilation system.

Two men and two women sat inside on folding chairs around a card table. They wore t-shirts, shorts, and jeans, and looked healthier and better healed than most of Stradley's other followers.

"I arranged this for you," Stradley said.

"Another sideshow," Nelson said. "You're wasting my time."

"You'll change your mind soon enough. Watch."

Stradley moved close to the sheeting. The four within gathered near him on the other side.

"Do any of you want out? Changed your mind? Reconsidered? You know I'll open the seal right now if you do."

The four shook their heads.

"Did I force any of you in here? Coerce you? Intimidate you?" Stradley pointed at the old man. "It's important that Mr. Nelson understands what he's seeing."

Again, the four shook their heads.

"Good, very good. We drew lots, didn't we? Because so many people volunteered for this." The woman nodded. "Excellent. Marybeth, please show us the container then proceed."

Inside the cube, Marybeth raised a steel container roughly the size of a thermos, waited several seconds while Nelson took a good look, and then set it on the table. She unscrewed the cap and set it beside it. Producing a new top with a nozzle, she screwed it onto the canister. Once it locked into position, she put the cylinder on the floor at the cube's center and then depressed a button on its side.

"Expensive stuff you're about to see in action. This one cost $15,000 alone," Stradley said. "You wouldn't believe how hard it is to find people selling, but they're out there, oh, yes, and money sure does grease those wheels."

A gray mist plumed from the nozzle and spread within the cube.

An instant later, the men and women inside crumpled to the floor. The spray continued for several seconds and rendered the interior of the cube invisible. To Nelson's eyes, it looked alive, writing to free itself from its meager cell, hungry to touch him. In minutes it dissipated. The four lay dead where they had fallen, eyes rolled back in their sockets, blood dribbling from their nostrils and lips, their skin pale.

Nelson staggered a step and used the walking stick to regain stability. "Why? Why did they kill themselves like that? Why did you ask them to do that?"

"So you would understand what the fortune you're going leave me will buy. They had no fear. You understand? They knew what you wish to know. Now, Mr. Nelson, if I ask *you* if you are ready, what will your answer be?"

SIX

Yes.

Of course, Nelson said yes.

With no real idea of his true readiness, he accepted whatever Stradley guided him to next. He hadn't paid his money to *not* take the ride, and despite the vileness of what Stradley had so far showed him, here he had seen more faith, witnessed more real power, and felt closer to the edge of the answers he desired than anywhere else he'd ever sought them.

The rest unfolded over several days. Stradley stayed with him through most of it.

They began with diluted poison mixed into fine scotch, a celebratory concession. The alcohol burned Nelson's throat, and the poison gnawed at his guts.

Next, he entered one of the tree cages and found it much worse than his first prison. He emerged three days later, dehydrated and confused.

His disorientation pleased Stradley, who spoke of breaking down barriers, killing the flesh until only the spirit remained and then killing the spirit until only the truth endured.

Two days buried up to his neck. Four tied to a Live Oak.

With every passing second, the world became a stranger and less certain place for Nelson until, in the end, he almost believed he had left it behind. Or that it had never existed. A dream of life, of being, from which he now awakened. Everywhere he looked, he saw strange shapes and colors, an infestation of unreality.

By the time Stradley and four of his followers brought him into the armory, Nelson couldn't walk on his own. His tremors rocked him. He ached for food and drink. Open wounds and sores riddled his sunburned, peeling flesh, and his limbs screamed with itching insect bites. They took him past the weapons to the back room. The plastic sheeting cube and the equipment that had maintained it lay piled in a corner. Eight gurneys occupied that space now, all but one of them bearing a motionless human figure under a dirty black sheet. On the one empty gurney, a folded black sheet waited at the foot.

Against one wall, a standing mirror reflected the overhead fluorescents and gave the light a hazy quality.

In a corner of the room stood two chairs and a card table, a manila envelope upon it.

Two of the entourage helped seat Nelson at the table, while the other two waited by the empty gurney. The old man eyed the envelope as Stradley took the other seat.

"What are these?" Nelson's hoarse voice barely broke a whisper.

"Don't you recall?" Stradley opened the envelope and slid out several pages printed with small words. Colorful sticky tags prodded out from some of the papers. "They're contracts and releases you promised to sign if I showed you where we go when we die. They leave all of your earthly fortune to me."

Nelson nodded, a gesture difficult to discern, considering how much his head bobbed. "I remember, but you just dragged me through the freak show. I'm waiting for the main attraction."

With a smirk, Stradley said, "It's going to begin once you sign the papers. Unorthodox of me, I understand, to ask you to keep your end of our bargain before I've kept mine, but, trust me, you won't be in any frame of mind to do this after you see the show. It's the only way we can keep our deal."

"What if you're tricking me?"

Stradley said nothing for several seconds. His red aura appeared, painting his person with a cold, ruby light. He lifted from his chair, rose several feet in the air, and regarded Nelson like a parent regards a doubtful child.

"Have I not shown you miracles enough to earn your trust?" he said. "I have but one mystery left to share."

"Yes, yes." Nelson pawed at the pen until he snagged it in quaking, arthritic fingers. He sifted through one page after another, signing where the sticky tags indicated until no papers remained. One of Stradley's people gathered the signed documents, looked them over, and gave a sharp nod of confirmation.

"You've done all of humanity a tremendous favor. Your resources will allow me to tear away the veil of falsehoods under which we suffer and show everyone what the universe really is and how awful our place in it is. Right now, humanity still thinks the world is a place for the living. They go on about their lives, worried about surviving and thriving, arguing over the right way, the best way, their favorite way to live, and they think killing one another is the greatest of sins. I'm going to show them all how wrong they are and teach them death is the way. Death of the flesh to free the spirit, death of the spirit to free the flesh."

Two of Stradley's people helped Nelson from his chair and over to the empty gurney, where the other two helped him onto it.

Stradley wheeled one of the other gurneys into place beside Nelson's and peeled back the black sheet. Virginia lay there, dead, discolored, and yet better preserved than Nelson expected for a days-old corpse.

"Are you ready to see, Mr. Nelson?" Stradley said.

Without shifting his gaze away from Virginia, Nelson said, "*Am* I ready?"

"Yes, I think you are."

He cupped a hand over Nelson's mouth, pinched the old man's nose shut with the other, and waited. Nelson jerked, tried to bat Stradley's hands away, but his body possessed so little life after all his tribulations, and tremors robbed him of his strength. Seconds became a minute, then minutes, and then a gray fog overcame Nelson's vision, darkened to black, and he died.

SEVEN

Nelson's eyes popped open.

The world dizzied him.

The room, the gurneys, the dismantled cube, the table and chairs, Stradley's people—it all looked as if it had sprung to life from a cubist painting. He saw the world as if cracked in two and pieces pressed together misaligned. He looked at the backs of Stradley's people with one eye and the fronts from another, both still part of his gaze. The disorientation should've nauseated him, but he felt nothing more than the light stinging his eyes as they adjusted.

The view tilted. He moved around the room, but not under his control.

He glimpsed the gurneys, on which the dead figures now sat up, black sheets peeled back, bodies wrinkled and spotted with rot. He recognized two of the dead from his first night caged in the Garden, the mystery of what happened to them now solved. He knew the other four from the makeshift gas chamber, Marybeth and the volunteers who died to show him what his wealth would permit Stradley to unleash on the world.

The scene lurched again.

Nelson felt none of it, only saw it.

He felt nothing at all beyond the grasp of his eyes.

A terrifying silence surrounded him.

The mirror gleamed.

One line of his sight approached it. From the other, he saw the back of Virginia's naked corpse shuffling toward the glass. He recognized her crisscross scars and cigarette burns. Then one of his eyes found the reflection, and he stared at himself while the other watched Virginia sway in front of the mirror. Long seconds passed before Nelson made sense of what he saw.

The single eye staring into the mirror looked upon itself, peering out from folds of skin at Virginia's waist above her right leg. Someone turned Virginia to face a second standing corpse, and Nelson met the gaze of his second eye staring out from the dead flesh of a man he had watched die. His two eyes regarded each other. The rotted skin around them blinked.

Nelson wished to scream, but he had no lungs, no throat, no voice. He wished to run but found no footing. He wished to die—and then understood: He already had. Stradley had killed him then resurrected him to show him what he had so long desired. *Where do we go when we die?* The main attraction unfolded within Stradley's secret big top. More eyes peered from the other corpses in the room. All stark with confusion and shock. None able to communicate even with the flesh they inhabited. Only passengers now, their life's energy imparted to dead flesh, reallocated and... preserved?

How long would this last? Was this the eternal afterlife?

Nelson's view whirled again as someone forced Virginia to sit. Stradley sat across from him, smiling, looking him right in the eye. At the same time, his other eye focused on him from across the room. Stradley's gaunt face resembled a skull.

No, Nelson thought. *Not eternal life.*

Death. He is death.

Eternal death.

THE DISTANCE TO LOHATCHIE

The Dead in Their Masses—unlike some of the other Corpse Fauna stories—enjoyed a fairly straightforward path to publication. It was a story I wanted to tell as soon as I finished "The Dead Bear Witness" so when Vince Sneed asked me to contribute to a new anthology of zombie stories he was editing to follow up *The Dead Walk*, I knew the time had come to write it. I picked up only a short time after Cornell, Della, and Mason break out of prison and chronicled their attempt to journey to Lohatchie. In retrospect, I went a little easy on them for the first leg of their trip, so their lives only got harder when I revised the story for this new edition. Regardless, Vince was pleased with the original version and included it in *The Dead Walk Again*, published by Padwolf Publishing in 2007 with a cover painted by Steve Blickenstaff.

The threads of the overarching Corpse Fauna cycle really start coming together here. Cornell and Della strengthen their relationship. Cornell meets Birch. And then he meets the Red Man, a dark counterweight to St. Bianco from *Tears of Blood*. Before this Cornell thought he was only struggling to stay alive and find a safe place to live—but after his encounter with Darrell Philip Stradley, he is made into something more. A man with a role to play in something greater than himself. And that's not something that sits well with someone whose entire existence has been a stick poked in the eye of authority.

I revisited some of the themes from *The Dead Bear Witness*. Cornell's unease being part of society. His resentment of authority both spiritual and worldly. His sense that a terrible fate awaits him sometime in the future. But also his need—despite what he believes about himself—to not be alone. In a world overrun by the living dead, most people would see Camp Cady as luxurious sanctuary, but Cornell sees it for what it really is: a comfortable trap. That's all life can ever be unless you're making your own rules. But how does an outlaw define himself in a world where there are no longer any laws? Cornell may be a robber, but he's no savage, and in many cases, he proves the better of those who represent any kind of authority. His friendship with Birch reflects Vale's experiences from *Tears of Blood*. No matter how weird he thinks it is, Birch lives in the world as it is not as he wants it to be—at least as far as he understands it. Keep up or fall behind. Adapt or die. Or be damned to a living death. Trying to understand a new world isn't easy, but the ones who make the attempt are the ones who matter most.

When I began work on *The Dead in Their Masses*, I intended it to conclude Cornell's story. It wouldn't have been the end of Corpse Fauna, but it would've brought everything in Cornell's piece of it full circle and shown how things turned out for him. As I wrote it, though, I realized there was much more to Cornell and his role in the dead world than I could cover in this one story. Then I began to wonder what might happen if Cornell and Vale should meet, and *The Dead in Their Masses* turned out to be the only next major chapter in the Cornell's story, not the last.

Around the time *The Dead Walk Again* was published, Vince and I talked plans for a Corpse Fauna collection, a thick volume collecting all the published material, some new short pieces, and the last big chapter of Cornell's story, all to be published by Die Monster Die. It would pick up from where *The Dead in Their Masses* left off and it would answer all the open questions and explain many of the secrets of the walking dead. We were excited. I started writing. Vince was looking forward to designing the book and creating the cover. As sometimes happens, though, the real world derailed our plans. When Dark Quest Books revived Corpse Fauna, this volume stood ready to go. We made it as far as Glen Ostrander's gruesomely stunning cover, which, thankfully, adorns this edition before those plans also collided with unpleasant realities and derailed.

Twelve years later, Corpse Fauna returns from the dead once more.

James Chambers
September 2019

THE EYES OF
THE DEAD

FOR DAVE,
WHO NEVER WOULD'VE READ
THIS CRAZY HORROR STORY BUT
WOULD'VE LOVED THAT I'D PUBLISHED IT.

THE EYES OF THE DEAD

ONE

Inside the crashed yellow school bus, the dead partied.

At least, it seemed so at a glance: a teenage jumble of football, cheerleading, and marching band uniforms, slow-bopping to music only they heard, knocking around a handful of teachers and coaches playing chaperone. They mimicked a wild homecoming party coming off the high of homemade speed from a punch bowl spiked by the school science nerd. Then they saw me, Della, and Christopher stepping out of our Toyota Camry. As if a silent, invisible DJ doubled the beat and pumped up the volume, they thrashed at the windows and rocked the bus.

"Party bus from hell," I said.

"You think they were coming or going?" Della said.

"Hmm, let's say, coming home."

"Okay, Cornell, but did they win or lose?" Christopher said.

"Let's give them the win. Figure they checked out on a high note."

"Could they have been trapped in there from the start of the dead plague?" Della said.

"Safe bet, looking as intact as they do," I said.

"Sucks for them," Della said.

I slapped a hand against a bus window. The dead boogied down for me.

Clustered against the glass, they bared blackening teeth and stared at me with dozens of impossible eyes, the eyes of lost souls that never belonged to those cold bodies. They watched from every limb and wrinkle of exposed flesh, a winking pox. I used to pity the dead, raised up and filled by those invading eyes full of hate and envy. After so many hundreds of miles and months of living in this rotten world, after standing up over and again to the glare of those eyes, of them watching me fight for my life, I couldn't muster an ounce more of sympathy.

I waved my hands in the air and yelled, "Like you just don't care!"

It drove them wild.

"Maybe we shouldn't mess around with them," Christopher said.

Only twelve years old, his voice carried a layer of fear. Dirty blond and with a lanky build that would bloom into muscles in a few years, he put on a brave face, but horror remained fresh in his eyes, deepened by the reminder that the future he should've grown into no longer existed. The young adapt fast, yeah, but they feel things more acutely than grown-ups, especially the thick-skinned criminal kind like me or an ex-prison nurse like Della. Christopher had survived his own hell before we met, lost his entire family to the dead, but a light still burned in him, and I never wanted to be the one who dampened it.

"Don't be nervous," Della said. "They aren't getting out of that bus."

"No, he's right," I said. "We shouldn't push our luck. Good call, Christopher."

He smiled at me, anxious but a little proud.

The wreck had stopped us dead in our path.

The bus blocked the lanes on our side of the highway, part of a line of piled-up vehicles that stretched from shoulder to shoulder and clogged up the oncoming lanes, too, leaving no way to pass. The bus lay tilted about forty-five degrees on its side, propped on a BMW crushed under it. The twisted metal of the Beemer blocked the front door. A smashed Lincoln kept the dead from escaping by the rear emergency door. A street-lamp toppled in the collision pinned shut the rooftop exit hatches. Thick windows held but trembled in their frames as the dead surged against their glass.

All their hungry eyes focused on us. So many eyes peering out from every inch of their exposed dead flesh. Their stares burned with a critical mass of resentment and violence wrapped up smack in our path and packaged inside what, in the old, living world, would've been a microcosm of the next generation's promise.

A breeze tickled the overgrown roadside grass. Empty blue sky sprawled above us.

The air reeked of the dead. No signs of the living anywhere—except for us.

Right then, a familiar, deep bark rattled in the back of my mind. The cackle of my old pal and constant companion, the jackal waiting somewhere in the world to claim me the way death claims us all one day. His breath blew hot across the back of my neck as it had so many times before when he crept up from the depths of my subconscious to remind me of my mortality.

"Shit, we have to make a way through," I said. The jumble of torn metal and machinery hung together like a house of cards with no obvious move that wouldn't upset the pile that sealed the school bus.

"We should double back and find another way." Della wore jean shorts and a navy blue tank top, and the breeze plucked at her silky, black hair, sweeping it across her shoulders and the back of her neck. "Better not to fool with this mess."

We'd fled crowds of the dead together for longer than I liked to remember. On the road, wormfeeders turned to give chase when we raced by, but, slow as they were, they'd never catch up to us on the move. Turning back meant driving into the thick of them.

I shook my head. "We go forward. Christopher, drag Birch out here. We need his help."

Christopher jogged to the Camry and opened the rear passenger-side door. Fascinated by the dead on the bus, Della stepped into the glare of hundreds of eyes that watched us from hands, arms, necks, foreheads, even from tongues visible on one whose lower jaw had rotted out.

I knew more about those eyes than most, but I still didn't understand the phenomenon of the disembodied dead returning from insubstantial limbo to reanimate rotten flesh. Not why it had happened or what it meant.

The dead pressed together on one window by Della, decomposing bodies a single, writhing mass—until, with a sharp snap, a hairline fracture cracked the glass.

Della jumped back.

"Shit."

"Get away from there, Della," I said. "Don't rile them up."

The rooftop hatches bumped and clanked against the lamppost as dead hands shoved at them from inside.

"Why do they have so many damn eyes?"

I met Della's gaze for a moment, then shrugged and looked away. I knew one possible answer to the question, but until I believed it myself, I wouldn't ask anyone else to do so either.

"They're hardened," Della said. "Flesh cured, like leather. Mummified, like."

"They haven't been out in the elements or fighting with the living. It's a soft life on the school bus, all those cheerleaders with their pom-poms to keep your spirits up," I said.

Della smirked. "Wise-ass."

"You're right, though. Thank your nurse's eye for that. I've seen so many of these things, I can't make heads or tails of them but to keep my distance."

"That ought to be enough until we get where we're going," she said.

Lohatchie. The town on the edge of the Everglades where I grew up, where I kept a cabin hidden outside that forgotten scrap of civilization. I hoped no one, dead or alive, would ever find us once we settled in there.

Christopher returned with Birch, a former soldier turned microbiologist, who resembled a ghost—gray-haired, gaunt, eyes fixed on sights only he saw, his black cargo pants stained with mud and blood, but the Hawaiian shirt we'd found him clean and bright. His uncombed gray hair resembled a patch of dead weeds. He'd done no more than stare at us and nod or shake his head for days since he and I escaped a place called Deadtown.

"It's going take all of us to fix this mess, Birch," I said, "See the Buick sitting sideways against the bus?" Birch nodded. "That's the only car not tangled up with another vehicle. It's on the far side of the bus, which means we can push it out of our way, clear a path. The catch is the lamppost pinning shut those emergency exits is resting on its trunk. We have to heft that off there before we can move the Buick, which means we risk those hatches popping open and releasing the teen spirit brigade."

"Why don't we tie them shut?" Christopher said.

"Nothing there to tie onto," I said. "All the hardware's inside. Outside is smooth and aerodynamic."

"Can we shove something else up onto them?" Della said.

"Won't need to if we move fast," I said. "It'll take all four of us to lift the post, but if the Buick rolls, Birch and I can push it clear. Once we move the post, you and Christopher hop into the Camry and drive right up to the opening. Birch and I will jump in. We'll be gone before that dead quarterback can call a play."

"I don't like it," Della said.

"Neither do I, but that's how it's got to go."

Della frowned. Christopher, I give him credit, kept quiet and listened.

"Birch, you in?" I said.

One nod. I studied his eyes, worried he might flake, but I saw enough of the old, scotch-swilling, mad-scientist Birch there to trust him for this.

I inspected the Buick for the dead and found it empty. Reaching through the broken glass of the driver's side window, I put the car in neutral and hoped for the best. At least none of the damaged parts looked like they'd interfere with the tires.

"Everyone grab some lamppost," I said.

We spread out, Birch and I along the length laying on the school bus, Della next, then Christopher at the top, the light itself embedded in the Buick's trunk. Everyone gripped, then I counted down from three, and we pulled. The damn thing refused to budge. Our second try came no closer to freeing it.

"Christopher, you got the light end there, kid. What's happening?" I said.

"The metal's wedged into the lamp, kind of hooked on, but I see how to get it loose now. Give it another try, okay?"

I counted three again. We put our muscle into it. With a broken steel moan and a shattered glass tinkle, the lamp jolted loose. The weight of it shifted to our hands, heavier than expected, but we eased it clear. The bus hatches rattled like loose shutters in a hurricane. We strained and lowered the lamppost to the ground.

Della screamed: "Wormfeeders!"

From the near shoulder, a group of the dead emerged from the brush, all their hate-filled eyes sighted on us.

TWO

"Della, Christopher, back to the car," I said.

"We're not leaving you to fight them alone," Della said.

"We're not going to fight them. Birch and I can handle this. Please. Get in the car."

Whatever Della meant to say next vanished into the clank of one of the bus hatches flipping open. Dead hands pushed through and groped for freedom. The second hatch opened. More dead shoved out into the fresh air. Another group of roaming wormfeeders appeared on the far shoulder, rambling toward us like our voices summoned them from a deep sleep in the roadside brush.

"Are you kidding me?" Della shouted.

"The car, Della. Please. Go. I've got this," I said.

Trusting her to trust me, I tugged Birch along to the Buick, and we set to pushing it. The car refused to budge.

"Damn it, Birch, put some muscle into it, you stringy old bastard."

He hunkered down, planted his feet, and threw his weight against the car. It rocked on its tires. Out of sight, the Camry doors slammed shut. My unwanted friend who lived deep in my head, my jackal, snickered in my ears as death approached. He breathed a hot gust down my collar. I pled with my eyes for Birch to push harder and saw the first signs of real life there in days. We nodded in unison three times then shoved again. The Buick rolled.

"Yeah!" I shouted.

The car moved smoother with each step we took. Three, four, five, six steps, then I stopped counting as the front tires reached the slight incline toward the center median and gravity took control. Birch and I jogged along to keep the hunk of metal and plastic moving until it slipped out of reach. It crossed the left-lane shoulder, knocked down a pair of wormfeeders scrambling onto the pavement, and then bumped to a stop on the overgrown median.

The path for the Camry gaped clear—except for wormfeeders.

The two roadside groups shuffled in our direction. The bus crew learned to let one at a time through the escape hatches. Already four football players aimed themselves at the Camry as two drum majors tumbled out onto the road. Cheerleaders lined up behind them. The dead kept coming. What had looked like a small gang inflated to a crowd with no end in sight.

Birch and I hustled to the space we'd cleared. The Camry came to life and shot forward, bumping aside three decomposed cheerleaders. Its engine noise excited the dead. They filled the road from every direction. Their stench hit like gut-punches. Birch and I gagged on it. If not for the wind, we would've smelled them the moment we'd stepped out of the car and never let them catch us by surprise. Their wordless moans drowned out the sound of the Camry. Their putrid bodies filled the gap we'd made for the car.

On the other side of them, Della stopped and honked the horn.

She screamed out the window, her words lost in the din.

Sit tight, sit tight, I thought, reassuring myself, willing Della to comply.

The dead swirled around me and Birch. We froze.

They came within inches of us, but not one of them touched us. They stared at us; I stared back, wondering who those eyes had belonged to in life.

They lost interest and shifted their attention to the Camry. The bus riders encircled it and pawed at the windows and doors. Birch and I approached the car; the dead backed off and kept their distance, providing us a clear path. We separated, using their aversion to us to reopen the gap. I waved Della through.

She drove clear of the crash zone. I jumped into the passenger's seat. Birch climbed in back with Christopher.

"What the hell was that?" Della said. "Why didn't they attack you?"

"It's a long story. Better I explain while we're on the move. Drive us out of here."

Della frowned at me, then glanced in the rearview mirror, and her frown deepened.

Ahead of us, more dead wandered into the road.

"Now, Della, please, before there are too many."

"Dammit, Cornell," she said. "You and your damn secrets."

She slammed her foot on the gas. The acceleration thrust me against my seat. I scrambled to put on my seat belt as Della wove through the gathering dead. She clipped a few, but it paid to avoid them to prevent damaging the car. They kept coming for almost a minute before open road stretched ahead of us. After a while of easy driving, Della calmed, settled the car into the middle lane, smooth and sure, then spared a glance at me and said, "Talk. *Now.*"

THREE

Where to begin?

I didn't want to keep it from Della. Hated to hold secrets. Only I didn't know how to explain so much of what had occurred in Deadtown. Della and I had forged a bond, running together since we'd escaped a prison transformed into a death house by a fanatic warden. We clung to each other even more after our friend, Mason, who'd broken out with us, died. Then came the mess at Camp Cady, a small, hidden community of the living, where we'd met Birch and Christopher. From there, Birch and I made the trip to Baxtonville, or Deadtown, where the dead gathered in their masses and the strange Red Man who could destroy them or control them with his touch or a thought waited for us. Especially for Birch. Thousands of the dead. Hundreds of thousands, maybe. Of all the living folks who entered that place, only Birch and I left, and the Red Man kept Birch's tongue. Making sense of it proved impossible for me, so how could I have explained it to Della? Part of me still wrestled with the dead walking, that they had a purpose, a resurrection for a reason. Thinking about it at all made me feel like an ant trying to understand a lawn mower as it rolled over my anthill.

Still, I told her as best I could.

"Fifteen, twenty years ago?" she said when I finished.

"Yeah, on a raid because Stradley and his death-torture cult stocked up on weapons, including nerve gas. Birch took part on behalf of the military."

"He shot this Darrell Philip Stradley guy?"

"Twice," I said.

Della glanced over her shoulder at Birch.

"How could someone who died so long ago come back now? Wouldn't he be a rotted-out pile of bones?"

"You'd think, but nope. He's the Red Man, one evil bastard when he lived, and a true-life monster now. Something made him different. When he resurrected, he got up as if he'd died only an hour before. He knows what made the dead rise. He knows whose eyes stare out from their flesh. He's part of why this is happening, maybe even caused it."

Christopher leaned forward between the front seats. "Why didn't you kill him?"

"Don't you think we tried? Every man who went to Deadtown died, except for Birch and me. The Red Man wants something from the two of us. With Birch, it's personal. I get holding a grudge against the man who killed you, but what the hell does he want from me?"

"How'd you two make it out of Deadtown?" Della asked.

"Stradley put his mark in blood on our foreheads," I said. "After that, the dead wouldn't touch us. I walked right through them."

"You figured that would protect you when you sent us back to the car," Della said.

"I hoped it would."

"*Bastard*. You should've told me. I thought you were dead for sure."

"No time for a chat. Anyway, I wasn't sure it would still work. Wouldn't look good if I started bragging then wound up chow for the wormfeeders."

"Hell of a way to test it."

"Got us out of there, didn't I?"

Della rolled her eyes and shook her head. "Idiot."

Christopher flopped back into his seat, jammed in beside boxes of stuff he and Della had grabbed from Birch's lab when they fled Camp Cady. "Is it like he says, Birch?"

Birch raised his head from scribbling in his notebook long enough to nod then resumed writing. He no longer spoke since Stradley ripped out his tongue.

"I wandered out of Deadtown. Stradley took Birch prisoner. Tortured him, maybe. I don't know, and he won't say. We met up later in a grocery store. Stradley meant us to, I'm sure. Let Birch go on purpose," I said.

"It's okay, now, Birch," Christopher said. "We'll look out for you. Right, Cornell?"

"Do our best." I swiveled in my seat to see Birch.

Christopher raised a hand for a high five. Birch squinted at him, then raised his palm and completed the gesture without enthusiasm. I swear the hint of a smile creased in his lips, though, before he resumed writing.

"Shit, we got more dead," Della said.

Ahead of us, the highway stretched long and open, marked in places by abandoned or wrecked vehicles. About half a mile up ahead, though, a line of bodies stretched from shoulder to shoulder. Shadows cast by the high sun hid the details, but the way they moved left no mistake. A wall of corpses crept toward us. They reminded me of when people in search parties link arms and move together, one giant, organism scouring the earth in their path for missing kids or dead bodies.

"Can we drive through them?" Della said.

The line looked at least four or five bodies deep, maybe deeper.

"We'd get stuck then surrounded," I said.

"Don't say we have to turn back," Christopher said.

"Back to what?" I said. "We got the dead behind us too. Only escape is to keep heading for Lohatchie. We keep moving southwest."

"Guess we take the exit then," Della said.

Between us and the oncoming dead, an exit ramp offered an alternate route. We stuck to the highway because sideroads and backstreets came with more blockages—and more places for the dead to hide. But I saw no other option.

"Yeah, let's do it," I said.

Della drove us away from the dead. The exit spilled us onto a two-lane road heading east, nothing around but sawgrass and trees. A U-turn directed us west again. Ten minutes later, we passed a gas station. A fast-food joint came next. Then a strip mall. Soon we rolled into a proper town with shops and buildings lining Main Street. Except for me and Birch in Deadtown, none of us had seen anywhere but the road or Camp Cady, tucked out in the woods, for a long time.

Della slowed the car to a crawl. Even Birch set down his pen and looked.

I don't know what I or the others hoped to see, but the instinct to seek life still kicked within us. That urge, after a long drive, when you first come into a civilized place, to search for the familiar, to orient yourself, and size up the people and places around you. Like a dead phone line, though, the town created expectations doomed to remain unfulfilled.

Della stopped the car. "Gun shop over there," she said. "Grab some goodies?"

"Maybe." I rolled down my window. Engine noise from our idling car. Birds singing in the trees amidst the rustle of leaves. No other sounds. "I don't hear the dead."

Christopher rolled his window down too. "Sounds clear. Not too much stink either."

I twisted around in my seat. "What do you think, Birch?"

Birch lifted his gaze from his notebook for a few seconds, then resumed writing.

"Gotcha," I said. "Thanks for your helpful input, Birch."

Della placed her hand on my arm. "Cool it. He needs time."

"He can have all the time he wants once we get to Lohatchie," I said. "Pull up in front of the store."

The Camry slid in at the curb, and Della killed the motor. The shop looked intact, front door shut, windows unbroken, not an item out of place in the meticulous storefront display of hunting and fishing gear. In the door hung a sign: "Closed. Please call again." The neighboring shops looked fine too, as if nothing bad ever happened in this town, and it had died in its sleep of natural causes. It looked like the perfect illusion of a town. A mask of life.

"Mayberry," Della said.

"Bedford Falls," I said.

Christopher frowned, confused. "What?"

"Like the dead never touched here," I said.

"How can that be?" Della said.

I scanned the street then climbed out of the car. Off to the south, the top of a Ferris wheel crested a line of trees. A traveling carnival. I called Della and Christopher out of the car.

"Think everyone was down there when the dead hit?" I said.

"At a carnival?" Della said.

"Small town like this? Sure. They all went for some excitement."

"Think they're still there?" Christopher said.

"Yeah, I do, or at least nearby," I said. "Smell that? We're getting too used to it, taking it for granted, but there's death and rot in the air."

Christopher sniffed a long breath through his nose, then frowned. "Ugh, wormfeeders."

"Let's make this quick."

I tried the gun store door, locked, of course. I rummaged a hammer out of the tools in the Camry's trunk, wrapped an old shirt around my hand and forearm, and took a whack at the door window. It shimmied in its frame. Another blow. It thumped but didn't break. My blows hit too close to the center of the tempered glass. Planting my feet, I put all my strength into a whack at the upper corner, and the glass cracked. Splinters flew back at me. Another strike. The upper portion of the door shattered. I knocked broken glass free until I could reach in, unlock it, then swing it open. I closed my eyes and counted to ten to prepare for the interior gloom, then stepped over the litter of glass. After a look around, I swore. Someone had emptied the place and not too recently, judging by the dust gathered on the displays. Figure the proprietor saw the writing on the wall when the first reports of the living dead hit the news, quietly packed out his inventory, then ran for the hills.

Della called me from outside: "Cornell!"

I left the store. "Someone beat us to it. Damn place is picked clean."

"Forget that," she said. "Look!"

My gaze followed where she pointed: a white church with a tall steeple down at the far end of the road. The double doors of its entrance hung wide. Wormfeeders streamed out. Even at that distance, I saw their sights set on us. Okay, so what? We had a car, and they were too far to catch us. Even as I formed that thought, a chorus of moans came from the direction of that Ferris wheel as the vanguard of another dead mob appeared on the side streets to the south. From an alley no more than a hundred yards away, another line of them straggled into the sunshine.

"We've got go," Della said.

"Sonofabitch," I said.

The few dead in sight posed no real threat, but small groups grew fast into big crowds. The dead had a way of sounding the dinner bell when they saw the living, a link beyond living senses. No point in waiting around for things to worsen.

I jumped into the car. Della jolted us as she made a wild U-turn, then gunned the Camry back the way we'd come. Along the road, more of the dead emerged from the houses and shops we'd passed. The path before us narrowed. A throng rushed us from a side street, stumbling against the Camry, scrabbling at the windows with rotted, gray-and-purple fingertips.

"Hang on," Della said.

She gunned the engine.

Half a dozen wormfeeders clung to our bumpers, door handles, fenders, anywhere they could grab on, dragging themselves along the road, weighing us down. With every bit of speed they stole, I watched more of them assemble and constrict the road ahead, narrowing our exit until I thought of that Bible adage about running a camel through the eye of a needle, except I was no rich man, and heaven didn't wait on the other side—only the way out of town.

More wormfeeders grabbed on as others dropped off.

The engine screamed against their weight.

"We're not going to make it," Della said.

FOUR

"Stop the car," I said. "Stop!"

"No way! We stop, we're done." Christopher thrust himself between the front seats. "There are too many."

"Trust me. It's the only way we get out of here."

"What the hell are you talking about?" Della said.

"They don't know who's in the car," I said.

"I don't think they give a good goddamn," Della said.

"They will when they see me and Birch."

Birch tugged Christopher into the backseat and leaned forward in his place. He tapped his forehead, showing Della the spot where the Red Man had placed his now invisible mark.

"What if it doesn't work this time?" she said.

"We're goners either way." Our speed slowed to a crawl. More dead surrounded us. Their wordless moans filled our ears, making my point for me. "It can't hurt to try."

Della slapped the steering wheel. "I hate these fucking wormfeeders." She lifted her foot off the gas. The car ground to a halt.

The dead covered it like beetles scrambling over a scrap of taffy, like maggots on a dead bird. I opened my door a crack then shoved. Birch did the same. I figured he sized things up the same way I did. Good. That meant at least some spark of the will to live still flickered inside him. The dead weighed against our doors. We cracked them open and shoved until rotting hands yanked them wide and groped for us. They dragged me from the car, leaned over me with their slack-jawed mouths full of broken teeth protruding from gray, melted-cellophane gums. Then their touch fell away. Their many eyes glared at me and Birch with unwelcome recognition. As I'd done far too often of late, I stared right back.

I picked myself up from the pavement and stepped forward; the dead retreated.

Another step. They backed off farther.

Birch followed my lead. Those clinging to the car let go and slunk away on limbs shredded by road rash. Not far, but they emptied the road east, a channel lined by corpse-spectators waiting for a parade. Word traveled, but only in one direction. Behind us remained a solid sea of dead flesh. My personal jackal laughed; the sound echoed through my head.

"Guess the Red Man still has plans for you and me," I said to Birch.

Birch frowned and flipped his middle finger at the dead.

"Yeah, right, fuck the dead, fuck the Red Man."

We dropped back into the car, shut the doors. I slouched in my seat.

Della stared at me, and I didn't meet her gaze.

"Well, go on. They won't stop us now," I said.

She put the car in gear and drove. The dead made no move against us.

Their myriad eyes only watched. Eyes connected to the dead, linked to a force out in the universe, full of rancid bitterness and concentrated hate, and headed our way in its full fury and malice. The Red Man had shown me that much in Deadtown even if I didn't understand it.

Soon we passed the last of the wormfeeders. Della floored the gas. The Camry shrieked and shot down the road, leaving them all behind. No one spoke until we reached more dead, a few hundred, maybe, blocking our road, leaving us only one way to continue, a direction we didn't want to go: north. We took the turn anyway.

"I swear I saw some of the same wormfeeders from back in that town," Christopher said. "A guy with John Deere cap. A lady in a Prince T-shirt. Anyone else see them?"

"Those ain't exactly uncommon items," I said.

"They looked the same. Same faces, same pieces rotted away. No one else noticed?"

I shrugged. "Like it says in that old vampire book, kid, the dead travel fast."

"What the hell does that mean?" Christopher said.

"Means the living travel slow," Della said. "We've been driving all day, and we haven't hardly made any progress with all this turning around and doubling back."

"Ah, forget it." Christopher slumped against his seatback.

We drove until the sun sank below the horizon. Worn out and wired, afraid to keep driving in the dark, we parked for the night at a gas station and garage. Pulled the car into the workshop, then shut and locked the door behind us.

Christopher raided the adjoining convenience store for food and brought back bags of chips, cans of chili, beef jerky, and bottled water. We ate the stale but edible chips and stashed the canned stuff in the car. Only Birch dared chow down on the jerky. We took turns standing watch and sleeping in a small, windowless back office.

All night the dead ignored us except in my dreams.

After my watch, I crashed hard. I'd slept little since fleeing Deadtown. Partly from being on the run, partly because I didn't want to dream. The night before we entered Deadtown, the Red Man reached into my head and sent me messages and nightmares the way he'd been sending them to Birch since the dead began to walk, and he peeked inside my head while he did it. I hated it almost as much as I feared it. Every time I slept, I wished his touch wouldn't come, but lately, it did more often than not, and tonight offered no exception.

I closed my eyes to find myself on the run, not from the Red Man, or the living dead, or even the police, but from a man with an oversized shotgun and a novelty hunter's cap, like those goofball foam hats sold in sports arenas. He tiptoed through a forest that resembled a watercolor painting more than anything real and took great pains to keep quiet, making exaggerated tiptoes with his shotgun tucked under one arm, the ends of its barrels like mouths eager to spit lead. He walked past my hiding place inside a hollowed-out tree. I poked my head out, saw things the hunter didn't. Behind a thick stand of trees hid a nurse straight out of a Tex Avery cartoon, full of curves and stuffed into a uniform straining at its buttons and seams. A boy hid behind another tree. He held a giant, all-day lollipop and wore a shirt that read "Little Orphan Boy." At a third tree hid a man in a long, white lab coat. His hair stuck out in all directions. A flask bubbled in his hand, streaming vapors into the air. Blood covered his fingers. An overblown, silly-looking gun hung holstered at his waist. The hunter came on, tiptoe after tiptoe, oblivious.

Little Orphan Boy dropped his lolly. It hit the ground with a soft thump.

The hunter stopped, listened, only feet away.

The boy eyed the dirty candy. His face screwed up, and tears brimmed from his eyes.

Foxy nurse tried to shush him. The scientist ignored them both, pulled a test tube from his pocket, then poured its blue fluid contents into the flask. Colors rippled in the mixture, and sparks shot out. A mushroom cloud appeared in the flask, sprouting tendrils of glowing steam. When it settled down, the scientist drank it.

Afraid to see, I looked down and found myself dressed in a black-and-white striped shirt, black pants, and black gloves—a cartoon bank robber.

"Holy hell," I muttered.

Little Orphan Boy lost it then and broke out bawling.

The hunter smiled and stalked him.

The wild-haired man's potion kicked in. With an explosion of smoke, he transformed into a hideous, hairy monster, popping the seams of his lab coat. He snarled, jumped from his hiding place, and rushed the hunter, who aimed his shotgun and fired, but the shot went wild. The recoil hurtled the hunter against a tree. He recovered and aimed again. As the beast-man reached him, another eruption of smoke signaled the reverse of his metamorphosis, and he reverted to human form. He grinned, embarrassed as the hunter raised the shotgun, and donned eyeglasses from his coat pocket. "You wouldn't shoot a man with glasses, would you?"

The hunter's finger wrapped around the trigger.

I didn't want to know the answer. I forced myself awake, snapped upright from the floor, and banged my thigh against the desk, waking Christopher, who slept beside me.

"What's wrong?" he said.

"Nothing. Bad dream. Back to sleep."

He closed his eyes, and his breathing soon settled into a deep rhythm.

I left the office and joined Della on watch. Birch sat in the Camry.

"Can't sleep?" Della said.

"Sleep just fine, but I can't not dream," I said.

"Oh, lord, here we go. We've reached the point in our relationship where we tell each other our dreams. *Oh, Della, what's it mean when my teeth fall out?* Can I just go fight some of the wormfeeders instead?"

I laughed. "I hear ya. This ain't actually *my* dream."

"Meaning what?"

"Someone sent it to me."

Della eyed me, assessing me, smart-ass or serious. "Okay, talk."

I did, and it resonated for her. I explained how the Red Man sent Birch dreams, how he'd started doing the same for me, and how I believed he'd sent this one, delivering a message whose meaning beyond the obvious eluded me.

"He knows about all of us?" she said.

"If he's in my head, why wouldn't he?"

"Think he knows where we are?"

"I think he's herding us."

"With the dead?"

"Yes."

"I wondered why they seemed determined to keep us from going the direction we want but never interfering with us heading north. Chalked it off to coincidence."

"He wants us up there for some reason, is my guess."

"What reason?"

"Don't know."

"Maybe it *is* just coincidence."

I shook my head.

Acceptance entered Della's expression. It hurt me to see it. Acceptance meant giving up hope for a better option. I put my arms around her and pressed her tight to me. She returned the embrace. We kissed. I sat the rest of the watch with her.

In the morning, we drove out and again found it impossible to head south or west, those directions clogged with wormfeeders. Any attempt to plow through them would only jam up the car on their bodies. We landed on a rural route north, no sign of the dead. Coming around a long curve, though, we found something even more terrifying: Fifty yards down the road, two living people stood beside a pair of motorcycles, one with a small cargo trailer hitched to it. At the sound of our car, they turned and looked our way.

FIVE

"Are the wormfeeders starting a biker gang?" Christopher said.

"Doubtful," I said.

"What do we do?" Della said. "Double back or roll up and meet the neighbors?"

"I've never been the neighborly type," I said.

"If we turn around, won't the dead send us back this way?" Christopher said.

"Kid's got a point," Della said.

I twisted in my seat to see Birch. "What do you say, Birch? Go forward or retreat?"

Birch only glanced at me, didn't even stop scribbling.

"Thanks for the advice," I said.

While we debated, the two bikers wheeled their motorcycles into the road, blocking it, and leaned against them as if waiting for us.

"There's the welcoming committee," Della said.

"Could be more of them hiding in the brush or farther up the road." I opened my door. "Stay here for now."

Outside, the steamy air carried the odor of death, less intense than it had been, which suggested fewer wormfeeders in our immediate area. I held a revolver at my side as I walked in front of the car.

"Hey there," I called.

One of the bikers waved back. "Hi."

"Haven't seen many live folks for a while," I said. "How're y'all getting by?"

The one who'd waved removed his helmet, revealing a gaunt, pale face and sunken eyes inside indigo rings. "We're alive. That's pretty much the whole ballgame these days."

"That it is," I said.

"Listen, man, we don't want trouble or nothing. You want to pass by, we'll move our bikes. I just wanted a chance to talk before you moved on. We hardly ever see anyone alive. Thought maybe you've heard some news."

"Nothing but the headlines, and they're all bad."

The second biker removed her helmet and shook loose her dark hair. She, too, looked thin and pallid, wasted, hungry, her eyes dull, expression flat. "My name's Rhea. This is Damon."

I nodded. "Name's Cornell."

Damon popped a hatch on the cargo trailer and reached into it. I cocked the hammer of my gun, ready to aim and fire, but then eased it back home when he produced a bottle.

"Y'all want to jaw a few minutes, I got some single malt to share."

"Haven't had that in a good long time," I said.

"Getting hard to come by."

One of the car doors behind me opened, and Birch emerged. He walked up beside me, eyed the gun, shook his head, and crossed the distance between us and Damon. His notebook poked out from under his arm. Birch took the bottle from Damon, read the label, and smiled. Damon stared at him, confused.

"You want a drink?" he said.

Birch nodded and winked.

"That's Birch," I said. "He's quiet, but he likes his whisky. Guess we're taking you up on your offer."

I gestured for Della and Christopher to hang back in the car, knowing they would cover us if things turned bad, then joined Birch and the bikers. Rhea pulled plastic cups from the cargo trailer. Birch returned the bottle to Damon, who opened it and poured us each a measure.

"Cheers." He knocked his back in one gulp then exhaled satisfaction.

I sipped mine, savoring the taste and the burn. So did Birch.

"The others in the car are welcome to join us. We don't bite," Rhea said.

"Pardon my asking," I said, noticing close up the extremity of their pallor, "but you both look a little, uh, under the weather."

"Yep, got us a cold or the flu or something. Been dogging us for days. Saps all the energy out of you, but what are you gonna do, right? Ain't bad enough the dead trying to kill everyone, naw, here's a fever and some chills to go with it."

"I hear you. That sucks." I watched Birch, and his expression told me the same question pinged around inside his head: *How can they be ill?* It had been months since either of us had seen anyone sick. Birch's research at Camp Cady had found that for the dead time had slowed to a crawl, maybe even close to stopped at a cellular level and that something similar had occurred in living people. That's the simple, explain-it-to-a-bank-robber version. I don't pretend to get all the science behind it or why it only worked on a microscopic scale while the world at large went on unchanged. Bottom line, the effect slowed rotting and aging, retarded cellular processes to the point of making bacterial or viral illnesses impossible to catch because cells didn't reproduce fast enough to make you sick. Damage by invader cells took so long to manifest that immune system cells, operating only slightly faster, wiped out pathogens before they took hold. Maybe Damon and Rhea mistook malnourishment for illness or lied to cover up for some kind of dope sickness. Or maybe things were changing.

"Do us a favor and cover your mouth if you sneeze," I said.

The pair chuckled with little enthusiasm. Standing around talking seemed to drain them. They moved slow, spoke softly, and squinted whenever the sun hit their faces.

"Where you heading?" Damon said.

"Hoping to go west, but there are too many wormfeeders."

"Yeah, they're thick in that direction," Rhea said. "Gets better going east. We're on our way to Miami. Heard word there are other living people there, and a lot less of the dead."

"Where'd you hear that?" I said.

Damon refilled our cups. "Fat Jake. He rode with us for a few days. He'd been there a while but left to look for his brother. Found him dead and decided to go back. We got overrun a few towns north of here, though, and he didn't make it. Bunch of wormfeeders came out of the grocery store we were scavenging. Bad day."

"Sorry to hear that," I said.

"You're welcome to ride with us down that way if you want," Rhea said.

"Might take you up on that. Have to talk to my people," I said.

"Sure, go on," she said. "We're in no rush."

I walked back to the car and clued in Della and Christopher.

"They seem like a threat?" Della said.

"Seem like they can barely keep their eyes open and their feet under them," I said. "Say they got the flu."

"They don't look too tough. We can take them for sure," Christopher said.

I frowned at him. "Take them? Like jump them and steal their stuff?"

"I didn't mean that. Like if they give us trouble, we could handle them. I don't want to jump anyone or steal anything," he said.

"Gotcha. Yeah, maybe we can take them if they give us a hard time. But they're alive, and that means they're tough enough to survive. Don't underestimate them or anyone else we meet."

I scratched the back of my neck, feeling for my jackal's hot breath. For once, it felt cool and dry. "All right, we'll drive with them for a while, see how it goes. We're heading the same direction now anyway. Safety in numbers, I suppose. Maybe there's something to this about Miami. We're seeing a lot less of the dead traveling this way, so who knows?"

I worked it out with Damon and Rhea to follow us. That limited the risk of them herding us into an ambush. They agreed without fuss, relief in their eyes at letting someone else run the show for a while. They rolled their bikes to the shoulder. After a last nip at the single malt, Birch and I climbed back into the Camry. Della drove past our new friends. Their bike engines growled as they fell in behind us, their ghostly faces hidden again inside their helmets.

We drove the rest of the day, finding more clear roads than not, but detouring around the dead in some places and finding alternate routes in others where wrecked vehicles blocked our path. Heading east offered much easier going than west, but pockets of the dead and abandoned or wrecked vehicles still made progress slow. In the side-view mirror, Damon's and Rhea's black helmets reflected sunlight, bopping up and down with the road. When twilight signaled time for us to stop for the night, I saw another dark shape far behind them. A four-legged shadow keeping pace with us, shimmering in the heat mirage rising off the road. A shape out of my mind. Its laugh echoed but only for me. Its breath burned the back of my neck. Then it vanished in a wisp of shade.

"Damn it," I said. "Where are all the dead?"

"Don't complain," Della said. "We haven't' had it this good for a long time."

"I prefer seeing the knife aimed at my throat."

We camped for the night in a fenced-in utility yard at the side of the highway. It held a pair of mobile, electronic road signs, which we wheeled out by hand to make space for our car and the motorcycles. We ate the last of the food scavenged from the gas station mart. Rhea and Damon produced another bottle of whisky, not as good as the first one, but no one complained. Even Christopher took a taste, his first. We all laughed at the face he made as he swallowed it and the sputtering cough that followed.

Afterward, our new traveling companions settled in by their cargo trailer to sleep. Della and Christopher took the Camry. Birch and I sat first watch. Cloudless sky and a waning moon lit the world bright. The night breeze blew around us, sweet-smelling and quiet.

"The air ain't right," I said.

Birch raised an eyebrow.

"No stink."

He inhaled a deep breath, exhaled it in a long stream, and then nodded. He pointed to his ears and shook his head.

"Right. No moans. Can't remember the last night I passed without hearing those fuckers. Goddamn, their voices carry." Tension knotted above my eyes. I tried to rub it away, but it persisted. "Either there aren't wormfeeders around, or they suddenly turned stealthy."

Birch shrugged.

"Used to be I couldn't shut you up." I stood, stretched my back and legs. "I'm not exactly the 'share-your-feelings' type, but you ever want to talk about what the Red Man did to you after things went south in Deadtown, I'm all ears."

Birch looked me in the eye. For a moment, it seemed he wanted to talk, but frustration crushed him as his physical inability to do so collided with his urge to communicate. He made an awful, hopeless face, then flipped me the bird.

"I hear you." I grabbed my flashlight from the ground. "Listen, I'm going to check things out. I won't sleep if I don't see what's out there. Keep the gate closed until I'm back."

The chain link rattled as I shut it behind me. The latch clicked home.

I kept the flashlight off. The moonlight made it unnecessary.

Earth and gravel crunched underfoot as I walked to the road. A hundred yards back the way we'd come, I found nothing but empty blacktop and overgrown shoulder. I returned, passed our camp, and stalked another hundred yards in the direction we headed. Found the same. If something out there meant us harm, it hid too well for me to find it.

I took my time walking, sniffing the clean air, listening for any sign of life bigger than a raccoon. For a while, I gazed at the moon and considered how low we'd fallen as a species, reduced from sending men to walk the lunar surface to scrabbling to stay alive. The visions the Red Man had sent to my dreams showed a cosmic darkness sweeping over the universe, a malignant force ravenous for every life it encountered. A shapeless consciousness of shadow, brimming with hate and anger, and all the rotten emotions that make people the utterly flawed creatures we are. All the burdens of darkness unbalanced by light of any kind. That balance differentiated people from other creatures, our equal capabilities to do both awful and wonderful things.

Our light. Our dark.

Our capacity to choose, to learn. Our mistakes taught us to be better.

Before the dead plague, before prison, I'd held that light within reach with the woman I loved, Evelyn, and both of us failed to grasp it.

Our last bank job ripped it away from us. One final hit of greed and recklessness before we quit, went straight to raise our child growing inside her womb. Two lives ended when bullets ripped into Evelyn. My own life was thrown into endless darkness when I killed the man who shot her and two more in the wrong place at the wrong time. Guilt and grief made me a willing prisoner. *Lock me up forever. Throw away the key, please.*

I deserved it for failing to protect the only lives other than my own that mattered to me in this rancid, corrupt world. I pled guilty to make sure I got a life sentence and not capital punishment. I didn't deserve to die and escape. I needed to feel it for the rest of my days. I'd thought I'd made my peace with it and with Evelyn's ghost, by later choosing to seek my freedom and live again in this dead world, but even when you're okay with grief, failure, and regret, even after you've put them in proper context, compartmentalized them, and moved on, they have a knack of shooting to the surface when you least expect it. Then they wrap their cold, raw tendrils around your brain. They suffocate you, and squeeze your heart, and drag you down into their darkness. In the first true respite I'd known since that deadly day, all that guilt rushed back to me.

The moon and the stars blurred as tears filled my eyes.

They burned down my cheeks.

I stood there, silent, and cried, and stared at the blank heavens and light generations older than me when it reached my eyes. I lost track of time. The moon shifted to the horizon. My tears dried up. I wish I could say I felt unburdened after releasing all that pent-up emotion, but I only felt drained as I returned to our makeshift camp.

Into that emptiness flowed fear when I saw the gate hung open.

Rhea's motorcycle stood outside the pen.

A voice whispered in my mind to stay cool, stay cautious. Every ounce of me wanted to rush in and investigate, but the smart part of me held back, reminded me that living predators still roamed the world, and they didn't stink like the dead or make brainless sounds.

I crept toward the open gate.

Footsteps came from inside the fence.

Shadowed bodies moved around the Camry.

A muffled voice made a frightened whine.

One of the bodies approached the open gate, wheeling Damon's bike with its cargo trailer attached. I waited until the bike and trailer filled the exit then flashed my light at the blacked-out face.

SIX

Damon squealed and recoiled from the brightness. The illumination turned his skin translucent, revealing veins running beneath it. His eyes bulged.

"Where the hell you going, Damon?" I said.

"Rhea, oh, shit! Rhea," he shouted.

I swept the light across the pen. Birch lay facedown in the dirt where I'd left him, red wetness smeared on the back of his neck. Beside the Camry stood Rhea, dragging Christopher, gagged and bound with cord, out of the passenger side seat. Della, who'd crashed in the back seat, remained out of sight.

"Get him, Damon, get him!" Rhea screamed.

A high-pitched snarl grated my ears as Damon charged me. He reached to draw something at his waist from under his coat, but before he cleared it, I rushed forward and planted an uppercut with my fist wrapped around the heavy flashlight to the bottom of his chin. His jaw clacked shut. His feet left the ground. When he landed on his back, I pinned him in place with my knee and cracked the flashlight against his nose. Blood gushed out. He gagged for breath. I grabbed his hand, still reaching under his coat, and found it wrapped around a revolver. Another flashlight punch, this one to his throat. His fingers loosened. I yanked the gun from him.

Rhea shrieked and opened fire, but the car interfered with her line of sight. Bullets whizzed by me. I tumbled off Damon, rolled across the ground for cover behind a low hill. I lost count of how many shots Rhea fired, but none of them hit me, and wouldn't you know it, the second I realized that fact, howling laughter rolled through the night, through my mind, from my old pal, the jackal.

"Yeah, real fucking funny," I muttered.

I lifted my head as Rhea dragged Christopher across the pen. She stopped in the gate, gun still in hand, and knelt to check Damon. He spluttered blood and tried to sit up.

"What the hell is wrong with you two?" I called out.

Rhea fired in the direction of my voice. Her shot went wide.

"Shut the fuck up!" she cried.

I eased my head up to check my shot on her. She spied my movement and fired. Two more shots, both into the dirt mound in front of me, sending a spray of soil and grit into my face—then came the click on an empty chamber. I didn't wait. I sprang up and fired four times. My first two shots went in low, but I corrected and took heart when I heard Rhea cry out and then topple over. Two shots left. I rushed in to finish her off but held my fire when I saw what I'd accomplished. My two low shots had hit Damon in the head and neck. The other two took Rhea in the stomach and lower chest. She lay gasping for breath, her gun spilled out of reach. She lay across Christopher's legs. I thanked the heavens none of my shots hit him.

After taking Rhea's gun and checking her and Damon for other weapons, I yanked the gag from Christopher's mouth.

"Holy shit, Cornell. They wanted to eat me!" he said.

I untied his hands and legs. "What are you talking about?"

"They left Della tied up in the Camry. They were kidnapping me to *eat* me."

"Della's okay?"

"I don't know." Christopher stood, rubbing his wrists where ropes had bitten them. "It was their watch. I guess they knocked out Birch, and I was afraid they'd killed you."

"Go check on Della while I see to Birch."

He ran off to the Camry. Birch's torso rose and fell as he breathed. I shifted him onto his back, and he roused. They'd hit him on the back of the head hard enough to stun but not kill him, a precious bit of luck. Della emerged from the car, walked to Damon and Rhea, spit on Damon, then kicked Rhea in the side. Rhea yelped and hollered, clutching her wounds with bloody hands.

We dragged her and Damon into the pen. A woozy Birch and I unhitched the trailer, then rolled their motorcycles down the roadside slope into the woods, out of reach, out of sight. While Della drove the Camry into the open, Christopher raided their trailer. Then he lurched away from it and screamed.

Unloaded liquor, ammunition, odds and ends such as rope, tarpaulins, camping lanterns, and similar gear circled him on the ground. Inside the trailer, though, lay Rhea and Damon's food stock, fresh meat wrapped in plastic. Human arms and legs, other bits I couldn't identify, even the partial remains of a head, all wriggling and twitching with unnatural life. Nauseated by the sight, I sifted through them, counting too many to have come from a single body. An eye opened on an ankle. I jolted from the trailer, stumbled, almost fell. When I forced myself to look again, more eyes looked back at me from all the limbs, staring at me with naked expectation.

I knew what they wanted. They wanted me to die.

I slammed the trailer shut.

Pointing at the stash on the ground, I said, "Load that stuff in the trunk."

Before Christopher did, I plucked one item out of the pile, a padlock with a key stuck in it, probably for locking the trailer, but Damon had gotten lazy. Rhea glared as I entered the pen.

"How long you been doing that?" I asked.

She spit blood at me. It fell short and landed in the dirt.

"It's not the flu, is it? You look all sick because you eat that rotten, dead flesh."

"Eat the flesh. Steal their power," Rhea said. "They don't hunt us. They don't bother us. We get a free pass."

"Guess you smell like them." I closed the gate then placed the padlock through the latch. It snapped shut with a metal click. I threw the key as far as I could into the brush beyond the road. "Maybe you're already half-dead inside. Whatever it is, at least you won't go hungry for a while in there since you got each other."

Rhea snarled at me, tried to lunge, but fell to her knees, hacking and spitting up blood.

I helped Birch into the car, then climbed in beside Della.

She turned the Camry around and drove down the road, honking the horn twice as we passed the pen. We risked night travel, hoping to leave the memory of Damon and Rhea in our dust. Few other predators I'd encountered left me so disgusted. As abhorrent as I found the idea of cannibalism for survival, it made a desperate kind of sense. I could understand it if not accept or excuse it. But this? No, not this. Eating the flesh of the living dead, eating toxic meat with living eyes that stared at you, hated you, wanted to murder you, flesh that held consciousnesses embedded where they had no business being. Eating poison. Literal corruption. Devouring the perverted version of humanity. Nourishing yourself on the worst thing imaginable a human being could suffer. That reached next-level repulsive, a taboo too horrible to contemplate breaking. I thanked my luck for walking off to scout the road, or else I might have wound up dead, leaving the others for meals.

"They planned on coming back," Christopher said.

"What do you mean?" I said.

"They wanted to take you out tonight, hit the strongest first, they said, then come back and pick us each off along the road. When they couldn't find you, they panicked and decided to butcher me, then follow the rest of you along the road, grab Della in a few days, then Birch, and then come for you, Cornell, when you were on your own."

"Their brains must be rotting if they thought they would get us that way. What reduces a person to that?" I said. "I'd rather die."

"You saw how they looked," Della said. "Like addicts, like that dead flesh altered their metabolism. There's more to it than survival. I wonder if they could even still eat normal food."

"That possible, Birch? Junkies for the flesh of the living dead?" I said.

Birch reclined in the seat behind me, eyes closed, head resting on a piled-up sweatshirt. Della had cleaned and bandaged the bloody bump where Damon had hit him. He raised his head enough to see me, shrugged, and then nodded once before closing his eyes again.

"What a world," I said.

"At least we know, we meet up with any other strung-out, pasty-looking people, we shoot 'em first and ask questions later," Della said.

"Amen," I said.

The road brought fewer and fewer signs of the dead as we traveled southeast, rolling on toward Miami. The air, unbelievably, grew even fresher and sweeter. Wildlife appeared. More birds in the sky. Squirrels in the trees. Snakes. Even a few alligators parked in a canal with their eyes and snouts prodding out of the water. Houses and stores looked cleaner and less broken than most, and we made good time. The rhythm of the road lulled me to sleep. I needed the rest, but I'd have paid a fortune for a giant, steaming cup of coffee to keep awake because as soon as slumber gripped me, the Red Man touched my mind.

I "awakened" inside my head, my body trapped in sleep.

Black nothing surrounded me. My dream flesh ran cold with the chill of the Red Man's touch. A ruby light winked in the distance, a channel marker bobbing in the waves. I approached it, my legs heavy with dream sensation, the feel of trying to run through water. The light blinked out, then on, out, on, out, on, and came no closer, as if a treadmill scrolled beneath my feet—until raucous laughter came out of the darkness. Part of it I knew well, the bark of my old jackal friend. Part of it stabbed my soul, the laugh of the Red Man.

The ruby light erupted into a searing bright sphere. I cast my hand across my eyes and stumbled backward. The light surrounded me. The red intensified. My existence turned crimson, and some immeasurable length of time passed. The brightness faded. My eyes adjusted to shapes and shadows, a world delineated in red and utterly alien yet familiar. As my sight recovered, I recognized Acme Wonderland, a cartoon theme park I'd visited as a kid. Death stained my frivolous memories of it. Charred and cracked skulls littered the fairway. The entrances to all the rides resembled cave mouths brimmed with jagged stalactite teeth. Slowed-down, carnival music played like a dirge. Red light flared and revealed a tower of skulls reaching toward the sky. High atop it sat the Red Man on a death throne. He lounged in his seat like an emperor sated on power. Coruscating red light crept from the many scars on his body. A hundred eyes opened and glared from every part of him, his body a window to the deranged dead. A thousand more blinked open and stared, many searching the vast darkness swirling above as it spread and reached for him. He offered me a paternalistic smile that made me shiver to my bones.

I wanted to scream myself awake but couldn't force the slightest sound from my throat.

Lazy, indifferent, the Red Man pointed in the direction of the park's largest ride, Connie Caribou Mountain. A force outside myself turned me—or held me still while the park swiveled. Who knew how things worked when a dead man controlled your dreams? The Connie Caribou Mountain roller coaster filled the red sky, an architect's nightmare of loops and knots, twisted tracks, and lines of cars racing along the rails at breakneck speed.

Connie and her gang of friends stood at the entrance, each a surreal blend of cartoon animal and actor inside a character suit, but all twice human size and putrescent. Connie's ribs showed through torn patches on her trademark maple leaf print dress, and one loopy, cartoon eye hung partway out of its socket on a bloody strand of optic nerve. Marvelous Moose posed beside her, his super-hero cape and costume pitted with holes. Skulls dangled from his antlers. His own skull peeked out from rotted flesh; his eyes glared livid in their exposed sockets. Foxy Pinewood came next, matted with blood, his fine three-piece suit torn and smeared with gore. Decayed fur exposed muscle and bone, but Foxy's face remained as roguish and handsome as ever, his sly tongue licking his chops. A sheriff's star hung from his suit. A pair of rusty six-shooters dangled at his waist. The motherly Darlene Deer paced beside him, her dress torn. Tumorous, apple-sized growths dangled from her throat and ribs. A fierce muzzle full of fangs replaced her placid face.

Saturday-morning cartoon, sugary cereal binges had never looked like this.

I didn't know if I should scream or laugh.

The piercing bleat of an airhorn filled the park.

Three figures appeared, fleeing from the mouth of the Polly Platypus River Run.

Little Orphan Boy. Mad Lab Coat. Red-Hot Nurse.

I clamped my eyes shut tight, counted to ten, and looked again. Still there, as if the entire dream hit pause while I couldn't see it. I checked myself for my cartoon robber outfit, but I wore only my regular clothes, a hint that I did not play the same game as the others.

The three huddled together, unaware of Connie Caribou's crew eyeing them from the Mountain. Again, I tried to shout, to warn them, but my lips produced not so much as a whisper.

I ran toward them on rubber legs and feet dripping invisible wet cement.

From his throne, the Red Man laughed.

Foxy Pinewood drew a gun and fired. The shot passed over Mad Lab Coat's head. Now the trio dashed to the next ride over, Captain Capybara's Congo Cruise. Marvelous Moose flew after them. The rest of Connie's crew joined the chase. Connie and Darlene switched to all fours. Foxy slinked along behind them. In the Congo Cruise's entrance awaited Captain Capybara, his nautical attire hanging in shreds from his decomposing body, a black tongue dangling from a mouth of overlong, razor-edged teeth.

I managed another step, then two more, a fifth, but drew no closer to the cartoon stand-ins for Christopher, Birch, and Della. Marvelous Moose reached them first and cut off the path to the next ride. The others soon surrounded them. Little Orphan Boy, Mad Lab Coat, and Red-Hot Nurse cowered, trapped.

A hand gripped my shoulder.

With a jolt, I screamed, at last finding my voice.

"Too late," the Red Man said.

He squeezed my shoulder until it ached.

The cartoon monstrosities closed on my friends.

Connie Caribou took the first bite, wrapping her rotting mouth around Little Orphan Boy's arm. Captain Capybara took the second, biting into Mad Lab Coat's leg. Darlene Deer snapped at Red-Hot Nurse, champing down on her shoulder in an enormous, bloody chomp.

"Go ahead, now, and scream," the Red Man said.

I did. My entire body trembled with it.

Then light filled my eyes. Hot air and stale sweat. The ugly, dry taste of waking up.

I banged my knee against the underside of the dashboard and yelped as I fought against a tightness pinning me until I recognized my seat belt and undid it. I sat alone in the unmoving car. A swift push opened my door, releasing me to stumble out onto all fours and dry heave into the weeds of a crumbling blacktop parking lot. When my convulsions ended, I clambered to my feet, steadied myself, and checked my surroundings: a gas station on the edge of an old shopping mall parking lot. Across from the Camry, Birch and Christopher siphoned gas from abandoned cars into our gas cans. Della approached me, concerned.

"We let you sleep. Figured you needed it," she said. "You all right?"

I nodded and squinted against the high sun. "What time is it?"

"Almost noon. We had to go slow in the dark. We passed pockets of the dead. Covered sixty, seventy miles. Best we've ever done, I think."

"Okay, good."

I leaned on the car and reached in for a bottle of water. I drained most of it at a gulp.

"If it keeps on like this, we'll reach Miami this afternoon, no problem," Della said.

What to make of that good news, I wondered? The water restored me enough to notice the clean taste of the air and the absence of the dead's anguished cries. Della offered me a worried smile. I returned it to reassure her while I struggled to regain my bearings and waited for the ground underfoot to feel solid and real. I tried to make sense of the quiet, ordinary morning occurring around me, hoping it could lift me from the terrifying remnants of my nightmare.

A mechanical sound broke the peace.

The grumbling motor of an approaching vehicle.

In unison, Della and I looked to the highway.

From back the way we came, a truck rushed into sight.

SEVEN

"Find cover, now!" I said.

I grabbed two rifles from the Camry then herded Della, Christopher, and Birch behind a rusting bulldozer parked in the high weeds beside the gas station building. I handed one rifle to Della. Christopher already had one slung on his shoulder, the kid always cautious and prepared the way I'd taught him back at Camp Cady. The truck grumbled along, visible through gaps in the mechanisms of the bulldozer. It brought a stench with it, a cloud of decay that rolled ahead, pushed into the air by the truck's motion.

Stains of gore and scraps of ripped flesh covered the front hood and grill, remnants from collisions with the dead. Armored all around with sheets of steel, the truck looked impenetrable except for openings for the driver and narrow windows along the side of the body. Gun ports. An armored car. I'd studied them a long time in my bank-robbing days. Never could find a sure way to knock one over. I understood the appeal of riding behind such defenses, able to crush the dead under the wheels or plow through crowds of them, but I also saw a rolling deathtrap ravenous for fuel, straining under the weight of its shielded mass and forcing constant stops to gas up. Such a motored fortification might breed overconfidence that might leave its driver and passengers stuck high and dry amidst a thousand pissed-off wormfeeders when they overwhelmed its unprotected wheels. Better to move fast, avoid them altogether how we'd done since hitting the road. Never any downside to making a fast getaway.

The truck slowed then crawled into the gas station, bumping over the curb apron before grinding crumbling blacktop beneath its tires. It stopped. Plates slid back from the side gun ports. Shadows moved behind them. People inside the truck looked out. Then they closed. The engine died and clanked as it cooled.

Seconds passed. A minute. Two.

I hated when circumstances forced me to sit tight and wait, to let tension and uncertainty rise while the world carried on in total indifference. Insects flitted in the hot sun. Birds chirped. On the far side of the gas station, two squirrels chased each other around the trunk of a tree. But the odor of death wafted from the truck into the clean air I'd grown to relish, a reminder never to take anything for granted.

The truck bounced and creaked.

The back door banged open. A woman emerged.

Tall and muscular. Dressed in jeans, a khaki tank top, and an equipment vest from which hung binoculars, a knife, and ammunition for the scoped rifle slung from one shoulder. She wore a black ball cap, her brown hair pulled back in a ponytail. Dark shades concealed her eyes. For a few seconds, she lingered at the truck, speaking with someone inside, then she slammed the door shut and walked toward the gas pumps. She lifted the nozzle from one, then, in a quick gesture that almost cracked me up, she pulled a credit card from her pocket, slid it into the pump's card reader, and then pulled the trigger on the nozzle. Nothing came out. I knew the other three pumps would produce the same results. We'd failed with the same trick so often we didn't bother anymore.

When she exhausted the pumps, she looked around and eyed the cars lined up along the far edge of the lot, looking right at our gas cans and siphon pumps and hoses, forgotten by Birch.

I steadied the others, kept them chill.

The woman tensed as she scrutinized our gear. She jogged out of sight on the driver's side of her truck. Muffled voices carried across the distance. The woman walked to the center of the parking lot and crossed her arms over her chest. An unexpected memory burst into my mind, dizzying in its intensity, a recollection of Evelyn in the moments before she died. The way she stood, her confidence, her presence as we worked the crowd on our last, fatal bank job.

She called out, "Hello," and her voice chilled me.

She even sounded like Evelyn.

We stayed quiet and watched.

The woman took off her shades and ball cap. She ran a hand over her head, then undid her ponytail, shook out her hair, then tied it back into a tail. She resembled Evelyn. Not in features, not exactly, but in her expression, in the set of her lips, in the way her eyes assessed everything around her, calm but alert.

"Listen, we didn't mean to intrude on you. We thought no one was here. No one living, at least. I see your gas cans. I guess we have the same idea about fueling up."

She looked the other way, then back to the bulldozer. She walked to the gas station shop, cupped her hands over her eyes, and peered through the window. She tried the door and found it locked like we had.

"We're going to take some gas from those cars," she said. "We won't take it all. We'll leave you some. If you want to keep your head down, fine. We don't want trouble. But we'd be happy to see some living people."

The whole time the woman's hands never moved toward her rifle. She kept them either crossed over her chest or loose at her sides. I'd spent a lifetime before the dead plague judging people in an instant. Good, bad, trustworthy, or a threat. I trusted that judgment always. It had never led me astray. But this woman reminded me so much of Evelyn I didn't know what to think. I wanted to see her up close. Because I sensed she was safe? Or because she stirred to life a part of me that died with Evelyn? I looked at Della crouched beside me and felt a pang of guilt for my traitorous thoughts. It must have shown on my face.

"You okay, Cornell?" Della whispered.

"Yeah, fine," I said, and then, not knowing precisely why I made the choice, "Listen, I'm going out there. I think we can trust her. Cover me."

Della shook her head and frowned. "Stay down until they leave. Let's not risk it."

"It'll be okay," I said. "She's not sickly like the biker cannibals. Maybe we can help each other."

I crept around the bulldozer, my rifle slung to my shoulder, same as the woman, although she wore hers with more ease and confidence.

"Hey there," I said.

She didn't flinch, only turned her gaze toward me and smiled.

"Hey there, yourself," she said. "My name's Vale."

"Cornell."

"Listen, I meant every word I said. My friends and I don't want trouble. We're surviving like the rest of the living. I lost track of how long it's been since we've met anyone else, though. Except for the dead-eater we found back up the road."

"Dead-eater?"

"Cannibals, sort of. They, um, eat the wormfeeders."

I scratched my cheek. "The one you found, she didn't happen to be locked up in a roadwork pen, did she?"

"You know her?"

"I'm the one who locked her up."

"They're gone in the head. The dead flesh melts the brain. Turns them into violent weirdos. It's a mercy to put them down. Makes the world safer too."

"I've never been one for killing in cold blood, though."

A white lie. An image of Evelyn lying dead on a bank floor flashed through my head. Then the flash of my gun as I shot the guard who killed her and two more who rushed me. Ice running through my veins.

Vale shrugged. "Me neither, but when everything wants to kill you first, what counts as cold blood?"

"Long as you don't turn that philosophy toward me."

"The living need to work together. Or at least let each other be. Speaking of which, I'm going to take that gas now. Like I said, I won't take it all. In case you get skittish, you should know my friends in the truck are covering me."

"I've got friends too," I said.

"Good. Keeps it fair."

"You gotta wash that truck. It reeks."

Vale laughed. "It's awful, isn't it? That's camouflage. The dead smell their own, they're less likely to swarm us."

"Where you coming from?"

"Up north quite a ways. The airport at Actsburg. We had a refuge there until the dead overran it."

"No place stays safe for long. How many in your group?"

"Back in Actsburg? More than a hundred before shit went south. Now? There's three of us, and in case you're a numbers guy working the odds, I guarantee no one in your crew is as good a shot as me."

I laughed at her mix of bravado and sweetness. I'd only ever seen the like in Evelyn.

"Numbers guy? Maybe, but not the way you mean. There are four of us."

"Thanks for sharing."

She retrieved two gas cans and a siphon from her truck and then started at the car farthest from where we'd left our gear. Once the first can started filling up, we made eye contact, sizing each other up. I wanted to take the next step in trust, maybe even lend a helping hand, but despite the risk I'd already taken, I couldn't surmount my fear of ambush, or lies, or being wrong again about throwing in with another human being like I'd been wrong about Damon and Rhea. That mistake had come damn close to costing us our lives.

After she filled her first can, she did the second. When that one filled, she carried them to her truck and poured the contents into its gas tank. She walked back to the same car, siphoned it dry, half a can, and then moved to the next car to continue. I watched her the way I used to watch Evelyn when she did simple things like put her clothes away after washing them or get dressed for a night on the town.

Footsteps crunching behind me broke the spell.

Della came out from behind the bulldozer.

"We've got some food if you're hungry," she said.

Vale scrunched her face, unsure what to make of Della, as if she thought we were playing a trick on her—or she had no idea anymore how to respond to kindness.

"I'm Della." She gave the smile she used to put panicked patients at ease. It worked.

Vale relaxed. Her tension gave way to a grin. "Oh, yeah? What you got?"

Della walked over to the Camry, rummaged around inside, and came up with a package of Oreo cookies she'd been saving for a special occasion. I swear a tear ran down Vale's cheek at the sight of them, but I stood too far away to say for sure. Vale waved to her people inside the truck. The doors opened. A man and a woman climbed out with guns handy but not a threat. The man wore jeans and a gray mechanics shirt. The woman sported running shorts and a fleece hoodie.

"This is Dawson and Gordon," Vale said.

I whistled. Christopher and Birch rose from cover.

"The young guy is Christopher. The other is Birch. He doesn't talk."

"Nice to meet you all."

Della ripped open the Oreos. We all dug in. Even slightly stale, they tasted magnificent.

"Where you heading?" Vale said around a mouthful of cookie.

"Long story. Right now, Miami."

"That so? We're heading there too."

EIGHT

We wound up driving down Route 27. Vale's crew took the lead, and we drove in their wake, windows up against the unrelenting awfulness of the odor, but it did the trick. The few times we passed clusters of the living dead, they paid us no attention at all. For a while, none of them showed up anywhere, then Miami embraced us. Route 27 became East Okeechobee Road.

After that, we only saw dead bits and pieces, twitching limbs, or single corpses too broken to move, stuck in place as if the sun had melted them to the pavement.

Around Miami International Airport, the welcoming committee rolled out to greet us.

A red convertible parked in the middle of the road. Two men and two women stood in front of it, one couple black, the other white, all dressed in beach clothes—bathing suites, linen shirts, and flip-flops. They waved us down.

Vale's truck stopped in the middle lane about fifty yards shy of them. Della stopped the Camry in the right lane so we could see. The locals spoke. I rolled down my window, but I still couldn't make out what they said. The back door of the truck cracked open, and Vale dropped out with her rifle in hand. She gestured to me: She would provide cover while I found out what they wanted. For a moment, I froze. Did Vale trust me that much already? Did I trust her? I felt no natural hesitation about her. When I looked at her, I saw Evelyn in my mind.

"Cornell?" Della said.

"Yeah, got this." I swiped a Beretta 92 from the glove box and stepped out of the Camry.

"Hey there," the black man called and waved.

I waved back and walked as far as the truck's passenger-side door. If shit went south, I could drop and roll under it for cover. Best I could tell, though, our greeters carried no weapons, and they'd come alone, not another car or person in sight.

"What can we do for you?" I asked.

"This may sound odd," the man said, "but we've been waiting on you for weeks."

"Waiting on who?" I said.

The black woman straightened from leaning on the car. "On you. You're Mr. Cornell, aren't you? Mr. Birch in one of these vehicles too?"

A warm breeze filled the silence. It carried a sound I'd lived with for far too long now, always on the edges of my thoughts: the jackal's laughter, no less cutting in its mockery of my belief that I controlled any part of my fate. The message came clear: I would never shake free of it. The world wasn't finished chewing me up, let alone ready to spit me out. Who could know me, know which direction I would go? Who could've sent all those dead to herd us down this path to here and now? Only the Red Man.

I pulled the Beretta 92 from the back of my waistband, where I'd tucked it as I left the car, held it low in front of me, ready to aim, to kill. The members of the welcoming committee flinched. Fear livened their expressions.

"You work for the Red Man?" I said.

"No, no, man, you got us all wrong," the man said.

"What the hell does Stradley want with us? Huh? Why does he keep playing with me? He still after payback for Birch?" I said.

"I don't know," the man said. "We've heard of the Red Man, but we don't work for him. We have no idea what he wants. Okay?"

The woman took a deep breath. She stepped forward, calm but frightened eyes darting between the gun and my face. I'd met half a dozen like her robbing banks. Terrified but capable of keeping composed, of navigating a fucked-up situation.

"I'm guessing you're Mr. Cornell," she said. "We don't want to hurt you. We only know of the Red Man. He's not here. He didn't send us."

"How the hell do you know who I am?"

"We see his mark on you," she said.

"What mark?" I said.

"On your forehead. Where he touched you," she said. "The Red Man isn't the only one with power over the dead."

"What the hell does that mean?"

"Listen, my name's Erika," the woman said. She pointed at the man who'd spoken, then at the white couple. "That's my husband, Octavio. That's Denny and Ruth. We're no threat to you. We can't answer your questions. If you come with us, we'll take you to the ones who can. They know better than us what the Red Man can do and what he is."

"If we don't come with you, what then?"

"I really don't know. We were told to expect you and Birch and another, a woman, Vale, and to show you the way into town, where it's safe. Where you can rest without fearing the dead will come knocking any second. We all have a part to play in... the end of the world, I guess, and if you do our bit, things go one way. If you refuse, things happen differently."

"That's it? Plans change?"

Erika shrugged. "Yeah. I mean, we can't force you. You've got to choose your own path for it to work."

"Hey, man." Denny pushed himself off the hood of the car. "We got no axe to grind with you. We're here to deliver an invitation and guide you to the ones who have answers. You don't want the answers? S'okay, cool, we go our own ways, the world keeps falling down this fucked-up rabbit hole of death, and everything turns to dust. That's all."

"What kind of answers?"

"The kind you get from a saint," Octavio said.

"A lot more sinners in this world than saints. Make some damn sense already," I said.

Footsteps crunched behind me. Instead of turning to see who'd stepped forward, I watched the eyes of our welcomers. Almost as one, their gazes shifted over my left shoulder, and their expressions widened with surprise.

"You got his mark," Erika said. "Mr. Cornell's is red, but yours is white. You must be Vale. St. Bianco told us you'd be coming too. We never figured you'd arrive together."

"St. Bianco is here?" Vale said.

"Friend of yours?" I asked.

Vale shook her head. "Not exactly."

"We don't understand all this stuff," Erika said. "The dead holy folk blessed us, which is why we can see your auras, see the marks on you, but none of us knows how it works. It sounds corny, but we're taking all this on faith."

"Come with us, get some answers," Octavio said.

"Or don't," Denny said. "Save the world or let it die. Your call, man."

"Dead holy folk?" I said. "As in living dead?"

Vale and I exchanged glances. She knew more about this than me. I read it in her face.

"They for real with this 'holy' talk?" I said.

"Could be, yeah," she said.

I squinted at her. "Oh, yeah? You got a lot of saints for friends?"

"Only the one," she said, "and when I knew St. Bianco, he didn't have much to offer the living except staying dead for good when you die. So, what's changed?"

"You'll have to come with us and ask him yourself," Erika said.

NINE

We followed the red Corvette into the big, bright city of Miami. Buildings shone in the sun. Heat filled the air.

As far east as I could see, hazy light emanated from a point down by the ocean and filled the sky. I recalled the crimson glow that had flowed along the streets of Baxtonville, heralding the arrival of the Red Man and death for everyone with us except me and Birch. The dead had ruled that town. Here I saw life. It gave me a tiny flicker of hope I expected reality to snuff at any moment.

The 'Vette led us south and east until we crossed Biscayne Bay via A1A and drove into South Beach. Erika and her crew guided us along the strip. The sight set my head spinning. On one side of the street stretched green grass and beaches filled with people in bathing suits and summer clothes. On the other, sidewalks punctuated by outdoor cafes where people drank coffee and ate, where faces peered out from hotel room balconies and windows.

Living people.

Eating, walking, sunbathing, jogging. Smiling. Laughing.

Going about life like it used to be.

Music played. I rolled down the window. A band performed an acoustic cover of an old Stones' song, "Gimme Shelter," in one of the cafes. The sound faded as we passed.

I hadn't been to South Beach in years. It looked like I remembered it. Alive. Set off from the rest of the world. Clean sand, lush strip parks, and the Atlantic Ocean rolling in on powerful waves. Untouched by the dead. It took more than Biscayne Bay and the Intracoastal Waterway to provide that kind of protection.

"So many people," Christopher said. "So many bikinis."

"Keep your eyes in their sockets, kid," Della said. "How's this possible?"

"Your guess is as good as mine." I twisted to face Birch. "Unless our resident mad scientist cares to enlighten us?"

Lifting his gaze from his notebook, Birch only shrugged.

Along the road, palm trees swayed in the breeze. A group played volleyball on the beach. Another group danced on the sidewalk to a hip-hop cassette playing on a boombox. Our caravan drew curious glances, even looks of disgust as the stink of Vale's truck spread in the air. The aroma of meat and spices sizzling on a charcoal grill drifted into the car. My stomach growled; my mouth watered. The world as it had been before the dead rose, except for little signs of the new reality. People on the beach, yeah, but only a tiny sliver of a fraction of how many would've once been there on a gorgeous day like this, and more than a few carried weapons or kept them propped up against their beach chairs. Men with rifles stood watch on the roofs of the tallest buildings. The inner darkness of the hotels, shops, and restaurants without electricity. The expressions of people who looked upon Vale's truck as if a horror movie had rolled into town, one they'd seen too many times already.

The convertible turned down an alley that connected to a parking garage behind one of the big, old art deco hotels. We followed. I kept my gun in hand. If we'd made the wrong call and Erika had led us to an ambush, we'd only have one choice: fight. But no attack came. Nor did I truly expect one. Something about all this felt, if not right, appropriate, as if whatever lay in our future, an innumerable array of alternate possible outcomes or a single, locked-in destiny, it lay on the other side of this place, a nexus through which we must pass to reach it. The Corvette rolled into a parking space far from the hotel entrance. Denny emerged and directed us to two nearby spaces. All the engines died, and the garage echoed with quiet.

Vale and I exited first, guns ready.

"You won't need those." Octavio pointed at our weapons.

"I'll make that call myself, you don't mind," I said.

"Nah, man, suit yourself," he said. "Trusting us is a lot to ask, I get it."

Dawson and Gordon climbed out of the rot van, Della and Christopher from the Camry.

"Sorry to park us so far from the door." Denny waved his hand in front of his face. "Need to keep that stink away."

"Ready?" Erika said. "What about Mr. Birch?"

I knocked on Birch's window. He gave me a look that said it all, and I heard his voice in my head, the way it used to sound: *Are we really doing this? There's no turning back. Why don't we walk our asses across the street and sit in the sand instead? Soak in the sun and the salt air. Let this rotting world keep rotting and enjoy what's left while we can.*

I crushed his hopes. "Come on, Birch. The bastards in charge here can't be any worse than the bastards in charge anywhere else, can they? So, let's go meet the mayor, even if it's just to tell him to fuck off and die."

Birch cracked the first smile I'd seen from him since before Deadtown. We both had our history clashing with authority. That grin lasted only half a second then vanished. He shoved his notebook into the box beside him on the seat then opened his door. I backed up, gave him a hand getting out, and then the lot of us walked toward the hotel entrance. I whistled that old tune from *The Wizard of Oz*: *We're off to see the Wizard, the wonderful Wizard of Oz.* Only Denny laughed. Octavio and Ruth held the doors. We entered into cool darkness.

Our eyes adjusted to the gloom. We stood in a small lobby that had popped wholesale out of a 1930s movie about big city life. Denny guided us along a corridor where a fuzzy blast of daylight glimmered at the far end, and we traversed it to a vast lobby. Accordion windows folded back along the front wall opened onto the street, permitting fresh air and light to enter. It overlooked a sidewalk plaza of tables, chairs, and palm trees, all with an ocean view. Daylight chased off the gloom, but another light illuminated the space too. A bright organic haze radiated from seven men and women seated in high-backed chairs in the lobby's lounge area. About half a dozen people sat around them in smaller chairs or on the floor.

My chest muscles clenched as I saw how much the glowing people resembled the Red Man, skin almost vivid enough to pass for living, but too dry, too tight. Deep wrinkles around their sunken eyes. Little scars that would never heal or fade. They wore clothes unsuited to their mystical appearance.

Tattered and stained shirts, ragged dresses, torn jeans, no shoes. Their bare feet mottled, black at the toenails. They looked asleep, eyes closed, expressions still. Every few seconds, I glanced away from them, let my sight focus on Della or Vale or the glorious day outside. Looking at them straight on for too long produced an ache behind my eyes that threatened to grow until it split my skull. Ideas and impressions pushed into my thoughts. Voices whispered at the edge of my hearing. Like the Red Man's dream. Invasive species of the mind. Outrage filled me.

My voice, harsh and righteous, cracked the silence. "Get the hell out of my head, you goddamn wormfeeders."

The glow of the dead holy folks brightened. Their eyes snapped open. Dusky, powerful glares, the whites of their eyes glimmering in dark pits. I glared back at them, fed up with staring down dead eyes. The walls and floor vibrated. A low hum quivered the room. The living people in the lounge area and our welcoming committee flinched and cowered. So did Vale's people and mine, except for me, Birch, and Vale.

Instead of shrinking from the show of power, we stepped toward it.

"You want something from us, we're here to listen," I said. "Otherwise, I might like to go crack a few beers on the beach and work on my tan."

Birch, of course, said nothing, but he put on a good show of looking bored.

The hum faded.

The dead holy folk stared a little longer.

The one in the center lifted a hand and blessed us with the sign of the cross.

"Don't take it personally," I said, "but I haven't been to church since the sixth grade."

Dressed in tattered black jeans, a once-white dress shirt, and a black leather jacket that looked like salvage from a motorcycle crash, he stood and took four steps toward us.

"Don't turn your back on God, Mr. Cornell. You'll need all the help you can get."

"God hasn't helped this sinner yet. Why would he start now?" I said. "How the hell do you know me, know any of us?"

He smiled, nothing pleasant in the expression. "Some of *you* know me. Vale. Gordon. Dawson. I trust your road here wasn't too much of a trial. I don't see Ms. Gallegos with you, though, so I gather you suffered a loss. Did she rise when death took her?"

We waited for someone to answer. Vale tried to bore holes into the dead man with her eyes until Gordon said, "She didn't."

"I'm gratified to hear it. May she rest in peace."

Vale's voice crashed out of her throat. "How dare you? How dare you leave the people we knew in Actsburg to die, then you come down here and set up your little beach party, and what— *what* the hell is it you want?"

"I understand your anger," the holy man said. "I did, indeed, show those people mercy. None would've survived, would've lived more than a day or two after leaving the airport where you took shelter. None would've arrived here, now, and stood safe from the living death astride the earth. Only you, Vale. You were the only one I *knew* would live on. If I hadn't blessed the others, they would've risen and added to the strength of the darkness aligned against the living. Do you understand?"

"No, I damn well do not," Vale said.

"Wait a minute," Gordon said. "You mean you thought me and Dawson would die, and you still withheld your blessing?"

"No. I gave you my blessing freely, as I did for Gallegos, then hoped for the best. Had you died, you wouldn't have risen. Now here you are, alive, I'm overjoyed to see."

Birch clutched my arm, gripped it so tight I winced. He looked at me, his face burdened by so much he wanted to communicate but couldn't say. I knew, though. The same terrible idea had formed in my head too.

"Only one other person I know can keep the dead from rising. Only one other person can put the dead to rest," I said.

"You're mistaken, Mr. Cornell. I don't put the dead to rest. I send the living to ultimate peace and remove their fear of rising," he said. "Others hold power like mine—or like that of the man you mean, Darrell Philip Stradley. But while we are many, there is only one man I know of who can send the Red Man to true death forever, and that man, Mr. Cornell, is you."

TEN

Seven living dead saints, holy folks, bodhisattva, prophets, whatever you call them, they set my skin crawling and tied knots in my gut. Their chests didn't rise and fall with breath. Their lips never moved, except for St. Bianco's. Their eyes never blinked, as if an artist had painted them on stone. I couldn't say if I stood in the presence of divinity, spiritual miracles, or simply dead bodies less rotted than all the rest. Flesh with enough brain cells still sparking to pretend to something more than death. It didn't matter.

For all their weirdness and formality, at heart, they were only another crew of people who believed they held the right to order me around, to control where I went and how I lived, to erase my wants and goals, and force their own into my head. Like Warden Lane Grove in prison. Like Sheriff Tom Weichert at Camp Cady. Like the Red Man. Self-appointed. Controlling. Arrogant. Indifferent to the hopes and desires of those beneath them. So unironically self-assured in their divine right to toy with the lives of others, they didn't see how they destroyed themselves.

"You're wrong," I said. "The Red Man is already dead. No one can put that rabid dog down for good except maybe one of you if you've really got the magic touch. Anyway, I've got other plans. You and your creepy-eyed friends can do the same thing everyone else who's tried to run my life has done, and go—"

"Mr. Cornell, you misunderstand us."

St. Bianco's voice boomed. It resonated in my bones, in the lobby walls.

It brought a cold wind that twitched at our clothes and hair.

Everyone, including me, flinched.

The misty glow around the dead holy folk intensified, deepened all the shadows in the lobby, and pushed the beautiful day outside away from the hotel. We stood in a bubble that his voice solidified. The sounds from beyond the open windows dimmed.

"You say we're arrogant. Yet it's you who assumes he can be a savior."

St. Bianco approached me. His body glided, legs barely moving. Energy radiated from him and tickled my skin. His light filled my eyes, entered me, suffused me with a calmness I hadn't known in years, and chased away my tension and anxiety. Even the breath of the jackal panting down my neck faded. His presence in the recesses of my mind vanished, leaving me free of him for the first time since before Evelyn died. All of this occurred so suddenly my head spun, and my knees trembled.

"We've seen many like you on this new dead Earth. People capable of adapting, of carving survival from the world no matter the obstacles stacked against them. People of spirit and willpower. Defiant, independent souls. The seven of us gathered here pooled our energies to repel the dead and create a haven for the living. The societies we knew, the natural order that once reigned, are decimated beyond recovery. A new world is quickening. We'll all witness to its birth. There's still time to tip the balance of things toward life and away from death, but it cannot be assured. Thus, we've followed the lives of people such as you and Vale, called to them in the night or touched their lives on our own journeys. We hoped for dozens, maybe hundreds of them to gather here. People with the spiritual stamina and the psychological surety to confront the Red Man. Since the early days of the dead plague, we've waited for you to come. Do you know many have arrived?"

All around me, confusion filled the expressions of my people, of Vale's, of the four who met us coming into the city. Sadness darkened their eyes too. Outside the windows, a new thing revealed itself. An awful, persistent fear and resignation in the faces of passersby. No matter how safe they felt here in this blessed city district, they knew—and could never forget—a world of the dead awaited them outside the city limits.

"Vale and I are the first?" I said.

"The first and only."

"What happened to the others?"

"Some died. Others broke under stress. Many ignored the greater needs before them and chose only survival in fortified pockets of apparent safety that one day will betray them."

"Can't blame them for surviving. That's prerequisite to everything else."

"Survival isn't truly living. It's scavenging off the corpse of the world."

"Like insects on a dead body."

"Yes."

"Yeah, well, we don't have the luxury of control over the dead like you do."

"You have more power than you think. Why else would the Red Man work so hard to turn you to his side? He's in your head, isn't he? And Mr. Birch's? He knows you're here. He tried to divert you, but he succeeded only in keeping you from going where you wanted. He lacked the power to force you to him as he desired. You skirted the edge of his influence and the limits of ours. You traveled the border between the light and dark, life and death, and your path ended at life. The Red Man sends you dreams because he fears you. He's done this to others. Many of those we hoped would join us turned to his side. None he's touched have held their ground like you."

"So, what? I'm supposed to play high noon with the Red Man? There can be only one? That kind of crap?"

"You're not supposed to do anything, Mr. Cornell. Your life is your own. You have free will like all the others. My sisters and brothers and I hoped for many like you—those who frighten the Red Man—to face him together with each other's support and protection. We wish a better future for the living. Only you and Vale have arrived. If I were you, I'd find those beers and head for the beach. The world belongs to the dead now. You and your companions, like everyone in this city, are dying by the second in a world that wants you only for raw flesh to house lost and angry souls."

The words stung. Was that all we struggled for? The opportunity to die on our own terms, to depart this world the way we'd always figured we would, and leave behind our bodies to the awful, new, unnatural order?

"Something's coming," I said.

"Something?" St. Bianco said.

"A dark thing. I don't know what it is or what to call it. The Red Man showed it to me in the dreams he sends. It's vast, angry, bitter, all the bad things you can imagine."

"We know."

"What are you doing about it?"

"What's to be done? If it is called, it will come."

"The Red Man's calling it?"

"Yes. And others like him. Stradley is only one of those who had a hand in bringing the dead to life. Others around the world have followed paths that parallel his. The details vary; the power doesn't. Others like us and like you exist around the world too. Events similar to these are playing out, have played out, or will do so soon in many places. We can only hope enough of the ones who can make a difference choose to keep that darkness from arriving. Here, at least, we've failed. So why not enjoy the light and warmth, live in the brightness, until it vanishes forever."

"That's not the life I want."

"What life do you prefer?"

Della held Christopher close, her arm around his shoulders. Her expression reminded me of when we first met, when she saw in me only a criminal, a convict, another untrustworthy man for her to guard against. Now she aimed that harshness and skepticism at the dead holy folks. She didn't trust them. Good. Neither did I.

"To be left alone," I said. "To get where we're going and live our lives in peace."

"If peace is all you want, I can provide it now. My blessing will stop you from rising after you die. We have a place here where you can go and the means to make it painless. Others have chosen that path. You can help the woman and the boy first, then see to yourself."

St. Bianco reached for my forehead.

I stepped back. "Don't touch me!"

I threw a punch at him, aiming for his chest, but my fist found only empty air. Without even appearing to have moved, St. Bianco stood six feet to my right, his hand lowered.

"Nothing ever against your will, my friend," he said, "but the offer stands."

Vale stamped up to him and slapped him, surprising him, connecting where I hadn't.

St. Bianco's face snapped sideways, then turned and glowered at her.

"Vale," he said.

"You bastard. All *you* ever offer is death. You're as much a part of this fucked-up world as any other rotting corpse. Just because your flesh doesn't stink, you think you're better?"

St. Bianco said nothing, only returned Vale's stare. Long seconds passed. The silence in the room developed an almost physical presence. Then the lobby darkened. It took me a moment to realize the glow of the holy folks had dimmed. St. Bianco returned to his chair and grew still, like the others, only their eyes betraying the faintest hint of animation. The gloom deepened. The holy folk faded into it. A sweet aroma like honey wafted into the air. I inched closer to the dead people and squinted, wondering if I saw what I thought I saw, wondering if wet, crimson tears really flowed from St. Bianco's eyes and down his withered cheeks.

ELEVEN

Erika and Octavio set us up with rooms on the fourth floor. No power, so we used the stairs.

The previous occupants had removed the electronic door locks. You could lock yourself in with the latch and the manual deadbolt, but you couldn't lock it from the other side. Not that stealing or any other crime posed much trouble, Octavio explained. We could take pretty much anything we needed or wanted from the shops in the city—and the dead holy folks had a way of weeding out bad apples upon arrival.

They housed us all in a row, our rooms overlooking the street-front and the beach. Clean sheets, comfortable furniture, and working bathrooms. A little taste of heaven to go with the saints. Della and I roomed next to Christopher, with Birch on the other side. Then Vale, and then Gordon and Dawson, and part of me felt herded, livestock penned in stalls for the night. Except that night, the locals invited us to their party.

A bonfire roared on the beach. Flames licked twenty feet into the air, spitting embers into the dark. The smoke almost vanished against the night sky. Surf rolled onto the sand and brought a rhythmic pulse, the beat of an enormous hidden heart. The pulse of the Earth itself, carrying on, indifferent, while humanity died and ravened its own bones. A crowd gathered, a few hundred strong, with beach chairs and blankets spread round the blaze, and I thought if this was everyone in Miami, then the living stood little chance of outlasting the dead.

A group of musicians played music by the fire. Mellow, relaxing songs. Bob Marley. The Grateful Dead. The Beach Boys. Eternal beach music. People knew all the words and sang along. Some got up and danced. Della and I watched Christopher throw a glow-in-the-dark frisbee back and forth with some kids his age. Nearby sat Dawson and Gordon, snuggled together on a beach blanket, singing, almost happy. Beside them but alone sat Vale, back to the fire, gaze steady on the enormous blank canvas of the Atlantic Ocean and the starry night sky.

This defined our world now, this little pocket of safety with our backs pressed to the sea. Nowhere left to retreat. Our trust in a group of beings we would've called monsters in another life. Too stunned and numbed to feel much horror anymore. We could stay, enjoy a comfortable room, the beach, the community of the living, but like the other places I'd found myself since I lost Evelyn, it didn't belong to me. I was living in someone else's space, living by their rules, by their authority, enjoying security they provided, and that always came with a cost, an obligation. It required trust too, but my reserves of trust had long ago scraped bottom.

Lohatchie called to me the strongest when I found myself like this, with time to catch my breath. My place down there beckoned. Lohatchie would be mine, Della's, Christopher's, and Birch's if he wanted, and the only authority there would be our own.

A truck grumbled onto the sand from one of the wide, paved paths through the park.

The music faded out. Voices quieted.

An old municipal pick-up truck with fat tires for the beach, it rumbled along, towing a cargo trailer equipped with an iron mesh cage. Probably once used to house tools needed to clean and maintain the beach, it now held half a dozen wormfeeders banging around inside, jostled by the motion and their own attraction to the living.

It stopped by the bonfire. The crowd gave a riotous cheer. They clapped and whooped when the driver emerged and waved his baseball cap at them.

The frisbee game ended. Christopher dropped to his knees in the sand beside me.

"What's going on?" he said.

The fire glowed dull against dead flesh but glistened in the living eyes glaring out from it. It flickered on the faces of the living, filled with child-like anticipation. People encircled the truck with ritualistic excitement, and the band launched into that old song about not fearing the reaper. It transported me back to the prison yard, back to a warden with the faith of a martyr, who built gallows and a bonfire to separate sinners from saints and send us all to our just reward. The driver and others reached into the truck bed and dragged out long poles with wire loops at the end.

"Cornell?" Christopher said. "You all right?"

Della put her hand on mine.

"They're going to burn them," I said.

"Where'd they come from?" he said.

Octavio walked up to us then and gave the answer.

"These are stragglers from the city limits," he said. "They never make it far, but we clean them out just the same. Catch a few every day. Then we bring them here and remind them this is a place for the living. Makes everyone feel better to see them burn."

"Not everyone," I said.

"Why don't you join in? You're the newbs. They'll let you throw one on the fire."

Della's fingers tightened around my arm.

"Can we?" Christopher said.

He didn't understand the harsh face I showed him. "No, we'll pass."

"Suit yourself." Octavio moved on to speak with Dawson and Gordon, who took him up on the offer and walked over to the truck. Vale declined.

A group of four men and women looped wires around the neck of the first wormfeeder then used the poles to wrangle it off the trailer. It stumbled and fell in the sand. Laughter rippled from the crowd. The dead thing rose to its feet and swiped at them, gnashed its teeth. People threw trash and seashells at it, ran up, and jabbed it with sticks. A kid, maybe fifteen years old, rushed in and stuck a beach hat on its head. That brought guffaws.

The four working the poles spun the thing around, the poles like spokes on a wheel, the walking corpse its axle. One of the women tripped, fell, and let go of her pole. The wormfeeder raged at her, dragging the others with it until another woman seized the loose pole. Laughter again. As if a slapstick comedy routine played out in jest. This was sport to them. The first round ended when they shoved the wormfeeder into the fire then yanked the poles free, decapitating it with the wire. The other corpses rioted in the cage while the first one burned.

"Let's call it a night," Della said. "We don't need to watch this."

"Take Christopher and go ahead," I said. "I'll come along soon. Need to think some more, or I won't be able to sleep a damn minute."

"Don't be long."

"Nope."

Della ushered Christopher off the beach. The boy glanced back at the fire half a dozen times, confused, fascinated, frightened, trying to make sense of what he saw and how Della and I had reacted to it. Trying to understand the adult world when even the adults didn't understand it anymore. I laid back on the sand and listened to the waves break on the beach, wishing for them to drown out the voices around me.

Someone screamed. I sat up, startled, but the scream turned into laughter.

Over at the fire, Dawson and Gordon each held one of the long poles and grappled with the corpse of an obese woman in a tracksuit. Two others angled their loops over her head, and the four wrestled the wormfeeder toward the blaze.

Vale stepped in front of me, blocking my view. I hadn't heard her approach on the soft sand. "Let's talk," she said.

I couldn't read her face. Too many conflicting emotions—and a kind of hard-edged nerve I'd never seen before. I stood and brushed sand off me.

"What's on your mind?"

"This place." She led us toward the water. "Doesn't feel right, does it?"

"Every place has secrets."

"St. Bianco has secrets for sure."

"How do you know him?"

"He turned up at the airport up in Actsburg out of the blue one evening. Set everything on its head, tried to warn us an army of wormfeeders would overrun the place. Everything turned to shit, and I lost a lot of friends."

"Was he right about the wormfeeders?"

"Yeah. Only me, Dawson, Gordon, and Gallegos escaped. Wormfeeders got Gallegos a few weeks later. But she didn't rise, like we said. That's what St. Bianco offered us, a blessing to keep us dead when we died. Real death. He came to see us all die."

"You'd think with all the people we lose these days, it'd get easier, but it doesn't. Still hurts the same. We just don't have time for grieving."

"Maybe that's why I don't like this place. I don't want time to think."

"There's more to it than that, though. I don't like this place because it's a prison like the one I broke out of at the start of this nightmare."

"You were in prison?"

"I robbed banks. On my last job, a dumbass security guard shot and killed my girlfriend. She was pregnant. I killed him and two other guards, then let myself get caught and pled guilty. I wanted to be punished, not for killing the guards, though I regret that, but for failing Evelyn. She could handle herself, never really needed me to protect her or watch over her—except that one time, and I blew it."

"I used to want that, to be protected. That's some bullshit, though. You take care of yourself, because when things go bad— really, really bad like they are now—all the protectors worry about their own ass first. My boyfriend, my parents, they all abandoned me, left me on my own for weeks alone in my apartment before I worked up the nerve to go out. I don't like this place because it's a daydream. A little pocket of pretending life can go on the way it did before the dead started walking. I gave up living in daydreams the day I set foot outside my safe, little hole. I prefer the real world even when it's doing its damndest to kill me. At least I'm living on my own terms then."

She sounded so much like Evelyn, my heart ached for my old life.

We stopped shy of the surf line. Waves broke and pushed froth and foam within inches of our feet, then dragged it back into the sea. The faint light of the bonfire danced across Vale's face. For a moment, I saw Evelyn in her features, and my chest tightened.

"We do what we do, what we have to do. We go on living," she said. "I never want to depend on anyone else again. Not my parents, not my boyfriend, not swaggering assholes who think they're better than everyone else, and certainly not a dead saint. No one. It hurt me bad to find my freedom. Wounded me, scarred me. I healed stronger. I won't ever give that up again."

My head throbbed, and my eyes welled up.

Reality cracked. For several moments, a cloud of confusion enveloped me.

I plunged back in time to a night before a bank job, standing beside Evelyn, each of us reassuring the other, sharing our confidence, our fates inextricably entwined.

Vale took my hand and pulled me close. Her warmth reminded me of Evelyn, and, god, she seemed so much like her, a woman who'd protect *us* before she ever needed me to protect her, a woman who understood life only counted if you played by your own rules.

The firelight glinted in her eyes. I stared into them, speechless.

"Cornell? You okay?" she said.

She leaned closer to my face, worried, watching me. Her breath glided across my lips.

She took my other hand and eased herself closer to me, our legs touching.

I sensed her desire to kiss me. My body responded with yearning. Part of me wanted it to happen, wanted to yield to the moment—but the rest of me knew what I felt I felt for a ghost, for Evelyn and memories Vale stirred, but not for Vale.

Back in the hotel, Della and Christopher waited for me, and somewhere far down the road, Lohatchie, but on the beach, men and women burned the living dead, while the world died all around us, and this woman offered me a connection to emotions that had lain dormant since Evelyn died. Why, when the world was ending, should I hold myself back from anything good? Anything that meant *life* meant *living*?

A high wave broke and flooded our feet. Vale yelped.

We let go of each other's hands and rushed to dry sand. The ocean washed the temptation away and left me grateful for its intervention.

Vale offered me a long, uncertain, possibly hopeful gaze. I looked away, walked away, left her standing alone on the beach, regretting every step. She might be the most "alone" person I'd ever met. I wished I could give her the connection she sought, but some people, that's their fate, their role in life, the only way they can survive and be who they are.

I looked back once from the shadows of the sidewalk.

Vale stood with her back to me.

Barely visible in the firelight, a thin, pale woman against the dead, blank ocean.

TWELVE

Whatever misgivings I had about shacking up in the Most Holy South Beach Realm of the Living, I couldn't deny how much Della and Christopher enjoyed sunbathing on the beach and swimming in the ocean. No matter where our path led, the destination could wait a few days while they enjoyed the respite. Birch, on the other hand, never left his room. I brought him food and found him in the same position every time. Hunched over at the little desk, scribbling in his notebooks. Vale and I avoided each other. Della didn't hide that she sensed the energy between us, but she said nothing about it.

Dawson and Gordon fell right into the beach life. They made friends fast and became part of the community. I envied their happiness and satisfaction to a degree. I couldn't wrap my head around it, but people need different things in life. For some, removal of fear beats confronting and eliminating it. Like a dog hiding its head under a chair. They can't see you, they figure you can't see them. But the cause of those fears remains.

Motivated by curiosity, I dropped by the dead holy folk a few times a day and peeked in the window or sat in the cool gloom of the lobby. Nothing about them ever changed. They sat on makeshift thrones in utter stillness, unblinking eyes staring straight ahead as if they saw past the world into another beyond it, a realm outside ordinary senses, a vision world that revealed its secrets only to them.

I dreamt every night. The Red Man showed me the approaching darkness.

In my dreams, it flowed like vantablack acid devouring the substance of the universe.

I couldn't tell if something drove it, or if it moved of its own volition.

It consumed the light, the planets, stars, galaxies, and nebulas, which all appeared like backgrounds for cartoons set in space where everything looks crammed together and close as hell and spaceships zip from planet to planet. The dark spread like ink spilled across an animation cell. When it ate enough of whatever scene played in my mind, it burst alive with human eyes, all looking my way as if they saw into my soul.

I woke up sweating then, every night for all the few days we spent in Miami. But I told no one about the dreams. I think Birch knew, though. From the way he looked when I brought him meals, I think similar visions invaded his sleep.

Those dreams wore me down.

Out on the road, with the dead everywhere, staying alive distracted me. I could wake up, shrug them off, and ignore them again until nightfall. Staying alive, keeping Christopher, Della, and Birch alive, held them at bay. But not here. Walking down pretty sidewalks, sitting on the beach, lounging in palm tree shade did not take them away. When I looked at waves breaking and crashing, the tide ebbing and flowing, the dreams rippled alongside. Sometimes I swam with Christopher and became lost in thought, afloat on the edge of an ocean that could swallow me in a moment. I walked the beach with Della, and the rhythm of the surf, the heartbeat of the earth slowed, wound down toward its last pump of blood to the body on which we lived.

Surrounded by beauty and peace, warmth and light, by people who smiled and didn't take every step, every breath in fear it might be their last, I sensed the world dying.

I lost track of how many times Della asked me what was on my mind.

How could I explain? To describe my dreams made them sound childish. I knew no words to convey the sense of abject nothingness, of despair, of anger that burned with more power and fury than the heart of a star in that vast darkness.

She let me be when I refused to answer. Let me work it out for myself.

My saddest point came the moment I did exactly that.

More than the dreams themselves, more than the dark horror they predicted, what left me most unsettled and fearful was that Miami provided a true taste of our future. We could run to Lohatchie, sure, and we stood a good chance of making it safe and sound given how good we'd become at navigating this world of the dead. We could escape the wormfeeders and the living alike. Make a home. But the dreams would come with me. That darkness would arrive one day. Until then, I'd live with it, every night, every morning. It would inhabit my mind. Rob me of the peace I sought. Once we hit Lohatchie, once we put the day-to-day struggle to survive behind us, I'd have all the time in the world to think about what was coming, to live life with that dream-imprinted horror, under the shadow of the Red Man, and, goddamn him, I understood then that what he'd done to me made it impossible for me to turn away.

I couldn't break out of this prison like I'd escaped Warden Grove.

I couldn't drive away down the broken highway the way we'd left behind Camp Cady and Deadtown.

The Red Man had latched onto my soul, a metaphysical tick bloating himself off my peace of mind. His burden would travel with me everywhere for as long as I lived or until the darkness snuffed us all out of existence.

Even if that happened tomorrow, it would be too long for me.

The morning I reached that conclusion, it came while Della and I sat high on a lifeguard's chair to watch the sunrise. In the growing dawn, she fell asleep with her head on my shoulder.

She sensed the change in me, the tension of confusion that left my body, the new tension of determination that replaced it. She woke and kissed me.

"There's something I've got to do, Della," I said. "And I'm sorry. So, so sorry."

She studied my face then kissed me again.

"I know," she said as if she had all along and only waited for me to catch up. "Promise me one thing?"

"What's that?"

"Wherever you have to go, whatever you do, do it for yourself, for *us*, not for *them*."

"Yeah, I promise you that. Everything I do now, I do for us. Always."

She kissed me once more. We embraced until the sun floated free over the horizon.

I dropped down from the chair, crossed the sand, walked to the lobby where the dead holy folk sat in motionless contemplation. They seemed different now, more substantial, more real. More credible. The calming effect of their proximity irked me. I walked to the lobby bar and plucked a straw from a bin there. I tore off one end of the paper and slid the remainder halfway off the straw. Standing before St. Bianco, I raised the straw to my lips and blew. The paper shot like a spear, struck his wrinkled nose, and bounced away.

After a few seconds, his eyes lowered to meet my gaze.

"All right, you crazy dead saint, let's talk about how we kill the Red Man."

THIRTEEN

How do you kill what's already dead?

The dead holy folks provided no straight answer.

Instead, they demanded I spend days fasting and meditating to prepare myself and my soul for the confrontation to come. I laughed at the idea, picturing myself sitting my ass on the beach and humming "Ommmm" for hours at a time while pondering the secrets of the universe, but they didn't mean that. Meditation doesn't begin to describe what they did to me.

After giving me time to say goodbye to Della and Christopher, they locked me in with them in part of the hotel basement. No food, only water. No light except for a single, battery-powered lantern.

In that milky darkness, the dead holy folks took turns putting me through an experience I'd only had once before, back in Deadtown—when the Red Man transported me into a vision of his past to show me how Darrell Philip Stradley had transformed from a convenience-store stock clerk to a death-cult leader to a master of the living dead. Stradley had touched me and sent me on a wild ride of visions. As each of the dead holy folks did the same, I learned they all shared a similar path. Each, like Stradley, heard a calling. Some believed it came from God, others from the universe, or the spirit world, or Nirvana, or some other deity, force, or entity I'd never heard of, and even one made up by a woman who'd believed in nothing at all before it spoke to her. She called it Princess, after her childhood cat.

One by one, they brought me into their heads. The dark basement faded away and filled with their histories. I lived the memories of their first contact with the spark that launched them to sainthood, priesthood, shamanhood, whateverhood...

A vision in a dream.

A voice from the oldest tree in the woods.

A fire in the sky only she could see.

A sense of infinite peace that shaped his every choice.

A fox and a deer in the wild.

The drumming of the surf upon the shore.

I heard each call the same as them, felt its compulsion in my bones, and saw the hope they'd found in it. Religion and its trappings never held much stock for me. If I didn't care for society's basic rules of the road, why would I want to bow to some invisible authority whose existence I had to believe in for it to matter? I understood its appeal, though. After sharing their experiences, I couldn't deny the substance of it—except as it turned out, I was right too, at least partly.

I'd relived St. Bianco's struggle with his inner darkness, the miracles that demonstrated its defeat. He beat the dark side of himself into submission, cast his entire being toward the light, worked wonders in our world—and what became of him when he died? What did he find waiting for him out in the grand hereafter?

The same damn thing as Darrell Philip Stradley, madman and vicious killer, and all the dead souls who'd returned to earth: not a goddamn thing.

Absence.

Void.

No heaven or hell. No reward, no punishment.

No return to life reincarnated in a higher or lower form.

No greater understanding of the path to Nirvana.

No unification with the fabric of reality.

No ultimate purpose designed by the Universe.

No community of spirits.

Not even the peace of their raw energy recycled by the cosmos, their lifeforce scattered to the stars and interstellar dust.

They found only themselves and the countless souls of others set adrift in the same utter blankness, where only the voice of Darrell Philip Stradley offered anything to cling to and orient themselves. Darrell Philip Stradley, who in life led a cult with the motto, "Death of the flesh to free the spirit, death of the spirit to free the flesh." Stradley, who'd killed, maimed, and tortured dozens, many with their consent and encouragement. Stradley, who'd built an arsenal and bought nerve gas on the black market to spread his gospel of death. Stradley, who'd died from a bullet to the heart fired by Birch. In the nothing that followed life, his voice ruled. His will rallied the souls of the dead for their assault on the living.

What did the dead holy folk do?

They watched.

Unlike ordinary souls, theirs remained tethered to their incorruptible corpses, and their faith led them to passivity. If utter emptiness followed life, it meant they hadn't fully grasped the purpose of the divine. They accepted it. The darkness flowed right in without any one of them lifting a finger to stop it. Thus Stradley rose again and became the Red Man, one of the guides and masters of the dead and the darkness. One of several around the world.

Whatever divinity existed in the universe, it looked and behaved nothing like what all the priests and prophets said. A damn big part of it boiled with… I don't know, hate? Evil? Words failed to equal the hostility and the craving for annihilation that lived in that darkness on its way to finish what the living dead had started.

Life and light repulsed it.

Warmth infuriated it.

Joy devoured its metaphysical guts like a violent cancer.

It sought to eliminate those things to preserve itself. Where was the light to balance the dark in all this? Somewhere in the vastness of existence, the dead holy folk assured me, light still existed, still shone on some far corner of reality, but not ours anymore. Not on humanity. Not on our very, very lost souls. The universe turns. Balances shift. Day follows night on a cosmic scale incomprehensible to me. And trust me, those dead freaks tried to make me understand, to show me what they knew. Every one of them.

I couldn't, though, not like them.

My brain could only wrap itself around the surface of their lessons. I couldn't explain or articulate it even to myself. The knowledge simply existed inside me, ready to guide me. All of this I saw and experienced, the memories of days, weeks, months, even years that unfolded around me in the span of seconds.

I watched souls leave their bodies and travel into the blackness.

I listened to ghostly screams of horror and despair.

Only their eyes remained vivid when they passed to the next world. Everything else about them turned amorphous and hazy.

Each dead holy person shared their death with me, and I died with them, over and again, witnessing their transcendence and the iridescent, ethereal tether that linked their soul to their corpse. The only lights in the void. A brightness other souls shunned because it reminded them that they hadn't lived a good enough life to escape the darkness. They clustered instead around the deep, red glow of Stradley's tether, moths to a terrible flame. When Stradley opened the way for their return, that light guided them into dead flesh.

The seventh and final dead holy person to share her memories with me reminded me of Della. A nurse, she'd died from a disease that infected her while she worked overseas to save the lives of children during a hemorrhagic fever outbreak. No coincidence, the healer went last. The experiences so far wore me down to a raw nerve, too tired to even sip water. The only saving grace came in escape from the dreams with which the Red Man afflicted me. After the last holy woman showed me her story, she embraced me, and her touch, her energy restored me.

I slept then on the floor of the basement.

Hours or days later, I woke alone and made my way to the hotel lobby.

The dead holy folks sat in their chairs, stony and impassive.

My whole body trembled with hunger.

Octavio came and helped me to a chair. Erika brought me food.

Minutes later, Della came, summoned by Ruth. She sat and held my hand while I ate, and my strength returned.

"How long was I down there?" I asked as Erika refilled my water glass.

"A week," Della said. "What did they do to you?"

"Showed me things."

Erika dragged over a chair and sat across from me. "What did you see? They know so much but tell us so little."

I tried to answer. I wanted to answer. I had no words to describe the vastness of the knowledge and experience they'd conveyed.

When I finished eating, Erika cleared away the plates and utensils. Octavio helped me up, but I needed less assistance now. I felt almost myself again, at least physically.

St. Bianco stood from his chair.

The lobby brightened. A honey-sweet aroma perfumed the air.

Crimson tears ran from St. Bianco's eyes, down his cheek, and soaked into his clothes.

The other holy folk bled too. Some from their noses or ears, some from their hands, some from their lips, from their gums. One bled from a hole in his throat. Permutations of stigmata.

An atmosphere of tranquility settled upon us. All fear and sadness evaporated. Joy and relief did not replace it. Only a sense of rightness remained, as if no matter what came next, all would soon be okay. Even Della relaxed against me, tension and worry drained from her body.

Yet, I still resisted.

In the back of my mind, red flags waved, and warning sirens blared, buried deep but still there. As St. Bianco tilted his head to speak, a hot breath of bad air tickled my neck, reminding me no matter how things seemed, that my jackal waited, always on the fringes of my life, ready to chow down on my corpse when death finally took me.

"You're as prepared as we can make you, Mr. Cornell," St. Bianco said. "I'd hoped to impart you with a better understanding, a deeper appreciation for the divine within us all, but your mind and soul resisted with great determination."

"I'm stubborn like that," I said.

"Indeed, you are. We grant you a day of rest. You shall leave tomorrow morning."

As I nodded agreement, Della dug her fingers into my hand.

The dead holy folks dismissed us, and then she led me to the beach.

"You're going to face the Red Man," she said.

"That's the plan."

"I don't want you to go. Let's leave tonight. You, me, Christopher, and Birch. We'll blow out of here for Lohatchie."

"Tried that already. The Red Man won't let go of me and Birch."

"Fuck this life. Someone's always got their claws in you, digging for a pound of flesh."

"That's why I robbed banks. Turn the tables on things."

"How'd that work out for you?"

I laughed, not a shred of humor in it.

"I'll go with you," Della said.

"What about Christopher?"

"He'll be safe here. He's already made so many friends. Dawson and Gordon will take care of him, I'm sure."

"Della, I don't know if..." About to say what an awful idea it would be for her to come with me, how much danger she'd face, it hit me hard how much I wanted her at my side and how often we'd saved each other's hide, and I said, "I don't know if I can do this without you."

Laughter trickled through the air then.

Not the kind that drifts up from people having fun on the beach.

The kind only I heard.

Jackal's laughter.

FOURTEEN

Next morning, Della and I packed our gear for the trip north.

We squared things with Christopher. He didn't like it, wanted to come with us, but one of his friends, a pretty, blue-eyed girl a year older than him, promised a beach picnic and eased the sting of staying behind.

We'd take the Camry, Della and I alone on the road again, uncertain of anything except our trust in each other and the need to buy our freedom at any cost.

Imagine my surprise when we stepped into the parking lot and found Octavio and Denny leaning against the hood of the Camry with AR-15s in hand. Birch stood with them, his hair a wild electric tangle in the morning sun, his wiry body back in those dirty old pants and the bright Hawaiian shirt, his traveling clothes. He kept one arm around Christopher, a protective gesture that raised every hair on the back of my neck. Our car sat parked beside Vale's truck, and Vale stood at the open back doors of the rot-mobile. Time did nothing to improve its odor. The sight that set my heart racing, though, was St. Bianco, poised between me, Della, and everyone else, left hand raised, palm outward, as if to bless us, his right hand hidden away inside his threadbare black sports jacket. He radiated no sense of calm now.

"What's all this?" I said. "You all here to wish us well?"

"In a sense, Mr. Cornell," St. Bianco said. "We're here to clarify matters for you."

"You spent a week inside my head doing that. If I don't see clearly enough by now, not much's going to change that."

"This matter is of a more worldly nature. You'll easily understand," he said.

Octavio stepped forward. "Something you need to get through your thick skull."

"What's that?" I said.

"The dead holy folks, Cornell, put fuck-all stock in material things, including existence. All this here in Miami? This was always only temporary, waiting for you and the others like you who never showed. Now they've done what they needed to here. No one else is coming. They're ready to move on."

"Okay, so? Who's stopping them?"

"Us," Denny said.

"If you destroy the Red Man, there's a chance for life to survive in this part of the world. If you fail, it falls to the dead," Octavio said. "We fall to the dead."

"High stakes, I know," I said.

"The Red Man placed his mark on you for a reason." St. Bianco lowered his hand. "He sees potential in you, as do we, potential for you to sway the balance toward the light or the dark because of your refusal to live as others demand. If you fall to him and fail to return here, we'll have to assume you tilted toward death."

"If that happens, they won't let the dead have us," Octavio said.

Into the uncomfortable silence that followed, an upbeat, happy pop song from someone's boombox on the strip intruded, all high-pitched voices and jangly percussion.

"If things go the dead's way, Cornell," Vale said, "the holy folks will bless everyone here like St. Bianco did for my people in Actsburg, then send them to the next life before leaving."

"You mean they'll kill them," I said.

"It will be a blessing for them, Mr. Cornell," St. Bianco said. "We won't abandon them to the world to come if you fail."

"We prefer to live either way," Octavio said. "So, to give you an incentive not to fuck up and to make it back here, we're keeping Della."

"No fucking way," I said. "Della goes with me. Christopher too. I won't leave them here if you're thinking this crazy."

Octavio raised his AR-15, aimed it at my face. "Not a discussion, Cornell."

Denny approached with his rifle ready, seized Della by the arm, then dragged her aside. "We're not making you go alone, though."

I looked at Vale. "You?"

"Yeah," she said. "And Birch. St. Bianco insisted."

"He, too, bears the Red Man's mark. He, too, has a part to play," St. Bianco said.

"Just like that, you take my people hostage and expect me to do you a favor? After all I've endured on your behalf?"

"Have you forgotten so much already, Mr. Cornell?" St. Bianco said. "You're helping all of living humanity, how little of it remains. A favor not to us but to the light that burns low in the universe now. There's so much more at risk than we were able to convey to you. If you saw as we do, you'd know this is the right way, that your individuality, your wants and desires, your *people* mean nothing compared to the endless struggle that defines universal existence."

"You son of a bitch," I said. "It always comes down to this, doesn't it? Saint, sinner, or butt-headed fuck-up, you never give a rat's ass for anyone else's life. You grind us down under your authority simply because you fucking *can* and destroy everything anyone under you tries to build. Do you do it because you're afraid we might challenge you, maybe surpass you? Or do you do it simply because you have the power? Or because we don't give a rat's ass what you think, and you can't bear to be ignored?"

Octavio nudged Birch with his rifle. Birch moved and picked up the bags and gear Della and I had brought. He threw it in the back of Vale's truck then climbed in after it. Vale shut the doors.

"You're wasting daylight, asshole," Denny said.

Della spit on him. The saliva slapped his cheek.

He let go of her and recoiled, swiping the moisture away. Della snatched the gun from his hands before he knew he'd lost it. When he realized it, he froze, eye-to-eye with the barrel of his own weapon. Octavio switched his aim from me to Della.

"Careful now, Della," I said.

"Give that back to Denny, or I'll shoot you," Octavio said.

I drew my Beretta, aimed at Octavio. "Not if I shoot you first, jackass."

The tension linked us all, and that damn pop song kept crashing along, all cymbals and a high-pitched refrain, so insufferably fucking mirthful, but none of it mattered because St.

Bianco, who I hadn't even seen move, now held Christopher by the shoulders, the fingers of his left hand spread across his throat, his other still tucked away out of sight.

"Mr. Cornell," he said. "If you wish to back out of our plans, we can simply give all the people here our final blessing today and move on to our next endeavor."

Della's eyes widened at the sight of Christopher, who'd paled, his eyes glassy with fear. She lowered the gun, handed it back to Denny. I put mine away. Octavio lowered his.

"Some kind of saint you are," I said.

Octavio glared at me. "Don't think any of *us* wanted this. Now, go."

I locked gazes with Della, and we reached a silent agreement. She nodded.

"I'll be back for you, I promise. For you and Christopher," I said, then switched on the voice I'd relied on to scare the shit out of bank employees and patrons, security guards, and even cops and FBI agents during my long-lost life of crime: "I come back and find either one of them hurt, mistreated, or worse, you'll learn exactly how much I understand about the true nature of life and death."

FIFTEEN

We drove almost an hour before we saw more than one or two of the dead at a time.

My skin bristled at the change in the air when we exceeded the last reaches of the dead holy folk's protective energy and rolled out exposed. Traveling in Vale's wide, bulky truck proved more difficult than the smaller Camry, which Della knew well how to steer through tight passages among ruined cars and other debris. Several times Birch and I hopped out to clear the road, once even to shove aside what looked like an entire household-worth of second-hand furniture spilled from an overpacked pick-up truck flipped onto its side.

None of us spoke more than necessary. Vale drove, eyes steady on the road. Birch scribbled in yet another damn notebook. I wondered what he wrote, but I feared the answer. Kept thinking of the scene in that old movie about the caretaker trying to write a novel in a haunted hotel, but only typing the same phrase, again and again, *ad infinitum.*

So, mostly, I stared out the window and counted the dead.

We passed a group of five, the largest yet. Their bodies swiveled to track our progress. Eyes opened on every bit of their flesh. Watching us.

The Red Man knew we were on our way.

What that meant, I don't know. Neither did I know what the dead holy folks intended for us to do to him. For all the knowledge they'd drilled into my head, they never said how to kill the Red Man for good. I'd have to figure it out for myself as if required by some cosmic rules of the game, as if it wouldn't count if someone slipped me the answer. Fine. Robbing banks fair and square was one thing, but I had never been a cheater.

Somewhere north of Fort Lauderdale, we rolled up on a roadblock, a line of delivery vans stretched across the road. A woman with a guitar sat in a lawn chair in front of it. She wore a tie-died tank top with a peace sign printed on it, a pair of denim cutoffs, and no shoes. A hand-scrawled sign beside her read *"Michele Kutner, Acoustic Stylings and Folk Ramblings, CDs $15."* Below the sign, an open suitcase held an untidy pile of CD cases. The cover art featured a photo of a hawk.

Vale stopped the truck.

The woman strummed, not even lifting her eyes to notice us. Matted, blonde hair hooded her face.

"That's a new one," I said. "Footloose and fancy-free."

"What's she doing?" Vale said.

"Free concert. You want to go throw money in her hat and ask her to play 'Freebird,' or should we turn this hunk of junk around and find another way forward?"

"Turn around?"

"Yep, that's my vote too. We got enough of our own troubles. Don't need whatever she's got to offer added to the list."

Vale put the truck in reverse, started to back it up, but then hit the brake as she looked in the oversized side-view mirror.

"Shit. Looks like the rest of the band showed up," she said.

Movement in the passenger-side mirror revealed a group of men approaching. They wore long-sleeve shirts, jeans, even jackets despite the heat and humidity, with caps pulled down over their eyes and mirrored shades. In their hands, baseball bats, rifles, and knives.

"Must be a death-metal group," I said.

Vale glared at me, surprised, then laughed.

"Run them over," I said.

She shook her head. "They attack the tires, give us a couple of flats, we're cooked."

I cracked the window. Guitar music drifted in, something lazy and mellow I didn't recognize. Low voices came with it.

"Sounds like a lot of them out there."

Vale lifted her rifle from where she'd stashed it alongside her seat. "I'll go up on top of the truck and give you cover. You get out and convince them to leave us alone."

"You make it sound easy."

"Trust me. Not one of them will get near you, and if they try, I'll send them running."

"Not a great plan. There's way more of them than us. If we stay here too long, we'll lose any chance at all to get away, but, okay, let's try it your way. I've bluffed my way out of worse odds."

I checked my Beretta and then stepped out of the truck.

The guitar music ended. The approaching men stopped. The driver's side door clicked open. Bumping and thumping told me Vale had gone up top. Guitar girl looked up from her instrument. Her hair parted from her face, revealing skin so pale it almost reached translucence and dark rings around her eyes. She appeared quite ill. A dead eater.

"Shit," I muttered.

One of the men threw a rock at me. It missed and pinged off the side of the truck.

"Hey! Don't look at her. You look at me," he said. "Over here. Look at me."

I did. "Go easy there, chief, I'm just an avid Michele Kutner fan. It's a treat to hear her play live. Or sort of live, I guess."

The man pushed his cap back on his head and revealed his own pallid, deathly face.

"Hey, Vale," I said. "Pretty sure they're hoping to make us dinner. *Their* dinner, I mean."

She didn't speak, only thumped the truck twice in reply.

"Go ahead and put that gun down, mister," the rock-thrower said.

"Nope," I said. "Listen up, we're going to turn around, go back the way we came, and you're going to let us go. I promise you don't want to mess with us."

"That so? You got an army hiding in there? Way I see it, there's twenty of us and two of you. I ain't no bookie, but those seem like good odds to me."

"Take my word, they're not. You don't know who you're dealing with."

"Oh, yeah? Who are we dealing with?"

I didn't know the answer. Me and Birch, sure, on our own we'd be screwed, going down with a fight. What had Vale meant to trust her? What did she intend to do? I leaned hard into the tone of voice that had sent bank patrons and workers face down on the floor and kept them there, while Evelyn and I collected loot. The tone of voice that ignited primal, animal fear in the base of their spines.

"You want to know you can find out the hard way. Or you can back off and let us leave."

The man hesitated, so slight someone else might've missed it. But I knew that pause. It meant uncertainty. "Can't do it, no way, no how. We're too damn hungry."

He gestured. The man at his left pressed the stock of his rifle to his shoulder and aimed at me. A gunshot cracked the air. Blood spurted from the rifleman's throat. He staggered backward, dropped his weapon, then fell over, dead. Three others with guns lifted them. More gunshots, one atop the other, rolling thunder that echoed along the road. Each gunman took a bullet in the same place, through the throat, out the back of the neck, then fell. A shot that severed the spinal cord and left the reanimated corpse paralyzed. What an incredible shot to make, and not one missed. It happened so fast my brain lagged at puzzling out that Vale was doing the shooting. The gunmen down, she turned to those with blades. Men dropped like wasps falling from a nest sprayed with pesticide. Rock-thrower hunched with an arm over his head, hopped this way and that to dodge the carnage. Bullets ripped into the knees of those carrying bats and other weapons, crippling them, and then only the rock-thrower and the guitar woman remained unscathed. All this in the span of seconds.

When the reverberations of Vale's last shot died, I approached the rock-thrower where he crouched with his arms covering his face and head.

"You found out the hard way," I said.

Trembling, he looked up at me, into my silhouette with the sun at my back.

"Who the fuck are you?" he said.

"We're the people you should've let go in peace, dumbass."

I braced my foot against one of his shoulders and pushed him down. He fell without any resistance and curled into a defenseless ball. I kicked him in the side to keep him there.

The truck clanked. Vale clambered down from the roof, smoke wisping from the barrel of her rifle. She grinned at me as she slung it from her shoulder.

I squinted at her. "Trust you, you said."

"Aren't you glad you did?"

"How the hell did you learn to shoot like that?"

Vale grinned, shrugged. "Just came naturally first time I picked up a rifle."

"Bullshit."

"True story, swear to God."

Vale crossed her heart, a childhood gesture, and laughed, and almost started me laughing too, but then the men Vale had killed began to reanimate. None of them could move with their spines severed, but they sure could grunt and moan. I wanted nothing more than to leave this ugly patch of road and continue our mission, but the road wasn't done with us. A scream burst into the air. In the corner of my eye, a flash of swirled colors and tangled, blonde hair signaled to me that Michele still contained plenty of fight. She swung a machete at my head. I dropped fast. The blade swished over me and clanked against the truck.

She raised it over her head for another blow, but I lunged before she could swing.

My right shoulder pounded into her abdomen as I lifted her from the ground and smashed her against the truck's armored fender. She growled in my ear.

The machete slashed wildly, missing my back, but soon enough, she'd hit me.

I'd lost track of Michele after the shooting started. She must have hidden until things calmed down. It made no sense for her to attack now. She should've run off and taken cover until we left. Hunger made people stupid, and Vale had called it: The dead-eaters weren't right in the head.

The machete scraped my lower back. I struggled to shift my weight and push the woman to the ground, but she tangled herself with me, tying up my limbs. The blade nicked my ass. She growled in my ear; a gunshot obliterated the sound as her head exploded in my face. Blood and gore showered me. All the tightness evacuated her body. Concert over, no encore. I staggered under her dead weight, then slid myself free and let her corpse flop to the ground, the machete still clutched in her hand.

After several stuttering steps, I dropped and sat on the road.

Vale's shadow fell over me. "You all right?"

"You could've hit *me* with that shot," I said.

"Only if I wanted to."

She offered me a hand, and I took it and pulled myself back on my feet.

Now I saw her through a wet, red haze covering my face. It seemed right, like staring at the angel of death, and I wondered what had made Vale who she was. She opened the back of the truck then returned to me with a towel. I wiped myself clean. Birch climbed out, looked around at the newly living dead, at the wounded crawling or dragging themselves to the roadsides. He looked me up and down, shook his head, then went back in.

I plucked a stone from the ground and hurled it at the rock-thrower. It struck his shoulder. He yelped and whimpered. I climbed back into the truck. Vale put it in gear and turned us around. Birch poked through the window from the back.

"Don't let us bother you, Birch. We're just keeping your ass alive," I said.

He nodded, then returned to his damn notebook.

The truck crunched over a body as we left the roadblock. I winced. Vale rolled her eyes.

The wheels sped up, and we returned to motion. The going only got tougher. The dead grew in number, the roads more clogged and difficult to pass. We drove north until dusk, then found a house to pass the night. The residents had boarded it up nice and tight as if preparing for a hurricane, and our truck squeezed into the attached two-car garage.

We heated canned soup in the fireplace and ate before taking turns standing watch.

Sometime after midnight, Vale woke me in the bed I'd taken on the second floor, rousing me from the first clean sleep I'd had in weeks. No dreams, not even my own.

"My watch already?" I said.

"No. You've got a couple of hours left, but you need to see this."

I clambered from bed and followed her to the master bedroom, where Birch sat on the edge of a king-size bed pointing at sliding glass doors that opened onto a small deck. I stepped out with Vale. The view overlooked a golf course, a manmade pond, and rows of houses like the one we occupied. Moonlight shone down, bright, austere, lighting the world like an old black-and-white movie. It took me time to process the view. The scale of it overwhelmed me. In the yard below, in the road, in the yards across the street, on the next block, as far as my eyes could see, the dead filled the world. Hundreds, more likely thousands. Wormfeeders in all states of decay and ruin, all facing our house—and all their eyes stared up at us, so many eyes opened in dead flesh, all turned to see the same thing at the same time, so many I imagined I heard them shifting wetly in unison, so many it looked as if the night sky with its stars and constellations had fallen to earth.

My stomach lurched. Sweat beaded on my forehead.

Vale used one of the deck chairs to boost herself onto the roof.

"Come up here," she said.

I did. From the roof peak, I saw the sight repeated on all sides of the house.

From every direction, the dead watched over us.

"The Red Man knows we're coming," I said.

"Oh, you think?" Vale said.

"This is why he didn't touch my dreams," I said. "He sent his nightmares in person."

"Why aren't they attacking?"

"Why would they? They're the welcoming committee."

SIXTEEN

By morning, the dead drifted off to wherever walking corpses go after dawn.

I had no idea how they came and went so quickly. I asked Birch what he thought, but he only scribbled a few words for me in his notebook: "The dead travel fast." I had told Christopher the same thing, and I glared at Birch, feeling like a patronized child. He shrugged. I knew the quote well, from *Dracula*, and it made me wish for a world where the monsters played by rules the way vampires did and the living outnumbered the dead. Such luxury!

We loaded into the truck then rolled out.

Here and there, a corpse watched us, its many eyes tracing our movements.

Vale drove slow, afraid of an ambush, but I knew none would come. The Red Man gained nothing from killing us. If I understood what the dead holy folks had shown me, he benefitted only if he turned us to his cause, to the service of the darkness.

A few miles down the road, a pattern emerged among the wormfeeders. The crowd from last night hadn't, in fact, wandered off so much as it had dispersed and now kept tabs on us. As we passed out of sight of one dead sentinel, another appeared.

The Red Man watched us through the eyes of the dead.

We traveled through his territory now, the territory of the dead, of the darkness.

Vale tensed, and her knuckles paled harsh white where she gripped the steering wheel.

"You and Della," she said, the first words spoken for almost an hour.

"What about us?" I said.

"I don't see it, don't see you two as a couple, I mean."

"Oh? You some kind of relationship expert?"

Vale laughed, much harder and longer than made sense to me.

"When the dead overran my town, I spent weeks alone in my apartment, worrying about my boyfriend trapped in his place on the other side of town," she said. "Eventually, when I left because I would've died if I didn't, I went to him. Guess what I found at his place?"

"I don't like guessing games."

"Fine. I found he'd been shacked up with another woman and gaslighting me the whole damn time. The one person I wanted to be with when the world ended wanted to be with another woman and lied to me about it. So, relationship expert? Not hardly."

"Sorry about that. He sounds like a world-class asshole."

"He was. That was another life. In the here-and-now, I see them with different eyes. I've lost everyone close to me. I'm more alone now than I was trapped by myself in my apartment, but I'm also, I don't know, happier, I guess, but that's not the right word. I'm not happy to live in this fucked-up world of the dead. But I know who I am better than ever before, and I know what I want and what I'm good at. I'd never have discovered my talent for shooting if the dead hadn't risen. Funny, right? Most people lost everything they had when the dead plague started. I gained everything I didn't have. I read people better than ever, and you and Della, I just don't see it."

"You think me and you make a better match?"

"Didn't say that. That's not what I'm saying."

"What are you saying?"

"That I... that I... well, I don't know what I'm saying. I don't see it. That's all."

"Duly noted, Miss Lonelyhearts."

"Whatever," Vale said.

The truck grumbled on along the road. The dead sentries doubled, came closer together, in pairs or trios now, all of them simply watching. I felt prison vibes, under constant scrutiny, laboring under the illusion of tiny liberties. We were all prisoners of some kind. Prisoners of the flesh, or our desires, or our blind spots, or destiny, or a world unrecognizable as our own. Even if we succeeded in killing the Red Man and the darkness never came, nothing much would change as long as the dead walked and things like St. Bianco and the dead holy folks existed. As long as people accumulated power and created authority to enforce their will on others, we remained imprisoned.

The sentinel groups numbered four, six, even ten in some clusters now.

"Getting closer," I said.

Half a mile later, we hit a four-way intersection, where the wormfeeder crowd stretched farther than the eye could see in all directions except west. Imagine the biggest concert or rally ever, an ocean of bodies, a sea of faces, painted gold by the sinking sun, but absolutely still and lifeless, except for the hard stare of innumerable eyes watching from wasting flesh.

Vale stopped the truck. "I've never seen so many of them," she whispered.

"I have," I said.

Deadtown streets filled with the dead in their masses. Here, though, even more gathered, maybe the entire southeast dead population. It took seven dead holy folks to create a bubble of life around Miami. It took the power of one, the Red Man, to fill an entire region with rot and death. The balance said a lot about our chances.

"If they attack, we're dead," Vale said. "Nowhere to run, and we can't fight them all."

"They're here to guide us. They left only one road open, heading west."

"It's a trap," Vale said.

"It always has been. We've been trapped since the dead rose."

A sad expression shaded Vale's face. "I was trapped long before that."

I didn't know what she meant, but it occurred to me I had been too. Trapped, physically, in prison, yeah, but, more importantly, trapped by my guilt for letting Evelyn die, for losing the future we planned together, for falling under the angry heel of the society I'd lived my whole life flipping off. Even afterward, trapped by circumstance, by dead people who pulled my puppet strings, trapped by my obligation to Della. That last notion hurt. I didn't want to think of Della that way. I *didn't* think of her that way. Vale had gotten under my skin. The way she'd talked about Della and me sounded an awful lot like what I imagine Evelyn would've said about us. I stopped myself from looking at Vale. Her face reminded me too much of Evelyn. I watched the dead. I shoved uncertainty from my mind.

"Good. We're on the same page. Keep driving," I said.

Vale shifted in her seat. I sensed her glaring at me but ignored her. I preferred to focus on the horror of a million walking corpses with eyes in every part of their flesh than look her in the eye and risk the cascade of old emotions she might instigate. I don't think I've ever heard the jackal laugh so loud and so hard in the entire time he'd stalked me.

"Well, fucking fine," Vale said.

She put the truck in gear and stamped on the gas. It lurched forward, and then she turned west. The dead didn't move as we passed them. Only their eyes did. The eyes of lost souls.

Clearer roads waited ahead, all of them lined by wormfeeders.

We made a one-truck parade for them to silently cheer. The odor of death permeated the air. It coated our nostrils, made our eyes water. Birch propped himself behind us, taking in the sight. We could've driven faster, but it seemed fitting to go slow, unhurried, as if unafraid, to let those greedy, malevolent eyes stare at the life they envied. A show of bravado, sure, but none of us were eager to reach the end of our journey. The route the dead allowed us led onto a highway. They blocked every exit, but one.

The road sign put a name to our destination.

Acme Wonderland.

The Red Man wanted to meet us on the site of one of my very few happy childhood memories. He wanted to confront us in a cartoon reality. I should have known.

I laughed hard.

Whether out of surprise or fear, I couldn't say.

SEVENTEEN

The entrance to Acme Wonderland loomed in the afternoon haze.

Wormfeeders streamed into the road behind us, cutting off our only escape route.

The theme park gates rose from either side of the road and formed an arch over the passage, once vibrant with color, now faded from neglect, painted with the most popular characters in the Acme Storyverse. Captain Capybara. Connie Caribou. Darlene Deer. Foxy Pinewood. Marvelous Moose. Polly Platypus. Clusters of decapitated heads hung down on wires and ropes from the top of the sign and covered the cheery cartoon faces, giving all the characters dead heads. A lazy rain of blood and putrescence drizzled onto the gates as the bodiless noggins squirmed and worked their useless jaws. A single lane stood open. Rows of Acme character costume heads—those big fuzzy ones actors wear to greet visitors—mounted on pikes funneled us toward it. The costume faces buzzed with flies dining on the stale blood and viscera smeared into the fabric and fur.

Vale drove us to the edge of the gate and stopped.

"I need a minute," she said. "Once we enter, we only leave if we kill the Red Man."

"We crossed that line quite a while ago," I said.

Birch placed a hand on my shoulder. I swiveled to see him. His expression confused me. Resignation and relief. Eagerness. The most relaxed I'd seen him since we met. Then it hit me how whatever came next would answer all the questions he'd hammered at since the dead plague began and free him of its mystery.

"The end is, indeed, fucking nigh," I said.

Birch smiled, his face full of deep wrinkles.

Vale drove through the gate.

Wormfeeders awaited us on the other side. Our persistent guides, shunting us through the maze of Acme Wonderland's many parking lots until we arrived at the entrance of Jubilee Town. Vale parked the truck. From here, we walked.

With no idea what to expect or how long we might be, we gathered guns and backpacks of food and water and ammunition. Vale yanked her overstuffed, bulky backpack on over her sleeveless back blouse, then swatted a mosquito away from the hem of her shorts. I wondered what she'd stuffed in there worth carting along. Birch tucked a notebook with a pen clipped to the cover into a pocket of his cargo pants, then smoothed the wrinkles of his Hawaiian shirt. I tugged off my sweat-stained T-shirt and replaced it with a clean, green concert shirt for a band I didn't know. I swept hair from my eyes, then wiped the sweat on my jeans and tucked my Beretta into the waistband at the small of my back. I grabbed my pack and slung it from my shoulders. The atmosphere of death thickened, imbued with cloying substance by the heavy humidity.

The turnstile awaited.

The dead lined the way.

When we entered Jubilee Town, they produced a horrible chorus of moans. An alarm? An announcement? Maybe a greeting? Whatever, it reached into my bones and filled me with cold dread. Icy perspiration crept across my back, the weight of my backpack plastering my shirt to my skin as it absorbed it.

Around us, shops and attractions offered delights and memories, all rotten and spoiled. Food overgrown with mold, overrun by insects. Toys and t-shirts caked with dust and mold. Photo rooms and novelty stores, abandoned. Places meant to inspire joy and imagination left to decay. No difference between this manufactured town and the many empty towns I'd passed through since escaping prison. Maybe the Red Man chose this place to send that message: no difference existed between the real and the imaginary. The real world held no more significance than a cartoon town deftly designed to move its visitors' money into the pockets of its creators. All societies, prison, the so-called real world, the microcosm of a theme park, even the apparent sanctuary of Miami, all of them charged a price, and all would one day die, cease to exist, rot, and decompose, and with time vanish from the earth, erased by history. Only death persisted. Only the dead knew permanence.

A headache exploded behind my eyes. I stumbled but kept on my feet.

"You okay?" Vale said.

"Yeah, fine," I said.

"You look pale."

"Pardon me for not sporting a hale and hearty complexion while we're walking through a theme park filled with walking corpses," I said. "I'll make sure I get my beauty sleep tonight."

"You don't have to be an asshole. I'm concerned, is all," she said.

"Thank you for that. Sorry. Sarcasm works wonders for my mood."

She smirked. "What, visiting the zippiest ol' town in the Storyverse doesn't brighten your day?"

"I was really hoping for cotton candy but looks like they're all out."

"That stuff will rot your teeth."

"Yep. Sweet, sweet poison."

I steadied myself, then resumed walking, passing Vale and Birch, who eyed me with a raised eyebrow and a face full of concern. I wished he'd share what was on his mind. Whatever the Red Man had done to him after Deadtown had changed him in a way I didn't understand. For the worse in many ways, yes, but it had also bred in him a steely resolve. Or indifference? Hard to tell. One way or another, Birch, as the saying goes, had no more fucks to give. Nothing made a man like him more dangerous to his enemies.

On the far side of Jubilee Town, the monorail station hummed with power.

The dead shepherded us there. When we hesitated to climb into the waiting car, they closed in, forcing us forward with their stench, their low groans, their nauseating presence. We boarded, took seats, and then the doors shut. A wormfeeder so rotted it resembled a dead tree stood at the front of the car in an Acme conductor's uniform, shirt unbuttoned. A cluster of eyes filled its chest, a line of them that ran up its throat to its face. Eyes stared from every bare scrap of flesh.

The monorail car jolted, then glided along the rail. I wondered where the power to run it came from. I wondered where it would take us. A goofy look came to Birch's face. He whistled the same song as me when we first went to meet the dead holy folks. *We're off to see the Wizard, the wonderful Wizard of Oz.*

"Wrong story, wrong universe," I said.

Birch didn't care. He kept whistling. Soon Vale and I joined in. Our conductor remained impassive.

Those eyes, though. The longer we whistled past their grave-yard, the angrier they grew, and so we whistled louder, filling the car with that cheery melody as we rocketed over artificial towns and landscapes, observed by corpses, hurtling toward a cosmic darkness.

Ahead of us waited Storyverse Castle, glowing with an ugly red light.

The Red Man's light, the light of death.

We whistled louder still until the monorail stopped, and the doors slid open.

Crimson shadows enveloped us at the base of a wide flight of steps.

At the top, arched doors banged wide and stilted music poured out. A recording playing on damaged equipment, hissing, crackling, warped. The Storyverse theme song. Wormfeeders came from all sides and herded us toward the entrance. Vale shifted her bulky backpack, groaned under its weight, and started up the steps. Birch and I disembarked after her.

Connie Caribou greeted us at the peak. A decayed worm-feeder, dangling strips of flesh filled with wide eyes, she wore a filthy Connie Caribou costume head, outsized and askew on her scrawny neck and stick body, like a giant bobblehead, its fur-and-mesh eyes watching us from a cockeyed angle.

"Ugh, that's not right," Vale said.

"What?" I said. "Storyverse is for all good people who like good stories, ain't it? You saying the dead don't deserve stories?"

"Smartass," Vale said. "Connie Caribou was my favorite."

"Favorites die like everything else."

Vale glared at me. I felt bad mouthing off, but it eased my tension.

The castle doors led to the ride's boarding station. A giant crown car sat ready to take us for the tour of King Koala's Realm. Hidden within the walls, a generator growled, and motors hummed. A flashback to childhood nibbled at the edge of my thoughts. I ignored it. Childhood never looked like this.

Impatient, Birch pushed past me into the crown car and waved for us to get in with him.

We did, and I closed the door. The car bounced, spun twice, then glided into a dark tunnel filled with more warbling, distorted music. I knew the tune, the theme song from King Koala's Kindness Castle. Everyone knew that damn song. My brain filled the gaps, maddening enough, but when I saw Birch bopping his head to the beat like a happy Koala Kid, it left me dumbstruck. What the hell gears turned in that man's head? We all had our own agenda, our own story to follow, me, Birch, and Vale, three more loveable goofballs twirling through Storyverse's most memorable stories, from the first Connie Caribou cartoon to Polly Platypus's Puppet Parade that had ruled Saturday morning television for a decade, on to Captain Capybara's Conservation Comet educational films, and finally to the king himself. King Koala, who sat on the Throne of Tales with the Book of Good Stories by his side and ruled over all of Storyverse. I wondered if our names, our lives, appeared within its pages.

Only King Koala knew—except the Red Man had staged a coup.

Atop the Throne of Tales sat Darrell Philip Stradley.

In the Throne Room, our crown car stopped, then spun twice again before the whir of machines driving our ride died. The music played a few seconds longer, squelched by a final staticky crunch. All the Storyverse characters surrounded us, giant, mock heads mounted on hideous walking corpses, the worst, most decomposed I'd seen still mobile. On the throne sat the Red Man, bathed in light from the setting sun pouring through picture windows that overlooked all of Acme Wonderland. The Throne Room, meant as a showstopping moment on the ride, gave a vista of the entire fantastic realm. It hardly caught my eye compared to the Red Man ten feet above us on the throne pedestal.

He looked less dead than I remembered. His scars and wounds, so pronounced the first time I saw him, had faded. Not healed, so much as retreated from existence. His flesh looked supple, nearly alive. He wore the same tattered blue jeans and worn-out boots, now caked with dirt and dried gore. On his head sat an awkward crown, ripped from the head of the King Koala animatronic figure, which lay broken at the bottom of the pedestal.

For long, burdensome moments, no one spoke or moved. We stared at the Red Man; he stared at us, his crimson aura coruscating. A terrible stillness gripped us, gripped the world. The silence of death. Time seemed petrified, preserved, halted, the rippling red light emanating from Stradley the only thing in the world still animate and mobile. Then the Red Man cracked a wide smile, stood before his throne, stretched wide his arms, and cried out: "Welcome to my realm!"

He descended from the pedestal by stairs along the left side.

Vale tracked him with her rifle the whole way.

The Red Man walked right up and pushed the barrel of her gun aside.

"If bullets could hurt me, we wouldn't be here now, would we?" he said. "At one time, they did, but not anymore. Birch can tell you all about that. Right, Birch?"

Birch and I exchanged glances, both thinking the same damn question: When the dead rotted and the saintly dead held just this side of decay, how could the Red Man possibly look *more* alive than when we saw him in Deadtown?

He sat cross-legged against the edge of the pedestal.

"So glad you came. I knew you would. Sooner or later. By hook or crook." His voice grated with the tone of glass ground between slate. "Our unfinished business brought you here. My mark upon your brows made sure you survived the trip."

"I didn't know you liked cartoons so much," I said.

The Red Man's smile deepened. "Oh, I do, I truly do, because when I asked myself what better place existed from which to toss the final handful of dirt onto the coffin of the old, living world, no more fitting monument to the ephemera of life came to mind." He waved his arms, an expansive gesture to our surroundings. "All this means nothing, *never* meant anything. Yet the living flocked to it, worshipped it, wore its icons on their clothing and personal belongings, even their goddamn cars. They painted its gods on their children's faces. Dressed them in the robes and gowns of its high priests and priestesses. They mimicked its romance for their wedding rituals. It became a new faith. The religion of escapism, the dogma of the juvenile bolstered against ugly reality. Think about life's necessities: to eat, to sleep, to breed, the need for shelter and protection, the urge for connectedness, the drive to conquer our environment. A uniquely human experience, that last one, whether it meant curing cancer or shooting rockets to the moon. All that human energy, ingenuity, devotion, and joy, all that potential for grand accomplishment, diverted to things that never existed and never, ever will exist. Football games. Fashion shows. High-priced coffee. Social media. TV series and 24/7 opinion broadcasts. Life got so damn good people thought those things counted. They forgot where they lived. Forgot what it *meant* to live. They poured their obsessions into nonsense. Slaved for years to pay for two weeks in this illusory wonderland, a break from an already hallucinatory society where they lived day to day. How many places like this exist in the world? How many piped themselves into your eyes and ears day after day? How many false idols commanded the living's devotion? No small wonder when they died, their souls found the light that should've awaited them had given up and moved on. They killed their gods and heavens in exchange for false prophets and worldly paradises."

Vale raised her rifle, aimed it at the Red Man's face.

"You can shoot me, dear. I won't stop you. I won't enjoy it, and it'll mess me up a while, but I'll recover. I contain the power of a million dead souls. More flock to me each day. But, no, wait, on second thought, I'd hate to be shot by someone I've only just met." He extended a hand to Vale. "Darrell Philip Stradley, pleased to meet you."

Ignoring his hand, Vale pulled the trigger. Her shot passed to the side of the Red Man's head and bit a hole in the throne pedestal. Birch and I flinched from the report. The Red Man didn't even blink.

"My name's Vale." She lowered her rifle.

The Red Man withdrew his offered hand. "Truth be told, I already knew that. I know all about you. I've been piggybacking in your friends' heads." He stood and walked past our crown car to the royal banquet table by the windows. Six seats surrounded a table painted with a mural of Storyverse characters. The animatronic figures who'd once filled them lay cast aside on the floor. "Come, sit. We'll talk all about how you've come here to kill me and how you never had a chance at success."

Vale and I hesitated, but Birch exited the crown car, walked right over, and took a seat. It unnerved me how matter-of-fact he acted, but I also sensed method to his madness. We had little choice, anyway. Wormfeeders had gathered in the throne room and left us nowhere to go. Vale and I joined Birch and the Red Man at a table that looked like it belonged in a spoiled rich kid's bedroom.

"I like this place," the Red Man said. "You can see all the way to the entrance where you came in. See?"

The three of us absorbed the sight of Acme Wonderland beneath a pale sky so clear it looked painted. I squinted against a sudden blast of light as a fireball erupted with a cloud of smoke and flame. The picture windows rattled in their frames. The sound of the blast followed. When the thunder and rumble died, Vale walked to the window and stared at the burning patch on the edge of the park, the black plume rising to touch the sky— surging from the wreckage of Vale's truck.

"Shit," she whispered.

"You came here to kill me. Figured, hey, maybe if we blow him up, the fire and shock will use so much of his energy, his body will rot before it can repair itself. So, you filled a truck with explosives and hoped to get it near me. Of course, I had other plans. Not that it would've worked. I'm beyond even that now. The energy of each soul contained inside me sustains my existence. They come so fast, two arrive for each one I expend," the Red Man said. "You'd have to burn me for a year to destroy me that way."

"Vale, what the hell is he talking about?" I said. "Was that really your truck?"

She met my gaze for a moment then directed her eyes to the floor. "It was St. Bianco's idea. With the Red Man in your head, he figured we needed a plan you didn't know about."

"We drove all the way here in a fucking bomb?" I said.

"Yeah, sorry, I couldn't tell you," she said.

"Hey, hey, it's all right, Cornell. Women are entitled to their secrets. It's the mystery that makes them so intriguing," the Red

Man said. "That's what gets you hot for Vale, right? How much she reminds you of your lost love? You want to be with her, that's cool with me. I won't rat you out to that pretty little nurse you're making time with. My lips shall stay sealed. Hell, I bet Ms. Vale has plenty of secrets from her old life, things she's done to survive, things she'd be embarrassed for you to know about. She does adore you so, after all."

Vale swung her arm to slap the Red Man. He caught her wrist before she made contact.

"Care to share, darling?" he said. "No? Then sit the fuck down."

He shoved her toward a chair. Vale landed in it and hung her head low.

"You're all going to be part of my vision as I remake the earth. You, Cornell, shall be my right hand of justice. Your lady-friend shall be my left hand of wrath. Birch, my old pal, my dear murderer, my original assassin, my nemesis, in many ways, my creator, my father, my genesis, you shall be my pet."

"No." Vale slung the awkward backpack from her shoulders.

"You object, darling?" the Red Man said.

Fear spiked through me. Part of me, I think, had suspected St. Bianco's demand for me to go with Vale amounted to more than it seemed. Sparing a moment to consider it, even the secret truck bomb didn't completely shock me. When Vale peeled the backpack's top flap open, I felt more resignation than surprise. My anger flared, not for the betrayal but for the idea of never returning to Della and Christopher. Vale implored me for forgiveness, her eyes wide and gelid with tears.

"I'm sorry, so sorry," she said as she flipped the detonator switch on the bomb concealed within her backpack.

EIGHTEEN

My heart skipped several beats. My breath caught in my throat.

No explosion. No heat, no light, no concussion, no shrapnel to shred my body.

The switch clicked.

Vale flipped it again.

Click.
Nothing.
Click.
Nothing.

The Red Man laughed, and, fuck me, but it sounded exactly like the laugh of my old pal, my jackal, prowling forever in the back of my mind. My death in whatever form it may come for me one day. The only thing from which I'd ever run. The end of my world. It laughed at me. *He* laughed at me. Reminded me how I didn't matter, how little control I possessed over anything.

The Red Man seized the backpack from Vale. She offered no resistance.

Tears cascaded down her face.

"I know, I know," the Red Man said. "I cry too when my bombs don't explode."

He handed the pack to the dead. They passed it among themselves down the tunnel and out of our sight. I can't say I was sorry to see it go. Can't even say I was entirely sorry that it had failed because I was grateful to be alive. The Red Man daubed Vale's tears with a cloth napkin from the table.

"This power of mine lets me do all sorts of things, allows me to control the world around me," he said. "I give you credit for getting that package so close to me, but you had no chance of setting it off. Maybe if you hadn't shown it before you flipped the switch. Who knows?"

Groups of the dead approached.

"Enough talking for today," the Red Man said. "Go where the dead take you. We'll get together again, real soon, I promise."

"Fuck that," I said.

"Excuse me, Cornell, you say something?" the Red Man said.

"What are you going to do if we refuse? Kill us?"

Hate radiated off the Red Man. For me. For the living. For whatever corrupt and evil core thrived inside him and had led him to this point in his existence. That insight changed everything for me in the span of a single breath. The Red Man hated his dead self as much as he had hated his living self. Here stood a man who'd gotten what he truly desired and now despised what it made of him. Yet he couldn't turn his back on it, couldn't let go, couldn't walk away, and risk sinking back into a useless, pointless existence. Like all of us pushing onward through a dead world to survive, human maggots on a rotting corpse, he needed to keep moving toward a future, a new life, a new existence. He wanted to remake himself as one of the living and damn the world if he wasted it in the effort.

"Oh, I'll do much, much worse than kill you," he said. "Then I'll find that pretty nurse of yours and that dumb little orphan boy you took under your wing, and I'll do worse to them than I did to you."

I stood to go with the dead, not because of the Red Man's threats, but because now that I better understood his nature, I wanted time to make sense of it.

He nodded at me. "Good. Let's do this like we mean it. I used to guide the lost to higher levels of consciousness, to surpass their physical limitations. I'll do that for you. I can open the door to the universe's pure fuel and help you plug your soul right into it. When all our work here ends, and you ride high in the new world, you'll shower gratitude upon me."

He ascended his throne, pretending to ignore us as worm-feeders guided us to the outgoing tunnel. From outside the castle, another explosion came. Vale's backup bomb. He had let go, released control. Either it had moved out of range, or he could force his will upon it only for a short time, nothing permanent. Another hint. More evidence that the Red Man couldn't be all he seemed or wished to seem.

Ain't that always the way with the high and mighty, the ones who seek power, control, and authority, the ones telling everyone else how to live, how to think, how to view the world through the same compressed, myopic, and homogenous perspective. Bullies at heart, every last one of them, in search of socially acceptable ways to impose their will, to apply threat of force or social exile to alter our behavior. The Red Man simply killed the world to do it.

True leaders accept power rather than dedicate their lives to gaining it.

They manage it; they don't cling to it like mother's milk.

They don't see the world in the worst terms of *us* and *them*.

In that light, the Red Man seemed no different to me than an overzealous prison warden, or a ham-fisted sheriff, or a murderous saint, or any of the endless chain of people who'd tried to force me to live their way from childhood until the world ended.

Despite all his power and fearsomeness, he seemed small.

The dead brought us to underground cells for park visitors who broke the law at Acme Wonderland. Cushiest damn cell I ever occupied. Plush chairs. Cartoon murals painted on the walls. Even a bathroom stall with a door that closed. Probably intended to stave off lawsuits from anyone security held there until the police arrived.

The wormfeeders locked us in separate cells then left.

I couldn't see Birch or Vale, but I heard Vale crying. Birch started snoring, and I shook my head to think he could fall asleep under the circumstances. Of us all, though, he knew the Red Man, knew Darrell Philip Stradley, the best. Had known him in life and had spent those lost days of which I knew nothing with him after Deadtown. If our situation didn't frighten him, I took that as a sign hope still persisted.

"Cornell," Vale said.

"Yeah?"

"I'm sorry," she said. "Sorry I didn't tell you about the bombs. I would've blown us all to smithereens if the detonator worked."

"I understand," I said. "I hate it, and I'm pissed you lied, but I understand. St. Bianco wasn't wrong about keeping secrets from me and Birch to keep them from the Red Man."

"What he said about me and you, I'm sorry for that too," she said.

"What do you mean?"

A long pause preceded her answer. "I wish we'd met under different circumstances, in another world, maybe."

"In a different world, we'd be different people," I said.

No answer. Time passed. I lost track. The light never changed in our cells.

Fatigue overtook me, and I slept.

The dead did not bring us food or water. The Red Man did not visit, even in my dreams.

Right when I feared he'd decided to let us starve to death and fill our bodies with the souls of his followers, he appeared with an entourage of wormfeeders.

"Showtime," he said.

The cells opened. The dead guided us out, all three of us moving slow and unsteady from hunger and thirst. They took us outdoors to Royal Square in the shadow of King Koala's Castle, where a life-size cartoon horse figure sat, a prop for photographs. Despite their rotted-out limbs, their shriveled, caved-in faces, their bones poking through putrid flesh, their leathery muscles, tendons, and ligaments, the dead fulfilled the Red Man's orders like well-drilled soldiers. They held me and Vale on our knees. They stripped Birch to the waist then tied him across the back of the horse. The statue's oversized googly eyes glinted in the sunlight.

One of the dead handed a whip to the Red Man.

He lashed it across Birch's back.

As best he could without a tongue, Birch screamed.

"Death of the flesh to free the spirit, death of the spirit to free the flesh," the Red Man cried out. "Your preparation for my new world has begun."

NINETEEN

We spent days in agony.

Birch's torture kicked off a sequence of abuse and mortification at the Red Man's hands that would've brought a blush to the most jaded sadist. Each of us in turn, strapped to the cartoon horse, or tied down spread-eagled to a picnic table outside Foxy Pinewoods' Fish and Chips Hut, or chained to the back of a golf cart decorated like old Marvin Marmoset's jalopy pick up and run around the park till we fell and shredded our knees on the blacktop. At Andy Eagle's Aviary Adventure, he locked us in giant birdcages hung in the air from the steel and vinyl limbs of Elder the Oldest Oak and let us cook in the relentless sun, a feast for mosquitos thriving in the absence of the park's pest control management. Cut with blades, lashed by the whip, pricked with needles, dusted with salt that seared our wounds. We bled. Sometimes the dead lapped our spilled blood. Always each in our turn, and the Red Man made us watch each other suffer.

All day. In the heat and humidity. Our skin reddened and peeled. Our lips cracked from dryness. At night, the dead dragged us back to our cells.

Cartoon murals decorated our walls, like those in a pediatrician's office to make getting pricked for a vaccination or probed with a thermometer less horrifying to the five-year-old psyche. For us, it meant hours spent haunted by once-loveable characters transformed into harbingers of pain.

Always we found scraps of food and water waiting in our cells. No more than enough to sustain us until the next day. We only ate the prepackaged stuff, the bags of chips and sleeves of cookies, afraid of touching anything that might carry more than the taint of having spoiled.

On day four, I noticed the Red Man's daily decay.

Each morning, the wormfeeders brought us to him, almost as healthy as a live man, even a touch of red in his cheeks. Although his multitude of eyes betrayed him, he could've passed for a living man with bad skin when he closed them all. By the end of each day, purple and gray blotches appeared. His skin flaked and tore along its dry folds. His scalp thinned, stretched tight against his skull, paled, grew more skeletal.

Every day by sunset, he looked dead.

Next morning, alive.

"That bastard's restoring himself somehow," I said to Vale that night.

I lay on my cot, my body too riddled with pain for sleep. The rasp in Vale's voice told me she felt the same. Birch, on the other side of me, snored like an idling truck. I envied him that Zen center that allowed him to bear our tortures with so much equanimity. It simmered in the Red Man's eyes how deeply it burned his ass that Birch didn't beg for mercy and showed no fear after his first shocked scream on the back of the royal horse.

"What?" Vale said.

I explained what I'd observed; she'd noticed it too.

"I thought it was me, seeing things after all the shit he's put us through," she said.

"Nah, he's fixing himself using the souls he's gathered," I said.

"You know how that sounds, right?"

"No weirder than anything else I've said or heard these past months."

"You've got a point there." Rustling sounds came from Vale's cell as she shifted on her cot. Her voice trailed off, slurred, as she said, "How does that help us?" then fell asleep.

I didn't have an answer, but the question kept me awake a long time.

In the morning, when the wormfeeders fetched us for another torture-filled day at Acme Wonderland, I roused with the spark of a plan. I spent all day fanning its flames, ideas filling my head to blot out what the Red Man and his dead puppets did to Birch, to Vale, to me. When the day ended, I studied his face before our decomposing chaperones marched us back to our cells. The decay looked worse than at first glance. Cracks behind his ears. Lips sliding sideways. Eyebrows crumbling. Black spots on teeth that had gleamed white in the morning air. Across his chest, faint lines of old scars returning. The eyes that mottled his flesh drooped. It strained him to make himself look alive. Would the darkness make his restoration permanent when it arrived? Did he need the three of us to make that happen? No other reason to keep us around, wearing us down. I didn't plan to play along. If I couldn't figure out a way to destroy him, another option lingered in the back of my mind. He needed us alive.

That night, I jammed the lock of my cell.

I'd studied it every night, recalling all the locks I'd picked or broken in my old life, and rigged it so the door would close without latching. Not that the wormfeeders noticed. They had little awareness of their own. If the Red Man watched through their many eyes, fatigue made him careless.

I crashed on my cot. Ate the meager food left for me. Waited several hours.

No one came. No one checked my door.

Cut off from the outside, I had little measure of time. Trusting my internal clock, I stepped out of my cell at what I figured for the middle of the night. Birch lay sound asleep. Vale, too, tempting me to wake them up, but I had no way to get them out.

I backtracked our usual route to the Royal Square with the cartoon horse.

No wormfeeders in the underground security space, none in the plaza.

Weird. They didn't need to sleep. Night or day made no difference to them. Why not have them watch us 24/7?

In the western sprawl of the park, a red light glowed. I walked there, hidden in shadows. I knew my way around the park by heart, having run its full course so often while sucking exhaust fumes from Marvin Marmoset's jalopy.

I passed listless wormfeeders on my way to the brightness, which burned atop Polly Platypus's River Run. High up the ride, where the log flume shot out from a tight curve before plunging down a waterfall, a fire burned. No water ran along the artificial river. The chains and gears that pulled the flooms gleamed in the flickering illumination. Wormfeeders surrounded the base of the ride, hundreds thick, and so still I mistook them for part of the park until my eyes decoded their silhouettes. What I'd taken for fireflies were the flames reflected in their innumerable eyes, all open and staring at the top of the ride, beyond it at the sky, which possessed a darkness like spilled ink runneling among the stars. Some of the eyes watched the steel-and-resin hilltop. Others drank in that darkness.

The fire flared. Sparks and embers floated away into the night.

At the edge of the rail curve that arched into open air stood the Red Man.

Two wormfeeders brought him a body rotted beyond mobility. Its ragged flesh twitched. Its teeth and jawbone caught the light. From every part of it stared impossible eyes, each filled with dread and despair, apparent even across the distance between us.

The Red Man placed his hand upon the wormfeeder's dented forehead.

The act took a second, maybe two.

The ruined corpse sagged, lifeless, in the arms of the wormfeeders.

All the eyes upon it blinked shut.

A burst of red light flashed and winked out so fast I felt it at the back of my eyes more than saw it. New eyes appeared on the Red Man's body. His skin recovered a measure of its living luster; mottled patches of decay shrank.

As wormfeeders threw the wasted corpse over the side, another trio brought a fresh one. Something had sheared away half of this one's torso and most of its right leg.

The Red Man welcomed it, caressed its putrescent face. The transfer occurred again.

Crimson brightness strobed. New eyes opened on the Red Man.

Wormfeeders discarded the exhausted corpse over the side.

The darkness caught my eye.

Had it spread?

Had it reached down toward earth, attracted by the Red Man's acts?

Circles of blackness churned within it. Blind eyes whose gaze set my skin alive with a cold, electric discomfort. I felt seen and exposed.

I backed away from the River Run, retraced my steps, and returned to my cell.

Inside, unable to sleep, I wondered how to explain what I'd seen to Birch and Vale. When the wormfeeders came for another day of suffering, I still hadn't figured it out—but I'd decided before another night passed, I'd see either the Red Man or myself destroyed.

TWENTY

The Red Man always tortured us one at a time. In the moments he focused on Birch or Vale, I shared what I knew with the other and instructed each on how to rig their cell locks to stay open. When the wormfeeders left us that night, we licked our wounds, ate our meager rations, then waited a spell before leaving our cells. Despite her fatigue, Vale looked nervous.

"You have another hidden bomb we should know about?" I said.

"I wish," she said. "Just shaky from my daily beating."

"Might as well smile, then, because they'll continue until morale improves."

We all hung just this side of the living dead after the Red Man's torture. Indigo rings circled Vale's eyes. Birch's too. Pale and gaunt, they swayed on their feet. I knew I looked the same. We shared the weakness of suffering, part of the Red Man's strategy to grind away at us until we either begged him to stop and agreed to anything he wanted, or lost ourselves so deeply we came to believe in him, brainwashed. We would last another day, maybe two or three at most, before we died from deprivation and the slow blood loss that came each day. I'd never break. I stared death in the face now and found it familiar and inevitable, my personal jackal waiting to laugh me along the path to oblivion. I hoped Birch and Vale would hold out to the end if it came to that, but you never knew how one might crack when their life lay on the line. As if to answer my unspoken question, Birch offered me a folded piece of notebook paper from his pocket.

I took it from his trembling hand, unfolded it, and read the words written there in wavery but legible penmanship.

Scenario 17

Death of the flesh to free the spirit = Releasing souls, life force, spiritual consciousness? Energy cannot be created or destroyed. The anima of life enters a void of their making, a pool of genesis energy, a vitality battery, a limbo-container that shields it from... what, from its return to the cosmic biofilm of matter and energy, its dispersion to stardust?

Death of the spirit to free the flesh = An exchange, a price, a sacrifice, the anima of the captured souls expended to "free the flesh." From what can flesh be freed? Aging. Mortality. Decay. The spirits given over to it make the flesh eternal, incorruptible. Who/what accepts the payment and grants the boon? *The Darkness.*

I lifted my gaze from the paper. Birch regarded me with such hope and yearning for me to understand what he'd spent hours pondering and working through in his notebooks. As if the theft of his voice had been a blessing that allowed him to focus his brain entirely on decoding whatever Darrell Philip Stradley hoped to achieve. Vale read over my shoulder.

"What's that? What's this mean?" she said.

Birch gripped my arm, squeezed, implored me to comprehend.

"I think," I said, "that the Red Man is trying to become fully alive again, that he needs to be alive for the darkness to make him... immortal?"

Birch nodded as he wept. Tears streaked his cheeks.

Yes, yes, yes.

"What happens if he does that?" Vale said.

Birch gestured, miming an eruption, things sweeping away, the end of everything.

"Nice pep talk, buttercup," I said.

Birch cracked half a smile through his tears.

"Scenario 17," Vale said. "What are the others?"

Birch shook his head, shrugged them off, tapped the paper in Vale's hand.

This is the one.

Vale returned the page to Birch, who refolded it into his pocket.

"Makes as much sense as anything," I said. "Doesn't help much with killing Stradley."

Be patient, Birch conveyed with his hands and expression.

The park's underground corridors ran in all directions like ant tunnels. Last night I'd spied an access door near Polly Platypus's River Run that let us avoid the wormfeeders on the surface. Stairs led to the door, emerging into an alley alongside the River Run gift shop. The smell of decay blasted us. We crept to the alley's end and spied the gathered dead. High up the River Run, the Red Man stood on his perch. The expanse of night sky writhed with darkness. Low and close now. Like storm clouds creeping in fast from the horizon, erasing blue skies and sunshine, stars and moonlight. The darkness felt low enough to touch, as if it would soon reach the ground and envelope the earth, maybe tonight, maybe a couple of nights from now, but soon.

Vale grasped my shoulder.

"Promise me," she said, "if you see a chance to kill the Red Man, you'll take it."

"That's the whole damn point," I said. "What's gotten into you?"

"Nothing," she said. "Just, if I can give you that window, you'll take it, right?"

"Dive through it headfirst. Likewise?"

"Yeah. Good." Vale clasped her hands to my face, drew me into an unexpected kiss. Her cracked, dry lips rasped over mine. Her breath tasted sour, but the contact, the surge of living warmth, the intimacy, the affection brought a moment's pure bliss before Vale broke it off. "For luck." She pushed past me out of the alley.

Birch flashed me a stupid grin like some goofy high school freshmen

I blushed. "You want a kiss for luck, don't look at me."

The three of us skirted the edge of the wormfeeders to a path that dead-ended against the edge of the River Run. We hopped a fence and landed in thick hedges, where we dropped to our bellies and crawled. We'd agreed to climb up inside the River Run in hopes of taking the Red Man by surprise. Our way through the faux mountain proved harder than expected, climbing narrow ladders and catwalks and stretches where we walked the ride's exposed rails, feet sliding, hands grasping at whatever hold presented itself. We met no wormfeeders. All of them, except for the handful serving the Red Man, stood below. The Red Man's ego made him cocky. He needed those bodies, those millions of unnatural eyes cast up at him, at the darkness speeding across the cosmos to touch him. Their worship made him the holy man, the leader he believed himself to be. The righteous savior of the dead. Herald of a greater, universal truth than anyone had ever revealed to the masses. Their devotion measured his power. Sent a message to the darkness and all the lost souls contained in rotting flesh that he could take them anytime he wanted, that they served him, not the other way around. He wanted them to know it, needed them to believe it.

Needed them to believe it.

Needed...

The power of narcissism.

It amazed me how much of Stradley's living psyche remained intact after dying.

What did that say about all the dead holy folk sitting on their hotel-lobby thrones back in Miami, all the supposed "good guys" in this battle between light and dark, all the similar groups of dead and living, who—if St. Bianco spoke true—played out final acts like us? People who demand you live according to *their* needs, who needed you to pretend *their* fiction equaled reality, for *their* benefit. And so very many people eager to comply.

I saw little difference between the dead who filled Acme Wonderland now and the living who'd filled it in the past. So easy back then for anyone to buy a life, a reality, a philosophy, a prefab set of values and opinions. Subscribe here. Join a tribe. Pick your favorite media flavor with a side of politics, religion, outrage, and bonus professional sports team and film franchise. Receive their daily newsletter beamed direct into your head. Enjoy ready-made thoughts to live by. Waste no effort generating your own. Take no time away from living your best life to think.

You get convenience; they get control.

St. Bianco exploited human vulnerability no less than the Red Man.

Saints. Sinners. Two sides of a coin of entitlement and aggrandizement.

The only escape: reject it all, carve your own path.

Ignore the sales pitch. Deny the programming.

Rob a fucking bank and stick your finger in society's eye.

Push past fear and comfort until you broke through to the other side: freedom.

Trust that knee-jerk reaction against the authority of the appointed, the cruel corrections of the mob. As much as people hated and feared me in my bank-robbing days, admiration and envy complicated their emotions. They wanted me caught and stopped for breaking the law and bucking the established order—but really, for showing them what living life on your own terms looked like and shoving their complacency in their faces.

For the first time in days, the laughter of my old friend, the jackal, lapsed mute.

Maybe he didn't like my line of thinking. Maybe he figured I no longer needed him to goad me to self-destruction. Maybe he shut up because I grasped the world in a way I hadn't ever before and that we—that *I*—might really be part of a cosmic design that transcended us all but never forgot us. Then and there, I sensed it in my skin that we *could* resist the darkness—and the *Darkness*. We mattered. Each one of us. Every individual. Our decisions and actions mattered. All the choices I'd made that led me here had been right, no matter how heartbreaking.

Yet, despite my newfound awareness, I still saw no way to destroy the Red Man.

We reached the last ladder, ascended, and came within sight of him.

A dozen wormfeeders surrounded their leader. Three tossed a corpse drained of its lifeforce off the side of the resin-and-steel mountain. Three more brought another broken shell, a man in the tatters of an American flag t-shirt. Fear burned in its dozens of wide-open eyes.

Truth revealed.

The genuine end of a mercilessly prolonged existence.

No heaven or hell awaited. No oblivion.

Only the anger, obsession, and desire of the one who guided them back and warehoused them in rotting flesh. From the ground, a million or more eyes stared, unperceiving.

Rot tainted the Red Man's not-yet-fully-restored face.

"I was wondering if you might join me," he said. "I've enjoyed our dance, but if you listen real hard you can hear the music winding down now. The party's almost over."

Behind and above him, Darkness ruled the sky.

Red light flashed. All the flag man's eyes turned glassy and shriveled as the life behind them entered Darrell Philip Stradley. The darkness thickened. A whip of utter black unwound toward the Red Man then snapped back to the sky.

"More," the Red Man said. "Bring me more."

From the base of Polly Platypus's River Run, the masses of the dead moaned.

"Death of the flesh to free the spirit, death of the spirit to free the flesh," he said.

The Red Man ingested more souls from another fractured corpse. Its putrescent flesh vanished over the side, landing on a growing pile. He smiled as the flush of life returned faintly to his skin then raised his arms to the black sky and made a sound I can't rightly describe. A scream, a roar, a cannon shot blasting from his throat, a deep reverberating bellow that erased all other sound. It filled our ears, rattled our bones. The world rippled in its sound waves. Now the Darkness sent three coiled whips of its void skin to caress the Red Man's face then withdrew them. Stradley dropped to his knees and cried out, a human sound this time, of anger, defeat, fatigue, and frustration. A crack in the façade of his power.

So close, yet fallen short, he struggled too.

"Another!" he shouted.

Wormfeeders brought him the legless body of an obese woman, terrified eyes staring out from every fold of its decayed skin. I couldn't see this last night, this fear in the eyes of the dead, the reality of Stradley's transactions with his reanimated followers. His desperation. Their final understanding of how he'd manipulated and used them.

Birch shoved a crumpled paper in my hand: **Scenario 17.**

A flash of red. Another spent corpse dropped to the bottom of the River Run.

The Red Man repeated his inhuman cry, channeling some resonance from the foundation of reality, then he reached for the sky, for the Darkness, which reached back, and brushed his fingertips before it vanished.

Birch took more pages from his pockets.

Unfolded them.

Showed us each one briefly before casting it over the side of the synthetic mountain.

Scenario 2. Scenario 23. Scenario 7. Scenario 4. Scenario 13. Scenario 18. Scenario 32.

All filled with his quavered script. Cast to the gentle wind. Snowing down on the dead. Fluttering across their eyes.

He poked the paper in my hand.

This is the one.

Stradley's followers in life had bought his bullshit about freeing themselves and his followers from whatever hell-afterlife he'd created to hold them, bought it about coming back to life. He had conned them all. They believed him because they had no other choice. Too late for questions now. Trapped. They signed on for the world he promised them, one that wouldn't—*couldn't*—ever exist. A world of ghosts and hollow promises.

"He's using the dead to power himself by taking their souls," I said. "They make him almost alive again, but he can't hold enough to bring himself all the way back. The Darkness needs the living."

A rotted arm flew at us, landed by our feet. We all flinched.

"Are you watching?" the Red Man said. "Tonight I become the world. This is your last chance to join me in the new reality. One way or another, I'll make sure you take it."

A flash of red, another corpse spent, and the Darkness reached lower, lingered longer brushing across Stradley's livid flesh.

Vale stepped forward. "Why us? Of all people, why us?"

The answer came as Stradley groaned at the loss of contact with the Darkness.

Freedom.

The dead have no choices.

Trapped in his promises.

Only the living retain free will.

"He needs us to choose," I said. "To push himself over the threshold, he needs the anima of people who join him of their own choosing. He's let us live because he sees that possibility in us. He's threatened us, bullied us, tried to bribe us to buy into his horseshit. We give him energy from living flesh, the Darkness can enter him, and then he becomes immortal. We become like he is. Dead, incorruptible, but tethered to him forever, always at his mercy. Another fucking prison. Ain't that right, Stradley?"

Birch raised his hand, three fingers held up.

He nodded his head, then lowered one finger.

Two fingers. He shook his head, then lowered another finger.

One finger and another head shake.

Reading Birch's meaning, I said, "He only needs one of us to succeed?"

Birch nodded. Message delivered, he shut his eyes. The exhaustion and trauma he'd hidden since Deadtown showed all at once. He looked one step this side of dead; he looked un-burdened. Vale, on the other hand, looked reenergized. And me, dancing around the obvious, I still saw no way to use what we knew to destroy the Red Man. Like the old saying goes, I was so close, if it was a snake, it would've bit me—and that's exactly how it felt when Vale spoke what my mind refused to see. A bite. Venom pumped into my blood. Death at my vision's edge. Even then, my thoughts only circled the truth.

"I'll join you," Vale said. "I want to live forever in the new world."

TWENTY-ONE

Vale's words sank in while Stradley flashed red, absorbed another batch of souls, and flirted with the Darkness.

"You understand now," he said after the Darkness withdrew. "Death of the flesh to free the spirit, death of the spirit to free the flesh. Whoever among you makes the sacrifice shall stand with me forever in my favor. I welcome you, Vale. I welcome all who come to me of their own free will."

I studied the other's faces, rage at Vale flaring inside me. Vale, an outsider, always alone, who I barely knew, but reminded me so much of my first true love. Vale, who'd tried to blow us to smithereens. I opened my mouth to speak, to say... what? I don't know, because before a word crossed my lips, Vale punched me square in the face, hard enough to rattle my brain and send clouds of stars and darkness across my eyes. I staggered into Birch, who caught me as best he could, crumpling to his knees, both of us winding up on the deck.

Vale stepped up to the Red Man.

"The men aren't worthy," she said. "They want the world back the way it was. They don't deserve the gift you're offering. They don't deserve to serve you."

Stradley's face lit with the smug self-satisfaction of being proven right. In his mind, it had only been a matter of time. Vale's words cut me, though. Deep. To my soul. Her voice brimmed with conviction and certitude. No trace of doubt. She chose the new dead world that had peeled back the curtain on her own self and set free the person hidden inside her for so long, one of the old-style living dead, with prefab lives and minds. She turned her back on that world, that existence, and I can't say I blamed her, but I couldn't forgive her for trading it in for the version Stradley offered.

My head spun as I struggled to my knees.

I stumbled and dropped to the ground again.

Birch tried to help me, my dead weight too much for him.

Stop Vale.

Get back on my feet. Steady my head.

Grab Vale. Kill her before she reaches the Red Man.

I couldn't pull myself together.

Blood ran from my nose, filling my mouth with metallic saltiness.

Birch and I braced against one another, clambered upright together.

The stars in my eyes faded to after images.

My head settled.

Pain cleared my thoughts.

"Vale, no!" I shouted.

I took three steps, only to stop when everything resumed spinning.

How hard had she hit me? Not that it took much after days of torture wearing me down.

I rubbed my head and shouted again. I'm not sure the words made any sense.

Vale paused, glanced back at me.

"Let me open the window," she said.

She knelt at the feet of the Red Man. He placed his hands on the sides of her head. Red light flared, brighter, burning with the intensity of pure life—first life—putting to shame the energy trapped in dead flesh. The flash seemed to go on forever, filling my eyes, blinding me—and then it intensified. I looked away, to the sky, where the red light penetrated the Darkness. I saw inside it. How can I explain what it contained? The Darkness wasn't monolithic, nor a single entity, nor a cosmic toxic cloud, nor an absence. It held multitudes of faces within faces within faces. Eyes within eyes within eyes. Infinity rolling out in fractal waves of shades of black and deeper black and the black of nonexistence. It churned with violence, hate, and chaos. Jets and sparks of black energy flared within it, visible only as black lightning currents. It made no sense how I could see any shapes, any features in that festering hegemony of darkness. They imprinted on my perceptions over the blank canvas of the Darkness, my brain rationalizing madness into a form it could comprehend—and it *hurt*. My brain swelled against my skull. My head throbbed with an ache like a thousand migraines.

Beside me, Birch dropped to his knees, stared at the sky, let it flow through him as he accepted the experience.

Vale screamed.

The Red Man roared.

No longer deep down in the back of my mind but right there at the surface, my jackal laughed—and I knew he saw something I hadn't yet perceived.

The red light faded. Ropy darkness twisted toward the Red Man.

He looked alive, hale, hearty, and full of life.

Full of life.

Life.

All life dies.

The impulse exploded inside me, so urgent and overwhelming, my body responded before I knew I was in motion. I rushed Stradley. I passed Vale's prone figure, passed the slow-moving wormfeeders, and hit the Red Man with my full weight, slammed him against the faux rocks and scrub brush alongside the tracks, steamrolled him out of reach of the Darkness, which lashed at the empty air where he'd been standing. Thrusting my legs, jumping, pushing, I carried us both over the side and into empty air.

If I can give you that window, you'll take it, right?

Dive through it headfirst.

Vale hadn't turned her back on us at all.

Stradley screamed, the first time ever I heard fear in his voice.

Instinctually, I thrust my hands out, seeking hold, finding the rough edges of sculptured vinyl, fingertips scrabbling to change my momentum. I swung hard against Polly Platypus's mountain. The wind rushed out of me, but I jammed myself into a crevice that stopped my plummet.

The Red Man found no such luck.

His body hit the ground, the thud and snap of it music to my ears.

For long seconds, the dead stared at him.

He sputtered blood from his lips, tried to rise.

Tried to stay alive.

Alive among the living dead.

It dawned on the wormfeeders slowly, but they figured it out soon enough.

Another living piece of meat to satiate their appetites.

They descended, ants to a dropped ice cream cone.

One more scream.

The Red Man's light failed.

Stradley vanished under corrupt flesh.

He *died.*

Birch helped me back to the ride's high outcrop.

The wormfeeder servants ignored us and descended, hoping for their share of the flesh of the man who'd lied to them.

We could do nothing for Vale, who'd sacrificed her life to empower Stradley and allowed the Darkness to make him mortal for the crucial seconds we needed to kill him before he attained immortality. The Darkness boiled in the sky. Cheated, it frothed and raged. Black whips snapped from it and lashed overhead, unable to touch us. A door Stradley had opened had slammed shut with his death. For a time, Birch and I sat, Vale's head cradled on my lap, while the Darkness stormed, and the wormfeeders sang their awful song of death and need to a deaf universe. Vale did not reanimate. Whether from St. Bianco's blessing or because killing Stradley had changed the equation in our little part of the world, I didn't know. I felt no less gratitude or grief for it, though. When the Darkness finally spent itself and fled the sky, a shaft of morning sun broke through the clouds and painted Vale's face so pallid and empty, a part of my heart broke for her. I slung her body across my shoulders in a fireman's carry. With Birch's help, I navigated the long descent through the mechanical innards of Polly Platypus's River Run. We emerged into sunlight and an electric tension I'd only ever felt before in the moments after a hurricane passed, revealing the full measure of its devastation.

Not only had the wormfeeders turned on the Red Man, they'd turned on each other.

Hundreds of them lay in broken shambles everywhere. Squirming limbs ripped from torsos. Broken bodies writhing on the earth. Viscera puddles sending ripples of steam into the humid morning air. Heads lolling as mindless jaws snapped and ground. Hands, even individual fingers, worming across the hot pavement. The dead had torn themselves to pieces, echoing the tumult and fury of the Darkness. Or in a conscious act of self-destruction to free themselves from the trap into which Stradley had tricked them. Or for some other reason I'd never know, could never understand. One thing about that charnel debris, though, struck me with amazement and the first real spark of hope I'd experienced in longer than I could remember.

From not one body, limb, spilled organ, or scrap of flesh did an eye look upon us.

The souls trapped in the dead were gone.

Only flesh remained.

Death of the flesh to free the spirit.

With the truth of how Stradley had used them revealed, the dead, when given a choice, threw a honking, big middle finger at the Red Man and whatever Darkness he courted and put themselves back to rest on their own terms.

"Hey, you hear that?" I said.

Birch eyed me, confused, and shook his head.

"That damn jackal isn't laughing anymore."

Confusion wrinkled Birch's expression, but I gave no further explanation. Any words I might've spoken would've been cut short anyway by the eruption of a white light from the perch atop the River Run. My chest clenched tight, fearing The Red Man had somehow returned, and I know Birch's did too. We heeled about, shaded our eyes, and peered into the brilliance. Instead of the Red Man, though, another figure stood there, light flowing out of him: St. Bianco. He looked down upon us, raised his hands in a gesture of... affirmation, blessing, congratulations? Who knows what goes through the mind of a saint? He vanished a moment later, but the light remained. It settled over us like a mist dropping from the sky. As far as we could see in every direction, the dead ceased moving. That light finished the job they'd begun. An unexpected sense of relief filled me. My mind still doubted, but my instincts knew some great part of the conflict between the living and the dead, the light and the Darkness, concluded in that moment—and in favor of the living.

I shifted Vale's weight on my shoulders. "Going to be a long road back to Miami."

Birch nodded, then together, we took the first step.

LOHATCHIE CODA

One morning, a pillar of black smoke stabbed the clear, blue sky.

I sipped coffee on the front porch and watched it billow, unfurl, and expand into a brown haze staining the sky over the town to the east, figuring its source for the intersection of Lohatchie's Main Street and Banyan Road. That raised my hackles, though I couldn't say why exactly. Nor could I guess the cause of the smoke. No one lived in Lohatchie anymore. Far as I knew, only me, Birch, Christopher, and Della lived within a fifty-mile radius of town, and the reanimated dead don't set fires.

The front door creaked open then clicked shut behind me as I eyed the smoke. Della slid an arm around my waist, leaned into me as she sipped her coffee. "Spontaneous combustion?"

"Fires like that don't set themselves," I said.

"Wormfeeder cookout?"

"Only if the wormfeeders are the ones getting cooked. The dead may be dumb, but they know not to play with fire."

I laced my arm around Della's shoulders and kissed her on top of her head, inhaling the scent of sleep still lingering on her hair. Her body warmed me in the morning air.

"Well, if it's not the dead and fires don't start themselves," she said, pausing to sigh, "we got company in town."

"There goes the neighborhood," I said.

Green and brown surrounded us. Sawgrass filled the spaces between cypress, mangrove, and mahogany trees, broken by colorful splashes of wildflowers, even a few orchids south of the house. The green buzzed and chirped, abundant with wildlife. The sawgrass swayed where unseen critters traveled. Less than a mile west of our place ran a river that flowed out to the coastal marsh, and the most motion around us came when the wind rustled the trees. A Toyota SUV in desperate need of a wash sat in front of the house, windshield still peppered with dead bugs from our last scavenging run into Lohatchie.

More and more time passed between each trip now. The town had little left to offer, and Birch's garden out back brimmed with vegetables year round thanks to his clever planning. Christopher and I brought in plenty of fish and game, and in time, the apple, lemon, and orange trees we'd planted would add to the bounty. It amazed me how well we could live off the land in the absence of competition and civilization. Paradise. A pocket of vibrant life on a dead earth. My Lohatchie hideaway delivered all the things I'd hoped for when I first set my sights on her in the early days of the dead plague. The road here took its toll, sure enough, but this scrap of a home carved from the green wild worked a kind of healing magic on us all. After every terror and torture we'd survived, we needed it. Hell, we deserved it.

So that column of smoke dispersing itself toward the heavens?

That tightened my chest and put tension in my brow.

The sight of it gripped my heart in a stony fist.

It reminded me of another darkness, one spreading itself across the cosmos—one I hoped never to see or contact again. And until now, I believed in that possibility. But such is this world that no matter where you go, no matter how you live, the darkness always finds a way to catch up with you.

"I'll wake Christopher," Della said.

"Let him sleep a little longer. He's a growing boy," I said. "Nothing to gain by rushing. Enjoy the morning. No telling how things will look this time tomorrow."

Della's arm tightened around me. With Miami a year-and-a-half in our rear views and the Red Man destroyed, the dead he'd rallied to torment us lost their way. They still roamed the world, but with less aggression and no purpose. The souls inside them that looked out through the eyes that pocked their corpses seemed to be winding down and losing coherence. We'd almost come to take for granted the predictability and routine of life on the edge of the Everglades. I knew better, but it still stung for that pillar of smoke to shatter the illusion.

I finished off my coffee, hugged Della, then walked inside.

Birch slept on the sofa, his body so long, his feet hung over one arm. He laid so still with his arms folded over his chest it creeped me out. He looked dead. Worse, when I kicked the sofa leg and barked out his name, he didn't move a muscle, only opened his eyes, rising from slumber instantly. He levered his legs around and sat up. Ran a hand across the gray stubble on his scalp, the dry skin of his palm scraping, then shot me a questioning look.

"There's smoke in town. Where there's smoke, there's fire. Where there's fire, there's..." I said. "Well, me and Della think we got company. Better we scope it out before they find us here, so we keep this place our little secret."

He nodded then stood and flashed me an open hand. *Give me five to get ready.*

Once we found time to heal, I'd hoped he'd find a way to regain his voice, lost when the Red Man ripped out his tongue, but he remained as silent as ever. I left him pulling on his boots.

My place outside Lohatchie, passed down from my great-grandfather, consisted of a living room, kitchen, two bedrooms, one bathroom, and a dirt-floor cellar, where we kept our guns, ammunition, and other weapons scavenged along our journeys. Funny how so much of it accumulated after we destroyed the Red Man and stopped getting into constant scraps with the dead. Without his influence, the wormfeeders lost their will and dispersed. St. Bianco, who possessed the power to still the living dead, did so for all those in the Red Man's inner circle of ghouls at Acme Wonderland, but, I guess, he couldn't swing it for all of South Florida. They still troubled us, but at least they no longer swarmed or forced us to fight for every inch of road. We ran circles around them now. If we avoided them, they ignored us. Whatever bond once drove them to hunt us no longer existed.

We hardly ever fired a gun or bloodied a blade these days except when hunting. Other dangers existed out there, though, as they always had. I preferred to face them well-armed. I gathered handguns, rifles, and shotguns, a crossbow, knives, hatchets, a slingshot, with which Christopher could take a crow out of the sky, and lugged it all upstairs to load in the SUV.

Birch, returning from taking a leak on the edge of the wild, helped me load them.

I slammed the hatch shut.

Birch nodded to me. *Good to go.*

Christopher emerged from the house, dressed and ready to roll, except for his hair mussed in six different directions of bedhead mayhem. Della followed. They hesitated a moment to study the distant smoke. Christopher yawned, but then his eyes narrowed with irritation at the intrusion into our solitude. None of us relished routine more than him. That's what the young need, if only for something to test and rebel against—and I'd noticed the signs of rebellion growing in him as he hit the age when boys commence figuring out how to become men. Good for him. We all took that path sooner or later, if we lived long enough.

We climbed into the SUV in silence.

I cranked the engine, circled us around, and rolled up the trail toward town.

The closer to Main Street we drove, the more wormfeeders we saw.

Only in ones and twos, though. They no longer traveled in mobs, flowing like rising whitewater.

They barely noted our passing. The numberless, unnatural eyes that pocked their bodies showed fewer signs of life with every passing day, as if the souls behind them clung to existence in a process of slow decay, their vitality fading, the hungry gleam they once turned on us dimming under a milky haze. They didn't care anymore about what had once burned so fervently in them that it enabled them to persist after death, return to the world in borrowed flesh, and prey on the living. How that worked or what they hoped to gain, I still didn't fully understand, but I gladly accepted their weakening.

I guided the Toyota along a side street lined with empty houses and parked half a block from the main road. We slipped out of the car, armed ourselves from the trunk, and then broke into two teams.

Birch and I strolled toward Main Street. Christopher and Della headed to the other end of the block to move in along Biscayne Road, parallel to Main Street, backing us up while keeping out of sight. The rank odor of burning rubber tainted the air, emanating from the heavy, greasy smoke forming a shroud over the town. At the corner, I crouched and peered around the side of a long-abandoned hardware store, most of its useful goods now stored at my place. Fire raged at the far end of Main Street. A car burned. In its open trunk a pile of tires seethed with heat and smoke. Maybe a quarter mile away, yet the heat tickled my cheeks. I withdrew, let Birch take a look.

"I didn't see anyone," I said when he pulled back and straightened.

He shook his head. *Me neither.*

"So why burn tires and a car in the middle of the road? No point other than to catch someone's attention, I'd say, because it makes one hell of a mess. Impossible to ignore." I scanned Birch's impassive eyes, saw no objection. "Which means they're assuming someone is here to see it. Or, worse, they *know* someone's here to see it."

Birch nodded.

I reached into my pocket and plucked out the handset from a pair of walkie-talkies Christopher had collected from the hardware store. I'd laughed at the time, but they'd come in handy hunting and even around the house. Smart kid, that one.

I kept my voice low as I held the transmit button and spoke into it: "Someone definitely set the fire on purpose. We can't see anyone, though. You in position? Over."

Seconds passed before Della came back. "We're on the west corner of Banyan and Biscayne, a block down from Main. We don't see anyone. No one living, at least, but we got a couple wormfeeders taking root in someone's front yard across the street. Over."

Taking root. What the wormfeeders did when they ran out of steam. Found a place out of the way then stood there and rotted to dust. It took a long time. I knew of "wormfeeder graveyards," where they clustered like living grave markers waiting to disintegrate. It paid to stay alert around them, though, because sometimes they sprang back into action in a resurgent burst of hunger.

"Watch 'em close. Don't turn your backs on 'em," I said. "Birch and I are taking a walk. Squawk if you see anyone living. Over and out."

In silent agreement, Birch and I stepped around the corner, moved into the road, and walked right up the middle of Main Street at a Sunday-stroll pace. Birch carried a .45 in his right hand, low at his side, a .30 caliber rifle slung across his back. I cradled a 12-gauge shotgun in my arms, my 9mm holstered at my waist. We each wore a knife and a hatchet tucked into our belts. Walking up Main Street in plain sight might seem foolish, but time and again I'd found the direct approach worked best when confronting strangers. Anyone who knew enough about us to want us dead would've known where to find us. We had no living enemies, none we knew of at least, and it paid to make a show of ownership, striding through town like we alone belonged here, no one else.

The closer we moved to the fire, the worse the smoke and stink grew, until my eyes itched and watered. We halted about a hundred yards from the torched car, glanced around, saw no one. The car sat right in front of Mona and Joan's, a diner and ice cream shop back in the day.

A voice I'd forgotten whispered in my memory.

French fries and strawberry shakes.

"Shit," I said. "It can't be. No fucking way it can be."

Birch raised an eyebrow. I ignored him.

"All right, we saw your smoke signal. We came. We're here," I shouted over the crackling flame. "You going to make us wait all day?"

My gaze darted from one doorway to the next, one rooftop to another, from shadow to shadow, seeking a man I'd never expected to see again, near seven feet of muscle and meanness I'd watched die. Or at least thought I had. I held my breath, waiting for him to step out of a patch of gloom into the sun and firelight. Instead, a smaller, far-more surprising figure appeared.

A girl, maybe twelve, thin, gangly, wearing ill-fitting clothes, dirty brown hair tied back in a ponytail, ash smudged on her face, emerged from Mona and Joan's. She eyed me and Birch with fear. The two of us stared back at her for long seconds as we processed the sight of her.

Finally, I said, "Hey, there. We won't hurt you. Do you need some help?"

She nodded then vanished into Mona and Joan's.

Birch raised his left hand, palm up, snapped the first two fingers of his right hand against it, then closed a fist around them.

A trap.

"Sure feels like it," I said. "At the same time, it doesn't."

Birch raised both eyebrows at me for that.

I shrugged. "Feels like something else, that's all."

I reported to Della over the walkie then, with Birch's silent resignation, approached the door to Mona and Joan's. The fire warmed the back of my neck. Its smoke spilled around me. I covered my nose and mouth with my hand. Birch coughed then did the same. We waited a few moments for our eyes to adjust to the shade inside the diner then pushed the door open and entered, carrying our guns, ready.

"Hey, there, Lohatchie boy. Long time, no see," a man said from the back of the diner.

That whispering voice given full volume.

Seated on one of the counter stools, he shifted his mass, putting his face into the light. I blinked several times, making sure I saw who I thought I saw. He looked scarred and thinner, no less powerful or muscular than I remembered, and at the same time, faded and withdrawn, his deep brown skin tinged gray as if he'd sunken deep inside himself, taking refuge in the shelter of physical prowess—but that had changed even more than I realized at first. I understood fully what my eyes told me when he stood. He had lost his left arm, from the shoulder, and a scarred, ragged stump protruded from his sleeveless, muscle shirt.

"Fuck," I said. "Last I saw you, it looked like the wormfeeders had torn open half your chest."

"Damn near did. Wound up smeared in so much dead gunk the others gave me up for lost and left me alone long enough to squirrel out of there. Hid out until the hornet's nest shitshow we started ran its course. You're one mean son of a bitch, Cornell. Anyone ever tell you that?"

"Who keeps track?"

Birch tapped my shoulder, glanced from me to the man and back again.

"Birch, meet Klug, aka the King Snake. Klug, meet Birch."

Klug spun on his stool, showing off his cobra tattoo. It covered the back of his bald skull and ran down his neck, along his spine, and under his shirt. "Hey," he said as he rounded to face us again. Birch said nothing. "Quiet type, huh?"

"Can't speak. Someone took his tongue," I said.

"Ouch, my sympathies, brother," said Klug.

"Yeah, I'm sure he appreciates that. You two can be the charter members of the Lohatchie Lost Appendages club." My shock surrendered to tension. I changed the pitch of the shotgun in my arms. Klug didn't overlook it. "I suppose you set that fire for a reason."

"Sure did, and you ain't gonna need that scattergun," he said.

"I have vivid memories of pinning you to a wall with a truck, then the two of us trying to get each other killed by wormfeeders while I stole the getaway keys from your pocket."

"I remember that too. Wild times, man, wild times. The things we do to survive. Who can blame us?"

"You saying all is forgiven?"

"That's exactly what I'm saying. Not only that, but you were right."

"I was?"

"Yes, sir. We should've stuck to the plan and broken out of that prison. You got no concept of the hell that place became after you ditched it with Della and Mason. One of those 'life-altering' experiences people used to jaw about back when there were still enough people to listen. As Warden Lane Grove might've said, 'The scales fell from my eyes.' That and months and months of surviving second to second without a left arm changed my outlook."

"How so?"

Klug gestured to the girl. "You already met Chloe."

"Hi," she said, her voice shy, hesitant.

Two other children crept out from behind the counter. A black boy half Chloe's age, clinging to a superhero plushie at odds with the defiant look on his face, and a black girl, almost a teen, wearing a belt of knives, her hair cropped close to her scalp. The two bore a family resemblance.

"Meet Merit and his sister, Tayna," Klug said.

I nodded to each one and spoke their names. "I'm Cornell. This is Birch."

"Hi," they said.

"All of you now, come on," Klug said.

"It's like a damned clown car. How many you got hiding back there?" I said.

"Only them and Nina. Let's go, girl. No one here's going to bite you," Klug said.

A girl of fifteen or sixteen and several months pregnant revealed herself, rising behind the counter as if she expected to need to take cover again at a moment's notice. She wore a dirty, blue sundress and stared daggers at me with her brown eyes.

"I ain't the father," Klug said. "That was Rennie. Lost him about a month back."

"What the hell is this, Klug? You running a mobile daycare?"

Klug chuckled. "Like a halfway house on wheels. Della still with you? If she is, they all could use a look over from a good nurse. Nina's gonna need all the help she can get in a few months. It's why I came here. That and my yearning for one last strawberry-and-banana milkshake. Not going to get that, though, am I?"

"I am at a loss," I said.

"I was too for a long time," Klug said. "Things changed the first time I found myself around kids who needed protecting." A frown soured his haunted face. "None of those first ones are here. I did what I could. We can only do so much in this fucked-up world. We all got our limitations. We all come to the end of our road one day. I'm getting to mine. I thought, well, where in this whole, wide, savage world could I leave these four that they might have a chance without me? I figured if you were smart and tough enough to outdo me back in prison, you might have made it all the way to Lohatchie. I liked the idea of coming home too. Don't have time to wander the neighborhood knocking on doors, so I figured I'd send up the signal. You'd have to come if you saw it because we can't afford mysteries in our own backyard these days, right? I underestimated you once, not again."

I found no words to respond. The children watched me with intense, curious stares. Klug had guided them to a turning point, but they didn't know which direction their lives would take from here. Klug stared at me with different questions. The kind I thought could never even occur to a man like him, who'd lived his whole life by force, intimidation, and treachery before the dead plague, a man who did everything he could to deserve the name King Snake. Merit stepped to Klug's side, reached up, and took Klug's hand. Klug's massive, knobby fingers wrapped around the boy's with a gentle touch I'd have considered beyond his capacity. Like me, Della, Christopher, and Birch, though, Klug had defied the odds on more levels than one.

I raised the walkie to my mouth. "Della, meet us at Mona and Joan's. We're inside. We've got some kids who need a little nursing. Over."

A crackle of static, then Della came back, "On our way. Over and out."

"Got something to show you," Klug said.

He gestured for us to go out the back door to the small parking lot behind the diner. The sickness inside him revealed itself when he rose from his stool. He hunched over, his right hand clutched against his belly, and winced at the pain from whatever ate away at him. He took a second to catch his breath then shuffled along to the door. Despite his frailness, my gaze roved over him, seeking weapons. I saw none, but old habits die hard, and trust doesn't wink into existence because someone surrounds himself with children.

I traded glances with Della, who paused examining Nina long enough to notice how bad Klug looked. She'd already checked the other kids and given them clean bills of health, except for their hygiene, which we could remedy easily enough, but Nina filled her with concern, and that worried me. She nodded the okay for me to go, though, so I did. Birch came along behind me as I caught up to Klug. Christopher started to follow too, rising from where he sat playing cards with Merit, Tayna, and Chloe. I waved him off. I wanted him backing up Della, wanted to spare him whatever Klug had in mind, because I couldn't imagine anything pleasant waiting for us.

Klug opened the back door. We stepped into the sunlight of a day on track for high heat and humidity, the kind of day when we got up early to finish all our chores so we could spend most of it in the shade of our porch. Across the parking lot stretched a garden of the rooted dead, casting shadows in unison like giant-sized sundials. I hadn't been this way on our last few runs into town and had no idea so many had planted themselves here. They took no notice of us as far as I could tell. The breeze twitched their ragged clothing and disintegrating hair. Some of them swayed a little as it blew.

On the sidewalk that ran along the asphalt square sat a red cooler stained with dirt.

"Check this out," Klug said.

He toed the edge of the cooler lid then flipped it open with a kick. I don't know what I or Birch expected to see in there, but neither of us could've guessed the reality: a dead arm squirming on the cooler bottom, a dozen eyes blinking from its rotting flesh. The eyes squinted at the sunlight suddenly permitted into their nest. The cooler barely contained the big limb. It wriggled like a lizard dying staked to the ground by its tail, until the proverbial light bulb switched on in my head, and I directed my gaze at Klug's stump.

"Fucking wild, right?" He laughed, but it turned into a horrible, hacking cough. It took him almost a minute of wheezing to get his breath back. "I keep it as a reminder of how easy it is to lose things we take for granted in this world. Get me? I have this connection to it, to the dead through it, like a window into what they know, what they want. Let me tell you, that shit has kept me up many a night. It don't make a lick of sense, but it's helped me stay a step ahead of them when it mattered. Like an early-warning system. Now, though... now, they don't hardly seem to care much about anything. Like they're winding down. You notice that?"

I gestured to the still figures that filled the parking lot. "I see it all the time."

Klug looked over his shoulder. "Yeah, true. Maybe that's what's killing me. Whatever's passing out of them is passing out of my arm and draining the life out of me too. Or maybe it's just cancer eating my insides. Who knows? Don't make it hurt any less or change the result. I got only so much strength inside me, and when it's all eaten up, I'm gonna be right there with them."

Klug flipped the cooler lid closed. It snapped back open, making all three of us jump.

"Oh, shit," Klug said.

Pain burdened his voice. Like a knife thrust into him forced the words from his mouth.

The dead fingers of his severed arm curled over the lip of the cooler. The hand flexed, dragging itself up. It spread its fingers, opening its palm, full of winking eyes, and shook so forcefully the cooler rattled on the ground. Those eyes hadn't paled at all, preserved and sustained, perhaps, by their link to Klug's living energy.

In the parking lot, the wormfeeders roused. Despite their aimlessness and decay, the dead sometimes still traveled fast. In the blink of an eye, they turned to face us, then took rough, shambling steps in our direction. A few toppled over, their bodies incapable of motion on bones too brittle to support them and muscles, ligaments, and tendons long-since shriveled and snapped. One, whose feet seemed glued to the asphalt by putrescence, dropped as its ankles cracked. It tried to crawl, but then its wrists cracked too, leaving it stranded to wriggle its stumps on hot blacktop. The mob of them emitted a discordant, collective groan, as if anguished over their return to motion.

"The fuck is this?" I said.

Birch tugged on my shoulder, drawing me toward the door.

I resisted, fascinated by the dead uprooting themselves, wanting to understand what had sparked them back to motion. Birch pointed at Klug and yanked on me again.

Klug blinked his eyes several times and swayed on his feet. His jaw rose up and down, and his lips quivered. They looked like smears of ash. He couldn't catch or hold a breath. For a moment, his hand clung to the side of his gut, where his pain seemed to originate, then it slid away and hung limp at his side. I still didn't get what Birch had already sussed out.

"Birch's right. Let's get back in inside, Klug," I said. Klug didn't reply, didn't move. I dropped my hand on his shoulder. "Let's go, man. Come on!"

The King Snake heeled around to regard me with empty, glazed eyes. A gurgling moan escaped from his throat. A death rattle. He lunged his right hand at me, trying to grab my face. I fell back against Birch, ducking Klug's reach. Birch and I bolted to the door, no need to drag me along now, the two of us bumping together as we rushed inside, and locked it shut behind us. Dead flesh pounded against the wood, but it held.

"Fuck me, did he just die on his feet while we were talking?"

Panting, his eyes wide, Birch nodded. *Yeah, looks like it.*

"Ain't that a stitch?"

We hurried into the diner.

"Time for a hasty departure," I said. "Gather everyone up. We're going for the SUV."

"Where's Klug?" Tayna said. Her hands rested on the hilts of the knives strapped to her belt.

"Klug's out back in the parking lot. He was a lot sicker than you knew. A man that strong can hide a sickness for a long time. Keep himself going like he's better off than he really is. Then it catches up with him all at once. That's what he did to get you all here, keep you safe. But he's not sick anymore. Do you understand what I'm saying?"

"Liar! I don't believe you! You did something to him. He said you wouldn't be happy to see him. You hurt him! What did you do?"

Tayna's expression turned feral. She moved in a blur, unsheathing one of the knives at her waist and throwing it, missing my face by inches so the blade sunk itself into the wall behind me. She grabbed Merit's hand and pulled him along as she dashed out the front door.

"Come back," I called out.

Della and Christopher jumped up to run after them. I stopped them with news of the dead in the parking lot. "There could be others out there rousing for a last gasp. Seems like Klug's death set them off, like whatever life went out of him restarted their engines. We need to be careful."

"So what's the plan?" Christopher said.

"Della, Birch, you take Chloe and Nina to the SUV, lock them inside, and protect it. Christopher and I will find Merit and Tayna and meet you there," I said. "Then we get the hell out of town."

Christopher cracked the door and poked his head outside. "All clear."

We exited Mona and Joan's, the thud of dead fists against the back door fading behind us.

The heat and smoke from the fire turned the street to hell. That car would burn a long time.

Della and Birch led Chloe and Nina away toward the SUV, moving fast but with caution, keeping the two girls between them. I gestured to Christopher, and we walked the other way, rounding the fire as close as we dared as we crossed the street. I looked for signs of which way Merit and Tayna had run but saw no hint. They might as well have vanished like ghosts.

"Merit said they stashed their car nearby," Christopher said.

"Did he say where?"

"No, only said his sister did the driving because Klug couldn't anymore. Klug told them where to park because he grew up here."

Weekends, holidays, Main Street in Lohatchie filled up with people running errands or enjoying the town, parents taking kids for ice cream, teenagers cruising, people on their weekly gossip-and-shop route. The parking lot out back of Mona and Joan's and every other under-sized lot filled up fast on those days, which meant street parking for latecomers. Smart locals often went for that first anyway because two nearby streets offered easy parking in the shade while the sun cooked the public lots, and it gave them an edge on the traffic when it came time to leave. Klug had grown up here. He had to know about that.

"I got an idea where to look," I said. "Follow me."

Christopher walked beside me to the end of Main Street. The road continued, but shops gave way to houses. A mile farther down, if we were to walk that far, it gave way to nothing but sawgrass and trees, but no one ever parked down there. We passed the first residential side street, Finlay Road. No cars, only a handful of the dead rooted and rotted in front yards. On the second road, Chestnut Street, my guess paid off.

A Cadillac Town Car sat halfway down the block, neatly parked in the luxurious shade of an old red maple tree. The dead surrounded it, pressed against it, pawing at the windows, groaning, struggling to find a way inside, where Merit and Tayna clung to each other in the front seat. Why hadn't they started the car and driven off, I wondered. Echoes of the past provided the answer. They didn't have the keys; Klug did. Probably in his front shirt pocket like he'd had the truck keys so long ago back in the prison of Warden Lane Grove when I'd stolen them from him and escaped.

The yards along Chestnut Street had comprised a few wormfeeder graveyards. Many of them had uprooted themselves to pursue the kids. The others remained planted in place, their eyes noting us, watching, but indifferent. Their deteriorated bodies swayed, from the breeze, or maybe excited by the action at the car. I figured a good number of the dead had wandered over from Finlay Street too. Dormant for so long, until Klug rang their alarm clock.

"There's too many to dodge or kill," Christopher said. "What do we do?"

Merit and Tayna spotted us. They slapped their palms against the windshield and screamed for us to *help us, save us, get us out of here.* Just kids, dumb enough to throw a knife at me in one moment then beg me for help in another.

The smart play would've been to walk away, rendezvous with the others, and head home. Leave behind what amounted to two more mouths to feed, that's all. No one had asked Klug to bring a bunch of kids here, to trust me to take them in. But he had. Down to his last breath, my enemy came to me for help. Once, we'd tried our best to kill each other. You couldn't say either of us had defeated the other, but we'd persevered. Beyond that, though, the look on Christopher's face made the smart thing to do an impossibility. His expression removed "walking away" from my lexicon of moves. He intended to solve this problem. He needed to save those kids as he'd once been saved. I refused to let him down.

"We shoot them, we'll be ringing the supper bell for the others out behind Mona and Joan's, over on the next street, hell, anywhere around here. That only gets us cut off from the SUV." I pointed to an Acura with four flat tires in a nearby driveway. "Hide yourself behind that car. I'll draw them off the Caddy. They'll scatter a bit when they come after me. I'll lead them the other way. Once it's clear, get the kids out and head back the way we came for the SUV."

"No way, you can't dodge that many," Christopher said.

"Don't worry about me. They're slow, old, and unmotivated. I won't have to dodge them all, just a few of the overachievers, I said. "Besides, I got a plan."

Christopher met my gaze. I didn't turn away. I needed to sell the lie, couldn't let him see it in my eyes that I had no plan except to play rodeo clown for the wormfeeders long enough for him to retrieve Merit and Tayna. That's what parents do: They make sacrifices for their children. Put themselves at risk for their survival. Give of themselves. I wasn't Christopher's father and never really would be, but there was a time when I would've been a father. A time before prison, death, the dead plague, and mad saints ruled a world sinking into decomposition. A time when long-dead Evelyn, who blessedly passed before all this insanity, would've made parents of us both—and I let her and our baby die, taking all the hope I'd ever had of living a normal kind of life with them.

This time, I promised myself, it would go differently.

Once Christopher hunkered down behind the Acura, I rampaged at the Caddy.

I skidded to a stop and poked one of the wormfeeders with the tip of my shotgun barrel. Then another one. I prodded a third, a fourth, then onward, one after another until half of them noticed me and scraped their attention away from the kids. I howled and whooped and jumped around, mocking them, keeping myself out of arm's reach and glancing over my shoulder to check the ones still rooted in the yards. Most of the wormfeeders, about a dozen, left the Caddy and trailed me as I led them like the Pied Piper leading rats. I guided them beyond the Caddy, toward the far end of the block. When they slowed, I darted in and poled the frontrunners. A few lingered at the car, dead faces pressed to the windows. I grabbed a rock from the ground and threw it at them. Another. One more. I hit them in their faces, aimed for their multitude of eyes, made them see me. The curb tripped me, and I almost fell, but the tactic paid off. The last three joined the free-lunch crowd hoping to eat me.

"Go, Christopher, go, now!" I shouted.

On the other side of the Caddy, Christopher appeared, running so hard he stopped himself by slamming into the driver's side door. He slapped at the glass, urged Merit and Tayna to unlock the door, get out, run with him. After several horrifying seconds of fumbling, they did. They scrambled free of the Caddy, too frightened to argue now, and bolted with Christopher. I watched them turn the corner and dash back along Main Street, out of my sight.

Left alone with fifteen wormfeeders, I evaded their clumsy assaults.

When I reached the next corner, I stepped from the proverbial frying pan into the fire.

A mob of new admirers more than twice the size of the Caddy crew approached from the direction of town, likely formed by uprooted wormfeeders from Mona and Joan's parking lot. They had missed out on their prey at the diner, but they'd caught the signal.

Come down to Chestnut Street. We got fresh meat.

It's a block party for the dead.

Chowtime, soup's on, get it while it's hot.

Or at least warm-blooded.

The two groups melded together, a handful of wormfeeders falling as they tripped over each other. None rose again. The others simply stamped them to a gory mush on the street. I backpedaled, stringing them along toward the road out of town. They came faster than I expected, but not fast enough to catch me. With Della and the kids on their way to safety, I hoped and prayed, I raised my shotgun and let loose into them. If the report drew more of them my way, so much the better. Each blast did much more damage than I'd expected. The rooted ones weren't sturdy. They were the difference between uprooting a healthy tree and a dead one. The former makes you work for it; the latter rips right out of the soil. Several wormfeeders collapsed in the road, bodies so disrupted by shot, they no longer functioned. Enough kept coming to worry me. I crept backward, firing a shell every couple of seconds. More dropped and lay in the street like earthworms dying in the sun after a rainstorm. The stragglers slowed. An end to my pursuit appeared. I reloaded the shotgun, fired four rounds in rapid succession, knocking down a seven-ten split of wormfeeders. The last two didn't worry me. Their knee bones showed through their broken dead flesh, clicking, sliding like gears out of sync, on the verge of failing.

"Enjoy the rest of your walk, folks," I said.

I heeled around and ran, intending to rush up the next side road back to Main Street and hook up with the others. Instead, I bolted into a solid mass of dead flesh and muscle, hard enough to stagger me back two steps.

Klug.

He stared me down with a hundred eyes, but his own milky set sent the worst chill through me.

His right hand swung, almost slow-motion, and easy enough for me to dodge, but I felt the wind from it and knew it would punish me if it landed. He stumbled closer, took another swing. I ducked, lost my balance, fell to the ground, and rolled with the motion, coming up on my ass at the curb. The two wormfeeder stragglers hooked up with Klug. The trio moved on me, the way Klug had so often moved on his enemies in the prison yard, with backup, a gang, the implication of overwhelming numbers, a show of force to remind you of your weakness. Except Klug's intimidation, dead or alive, no longer sent a chill through me. Back when I met him, I'd wanted to stay clear of the web that people like him use to draw you in and manipulate you, but I'd learned how impossible this world made that. No one stayed clean, no one walked away free—not unless you fought for it.

"Shit, Klug, look how far you came, saving kids, and making peace with me, and now, you're right back where you started, you fucking evil, deadhead bully," I said.

I didn't try to rise to my feet. I braced the shotgun to my shoulder and fired.

The recoil slammed me flat on my back.

Scrambling onto the sidewalk, I watched Klug's decapitated body wobble. The blast had vaporized his head, neck, all of what remained of his left shoulder, and most of his right. His one arm bobbed from a thread of tendon and ligament.

The stragglers moved past him. I stood, steadied myself, and blew their faces away too.

"Son of a bitch, Lohatchie just ain't what it used to be," I said.

Groans and the rasp of air whispering through dead flesh caught my attention. More of the dead came shuffle-stepping in my direction. Another sound reached me too. A car engine.

The SUV came bouncing and jolting across a nearby front yard as it swerved out of a side street, rounded a cluster of worm-feeders, and skidded to a hard stop. The passenger door swung open. Tayna leaned out from the passenger seat. A chorus of voices yelled at me to get in. Jumping into the SUV, I shoved Tayna onto the console between me and Della, behind the wheel. I yanked the door shut behind me then pulled Tayna onto my lap.

Della floored the gas. I counted heads in the back seat. Everyone there.

Christopher crouched in the trunk, covering our six out the back window. Merit and Chloe sat on Birch's and Nina's laps. I never saw so welcome a sight. Our little group, or unit, or family, or whatever the hell you called it, had just doubled in sizc, and something about that fact that I couldn't put into words made all the chaos and death around us fall away like scenery.

"Took you all long enough, kid," I said.

"You shut up before I throw another knife at you," Tayna said. "We saved you didn't we?"

"That you did. You saved Klug, too. No matter how he died, you did that for him in life. I hope you know that." I let out a long breath. "And I hope you like gardening."

Tayna flashed a questioning eye at me. I didn't bother to explain. Plenty of time for her to learn, for all of us to learn.

THE DEAD WON'T DIE

As of the publication of *The Eyes of the Dead*, I've lived in the Corpse Fauna world for twenty-five years. If you define the modern zombie as walking dead ghouls who feast on the flesh of the living versus traditional voodoo zombies and place their birth in 1968 with the release of *The Night of the Living Dead*, that's just short of half the lifespan of this most popular of 20th-century monsters. Back in 1997, when I conceived the first story in what grew into the Corpse Fauna cycle, a dedicated fan could have, with a little effort, seen all the modern zombie movies—certainly all the ones worth seeing—and read all the modern zombie books and comics. There were *no* TV shows. That last fact is hard to fathom today when there are, as of this writing, three series about a world plagued by modern zombies currently on the air, more announced to come soon, and several more available through streaming services. More remarkable is the unfettered torrent of zombie movies that shamble forth on a regular basis from all over the world.

With all this attention from creators and audiences, though, does the modern zombie still matter?

The godfather of the living dead, George Romero, imbued his tales of flesh-eating ghouls with social commentary, using reanimated corpses to weave satire and pointed observations into his movies. Many people once considered that element an essential ingredient of the modern zombie mythos, yet, that aspect has faded with time. Just as Bram Stoker's commentary on Victorian sexual mores in *Dracula* has faded from vampire stories. Even as Mary Shelley's themes of humanity's relationship with its creations and discoveries have faded from adaptations and retellings of *Frankenstein*. In many ways, the modern zombie now stands with werewolves, mummies, and slashers as merely one more menacing figure in the pantheon of horror tropes and cliches.

With all due respect to the many excellent stories of modern zombies told since 2005, it's tempting to declare the modern zombie complete and fully formed as of the release of *Land of the Dead*, George Romero's fourth and final film in the original Dead series. He followed it with two more movies, *Diary of the Dead* (2007) and *Survival of the Dead* (2009), and even continued to build on his ideas in various comic book series, such as *Toe Tags* and *Empire of the Dead*; an anthology, with Jonathan Maberry, *Nights of the Living Dead*; and a novel, with Daniel Kraus, *The Living Dead*. All of those explored ideas and possibilities in the world of the living dead, but few of them added substantially to the idea of the modern zombie or to its full realization as a true classic monster. That George accomplished in *Land of the Dead*.

The classic monsters, as defined in film and fiction, include ghosts, Frankenstein's monster, mummies, werewolves, vampires, and even the Creature from the Black Lagoon. What they have in common and what makes them classic is how they not only represent universal fears but that they exist as fully rounded characters, monstrous and frightening, true, but also sympathetic and imbued with humanity. We regard them with more than fear, with perhaps even sympathy and compassion. Consider the romance of Dracula; or the tragedy of Frankenstein's monster, shunned by his maker; or the vibrant, charming Lawrence Talbot afflicted by a beast within him beyond his control; or the Creature, a lonely prehistoric throwback upon whose tranquil home eager scientists intrude. We find something in these monsters to love or, at least, with which to empathize, an aspect, characteristic, or circumstance that makes them as interesting to audiences and readers as the human characters who confront them. In some of those classic stories, the most monstrous character isn't the creature but the humans around it.

Most of the classic monsters possessed those elements from their introduction. They sprang to dark life fully formed in their debut novels or films. For modern zombies, though, it took four movies made over a span of more than twenty-five years to get there. In *Night of the Living Dead*, the "ghouls" acted as little more than assassins. Random. Inexplicable. Single-minded. Blind appetites driven by mindless hunger. A mob overwhelming resistance from the living through thoughtless persistence and sheer numbers. With *Dawn of the Dead* (1978), they evolved into mute stand-ins for the worst traits in modern humanity. Consumerism. Materialism. Mindless adherence to convention. Then in *Day of the Dead* (1985), they exhibited the first signs of consciousness surviving death—or perhaps new consciousness emerging after death. As though resurrection of the body catalyzed a rebirth into which a new consciousness entered. All fascinating stuff in a sense of monster and world-building, shedding pure monstrosity for something more meaningful— but not yet on a par with the classic monsters that came before.

Another twenty years passed before Romero took us there in *Land of the Dead*, which fulfilled the vision the filmmaker had expressed decades before as the ultimate goal of his *Dead* movies. In *Land*, the dead show all the signs of having become a rival branch of humanity, a mutant species, fighting for their survival, even for the dignity of their new mode of existence. They become sympathetic like the classic monsters. Humanity must still fear them and cannot coexist with them because, no matter if we might understand their will to live and recognize their undeniable—though inhuman—consciousness, they still want to eat the living and make more of the dead. In *Land*, the modern zombie becomes the underdog triumphant. Audiences could finally root for these monsters and sympathize with their urge to live their undead existence to its fullest. Thus the modern zombie took its place among the pantheon of the truly classic monsters. As in all of the Dead films, there are far more monstrous humans in the story.

Romero took a long and roundabout path to that point with his creation—but the silver lining came in the form of four incredible horror films made at distinctly different points in history, allowing each to resonate in a different way and reach new audiences. Yet the question remains: Does the modern zombie still matter?

Are all stories of modern zombies since 2005 really about post-modern zombies? The challenge of working in a post-modern mode is to find new perspectives and themes in a thing considered complete and fully rounded. To breathe new life into creations so familiar they no longer evoke much of a reaction in their well-known form. To reinvent them.

What of Corpse Fauna, a series of novellas and stories that spans the modern/post-modern eras?

That has been one of the greatest challenges in writing these stories, publishing and republishing them, spending intense periods of time with these characters, then taking long vacations from them, then back again like a family reunion with your grimmest group of old friends. A strange experience. Some of the initial inspiration for Corpse Fauna seems less compelling to me today than it did when I began this story cycle. Some seem more important than ever. The theme of social authority and control versus individual freedom, identity, and will, which runs through all the stories, resonates even more for me today. So does the notion of an ambiguous power fueled by thousands or millions of trapped souls that watches and strives to control one's every move, every choice, every thought. And the challenge of simply being left alone to live one's life in a world where the masses feel entitled—even compelled—to interfere with the lives of people to whom they have no real connection. I leave it to my readers to ascertain what these ideas relate to in the real world.

In this sense, I consider the Corpse Fauna stories modern zombie stories, not post-modern, positioned squarely in the sweet spot Romero left open to those of us who cared to enter it in the zombie drought years between 1985 and 2005. Back when modern zombie stories were expected to be about more than mere survival, and the zombies needed to function as more than a generic threat in stories and movies that fit better into the sub-genre of survival horror than zombie fiction.

Still, does any of this answer the question? Does the modern zombie still matter?

It matters to me. I suspect it matters to my readers. For all the love of movie magic, special effects, and unforgettable characters that have made post-modern zombie stories, movies, and television shows so entertaining, the living dead seem a bit hollow without those essential elements that made them great in the first place. As long as writers seek those greater possibilities in what makes the modern zombie such a fascinating classic monster—and as long as readers and audiences continue supporting it—the modern zombie will continue to matter. And matter more than the post-modern zombie.

Coming to the end of the Corpse Fauna cycle with *The Eyes of the Dead*, I realize I've inadvertently followed even more closely in Romero's footsteps than I'd ever intended. It's taken a quarter-century to bring all these stories to publication and complete what I envisioned many years ago. There have been a number of false starts and setbacks not unlike those Romero experienced seeking funding for his Dead films. Yet here I am, having reached the end of the story (or the end for now...) because the Dead truly *won't* die—unless we let them.

I owe a tremendous amount of gratitude to all those readers who have followed Corpse Fauna's winding and circuitous path and its many resurrections. Your interest and support made these books possible. Thanks as well to the wonderfully supportive and professional folks at NeoParadoxa and eSpec Books, who not only provided the opportunity to fully realize what I'd imagined for Corpse Fauna but have gone above and beyond to make it the best it can be. A very special thanks to two artists who have been part of this journey with me: Glen Ostrander and Jason Whitley. I'm finicky about how artists visualize my characters and concepts, but Glen and Jason, apparently, can read my mind. Their interpretations and representations of Corpse Fauna have been pitch-perfect every time, and their enthusiasm has helped keep me going on the long trek from "Prison of the Blind Dead" (read my afterword in *The Dead Bear Witness* if you don't know what that is) to *The Eyes of the Dead*.

Thank you for reading.

—James Chambers
April 2022

BODY

Light and sky erase what seemed an eternal darkness.

Wind and blades of grass brush withered flesh, sparking dulled nerves.

Craving stirs in shriveled guts, a ravenous need beyond hunger.

You raise your hands to the sky, bend your legs, twist a rigid spine, rise—and walk.

Others shuffle along the shop-lined street across from the park where you stand. Equally empty, driven by urges equally misunderstood. One moans a wordless exhortation of confusion and anguish. Another answers. A third. Then all the bodies part their lips and join in the great gasping mystery of their existence, a discordant chorus asking: *Why do we still live?* But they don't live, not in the true meaning of the word—nor do you. You know it. You sense it. You intuit your unnatural existence, this extension of ambulation and awareness beyond true life and nature, but you can make no sense of it.

You don't think these things, cannot think at all in the way you once did, not with an atrophied brain and shriveled neurons, not with only the barest glimmer of consciousness and the absence of true self-awareness. You possess no memory, no echoes of identity, only a primal knowledge of having once been something different, something beautiful and vital, fleeting, ephemeral, and fragile that reached its conclusion. In this abominable extension of what once was, you see and hear as if wrapped in cotton mufflers. You walk without purpose. Your nose scents only decay and life—and you desire the life, wish to consume it, to regain what you lost, although you cannot name that thing.

Like the other bodies, you expel a groan of bafflement and hunger, then stagger and join the parade of the damned. They bump each other, taking no notice, making no comment. Flies and other insects cloud them, feasting on expired flesh. You don't know this place, these shopfronts of glass and wood, though perhaps you once did. They signify nothing to you. You collide with another body, which stands before a plate glass window. You stop to observe. The other plucks at the pink cloth that covers its mottling torso and then looks at its reflection in the window. Its head tilts to see the shirt, then rises to view its own ghostly image in the glass, then back to the shirt, to the glass, to the shirt....

You stand beside it, look, find a body opposite you, seemingly trapped in the glass. It matches every move you make. Dirty fabric printed with pineapples and palm trees covers its torso— your torso. Cloth of pastel squares hangs from its waist—your waist. You touch your chest. The other does likewise. You pull on the colorful fabric. The other mimics you. A meaningful gesture, but what meaning escapes you. In seconds, your interest dissipates. The one in the pink shirt has already moved on. You follow, rejoining the aimless march along the road.

You walk, slow, unsteady, but constant.

The sun drifts overhead, and the shadows of the bodies grow long until dusk absorbs them.

Night brings a different sky, one that appears to you not indigo and speckled with dots of light, as instinct says it should, but nacreous and milky, stained with dazzling specks of black, pulsating energy, and tainted by a creeping stain of utter dark that erases the universe. A flickering neon moon shimmers against the backdrop. It gleams and flashes above you all. The darkness connects to you somehow as if emanating rays of anti-life, un-life, un-death, whatever fuels your thoughtless shuffle amongst this mad march of the dead.

Night animals emerge. An owl hoots, the sound muted and mysterious to your ears.

Different insects surround you.

The bodies walk on, regardless.

You walk on.

The night dark holds no fear for you, presents no obstacle. You follow an invisible road, a path sensed, not seen, summoned, and directed as if by magnetism, traveling together but apart, sharing no communication, no community with those around you. They walk. You walk. That is all. There is no more.

Dawn brings the sun and steals away the strange night sky.

Night creatures depart. Fresh insect clouds descend.

You walk.

They all walk.

You walk.

They walk.

You walk.

A melee of voices fills your head.

What did I do to deserve this?

Who are you?

Where are we?

Who am I?

Everything hurts, oh god, it hurts so much, please make it stop.

Barbara, are you here? Barbara? Where are you?

I only ever wanted what was coming to me.

How could there be nothing there? How could my life mean so little?

Why are we here again?

I was a good person! I didn't hurt anyone.

I prayed every day. Every damn day!

I can't move my legs or arms. Can't even feel my hands! How am I moving?

Where's my baby? Where is she? She's crying. She needs me.

What do you want from me? What?!

For god's sake, leave me alone. Give me peace.

Make it stop!

I lived a good life. Why am I being punished?

I don't want this. Let me out of here. I have money. I'm rich!

This can't be. I can't be here. Existence ends in death, dammit. Nothing comes after. Nothing! I shouldn't exist, for fuck's sake.

Darkness. There's darkness after death, not nothing.

There was me. There was us. There is this. We surrendered to the Darkness.

What the fuck does that mean?

Who are you? Why are you all here with me? Leave me alone! Didn't I suffer enough?

So much for pearly gates and angels playing harps. This sucks.

Stop talking! All of you, shut up! I can't hear myself think.

Those bastards! They lied, lied, lied. They lied to us all.

Is this what comes after? We're reduced to this?

How do we even exist?

COME. FOLLOW. JOIN ME. ALL SHALL BE REVEALED. I SHALL RAISE YOU UP FROM YOUR DARKNESS AND CON-FUSION. I SHALL MAKE GODS OF US ALL.

Who said that?

Who was that? What does that mean?

Was that... God? Or the Devil?

There's no God, no Devil, only the Darkness. It was the Darkness.

No, the voice in the Darkness.

You heard it too?

I heard it.

So did I.

Me too.

We all heard it. We all followed it.

COME!

We're following it still, you dumb fucks.

You struggle to make sense, any sense, but ideas and impressions gather like handfuls of cracked eggshells in your atrophied brain, spilling between the fingers of your proto-thoughts.

Where you saw one sky above, one earth beneath your feet, you now perceive a multitude, each glimpsed or felt from a different perspective. A dozen or more skies broken into shards of crisp blue and fulsome clouds. You see trees, grass, empty cars, darkened shops and houses, bodies making this aimless journey. You see them in full circle, glimpse them in broken fragments of reality that should form a whole; see, literally, with eyes on the back of your head, your neck, your arms and legs. But you cannot assemble the sights into a coherent perception, or fill the gaps among them, or find what ties them together.

Your hunger multiplies. You crave the life you once possessed. You seek flesh.

All the bodies share this need. They cry out in grief, in ceaseless, inarticulate protestations of hunger. Each mouth serves many voices. They take turns expelling their despair. You do the same. You cannot stop yourself—but the act brings no relief, no lessening of the urges.

You look at your right arm. Your arm looks back.

You gaze at your left hand. Your hand gazes back.

You stare at your kneecap. Your kneecap stares back.

In the same moment, you see your limbs and see yourself from their perspective, see earth, see sky, see trees and other shambling bodies, your own feet take step after step, shuffling. This is wrong, so wrong, you intuit, but you think and feel nothing beyond that. Your dulled senses prevent overload from addling or distracting you. The anomalous sensations seem merely part of your renewed existence. You accept them and continue on your invisible path.

A disturbance rises in the stability of the crowd.

The scent of life drifts to your decayed nostrils.

Every inch of your dead flesh crawls with enlivened need.

Your strange hunger erupts, and the air fills with a red haze.

A body strikes you, causing you to stumble, but you remain on your feet, your multitude of sensory input coruscating through your shriveled nervous system. You find your footing and step faster, attracted by the blossoming aroma of vitality. The current of the bodies alters. You flow with it. Ahead, the air shimmers with ruby energy, viewed by you in fly-eye multitudes. Your many eyes trace it to live people fleeing the dead. They are too slow and clumsy, panicked, perhaps fatigued. The dead overtake and surround them. You reach the frenzy, thrust yourself between rotting limbs to reach living, healthy ones, and sink your teeth into one of them. Liquid warmth fills your mouth, runnels down your throat, and coats your organs. Sparks sizzle in your brain. Proteins and sugars flood you.

Memories stir.

You take another bite, then another, chewing flesh and muscle between creaking jaws, slurping the blood with withered lips, swallowing half-chewed gobs of living meat. Signal fires flare in your brain, guiding you back to what was before. Another bite, more flesh, more blood...

You held a woman's hand in yours.

Shorter than you, she tilted her head back to show you her smile as you walked side-by-side along the quaint shop-lined street. She wore an airy, floral print dress that clung and draped from her body as she moved in a way that aroused a different kind of hunger for flesh and life. You relished the soft warmth of her palm against yours, the way her hip brushed against you every third step.

Her name floats to your memory's surface. *Berina.*

You met six months before this. A party at your best friend's restaurant. Thrown in part to lift your spirits after a vicious split with your ex-wife. There you met Berina, two years moving on from her own dead marriage. You seemed so perfect for each other, but you took things slow, cautious from still-healing wounds, learning each other, waiting, until this trip, this getaway for just the two of you, until last night when you dropped all defenses and slept together for the first time, giving form to what had grown between you, planting a seed for the future you both hoped to share.

In the morning, you awoke with the same thought in your minds.

This is forever.

Then you walked through the little town, looking for a late brunch after a morning spent in bed.

A filthy man in rags approached you, cornered you. Two more people joined him, another three. Pungent with odor, their mouths moved as if chewing on invisible food. All sickly gray, blotchy skin, with blood stains on their clothes, dead-eyed and fierce in their need, they surrounded you.

You thrust Berina behind you, but...

The flesh's warmth fades. Your teeth click against cleaned bone.

A sensation lingers in your brain. Did you remember something?

A floral print sundress clinging to curves.

It felt good, right.

You want to go back there and remember again.

A living voice screams. You extract yourself from the feeding frenzy, gaze all around.

On the next corner, two living women fight against the few that ignore the buffet at hand to chase them. Lines of red haze trail the women's every move, multiplying their limbs, blurring their faces, forming fogs of life. You stagger over and around the feasting bodies, stumble clear, hurry as much as your dead limbs allow. One woman holds a shotgun. It barks flame and smoke. The head of the nearest body evaporates in a cloud of blood and brains. The body falls backward, lies still for a moment, then clambers back onto its feet. Even without a head, it sees. Eyes wink from the sallow wrinkles on its arms and chest. You keep your pace. The women shriek with terror as the headless body limps toward them. They don't notice you approach. Their red auras flicker and vibrate. The other woman holds a baseball bat. She swings it to keep the bodies from reaching her, but she looks tired, overwhelmed. If you don't get there soon, the others will claim the life in her blood.

You force yourself faster, chasing *a floral print sundress clinging to curves.*

You want to see it again, maybe understand it.

Step faster.

Faster.

The woman concentrates on fending off the bodies in front of her. She doesn't see you until you wrap your arms around her from behind and sink your teeth up to their dry gums into her shoulder. You bite through cloth, through flesh, clench your jaw on bone, suck blood into your mouth, and slake your profane thirst. Her flesh sets your tongue aflame with warmth. You chew it greedily, swallow, then rip her shirt to expose her smooth back and take a second, larger bite. Less bone, more meat, muscle, and life. It fills you with a surge of vitality, lifting you above the multitude of voices that chatter in your head, and mutes them.

The woman weeps and drops her baseball bat. It clunks to the ground.

You take a third bite as the other bodies move in and begin to rip the woman's limbs apart.

You feast.

You feed

For a moment... you live.

Berina tickled your shin with her toes under the table.

An acoustic reggae band played at one end of the restaurant, near the outdoor patio, but you preferred this dark booth near the back, a small bubble of intimacy on the fringe of the nightlife. You and Berina sipped cocktails as the music flowed through you, and you struggled to think of fresh jokes to share only so you could hear Berina's laugh, which rang for you like crystal wind chimes. It sent a shiver of excitement through you even as it chased away your anxiety and uncertainty. You decided you could listen to that laugh every morning, day, and night for the rest of your life.

You reached across the table, took her hand, and turned it palm up. You traced lines in it with your fingertip. Berina narrowed her eyes and sighed.

She spoke then.

What did she say?

You can't understand the words in memory.

You hear them.

Clear, familiar, yet they hold no meaning.

In recollection, they've lost their intent.

You responded. The words that left your lips equally meaningless now.

The band played. A waiter refreshed your drinks. Later you danced, waiting for the slow songs so you could embrace each other and sway to the rhythm of that moment, together, your shared warmth, a micro-ecology where only you and Berina existed.

What did she say?

What?

You ache to hear...

...but the voices intrude.

Stop it! Give me a turn.

No! Me, I'm next. Let me remember.

Why does he get to remember? Why him?

Shut up! Who wants to remember anything? It'll only make this worse.

How can this be any worse?

I remember Barbara. Barbara, are you here?

I was better off in the Darkness.

Let's find a way back there.

No! Don't! If we open that door again...

What? What happens?

I don't know.

Who does?

No one.

You're all insane. None of this is even real.

His memories are real. I want to remember.

Not me.

Better to forget.

My baby is crying. Can someone help me find her? Please!

The Darkness is all that matters.

HUSH. COME TO ME. YOU ARE NOT HERE BY ACCIDENT. YOU HAVE A PURPOSE. YOU FULFILL A NEED IN THE UNIVERSE. COME AND LISTEN. I SHALL HELP US ALL TRANSCEND TO GREATNESS THAT AWAITS IN THE DARKNESS.

Aagh, stop that voice. It hurts me.

It rips at me.

It's like acid, like fire.

Like glass shards.

Metal spikes.
Hot needles.
Claws.
Thorns.
Barbed-wire.
Let me rest.
Why won't it let me rest?
BIRTH IS ALWAYS PAINFUL.
Noooooo!
Stop, please, stop.
Quiet. I only want quiet.
Send me to my reward or to nothingness, please.
YOU ARE NOT AND NEVER HAVE BEEN NOTHING. YOU ARE ALL. COME. I SHALL SHOW YOU.
Why?
Why do this?
Why do I exist?

What do words mean?

The woman holding the shotgun screams so many words as you devour the other woman. They shed all meaning when they reach your ears. You glimpse emotion in the woman's face, but the red haze obscures it, renders it nothing but a burning flame you want inside you. The mosaic impressions caught by your multitude of eyes elude your comprehension. Her expression changes too quickly to make sense to you. Life moves too fast for the dead to follow it. Words fly from her lips, louder. Other bodies catch up to her and drag her to the ground. Only the red energy matters. Bodies fall upon her, consuming her life. You greedily snatch another mouthful from the woman in your grip. Chew and swallow. The more you consume, the less satisfying the flesh becomes. The life leaves it so quickly. You ingest dregs now, a pale aftertaste of those first vibrant mouthfuls.

You stagger away from the fading corpse toward the other woman.

Too late. The others have taken the best of her.

Already, her red shimmer dwindles and pales.

Your disjointed jaw clicks open, and you scream. All that leaves your mouth is a dull, blood-gurgled dirge of need.

A red flash catches your eyes.

The scent of life sparks your senses.

Far down the street, a red cloud glows and then vanishes quickly out of sight behind the corner of a shop building. You trip over body parts, over wriggling dead limbs, over your own two feet, then find your balance and drag yourself toward the vanishing red. A few others, noticing your departure, follow in hopes you'll lead them to another feast. There are so few of the living left in this town and so many of the dead. Like survivors on a lifeboat, stranded afloat without provisions, ready to tear each other apart for another bite of flesh, for another glimpse of what the flesh brings.

A floral print sundress clinging to curves.

Maybe the others see similar scraps of remembrance. Totems of the red, of life.

Do they know what they mean? Why those visions hold such sway over them? Why their flesh full of eyes desires it so deeply? You envy them if they do. All you know is the red/life/flesh brings coherence to your mind, your existence, your purpose.

The eyes that pock your body see your surroundings from too many perspectives to count. Some see only the dry gloom beneath your ragged clothes; others see a wet dark that mystifies you, as if they lie beneath your skin. The world becomes a swarm of overlapping visions and blanks where gaps exist. The faster you walk, the smoother it appears, but you can hardly keep your balance. The muscles and bones of your feet, ankles, and legs feel brittle and leaden. You stamp forward as best you can, as fast as you can, until you reach the corner, round it—and confront half a dozen live people, all armed with guns and poles with blades strapped to the tip.

They scream, a barrage of sounds you know have meaning to them even though it cannot reach you. They fire their guns and thrust their makeshift spears. Slugs of lead rip at your dead flesh, through your torso and limbs, splattering several eyes. Their visions wink out, leaving new gaps in your sensory mosaic. Fresh eyes appear to replace them almost immediately, bringing new voices to the din in your head. You reorient yourself and push ahead, reaching for the magnetic red, the pulse of life.

Other bodies push past you, thrusting themselves against weapons, reaching the living.

More come, summoned by the life-scent and the transference of energy from the living to the dead as bodies feast on bodies. Soon the dead outnumber the living, and you have yet to taste a single bite of the flesh you discovered.

You walk without advancing, shuffling your feet in place. A bladed pole thrust through the side of your torso holds you pinned. You grasp it with both hands, tug, tug, yank, and—free. It slides through you, releases you, and you move into the feeding melee. There is little red/life/flesh left. Your despair deepens. Then a crimson glimmer enters your patchwork sight.

Farther down the road, it emanates from an alley between two shops.

While the other bodies focus on their meal, you strive past them for the light.

You enter the shadowed alley.

A dead end.

Three people hunker against the far wall.

A man in a uniform you don't recognize.

A child.

A woman in a *floral print sundress clinging to curves.*

The man waves a pipe as you approach, raises it to strike, revealing a vibrant red fountain where one of the dead ripped him open from armpit to waist. The pipe lands against your head. The man lifts it again, struggling, chest heaving, face pallid. He never lands a second blow. Instead, he collapses to the alley pavement. The child shrieks and rushes past you, a tiny red comet blazing toward the street. You ignore her. Let others devour the snack she represents.

The sundress fascinates you. Blood and dirt mar it, but the floral print shows through.

The face of the woman wearing it brings you no spark of recognition, though.

You might know her face, except you never saw it so contorted with pain, fear, and panic.

She raises a fire ax in both hands. Violent, meaningless words flow from her lips.

You step toward her. The fire axe lands against your shoulder. Your arm comes partly loose from your body. You ignore the damage, seize the woman with your other hand, fall upon her, drag her down, and bite into her as she bucks and slithers to break free. She cannot escape your mass, though. As you chew and slurp her sustenance, her red/life/flesh transfers to you, and…

You saved her.
That much rings clear in the memory that erupts within you.
You couldn't stop your attackers, but you slowed them.
Enough.
Berina slipped away and ran.
Her pretty dress fluttered as she rounded a corner out of sight.
You never saw her again.
You knew fear, then pain, then nothingness…

…a void that erased all the joy and wonder that gushes back to you while her warm flesh and muscle fill your mouth, while her blood runs down your throat. Her face in the morning sun. Her breath when she leaned in for a kiss. The first time you saw her at the party. How your heart pounded with fear at how beautiful she looked to your eyes. The short, potent path you walked hand-in-hand. You hoped it would be a prelude to an enduring journey to the end, and in a sense, it was, for here you are together in her last moments. The intensity of memory sears your being, doubled, tripled in power for how the same recollections and emotions course through her as you. A sensory collage rips across your Novocain brain.

Perfume. Breath.
Soft, supple skin. The knots in her unruly hair.
The saltiness of her lips.
The crystalline music of her voice.
Her gentle fingertips against your chest.

The aura cast around her face by a setting sun.

The dimple in her left cheek.

Berina rushes back to you.

Your nascent being fractures, then shatters, sundered by your need to devour her to regain the things you lost, the paradox of destroying her so she may live inside you once more, if only for moments.

Her face, illuminated by love and desire, by grace and intelligence, by certainty and faith.

You stare into its image coruscating across your dead synapses and withered nerves.

You reach for it. In your mind, your hand and arm look alive.

In the world, you see your pallid, rotting limb from three dozen points of view as your blackening fingertips dip into her rushing blood.

The heat cools.

Her red glow dims.

Her face fades.

She becomes a ghost then...

...vanishes.

You scream, striving to rend the world with your grief, but all that rises from your gore-choked throat is a liquid moan.

More.
Give me more.
I want my turn.
Let me remember next.
No, me!
No, I'm next.
I've been here the longest. I go next.
Let me remember.
Find more. Do it again.
Set me free.
Bring me back to life.
Give me another chance.
I don't want to die.
Life! Life! Life!

Remember, please, let me remember.

HUSH, ALL OF YOU. LIFE LIES IN THE PAST. I AM YOUR FUTURE. YOU ARE THIS WORLD'S FUTURE. JOIN ME IN THE DARKNESS. IT OFFERS YOU NEW LIFE AND FREEDOM FROM REMEMBERING.

What does that mean?

What happens to me when we forget everything?

Why do you want me?

Who are you? Tell me, dammit!

I AM YOU, AND YOU ARE ME. I AM LIFE IN DEATH. YOU ARE DEATH IN LIFE. DEATH OF THE FLESH TO FREE THE SPIRIT. DEATH OF THE SPIRIT TO FREE THE FLESH.

GIVE UNTO ME, AND YOU SHALL RECEIVE THE WHOLE WORLD.

YOU SHALL WIN FREEDOM.

You wander from the alley, unaware of your movements.

The voices carom through your head, frustrating you, maddening you, degrading your lingering impression of beauty and life. The blood and flesh that resurrected it now dry, caking your body and ragged clothes. A sense of loss overwhelms you. But what did you lose? You don't know. Can't even form thoughts enough to acknowledge your ignorance. Instinct only tells you once you had something magnificent that you no longer possess.

Far ahead, you see the red/life/flesh glow.

It fills the sky, a miniature sun against the inverted night that assaults your many dozens of eyes. You walk toward it. It emanates from a man standing high atop a water tower.

His voice booms loudest in your mind. His orders. His desire overcomes yours.

One by one, the other voices quiet. All your many eyes come into alignment, forming a singular vision of the Red Man, who returned from beyond, who speaks to the dead, who pulls the strings that make your stiffening limbs move, who blazes the invisible trail you follow.

You ramble closer.

His power fills you with a warmth that tastes like life on the tip of your tongue, but it doesn't fill you with vitality or raise your memories from the dead.

It commands, demands, orders, and instructs.

All your eyes meet his.

Red fills them.

Around you, the dead fall into order, slaughtering chaos.

They gather.

They listen.

They look. No matter how hard you try to turn your gaze toward the town behind you, the others drag your sight back to him.

And when the Red Man speaks, they obey.

You obey.

ABOUT THE AUTHOR

James Chambers is an award-winning author of horror, crime, fantasy, science fiction, and other genres. He wrote the Bram Stoker Award®-winning graphic novel, *Kolchak the Night Stalker: The Forgotten Lore of Edgar Allan Poe* and was nominated for a Bram Stoker Award for his story, "A Song Left Behind in the Aztakea Hills." *Booklist* described his collection *On the Night Border* as "...a haunting exploration of the space where the real world and nightmares collide," and, in a starred review, said of his collection *On the Hierophant Road*: "For fans of the new breed of dark-speculative-fiction writers who actively play with genre confines to create reads that are inventive, thought-provoking, and creepily fun." *Publisher's Weekly* gave his collection of four Lovecraftian-inspired novellas, *The Engines of Sacrifice*, a starred review and described it as "...chillingly evocative..."

He is also the author of the short story collection *Resurrection House*, the Corpse Fauna novellas, including *The Dead Bear Witness, Tears of Blood*, and *The Dead in Their Masses*, as well as the dark urban fantasy, *Three Chords of Chaos*, and *Kolchak and the Night Stalkers: The Faceless God*. His short stories have been published in numerous anthologies, including *After Punk: Steampowered Tales of the Afterlife, The Best of Bad-Ass Faeries, The Best of Defending the Future, Chiral Mad 2, Chiral Mad 4,*

Gaslight and Grimm, The Green Hornet Chronicles, Kolchak the Night Stalker: Passages of the Macabre, Qualia Nous, Shadows Over Main Street (1 and 2), *The Spider: Extreme Prejudice, Truth or Dare, TV Gods, Walrus Tales, Weird Trails*, and the magazines *Bare Bone, Cthulhu Sex*, and *Allen K's Inhuman*.

He edited the Bram Stoker Award-nominated anthology *Under Twin Suns: Alternate Histories of the Yellow Sign* and co-edited *A New York State of Fright: Horror Stories from the Empire State* (a Bram Stoker Award finalist), and *Even in the Grave.*

He has also written and edited numerous comic books including *Leonard Nimoy's Primortals*, the critically acclaimed "The Revenant" in *Shadow House*, and *The Midnight Hour* with Jason Whitley.

He lives in New York.

Visit his website: www.jameschambersonline.com.

ABOUT THE ARTISTS

Glen Ostrander (cover) is a Freelance Artist and Illustrator who has created artwork in the fantasy/horror genre for a wide variety of commercial clients. He is known for his evocative work and continues to bring his creations to life by finding daily inspiration near his home, in the wild mountains of New Hampshire, where he lives with his wonderful wife Anna, his devilish dog Jojo, and his fiendish feline Floyd.

Jason Whitley (interior) is the illustrator and co-creator of *The Midnight Hour*. Jason's work as a newspaper illustrator has appeared across the country and won many awards. His portrait of civil rights leader Charlotte Hawkins Brown is in the Charlotte Hawkins Brown Museum.

With writer Scott Eckelaert, he co-created and illustrated the classic comic-strip, *Sea Urchins*. Sea Urchins has been collected into four volumes. The fourth volume, *So Long, Frozen Ocean* will be released in 2020. Jason leads a Hermes and Telly Award-winning multimedia team of five in North Carolina. He's working on a crime-noir graphic novel with no set release date and looking forward to the complete *The Midnight Hour* collection from eSpec Books in 2023.

OUR LEGION OF THE UNDEAD

ABD
Agnomaly
Amy Grech
Angela Yuriko Smith
Anna Taborska
Annelise Pichardo
Anonymous Reader
April Grey
Arthur Kinsman
Aven Lumi
Avis Crane
Becky Wood
Bill Ginger
Brian W. Matthews
Carl W Bishop
Carlos Valcarcel
Carol Mammano
Chandler Klang Smith
Charles E. Wood
Cheri Kannarr
Chris Ryan
Christopher J. Burke
Cori Paige
Craig Hackl

Curtis Steinhour
Dale A. Russell
Damon Griffin
Dan Dalal
Danielle Ackley-McPhail
David Swisher
Diane Raimonde
Drew Biehl
Drew Cucuzza
Dusk Zer0
Ef Deal
Fiona A. Elder
Frieda Schultz
Gail Trotter
Gary Phillips
Giusy Rippa
Hank Blumenthal
Howard Blakeslee
Isaac 'Will It Work' Dansicker
J.R. Murdock
Janet Lees
Janito V. F. Filho
Jeff LaSorsa
Jenn Whitworth

Jennifer L. Pierce
Jessica Sarchet
John L. French
Jonathan Lees
Jp
Karen M
Karl Markovich
Kierin Fox
Kirk Larson
KJSP
L. E. Daniels
L.E. Custodio
Lakota Lara
Lara Frater
Lark Cunningham
Laurel Anne Hill
Laurie Jones
Lisa Kruse
Lisa Morton
Liz
Lorraine J. Anderson
Lou Rera
Lynne Hansen
Mallory N Pate
Mandi
Marc "mad" W.
Marc L Abbott
Maria T
Martha Huggins

Maya G Goldstein
Meghan Arcuri
Michele Clemente
Michele Kutner
Nathan Toby
Nicholas Diak
Nicholas Stephenson
Rachel & Jim Larson
Rachel Brune
Randee Dawn
Rebecca E. Hoffman
Reckless Pantalones
Robert Claney
Robert P. Ottone
Sarah
Sasquatch N
Scott Schaper
Scout McLoud
Sherry
Steph Parker
Stephen Ballentine
Steven Van Patten
Tasha Turner
The Creative Fund
Thomas Alan Horne
Timothy DuBois
Venessa Giunta
Victoria Navarra
WD Stancil